"My favorite part is when Hilo travels through galaxies. If I had to describe it in three words, I'd say it's **'SUCH A BLAST!'** D.J. is my favorite because he's a really good friend!"
—Matt A., age 10, Bloomfield, N.J.

"I love the Hilo books. Thank you so much! I really, **REALLY LOVE** the Hilo books."
—Angel O., age 10, Brooklyn

"**GINA WAS MY FAVORITE** character because she's into science and soccer like me! I also liked D.J.'s family because it looks like mine!"
—Kiran M., age 7, Carlsbad, Calif.

"*Hilo* is really cool and funny. It's **FUNNY** that he likes mangoes. You should read it because it's actually just **REALLY FUNNY!**"
—Gerard A., age 8, Bloomfield, N.J.

"**HIGH ENERGY** and **HILARIOUS**!"
—Gene Luen Yang, winner of the Printz Award

"**FANTASTIC. EVERY SINGLE THING ABOUT THIS . . . IS TERRIFIC.**"
—Boingboing.net

"My students are obsessed with this series. **OBSESSED!**"
—Colby Sharp, teacher, blogger, and co-founder of the Nerdy Book Club

"More **GIANT ROBOTIC ANTS** . . . than in the complete works of Jane Austen."
—Neil Gaiman, author of *Coraline*

"Anyone who loves to laugh should read *Hilo*. It is **ACTION-PACKED** with a robotic touch."
—Breslin S., age 10, Jackson, Mich.

"*Hilo* is loads of **SLAPSTICK FUN!**"
—Dan Santat, winner of the Caldecott Medal

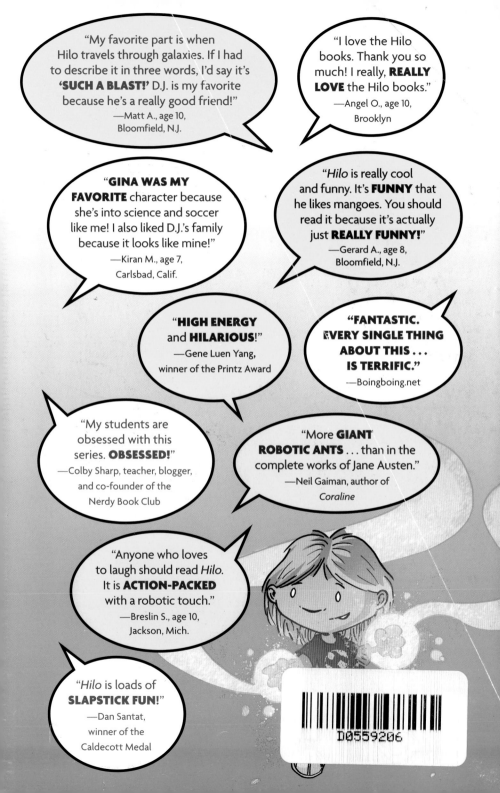

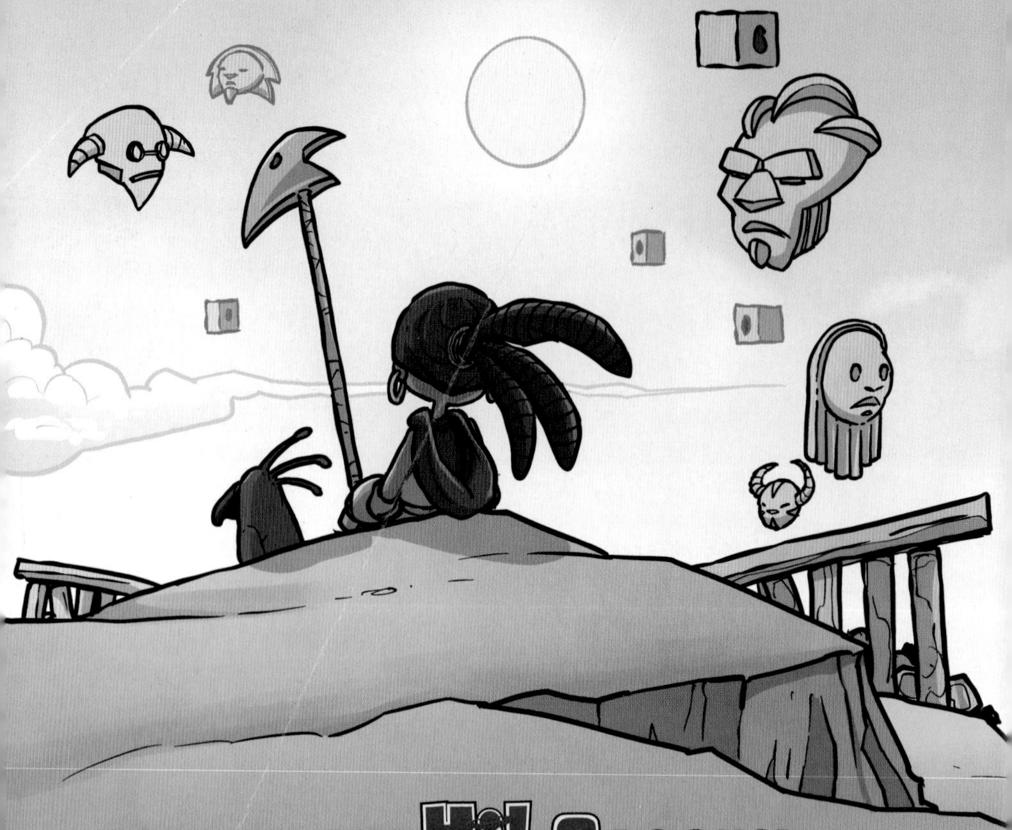

READ ALL THE HILO BOOKS!

HILO #1 THE BOY WHO CRASHED TO EARTH

HILO #2 SAVING THE WHOLE WIDE WORLD

HILO #3 THE GREAT BIG BOOM

HILO #4 WAKING THE MONSTERS

HILO #5 THEN EVERYTHING WENT WRONG

HILO #6 ALL THE PIECES FIT

HILO #7 GINA — THE GIRL WHO BROKE THE WORLD

HILO #8 GINA AND THE BIG SECRET

HILO #9 GINA AND THE LAST CITY ON EARTH

BOOK 9

HILO

GINA AND THE LAST CITY ON EARTH

BY JUDD WINICK

COLOR BY MAARTA LAIHO

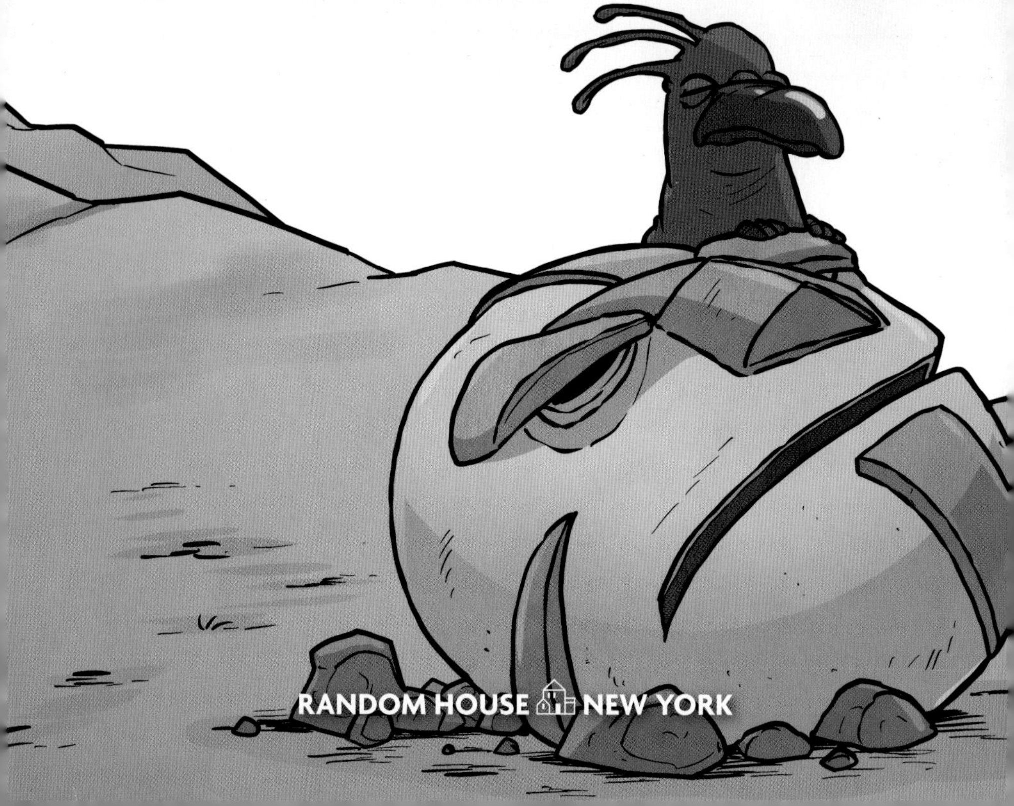

RANDOM HOUSE NEW YORK

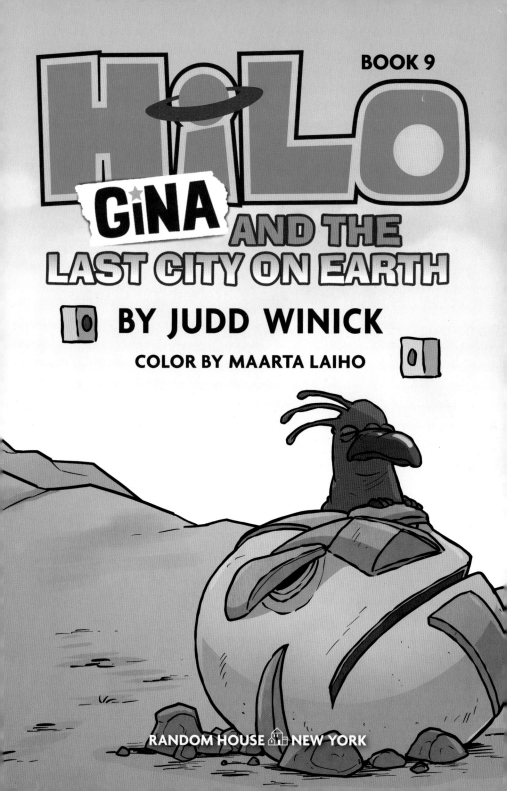

With thanks to Shasta Clinch, for her thoughtful feedback, insights, and perspective

All rights reserved. Published in the United States by Random House Children's Books, a division of Penguin Random House LLC, New York.

Random House and the colophon are registered trademarks of Penguin Random House LLC.

RH Graphic with the book design is a trademark of Penguin Random House LLC.

Visit us on the Web! rhcbooks.com

Educators and librarians, for a variety of teaching tools, visit us at RHTeachersLibrarians.com

Library of Congress Cataloging-in-Publication Data
Names: Winick, Judd, author.
Title: Hilo. Book 9, Gina and the last city on earth / Judd Winick.
Description: First edition. | New York: Random House Children's Books,
2023. | Series: Hilo; book 9 | Audience: Ages 8–12. | Summary: "Gina saves the world and restores the earth to what it was before magic took over"—Provided by publisher.
Identifiers: LCCN 2021050275 (print) | LCCN 2021050276 (ebook) | ISBN 978-0-593-48809-6 (hardcover) | ISBN 978-0-593-48811-9 (library binding) | ISBN 978-0-593-48810-2 (ebook)
Subjects: CYAC: Graphic novels. | Magic—Fiction. | Imaginary creatures—Fiction. | Science fiction. | LCGFT: Graphic novels. | Science fiction.
Classification: LCC PZ7.7.W57 Hq 2023 (print) | LCC PZ7.7.W57 (ebook) | DDC 741.5/973—dc23/eng/20220202

The artist used digital medium to create the illustrations for this book.
The text of this book is set in 11-point ImaginaryFriend BB.
Book design by Bob Bianchini and Juliet Goodman

MANUFACTURED IN CHINA

10 9 8 7 6 5 4 3 2 1

First Edition

Dedicated to . . .

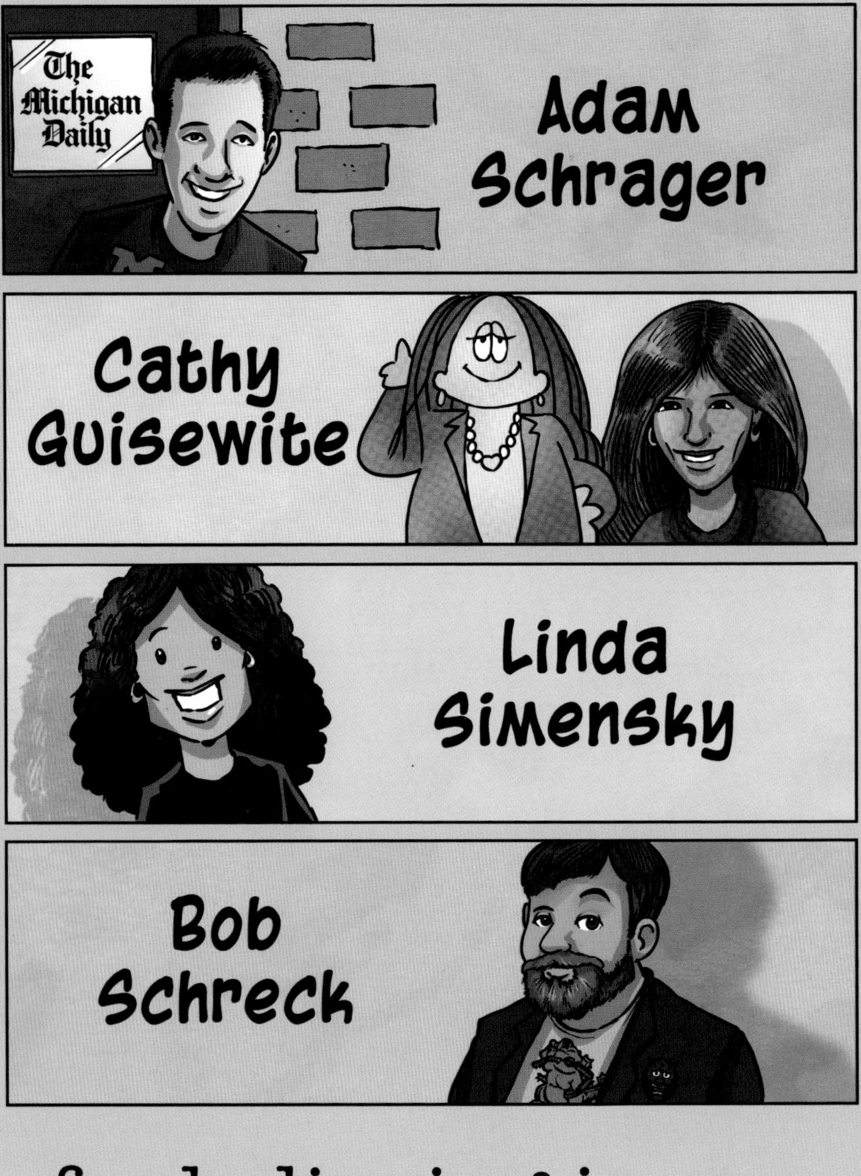
The Michigan Daily
Adam Schrager
Cathy Guisewite
Linda Simensky
Bob Schreck

for believing in me.

TWO DAYS AGO.

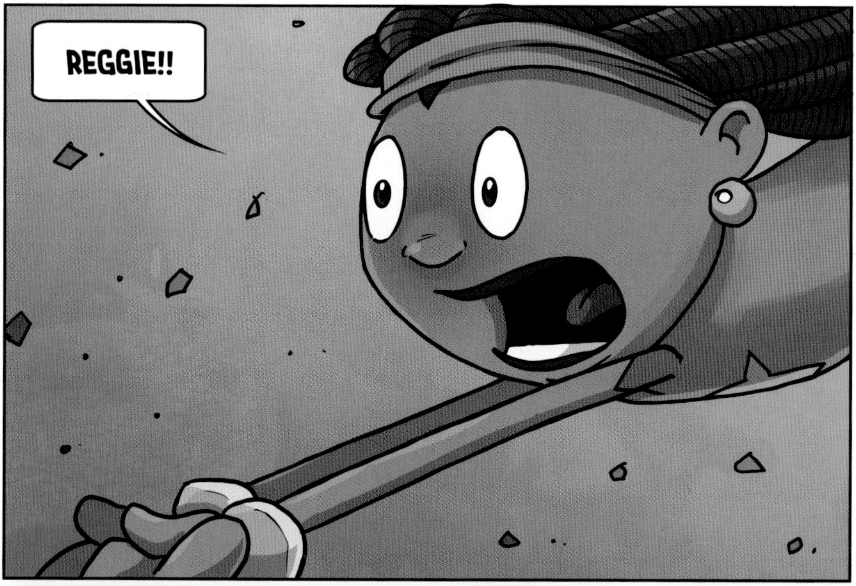
REGGIE!!

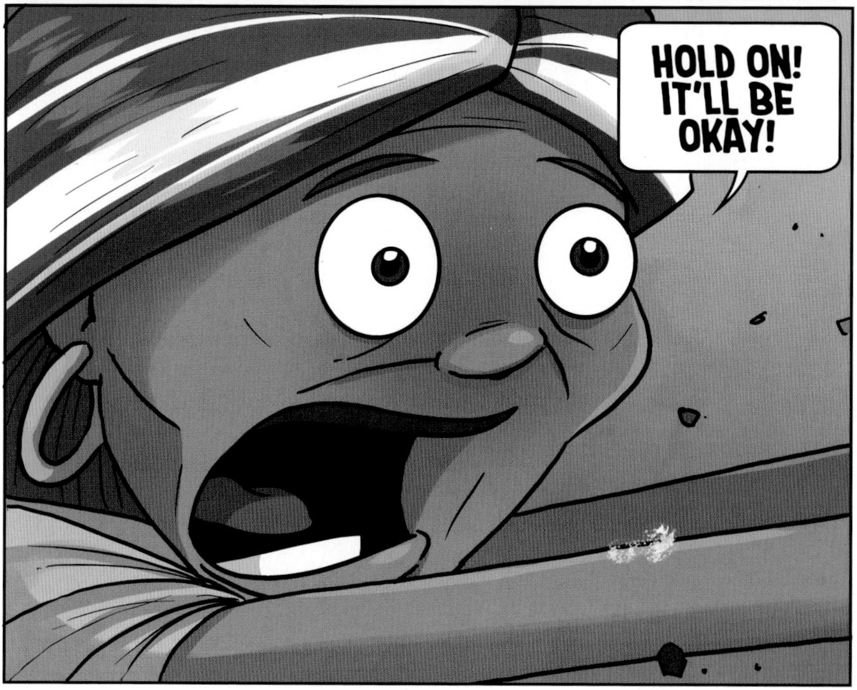
HOLD ON! IT'LL BE OKAY!

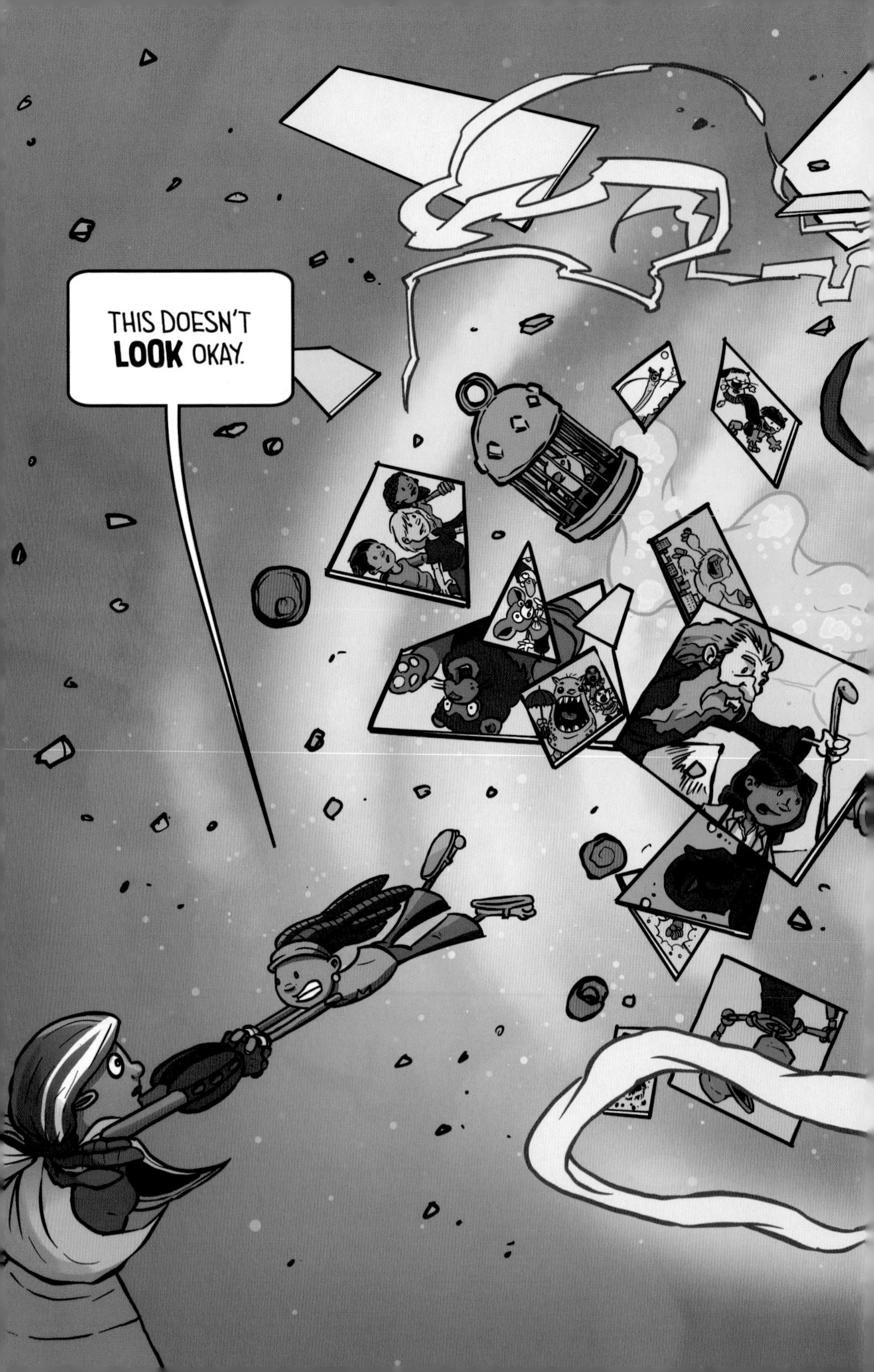
THIS DOESN'T **LOOK** OKAY.

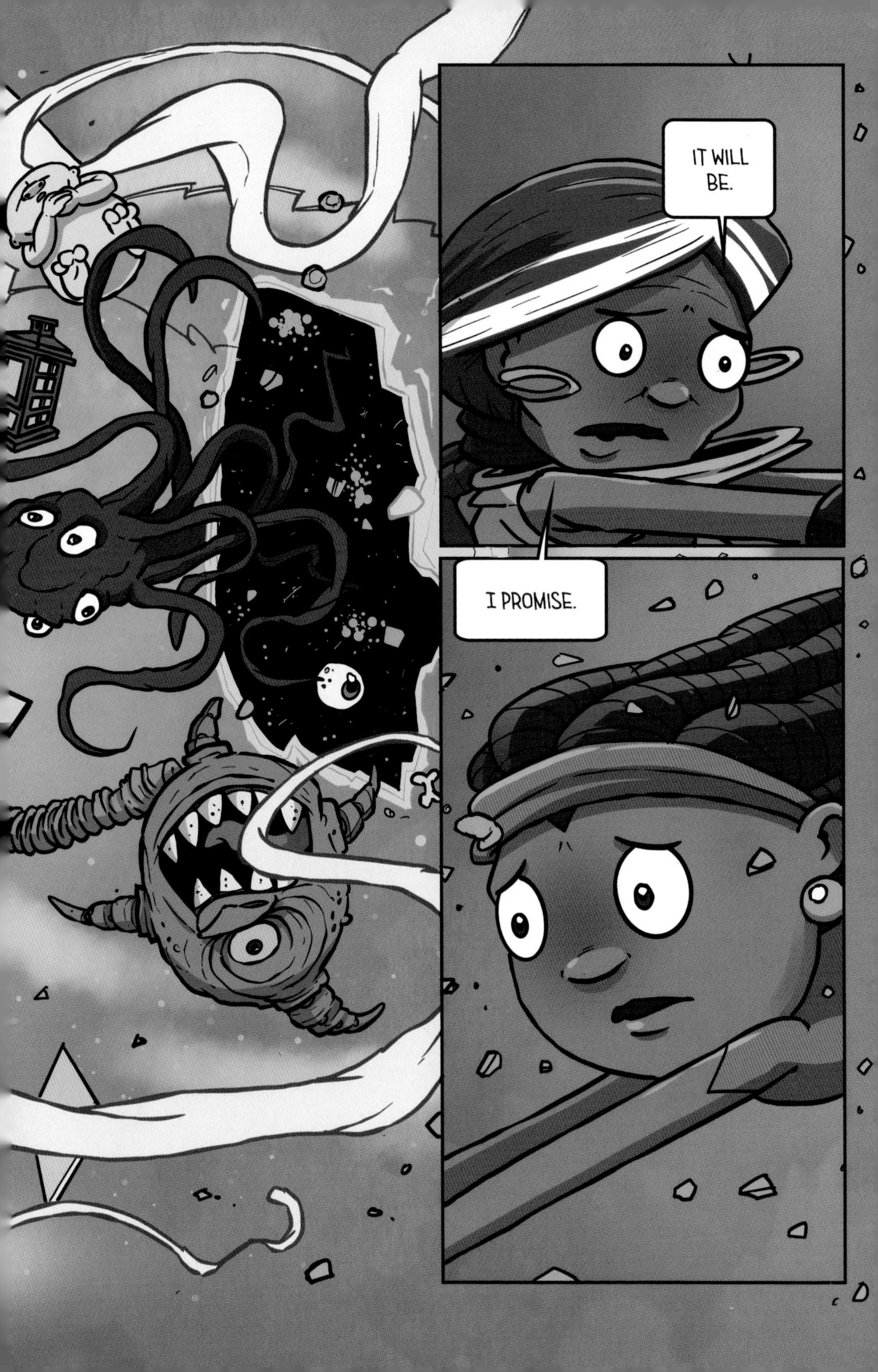
IT WILL BE.
I PROMISE.

1

REGINA LEE COOPER

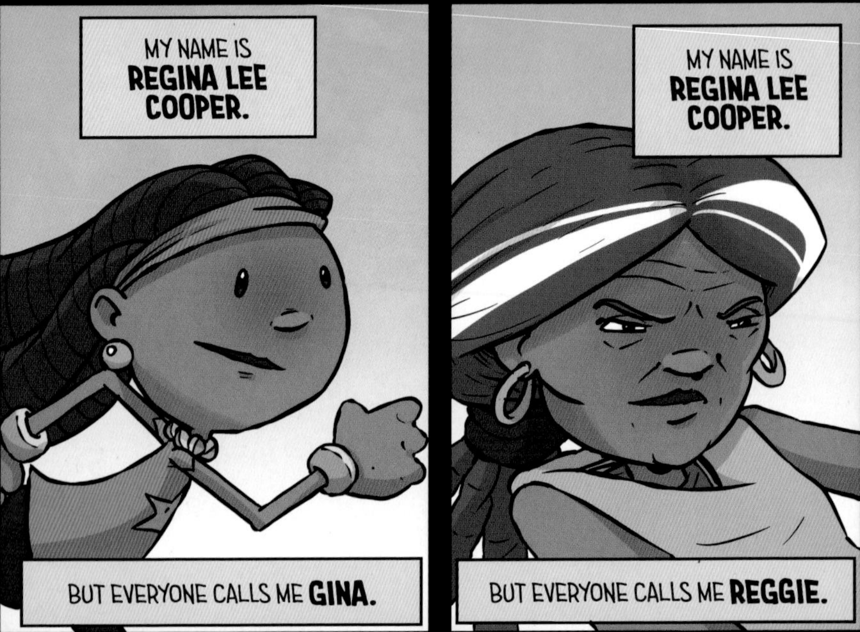
MY NAME IS **REGINA LEE COOPER.**
BUT EVERYONE CALLS ME **GINA.**
MY NAME IS **REGINA LEE COOPER.**
BUT EVERYONE CALLS ME **REGGIE.**

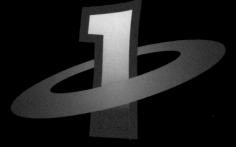

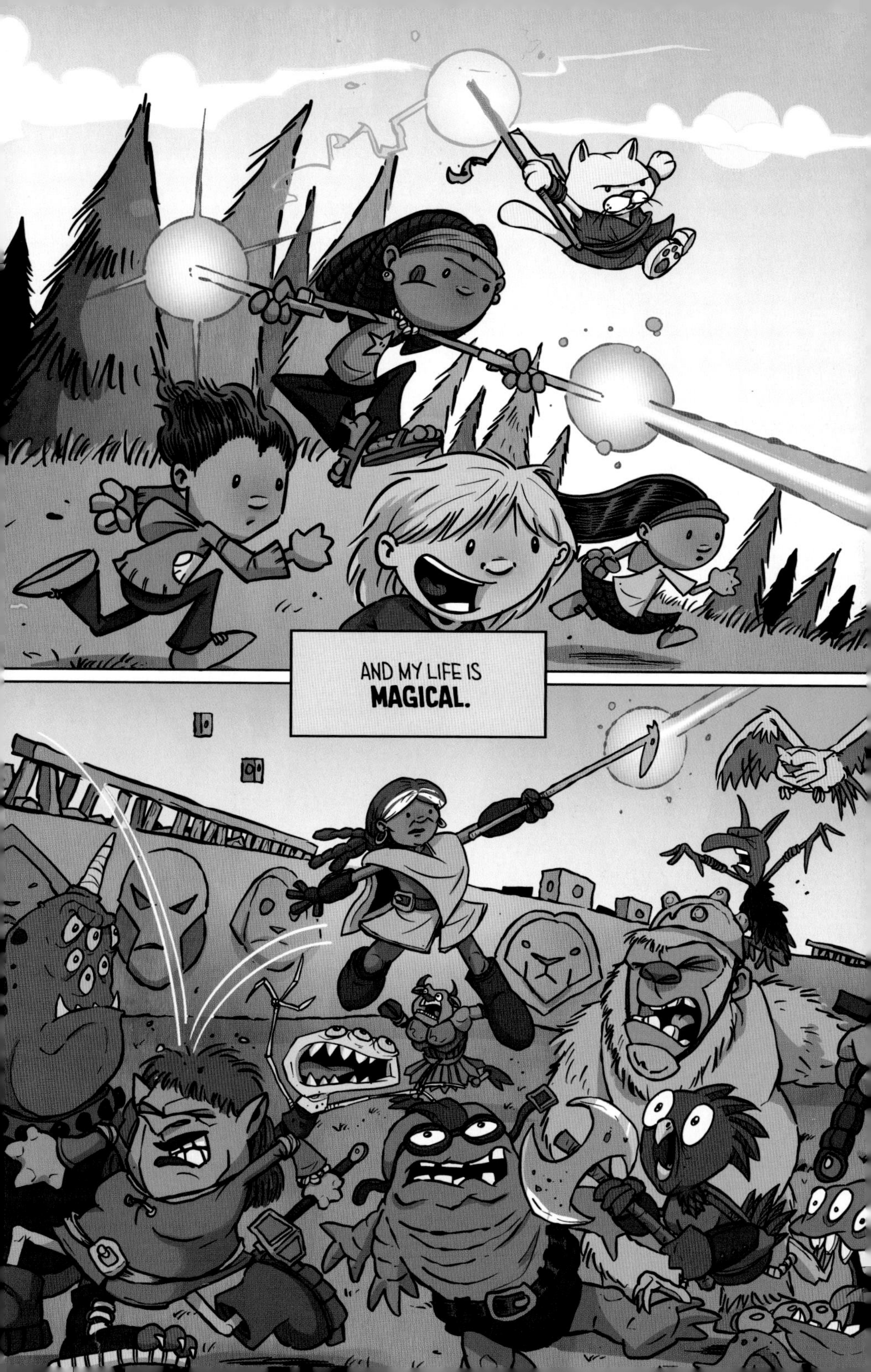
AND MY LIFE IS
MAGICAL.

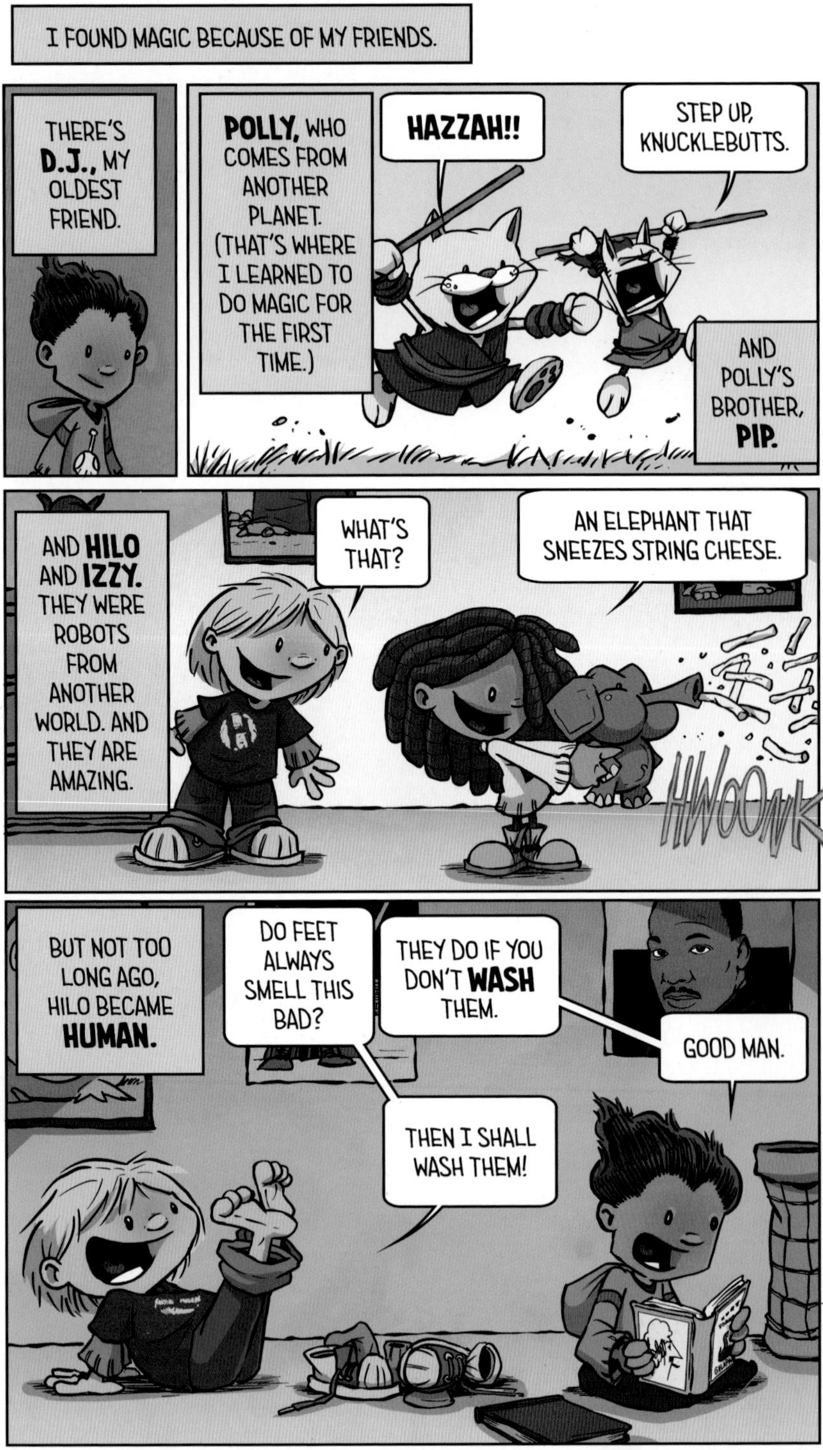
I FOUND MAGIC BECAUSE OF MY FRIENDS.
THERE'S D.J., MY OLDEST FRIEND.
POLLY, WHO COMES FROM ANOTHER PLANET. (THAT'S WHERE I LEARNED TO DO MAGIC FOR THE FIRST TIME.)
HAZZAH!!
STEP UP, KNUCKLEBUTTS.
AND POLLY'S BROTHER, PIP.
AND HILO AND IZZY. THEY WERE ROBOTS FROM ANOTHER WORLD. AND THEY ARE AMAZING.
WHAT'S THAT?
AN ELEPHANT THAT SNEEZES STRING CHEESE.
HWOONK
BUT NOT TOO LONG AGO, HILO BECAME HUMAN.
DO FEET ALWAYS SMELL THIS BAD?
THEY DO IF YOU DON'T WASH THEM.
GOOD MAN.
THEN I SHALL WASH THEM!

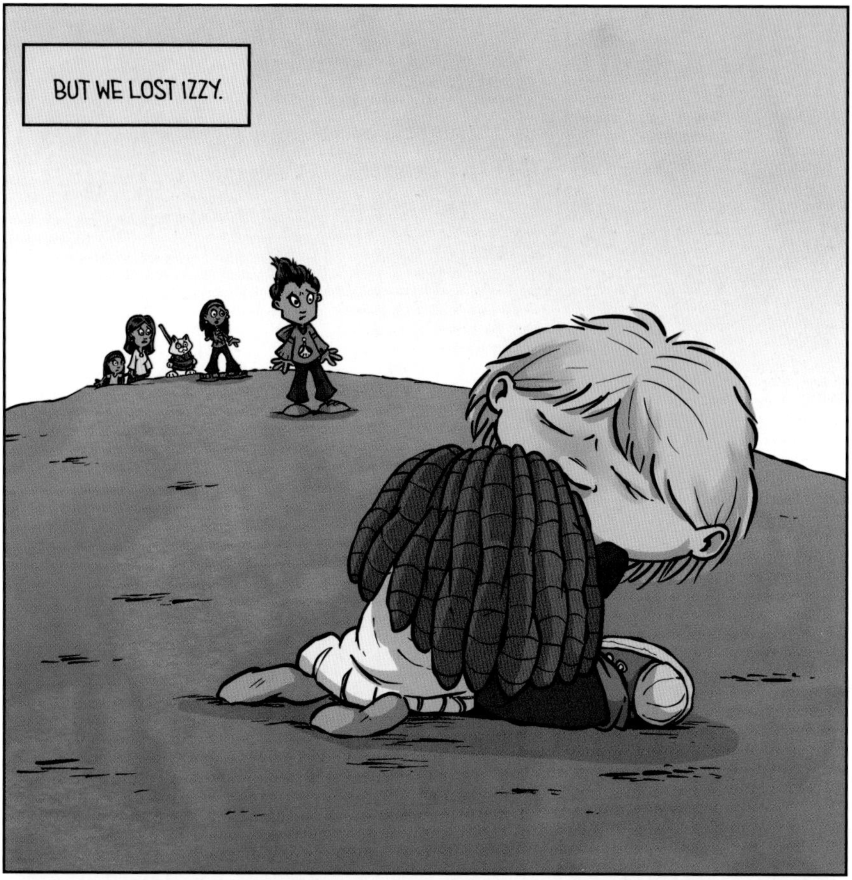
BUT WE LOST IZZY.

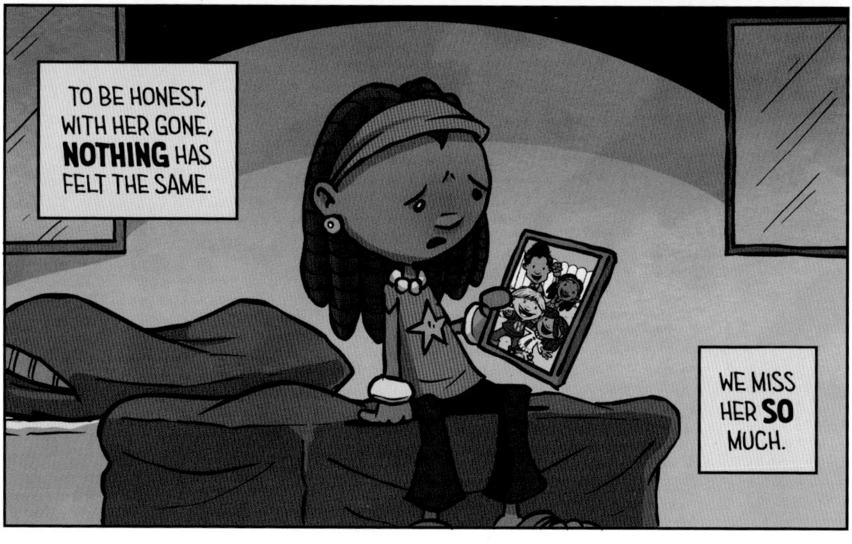
TO BE HONEST, WITH HER GONE, **NOTHING** HAS FELT THE SAME.
WE MISS HER **SO** MUCH.

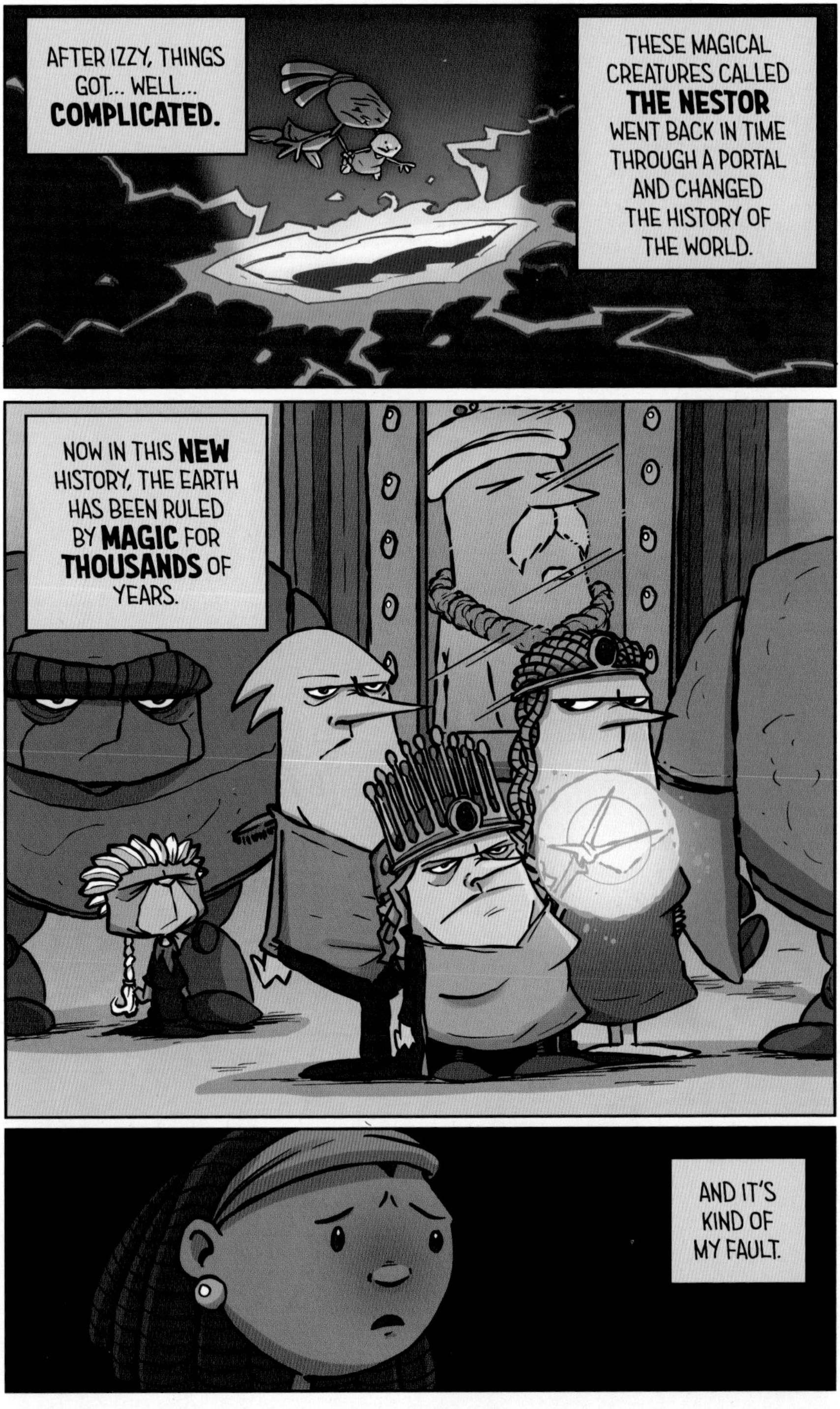

AFTER IZZY, THINGS GOT... WELL... **COMPLICATED.**
THESE MAGICAL CREATURES CALLED **THE NESTOR** WENT BACK IN TIME THROUGH A PORTAL AND CHANGED THE HISTORY OF THE WORLD.
NOW IN THIS **NEW** HISTORY, THE EARTH HAS BEEN RULED BY **MAGIC** FOR **THOUSANDS** OF YEARS.
AND IT'S KIND OF MY FAULT.

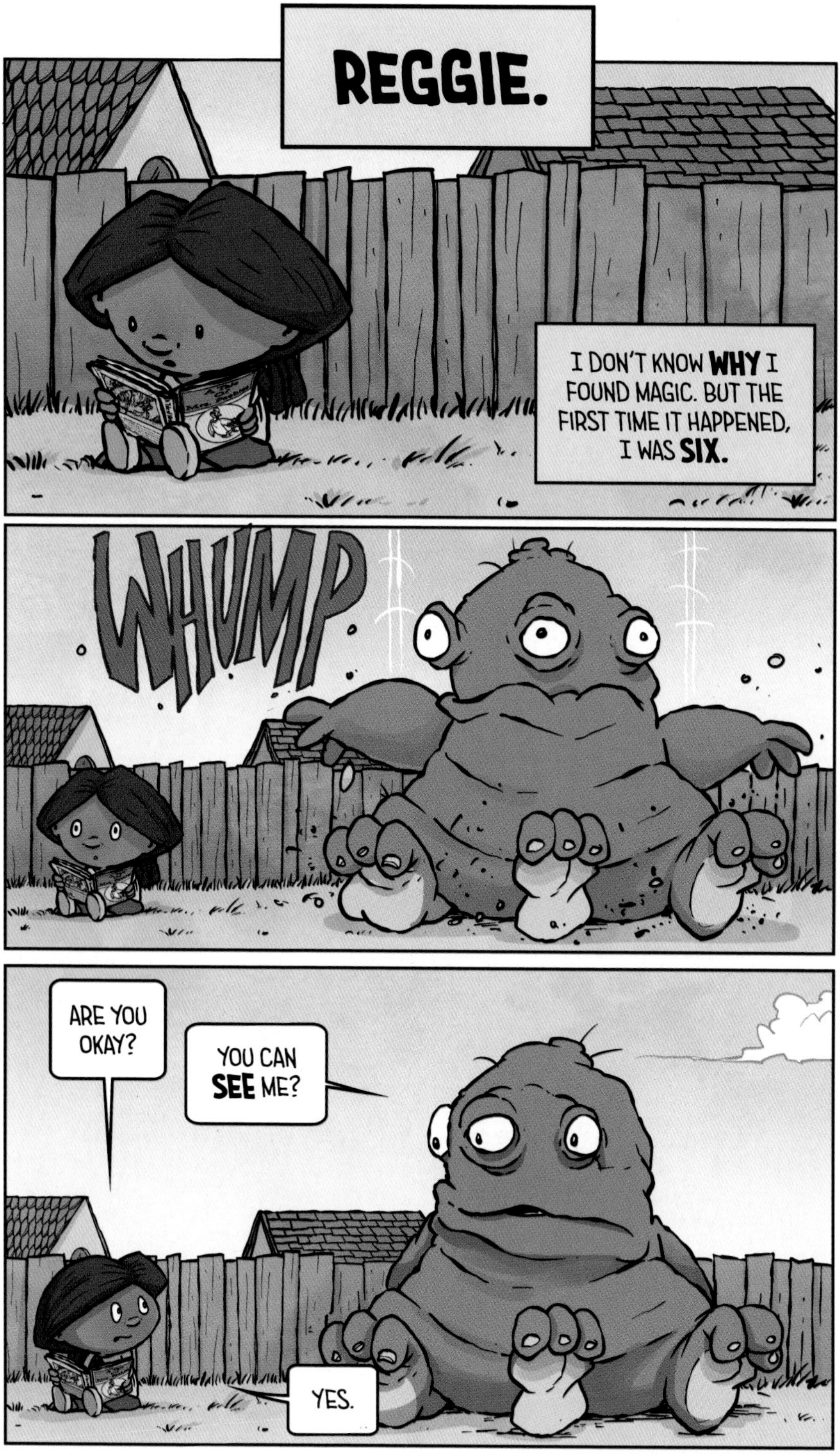
REGGIE.
I DON'T KNOW WHY I FOUND MAGIC. BUT THE FIRST TIME IT HAPPENED, I WAS SIX.
WHUMP
ARE YOU OKAY?
YOU CAN SEE ME?
YES.

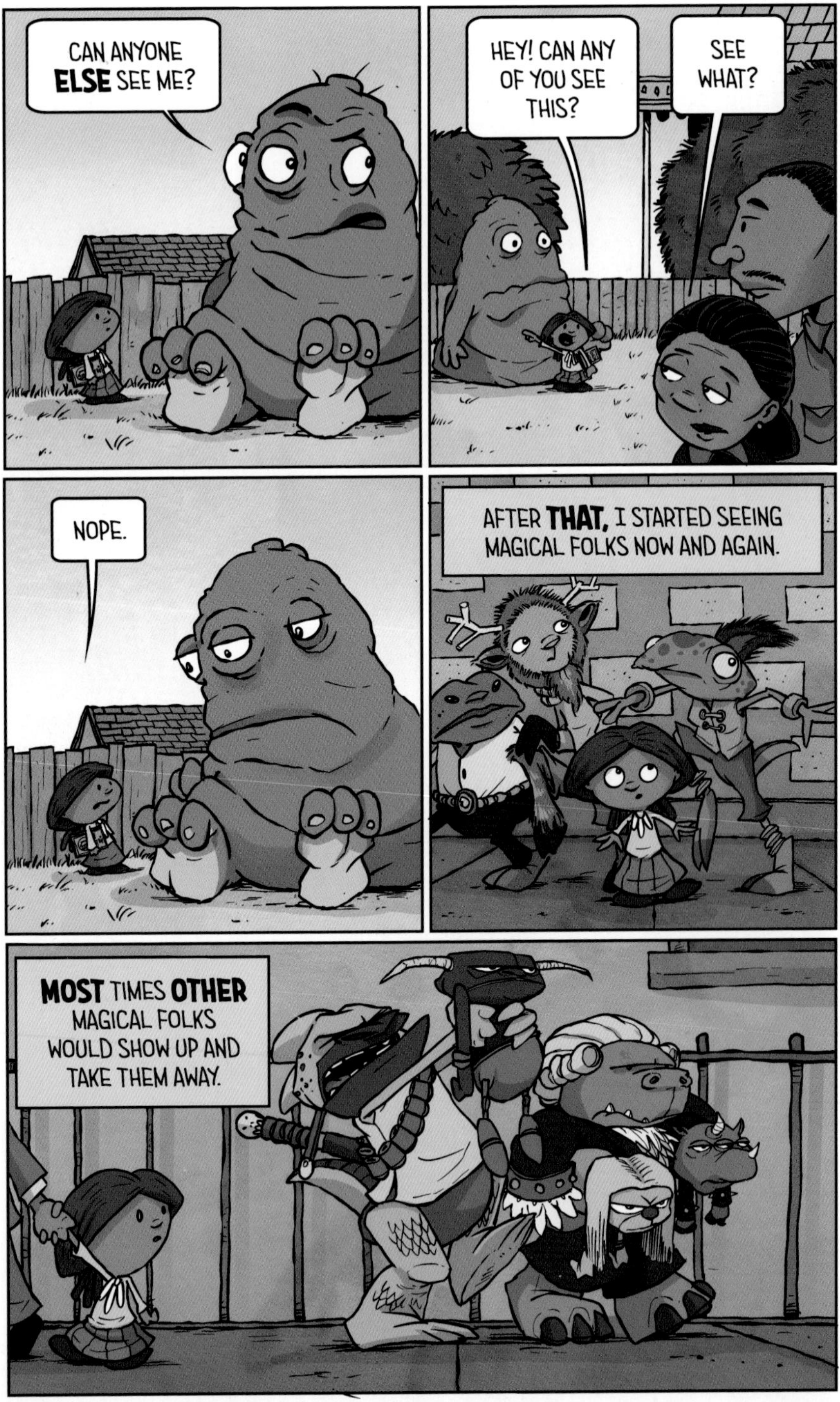
CAN ANYONE **ELSE** SEE ME?
HEY! CAN ANY OF YOU SEE THIS?
SEE WHAT?
NOPE.
AFTER **THAT,** I STARTED SEEING MAGICAL FOLKS NOW AND AGAIN.
MOST TIMES **OTHER** MAGICAL FOLKS WOULD SHOW UP AND TAKE THEM AWAY.

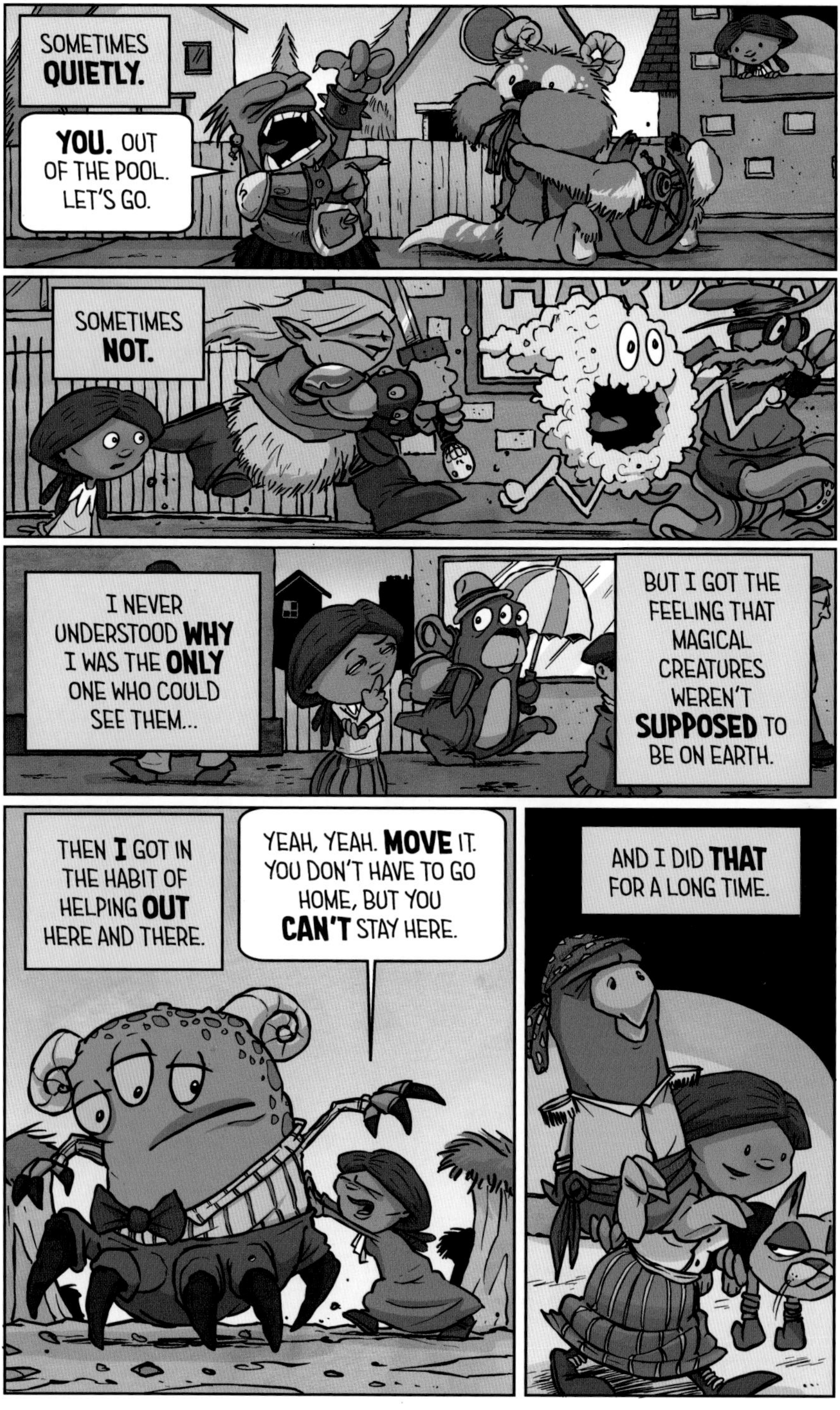

SOMETIMES QUIETLY.
YOU. OUT OF THE POOL. LET'S GO.
SOMETIMES NOT.
I NEVER UNDERSTOOD WHY I WAS THE ONLY ONE WHO COULD SEE THEM...
BUT I GOT THE FEELING THAT MAGICAL CREATURES WEREN'T SUPPOSED TO BE ON EARTH.
THEN I GOT IN THE HABIT OF HELPING OUT HERE AND THERE.
YEAH, YEAH. MOVE IT. YOU DON'T HAVE TO GO HOME, BUT YOU CAN'T STAY HERE.
AND I DID THAT FOR A LONG TIME.

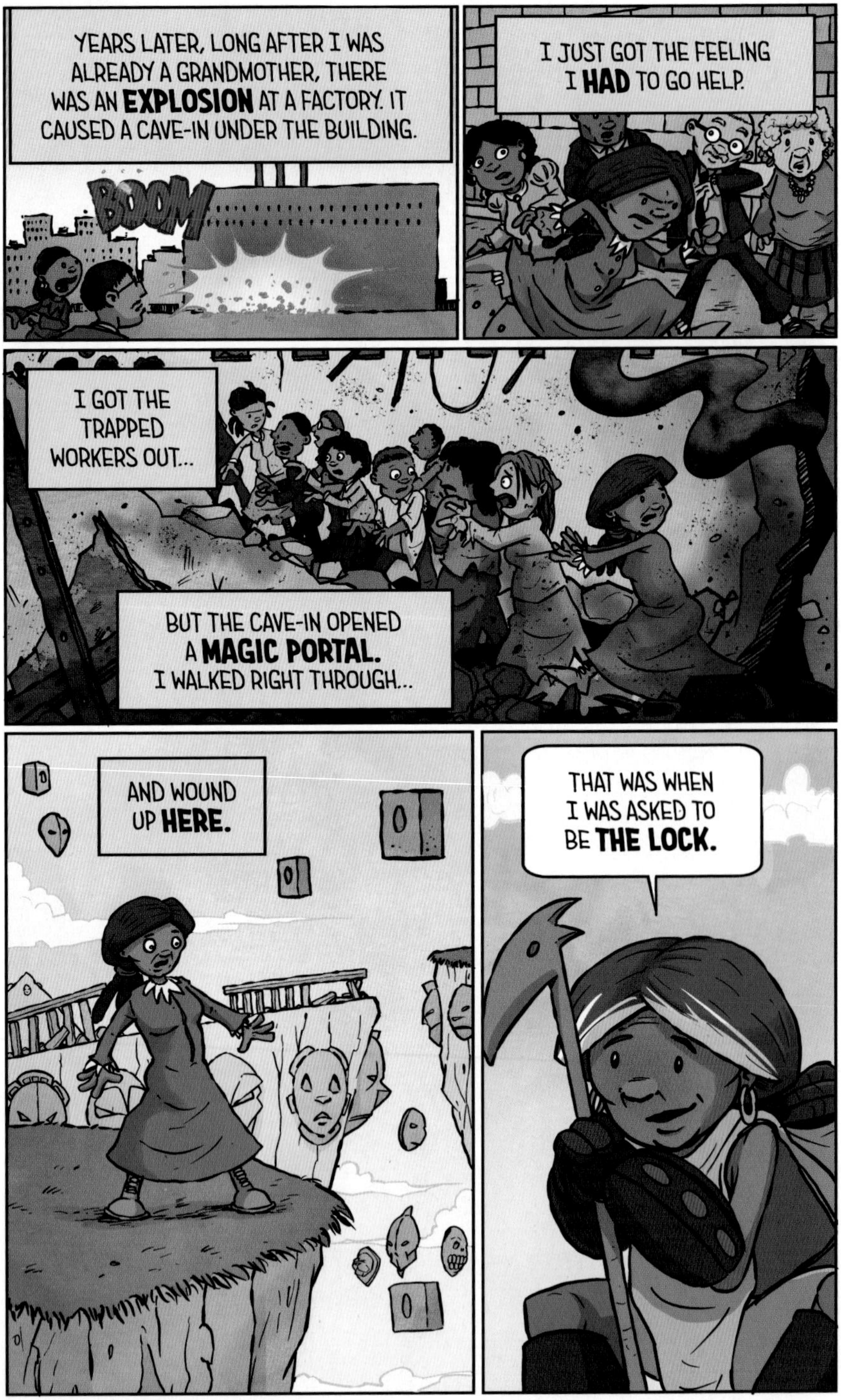

YEARS LATER, LONG AFTER I WAS ALREADY A GRANDMOTHER, THERE WAS AN **EXPLOSION** AT A FACTORY. IT CAUSED A CAVE-IN UNDER THE BUILDING.
BOOM
I JUST GOT THE FEELING I **HAD** TO GO HELP.
I GOT THE TRAPPED WORKERS OUT...
BUT THE CAVE-IN OPENED A **MAGIC PORTAL.** I WALKED RIGHT THROUGH...
AND WOUND UP **HERE.**
THAT WAS WHEN I WAS ASKED TO BE **THE LOCK.**

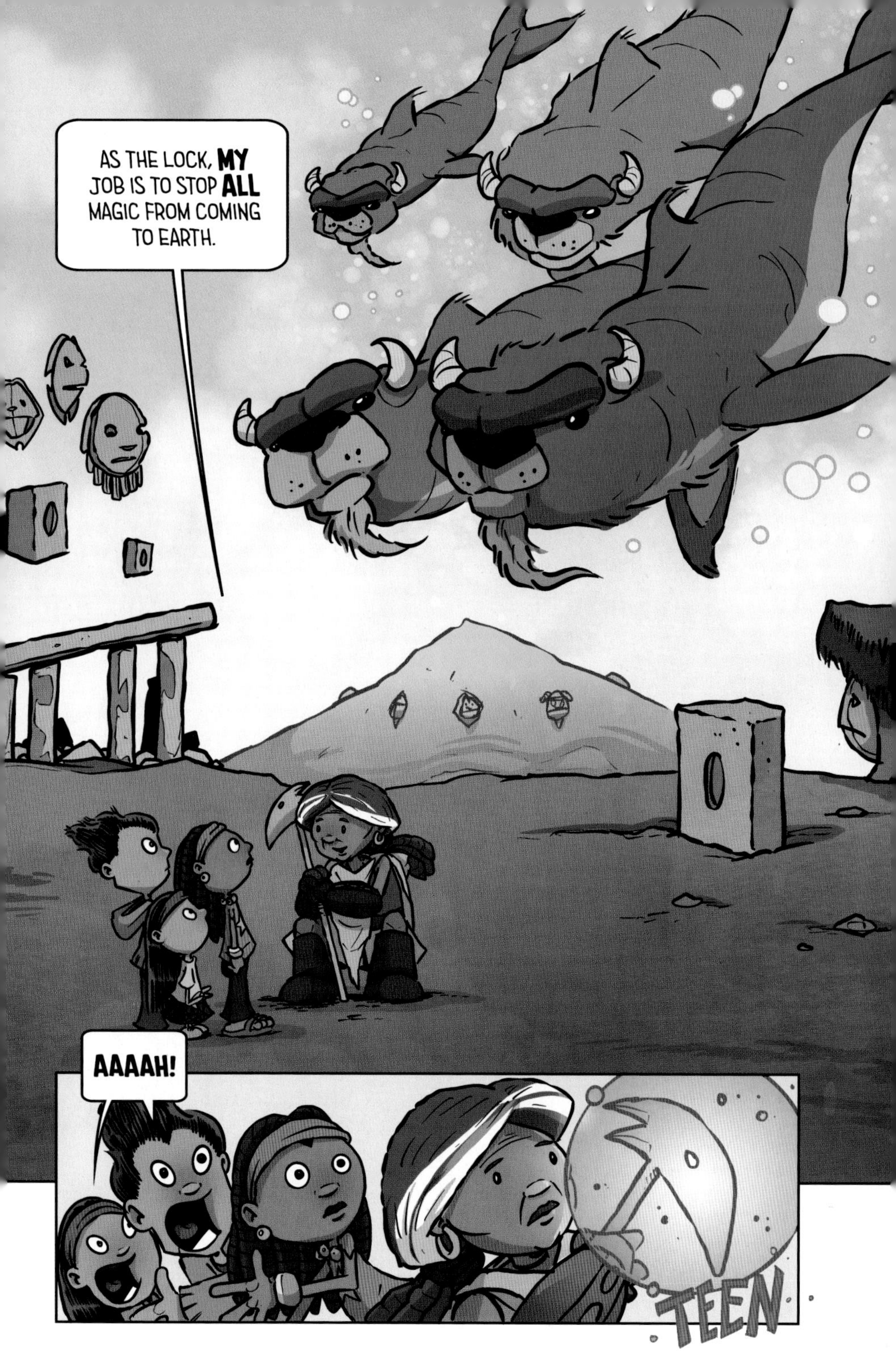
AS THE LOCK, **MY** JOB IS TO STOP **ALL** MAGIC FROM COMING TO EARTH.
AAAAH!
TEEN

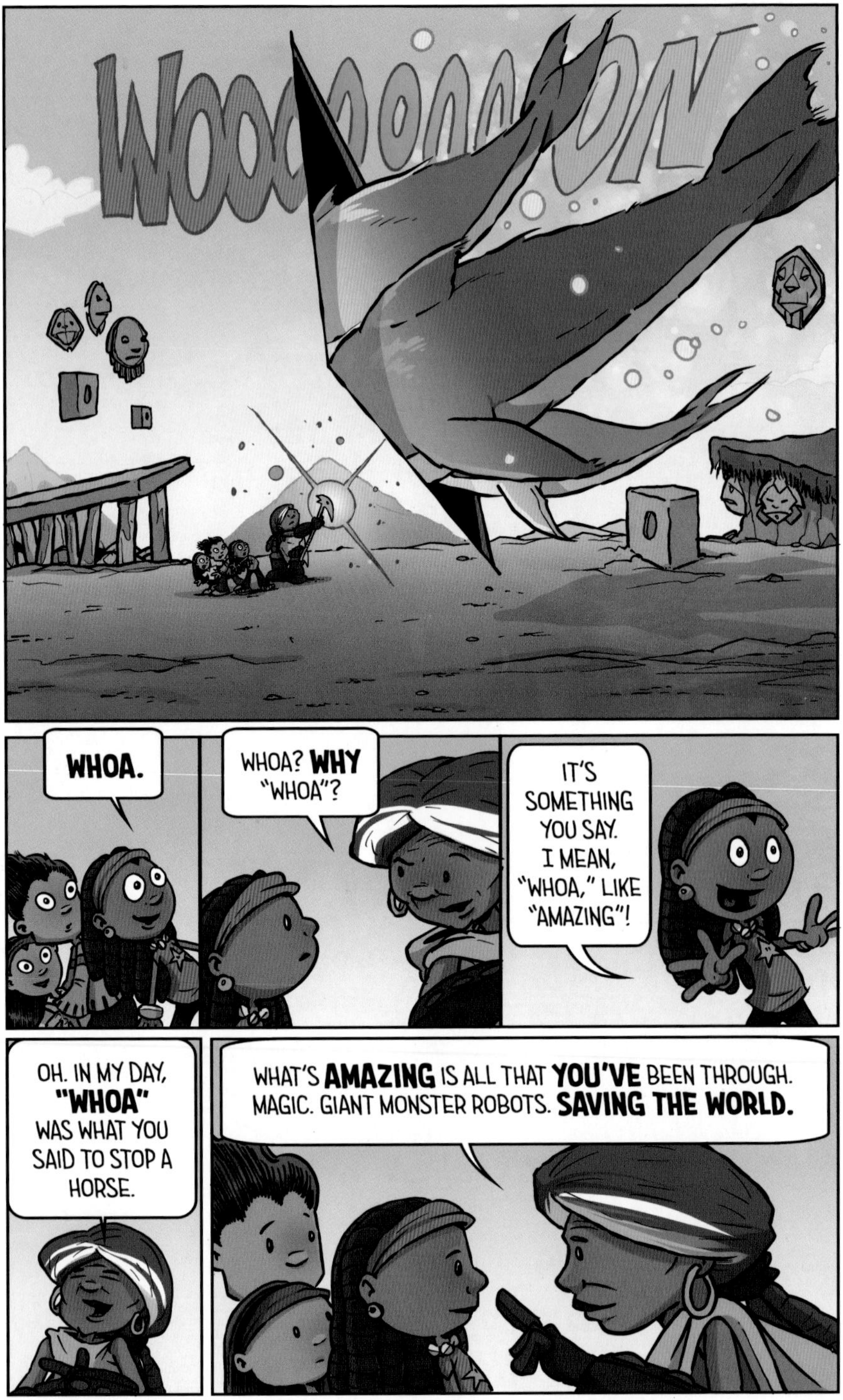
WOOOOOOOOOON
WHOA.
WHOA? WHY "WHOA"?
IT'S SOMETHING YOU SAY. I MEAN, "WHOA," LIKE "AMAZING"!
OH. IN MY DAY, "WHOA" WAS WHAT YOU SAID TO STOP A HORSE.
WHAT'S AMAZING IS ALL THAT YOU'VE BEEN THROUGH. MAGIC. GIANT MONSTER ROBOTS. SAVING THE WORLD.

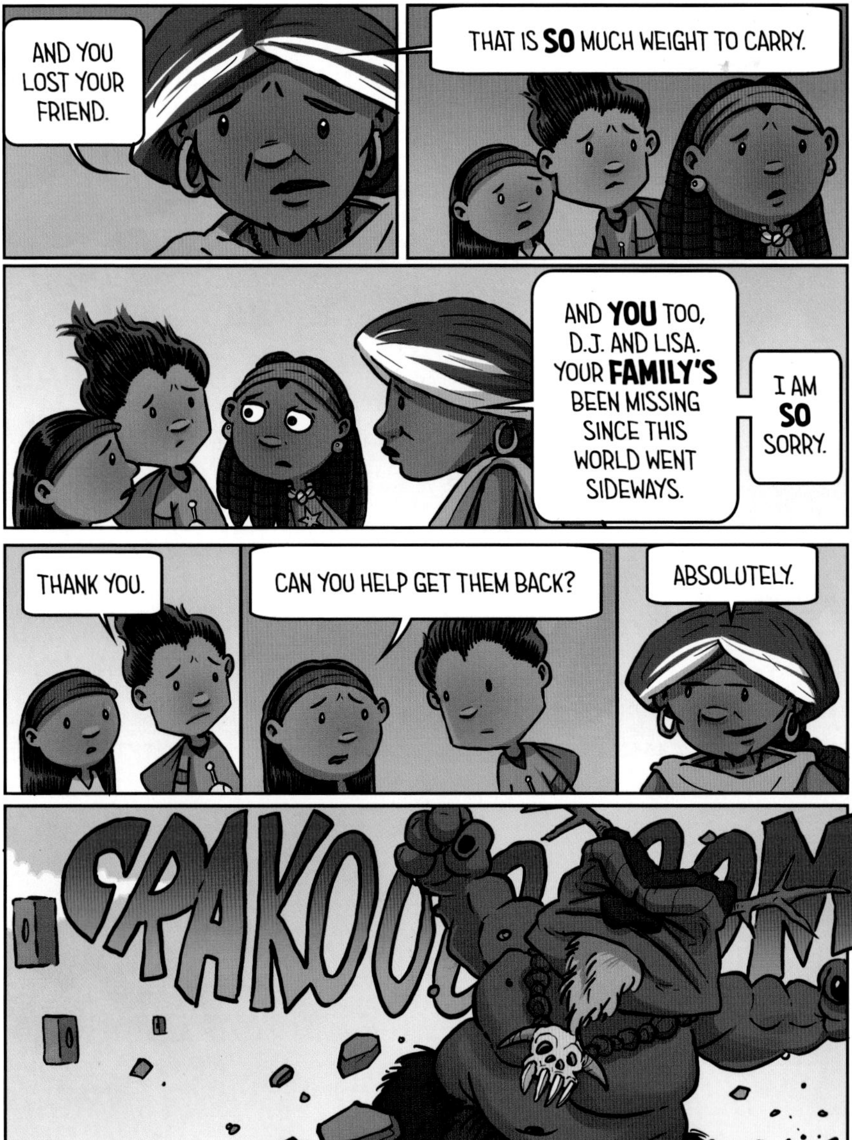
AND YOU LOST YOUR FRIEND.
THAT IS **SO** MUCH WEIGHT TO CARRY.
AND **YOU** TOO, D.J. AND LISA. YOUR **FAMILY'S** BEEN MISSING SINCE THIS WORLD WENT SIDEWAYS.
I AM **SO** SORRY.
THANK YOU.
CAN YOU HELP GET THEM BACK?
ABSOLUTELY.
CRAKOOOOOOM

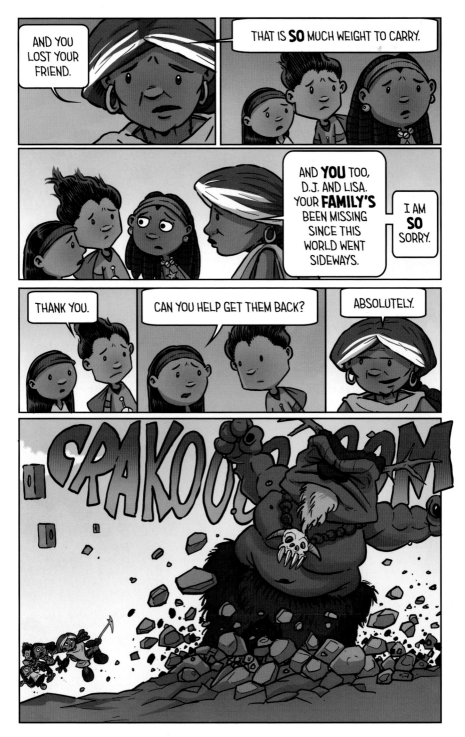

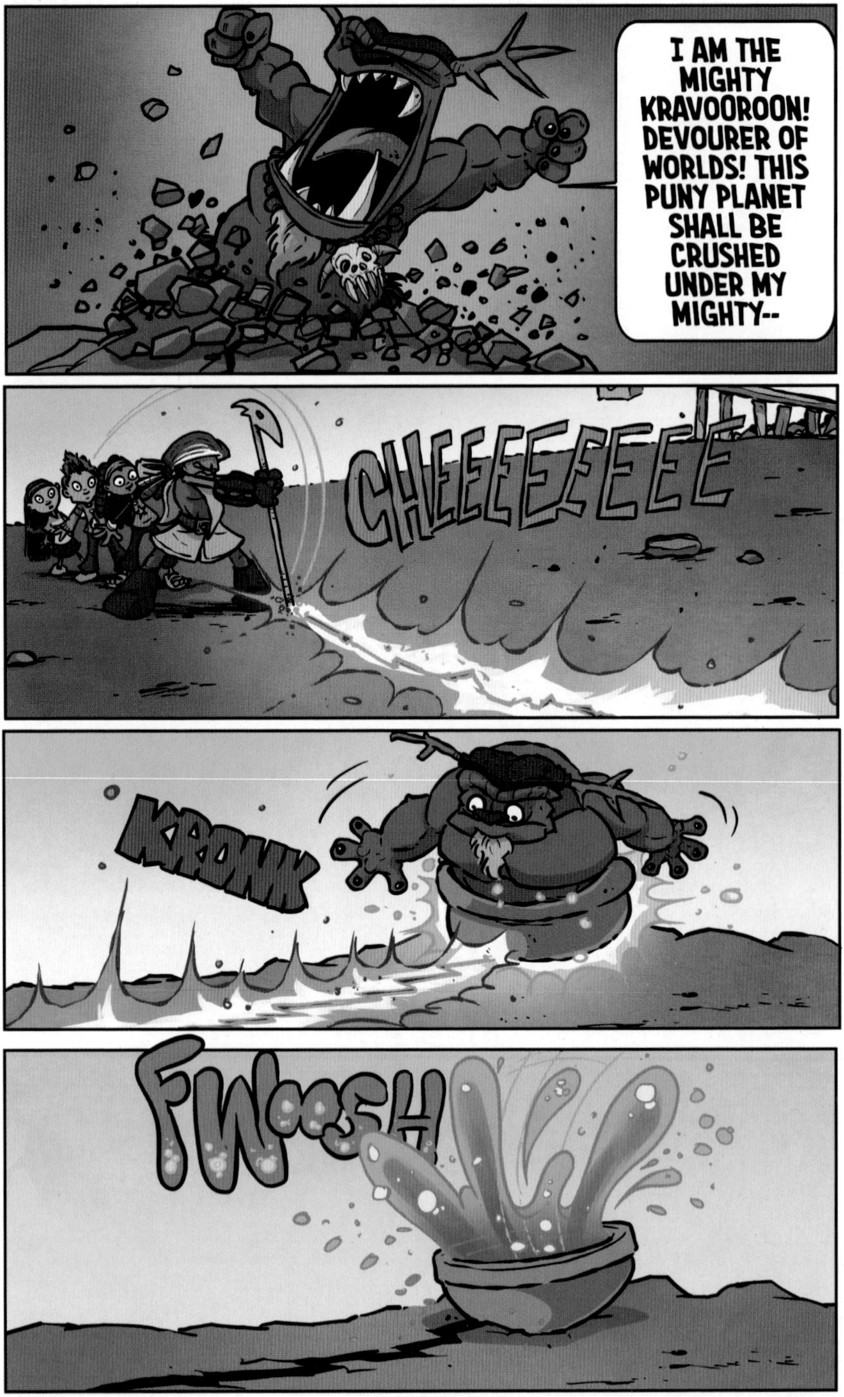
I AM THE MIGHTY KRAVOOROON! DEVOURER OF WORLDS! THIS PUNY PLANET SHALL BE CRUSHED UNDER MY MIGHTY--
CHEEEEEEEE
KRONK
FWOOSH

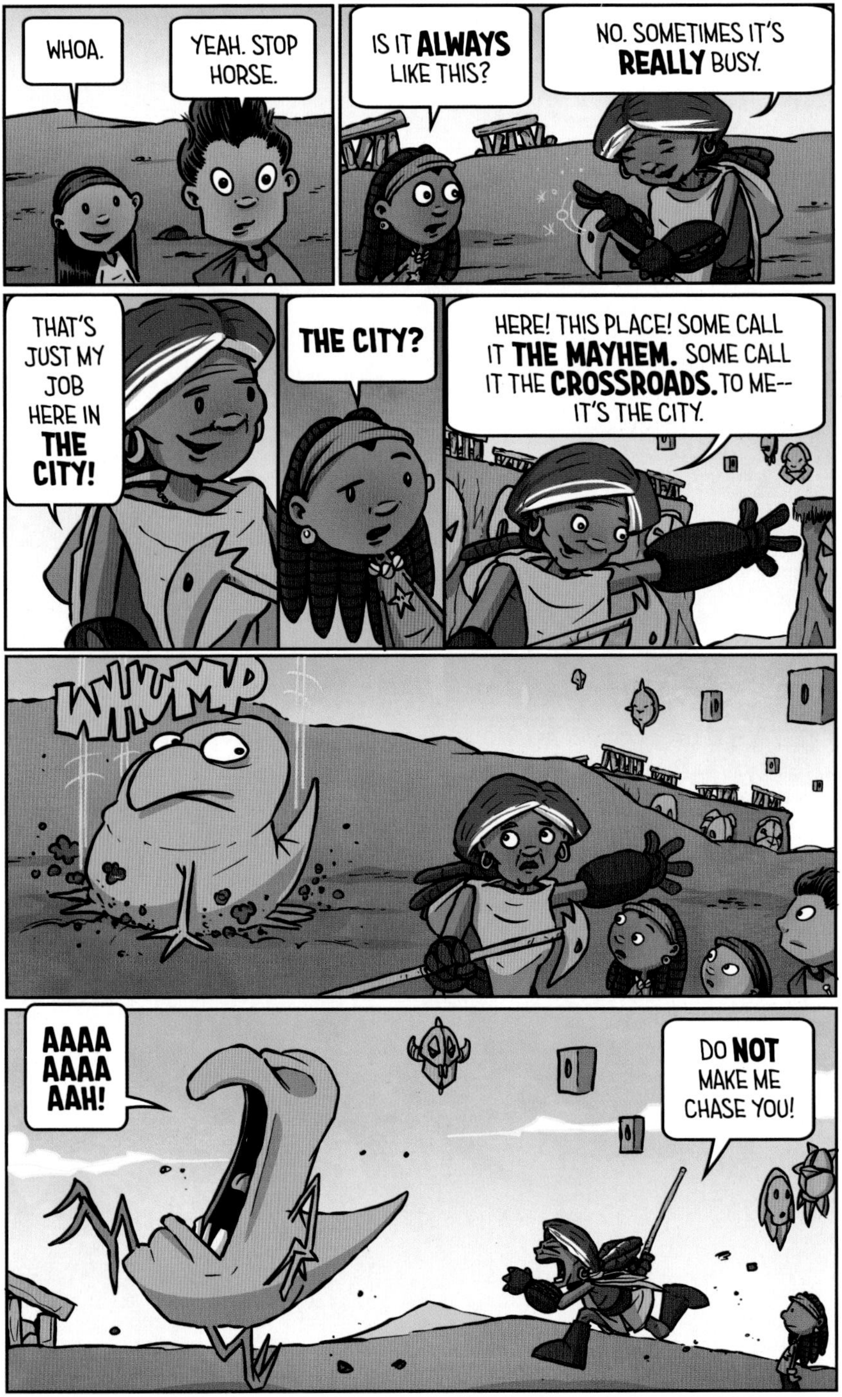

WHOA.
YEAH. STOP HORSE.
IS IT **ALWAYS** LIKE THIS?
NO. SOMETIMES IT'S **REALLY** BUSY.
THAT'S JUST MY JOB HERE IN **THE CITY!**
THE CITY?
HERE! THIS PLACE! SOME CALL IT **THE MAYHEM.** SOME CALL IT THE **CROSSROADS.** TO ME-- IT'S THE CITY.
WHUMP
AAAA AAAA AAH!
DO **NOT** MAKE ME CHASE YOU!

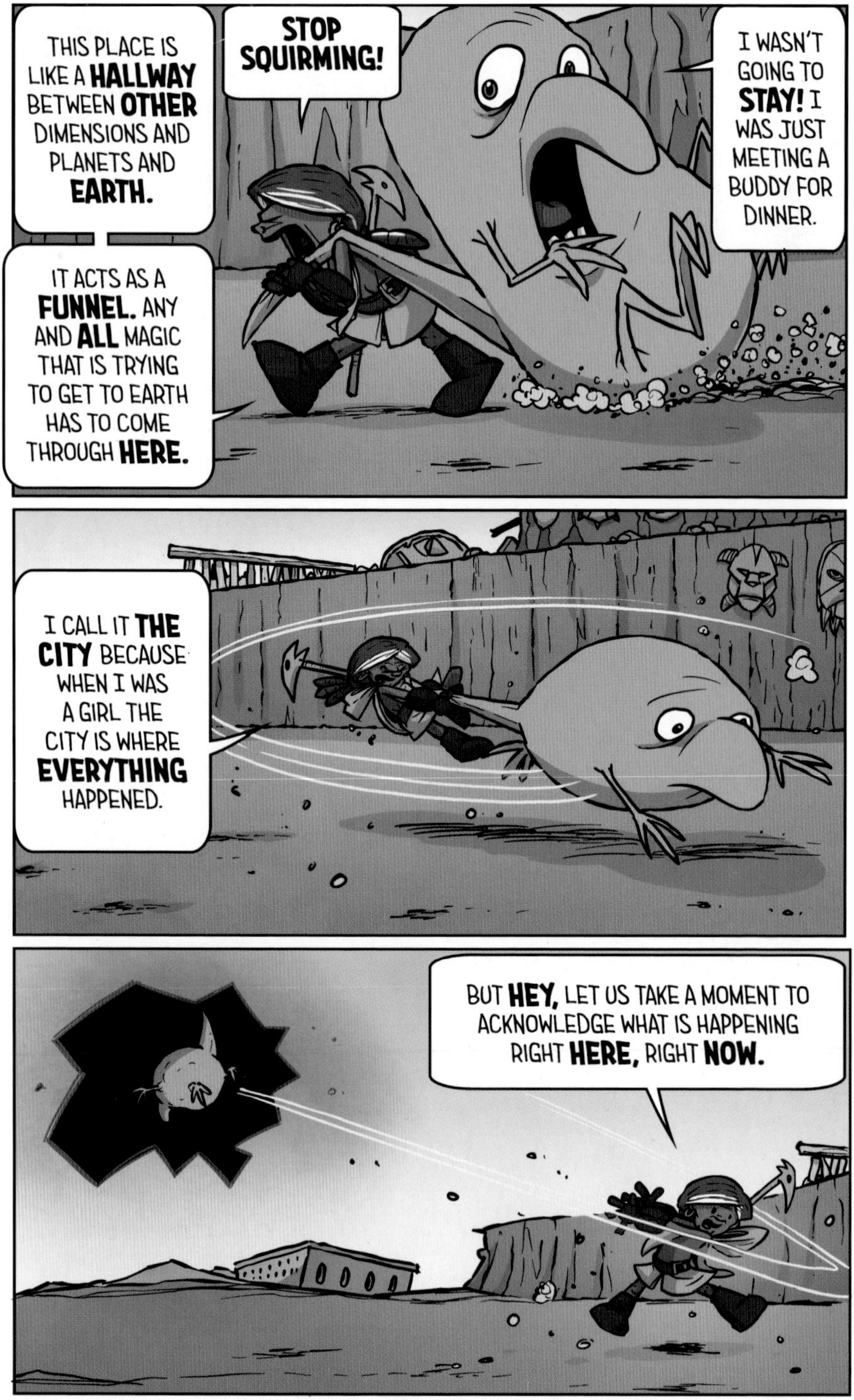
THIS PLACE IS LIKE A **HALLWAY** BETWEEN **OTHER** DIMENSIONS AND PLANETS AND **EARTH.**
IT ACTS AS A **FUNNEL.** ANY AND **ALL** MAGIC THAT IS TRYING TO GET TO EARTH HAS TO COME THROUGH **HERE.**
STOP SQUIRMING!
I WASN'T GOING TO **STAY!** I WAS JUST MEETING A BUDDY FOR DINNER.
I CALL IT **THE CITY** BECAUSE WHEN I WAS A GIRL THE CITY IS WHERE **EVERYTHING** HAPPENED.
BUT **HEY,** LET US TAKE A MOMENT TO ACKNOWLEDGE WHAT IS HAPPENING RIGHT **HERE,** RIGHT **NOW.**

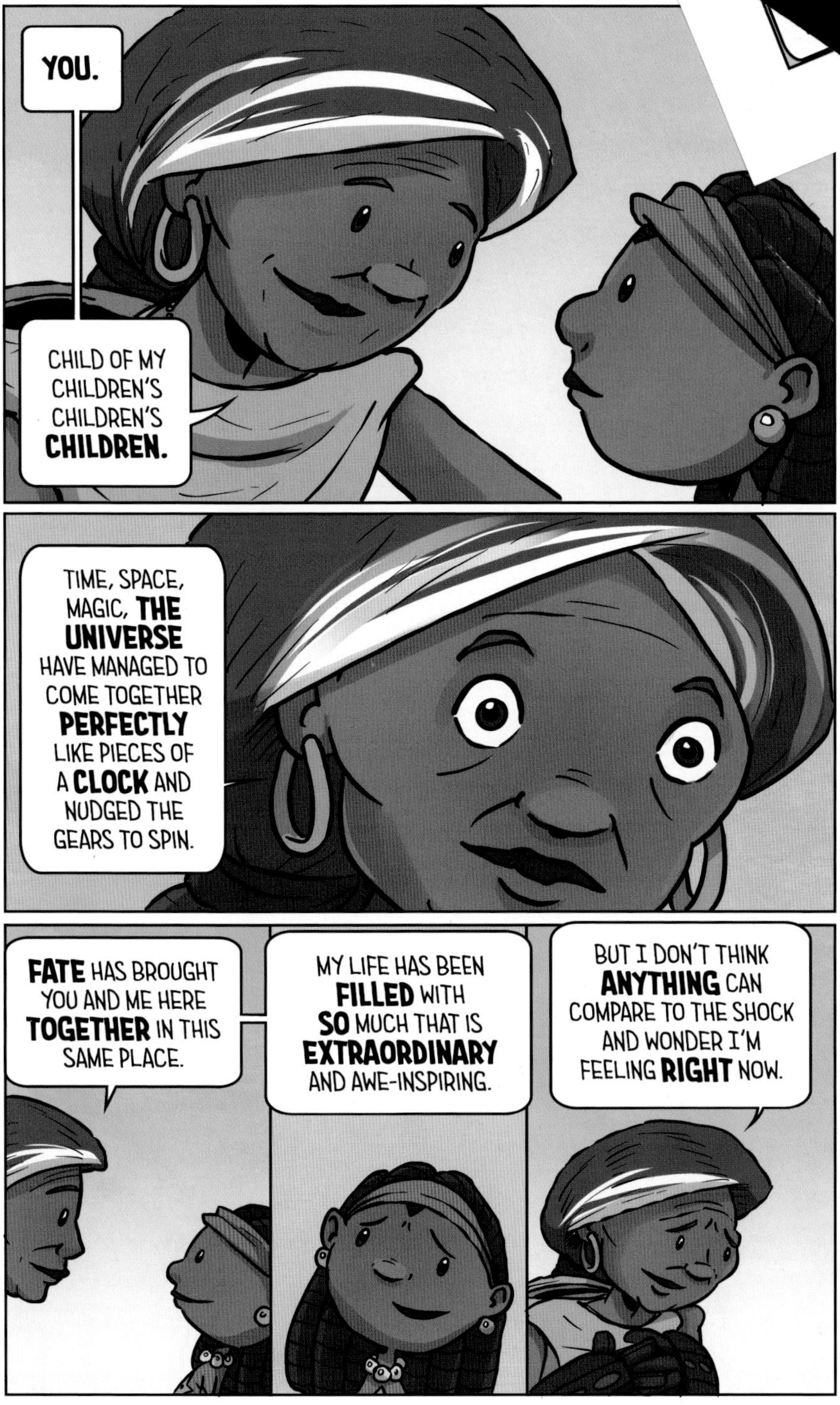
YOU.
CHILD OF MY CHILDREN'S CHILDREN'S CHILDREN.
TIME, SPACE, MAGIC, THE UNIVERSE HAVE MANAGED TO COME TOGETHER PERFECTLY LIKE PIECES OF A CLOCK AND NUDGED THE GEARS TO SPIN.
FATE HAS BROUGHT YOU AND ME HERE TOGETHER IN THIS SAME PLACE.
MY LIFE HAS BEEN FILLED WITH SO MUCH THAT IS EXTRAORDINARY AND AWE-INSPIRING.
BUT I DON'T THINK ANYTHING CAN COMPARE TO THE SHOCK AND WONDER I'M FEELING RIGHT NOW.

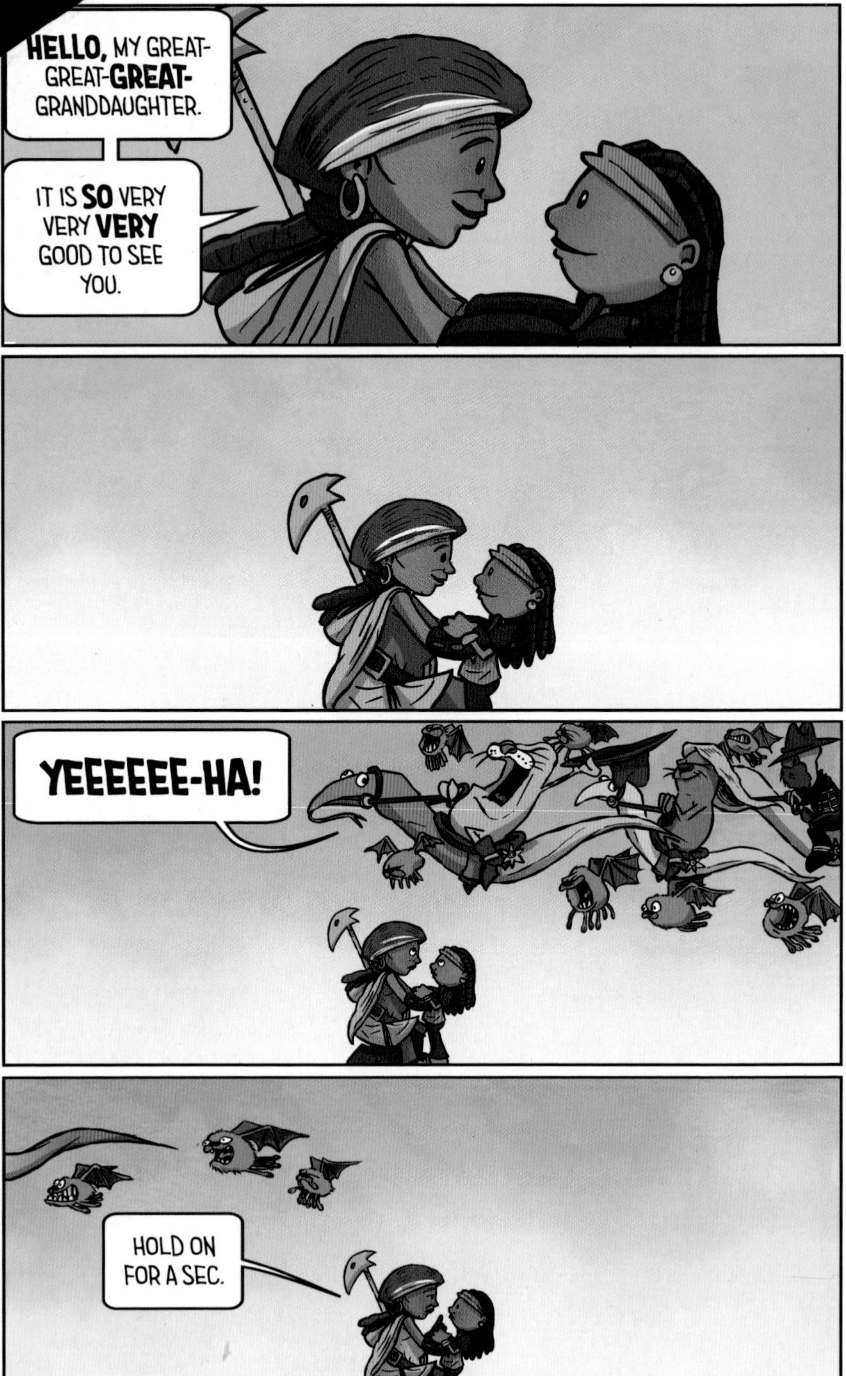
HELLO, MY GREAT-GREAT-GREAT-GRANDDAUGHTER.
IT IS SO VERY VERY VERY GOOD TO SEE YOU.
YEEEEEE-HA!
HOLD ON FOR A SEC.

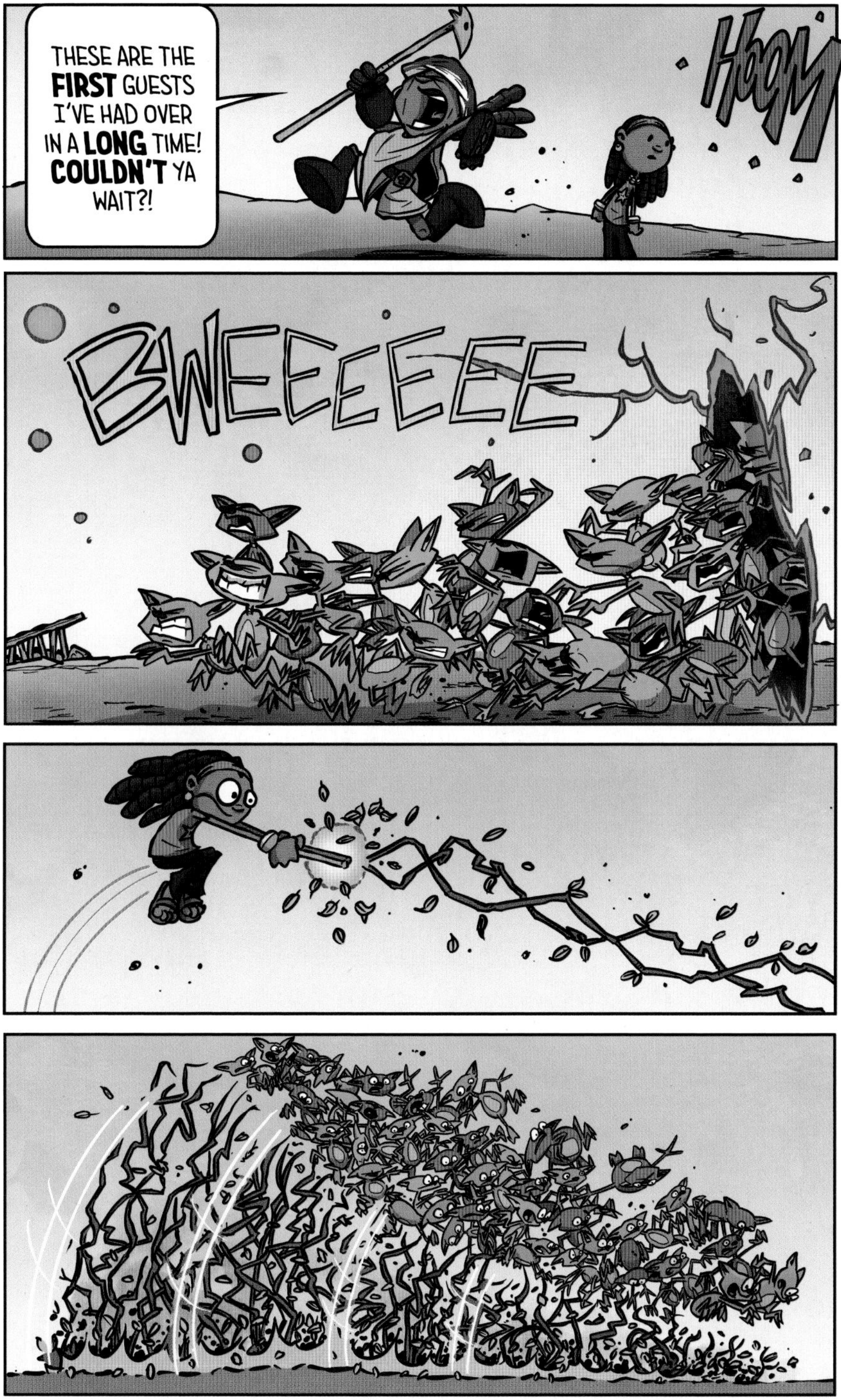
THESE ARE THE **FIRST** GUESTS I'VE HAD OVER IN A **LONG** TIME! **COULDN'T** YA WAIT?!
BWEEEEEE

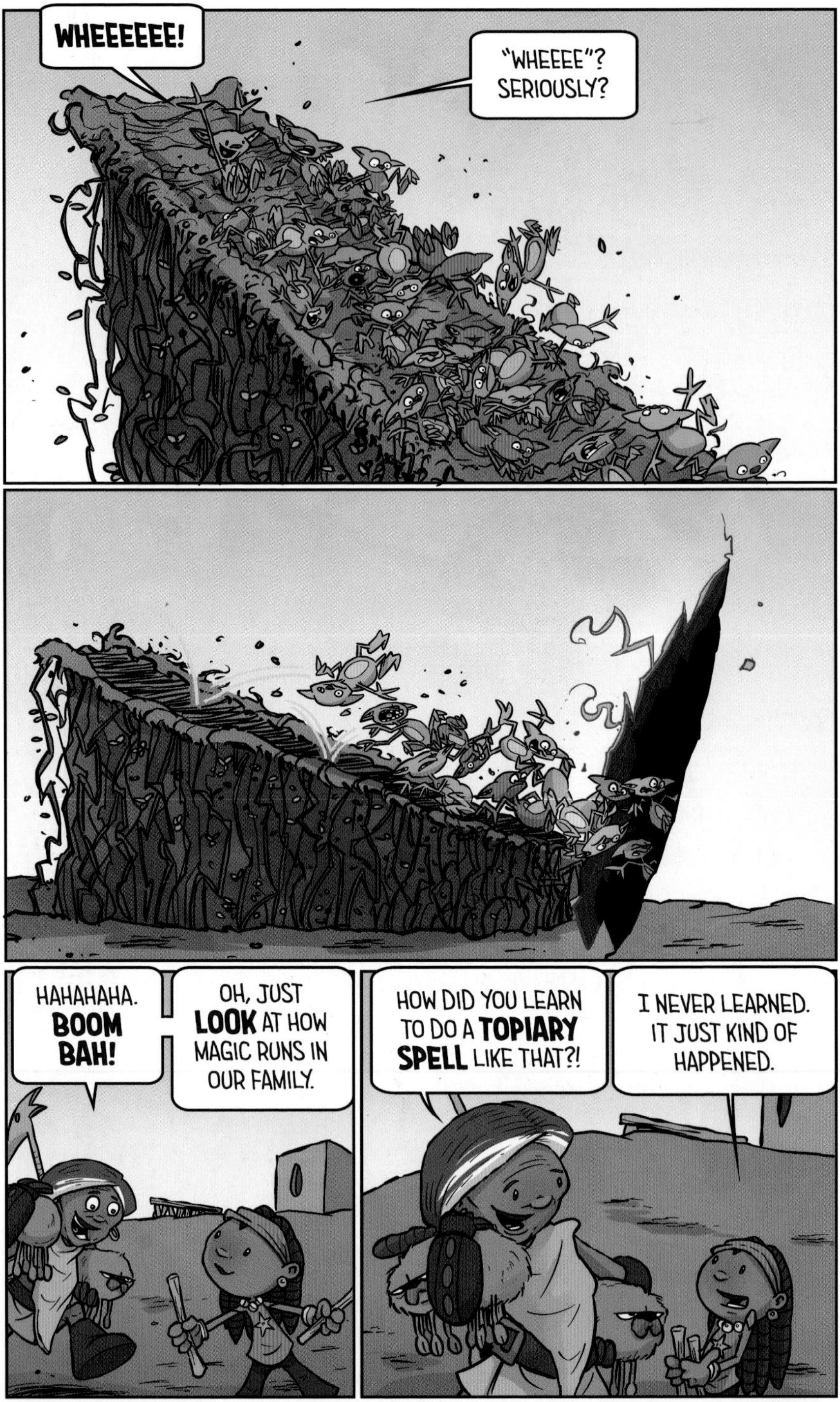
WHEEEEEE!
"WHEEEE"? SERIOUSLY?
HAHAHAHA. BOOM BAH!
OH, JUST LOOK AT HOW MAGIC RUNS IN OUR FAMILY.
HOW DID YOU LEARN TO DO A TOPIARY SPELL LIKE THAT?!
I NEVER LEARNED. IT JUST KIND OF HAPPENED.

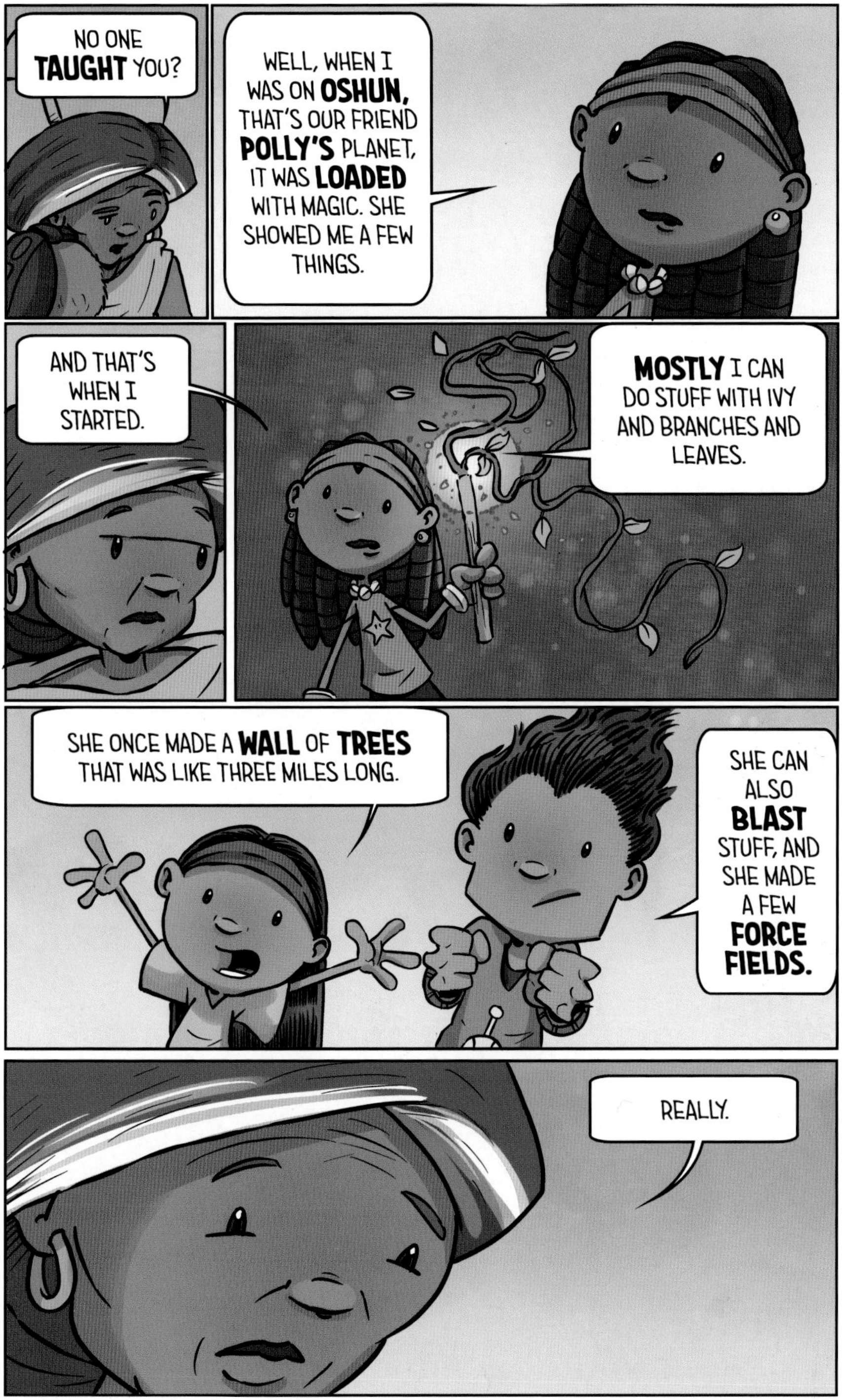
NO ONE TAUGHT YOU?
WELL, WHEN I WAS ON OSHUN, THAT'S OUR FRIEND POLLY'S PLANET, IT WAS LOADED WITH MAGIC. SHE SHOWED ME A FEW THINGS.
AND THAT'S WHEN I STARTED.
MOSTLY I CAN DO STUFF WITH IVY AND BRANCHES AND LEAVES.
SHE ONCE MADE A WALL OF TREES THAT WAS LIKE THREE MILES LONG.
SHE CAN ALSO BLAST STUFF, AND SHE MADE A FEW FORCE FIELDS.
REALLY.

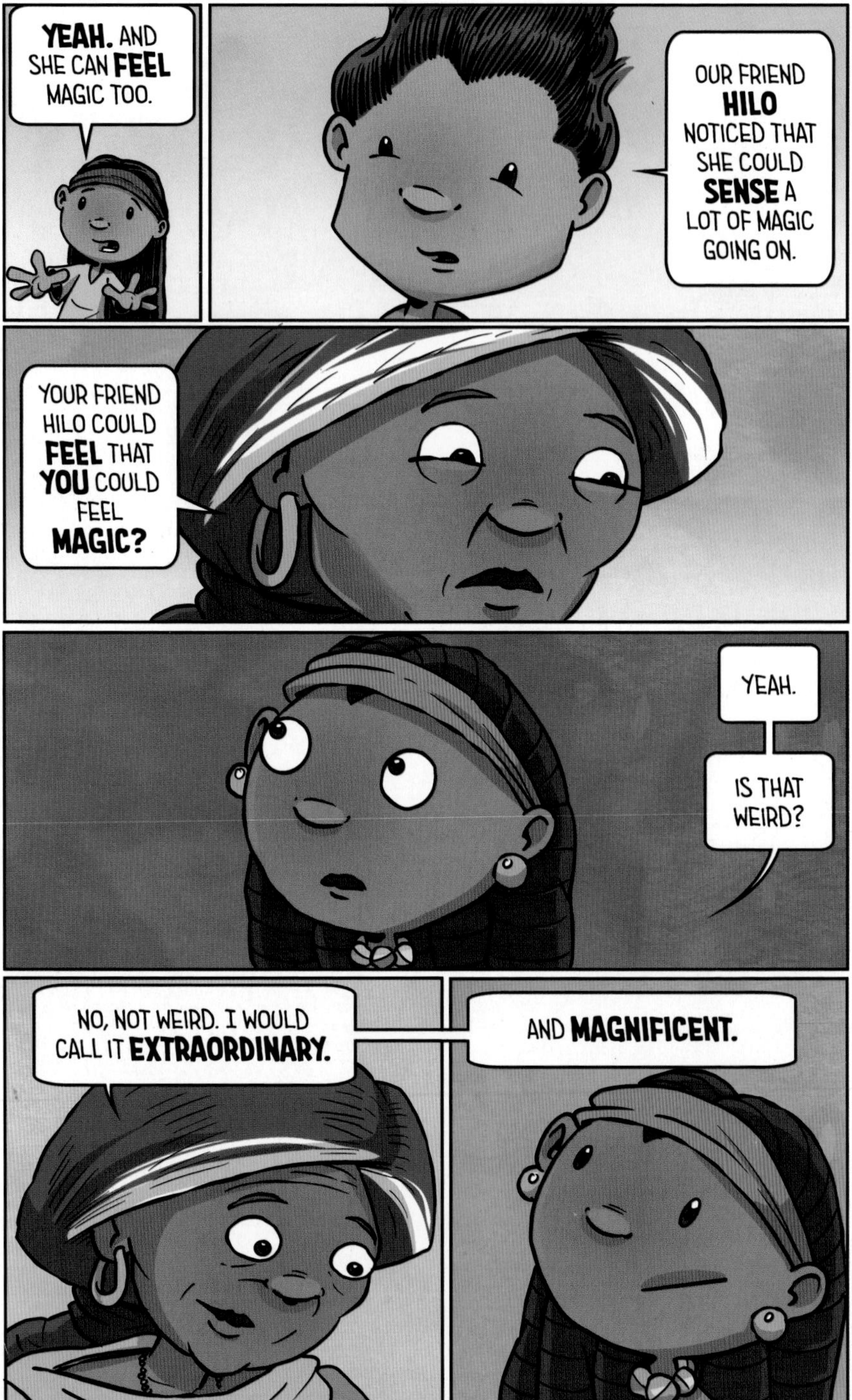
YEAH. AND SHE CAN **FEEL** MAGIC TOO.
OUR FRIEND **HILO** NOTICED THAT SHE COULD **SENSE** A LOT OF MAGIC GOING ON.
YOUR FRIEND HILO COULD **FEEL** THAT **YOU** COULD FEEL **MAGIC?**
YEAH.
IS THAT WEIRD?
NO, NOT WEIRD. I WOULD CALL IT **EXTRAORDINARY.**
AND **MAGNIFICENT.**

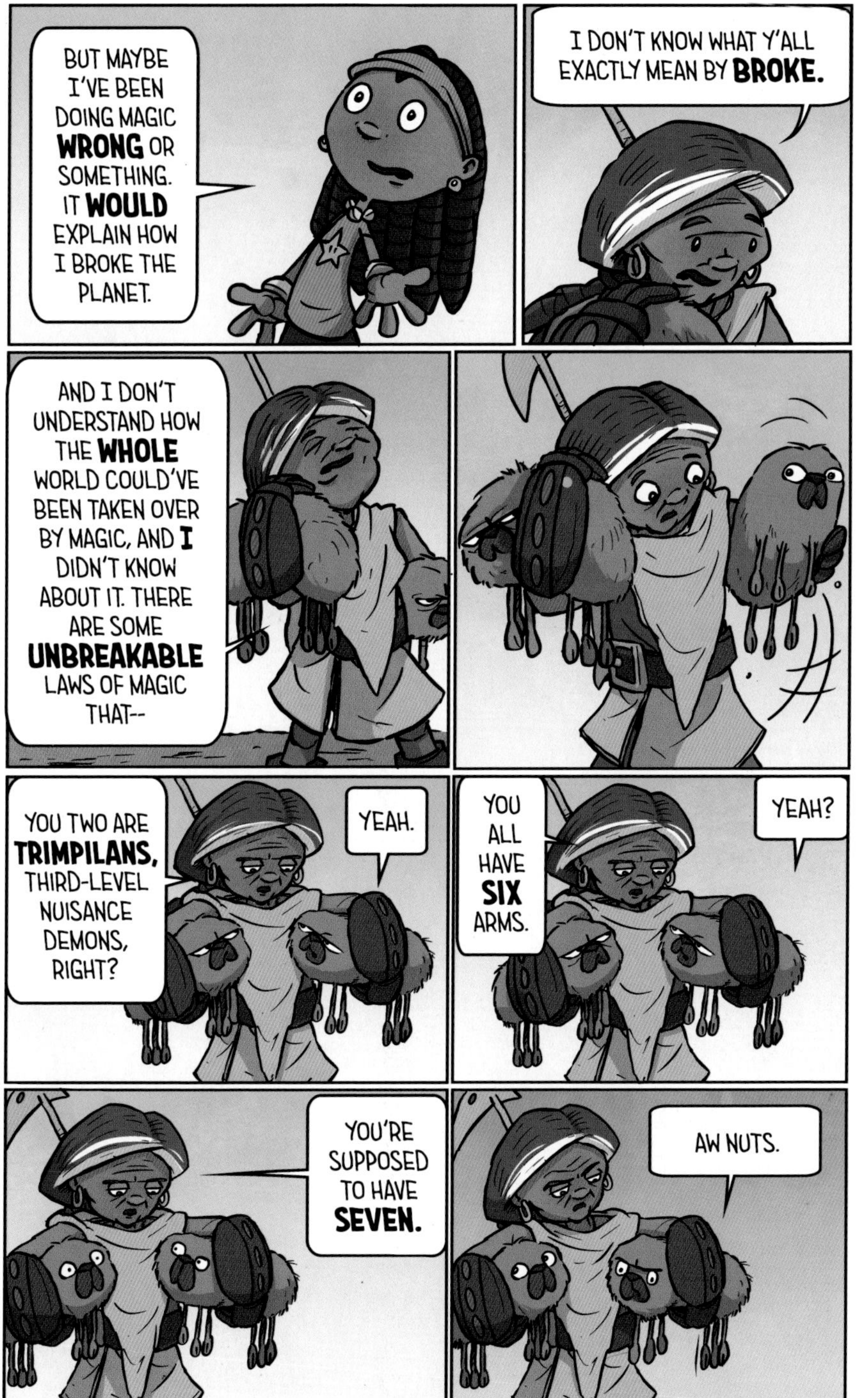
BUT MAYBE I'VE BEEN DOING MAGIC **WRONG** OR SOMETHING. IT **WOULD** EXPLAIN HOW I BROKE THE PLANET.
I DON'T KNOW WHAT Y'ALL EXACTLY MEAN BY **BROKE.**
AND I DON'T UNDERSTAND HOW THE **WHOLE** WORLD COULD'VE BEEN TAKEN OVER BY MAGIC, AND **I** DIDN'T KNOW ABOUT IT. THERE ARE SOME **UNBREAKABLE** LAWS OF MAGIC THAT--
YOU TWO ARE **TRIMPILANS,** THIRD-LEVEL NUISANCE DEMONS, RIGHT?
YEAH.
YOU ALL HAVE **SIX** ARMS.
YEAH?
YOU'RE SUPPOSED TO HAVE **SEVEN.**
AW NUTS.

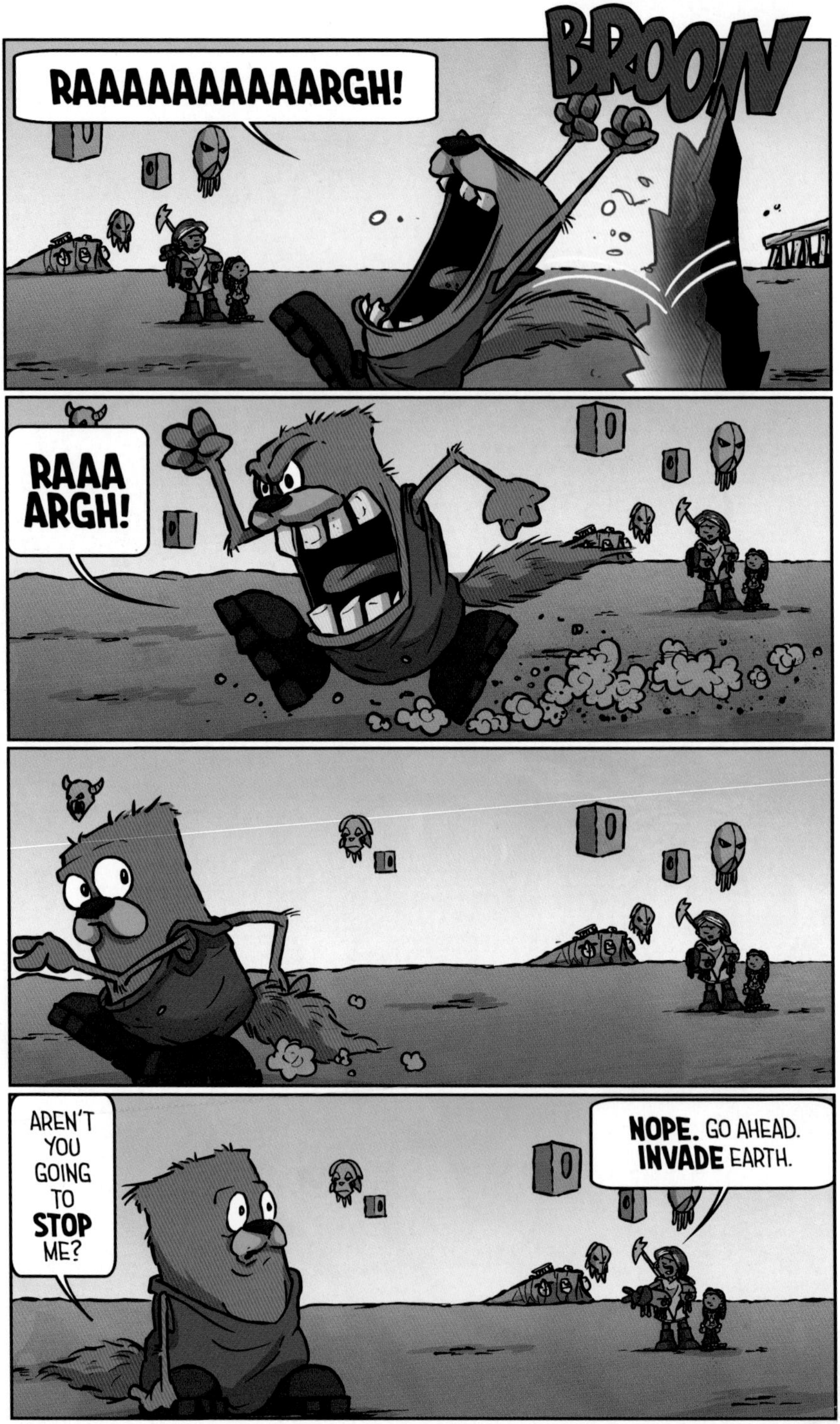
RAAAAAAAAAARGH!
BROON
RAAA ARGH!
AREN'T YOU GOING TO STOP ME?
NOPE. GO AHEAD. INVADE EARTH.

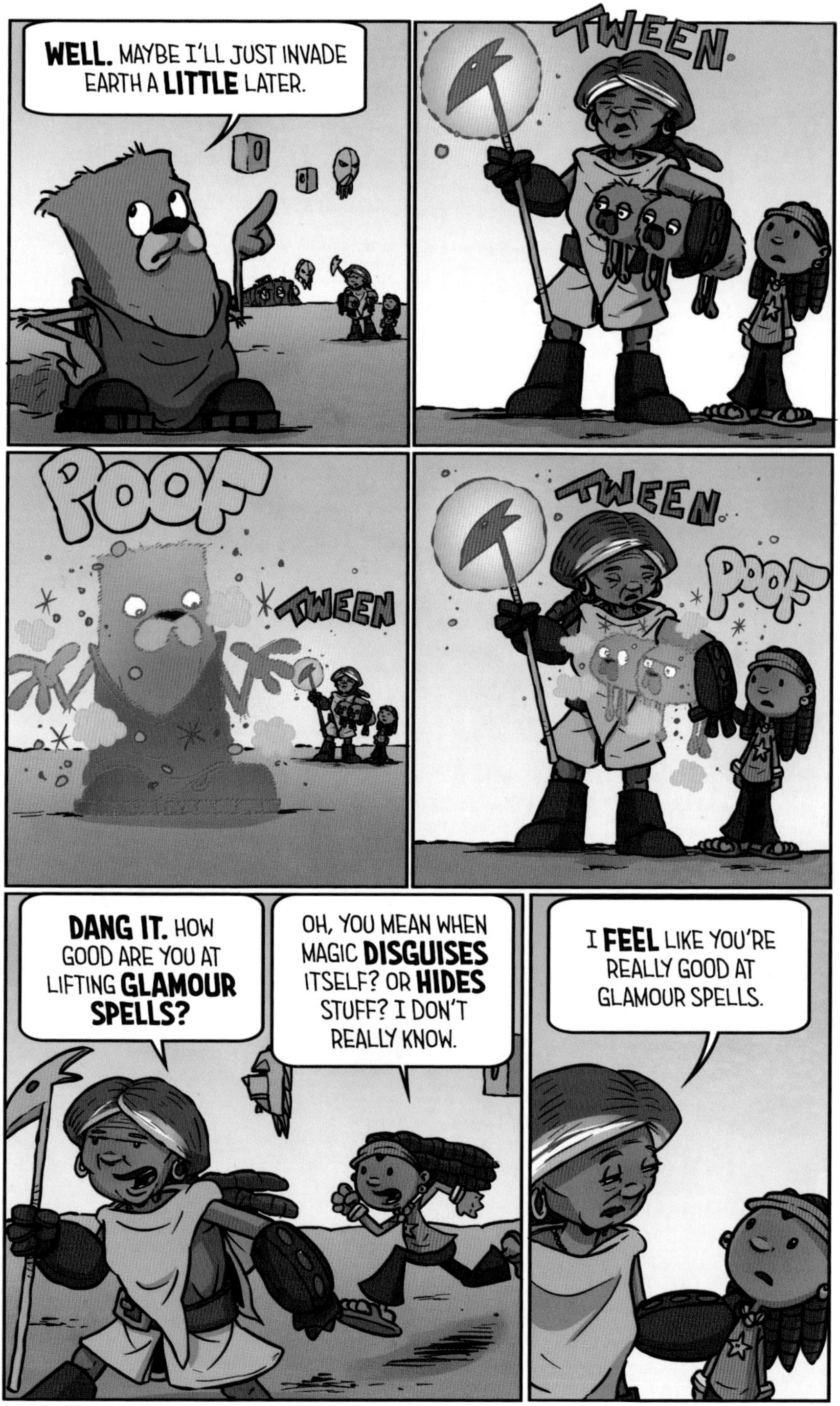
WELL. MAYBE I'LL JUST INVADE EARTH A LITTLE LATER.
TWEEN
POOF
TWEEN
TWEEN
POOF
DANG IT. HOW GOOD ARE YOU AT LIFTING GLAMOUR SPELLS?
OH, YOU MEAN WHEN MAGIC DISGUISES ITSELF? OR HIDES STUFF? I DON'T REALLY KNOW.
I FEEL LIKE YOU'RE REALLY GOOD AT GLAMOUR SPELLS.

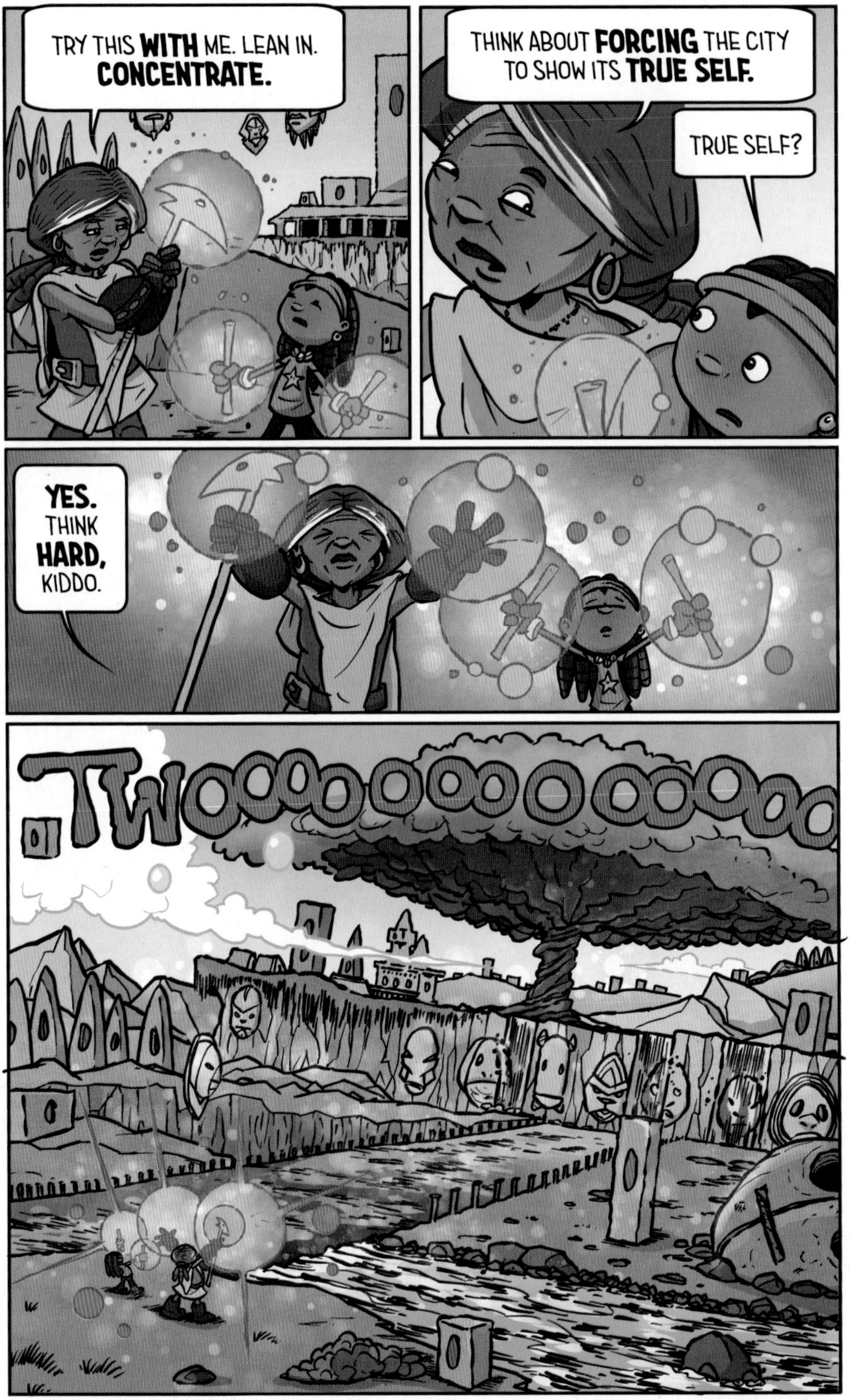
TRY THIS **WITH** ME. LEAN IN. **CONCENTRATE.**
THINK ABOUT **FORCING** THE CITY TO SHOW ITS **TRUE SELF.**
TRUE SELF?
YES. THINK **HARD,** KIDDO.
TWOOOOOOOOOOOO

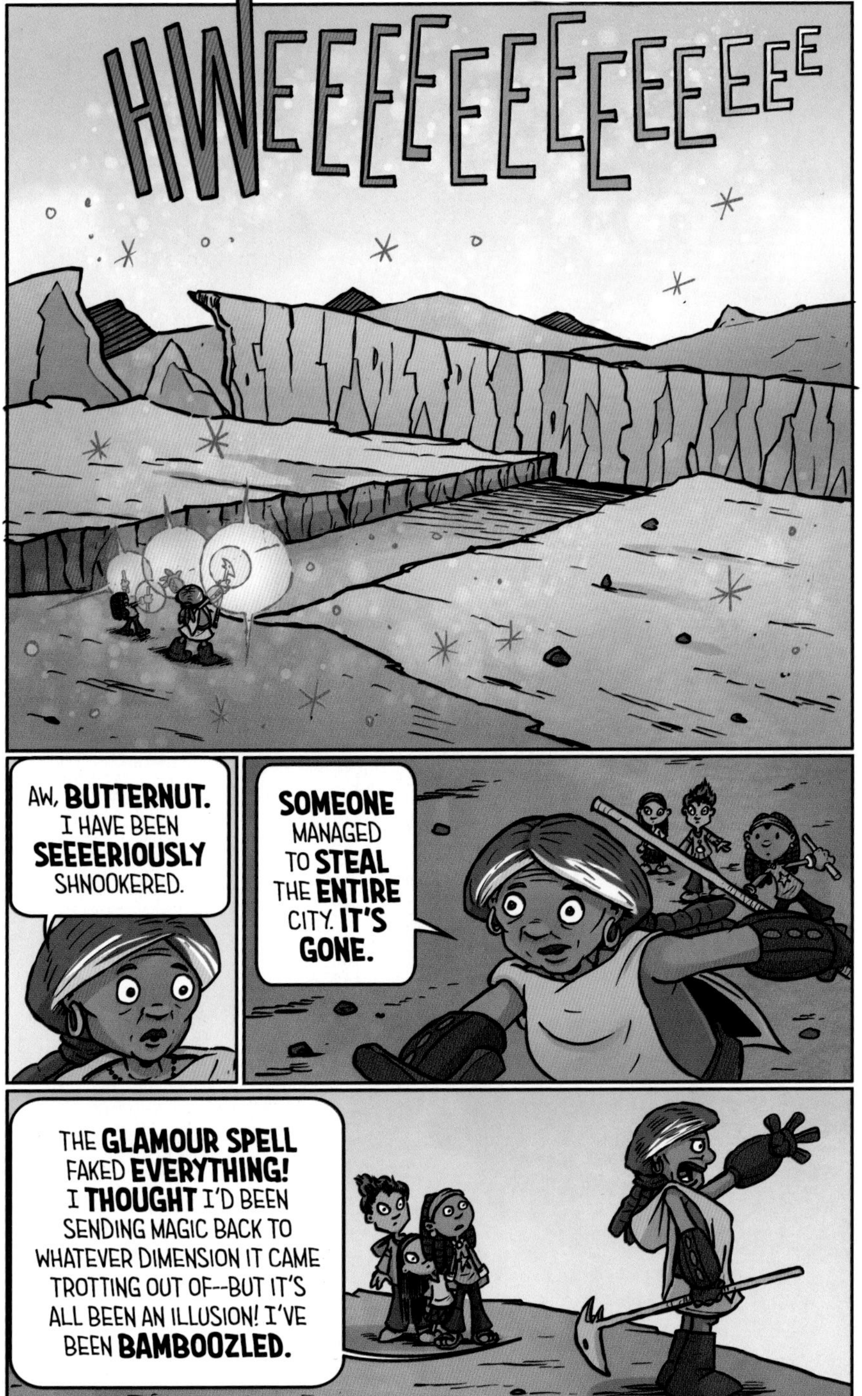
HWEEEEEEEEEEEE
AW, BUTTERNUT. I HAVE BEEN SEEEERIOUSLY SHNOOKERED.
SOMEONE MANAGED TO STEAL THE ENTIRE CITY. IT'S GONE.
THE GLAMOUR SPELL FAKED EVERYTHING! I THOUGHT I'D BEEN SENDING MAGIC BACK TO WHATEVER DIMENSION IT CAME TROTTING OUT OF--BUT IT'S ALL BEEN AN ILLUSION! I'VE BEEN BAMBOOZLED.

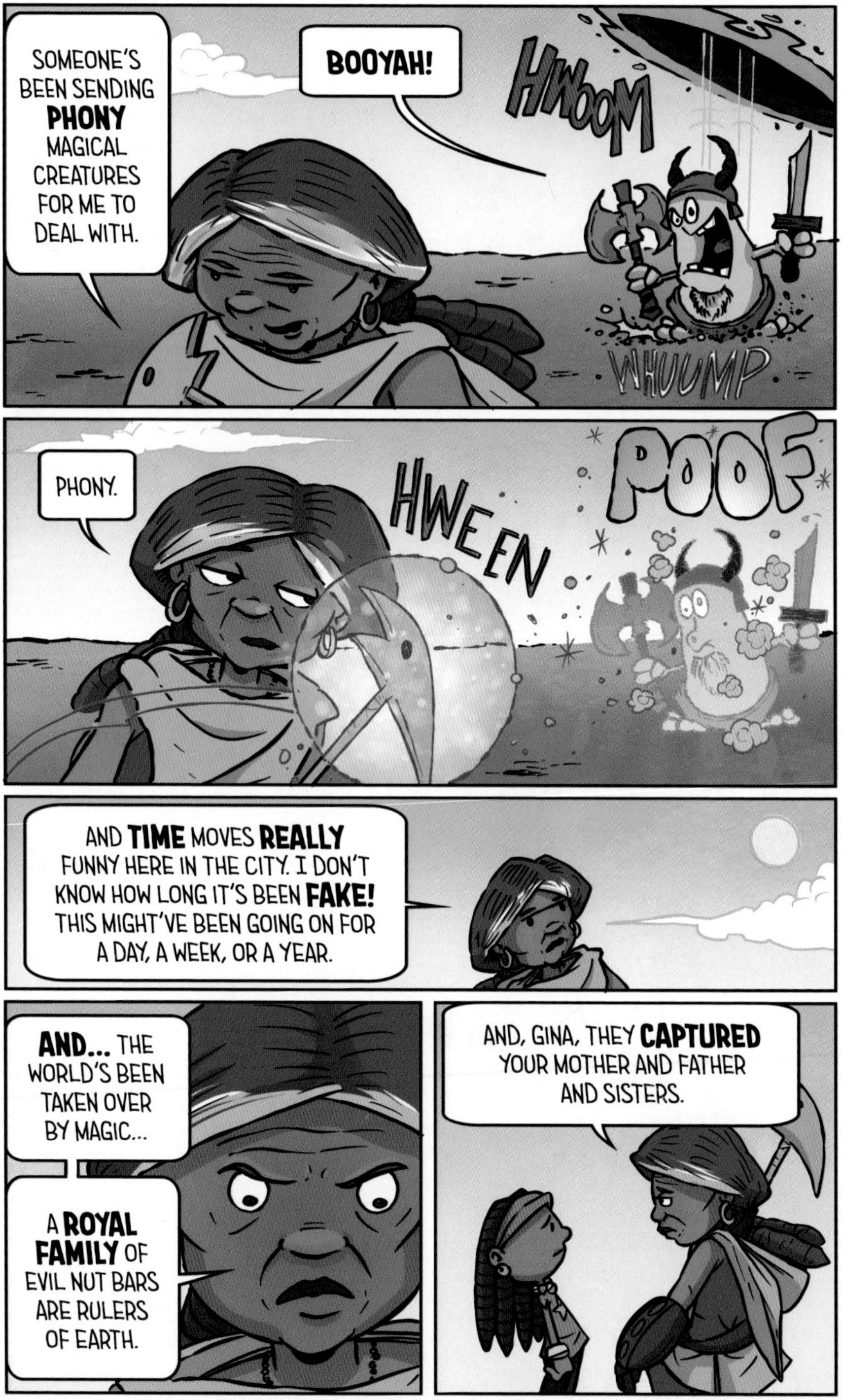
SOMEONE'S BEEN SENDING **PHONY** MAGICAL CREATURES FOR ME TO DEAL WITH.
BOOYAH!
HWOOM
WHUUMP
PHONY.
HWEEN
POOF
AND **TIME** MOVES **REALLY** FUNNY HERE IN THE CITY. I DON'T KNOW HOW LONG IT'S BEEN **FAKE!** THIS MIGHT'VE BEEN GOING ON FOR A DAY, A WEEK, OR A YEAR.
AND... THE WORLD'S BEEN TAKEN OVER BY MAGIC...
A **ROYAL FAMILY** OF EVIL NUT BARS ARE RULERS OF EARTH.
AND, GINA, THEY **CAPTURED** YOUR MOTHER AND FATHER AND SISTERS.

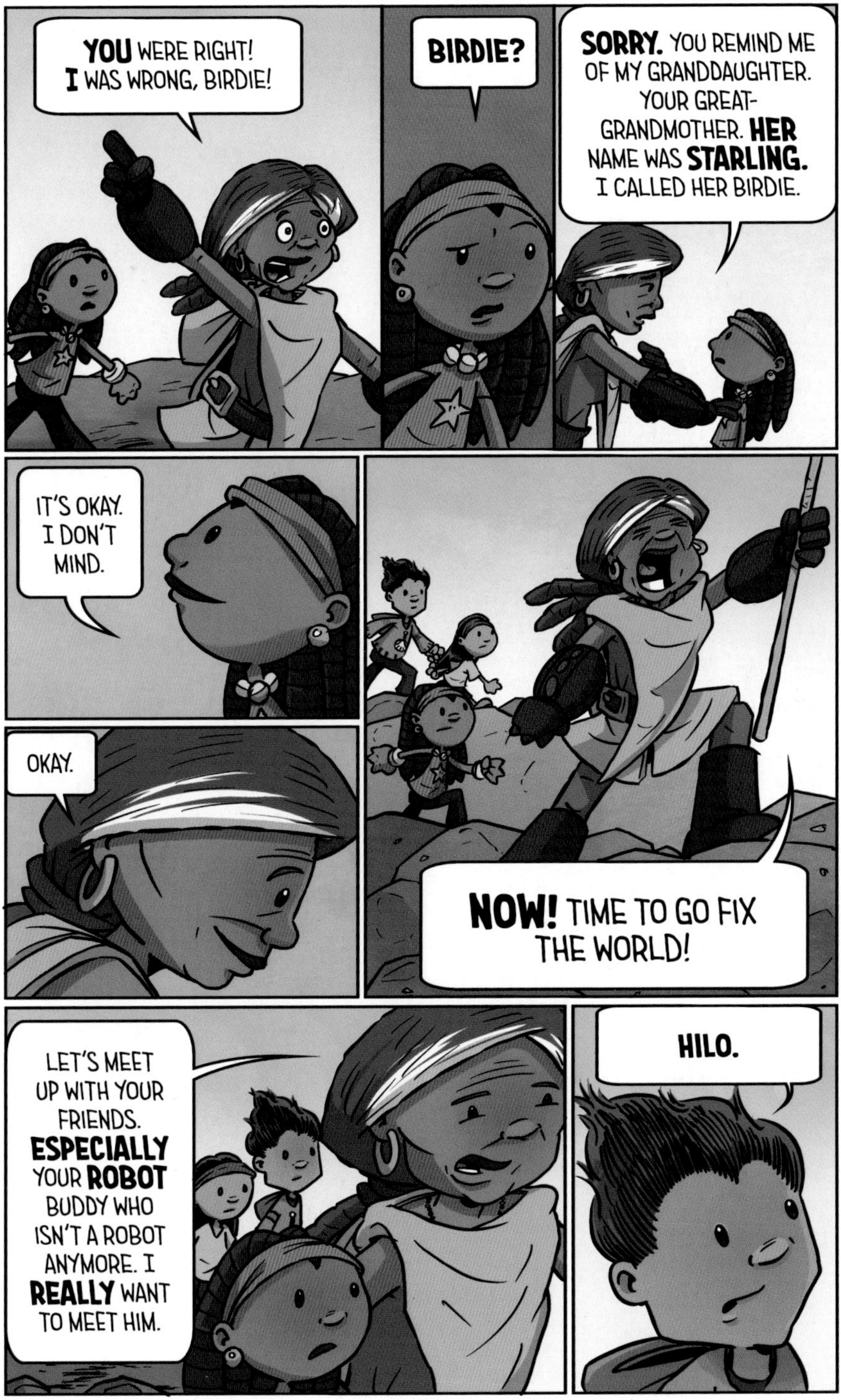
YOU WERE RIGHT! I WAS WRONG, BIRDIE!
BIRDIE?
SORRY. YOU REMIND ME OF MY GRANDDAUGHTER. YOUR GREAT-GRANDMOTHER. HER NAME WAS STARLING. I CALLED HER BIRDIE.
IT'S OKAY. I DON'T MIND.
OKAY.
NOW! TIME TO GO FIX THE WORLD!
LET'S MEET UP WITH YOUR FRIENDS. ESPECIALLY YOUR ROBOT BUDDY WHO ISN'T A ROBOT ANYMORE. I REALLY WANT TO MEET HIM.
HILO.

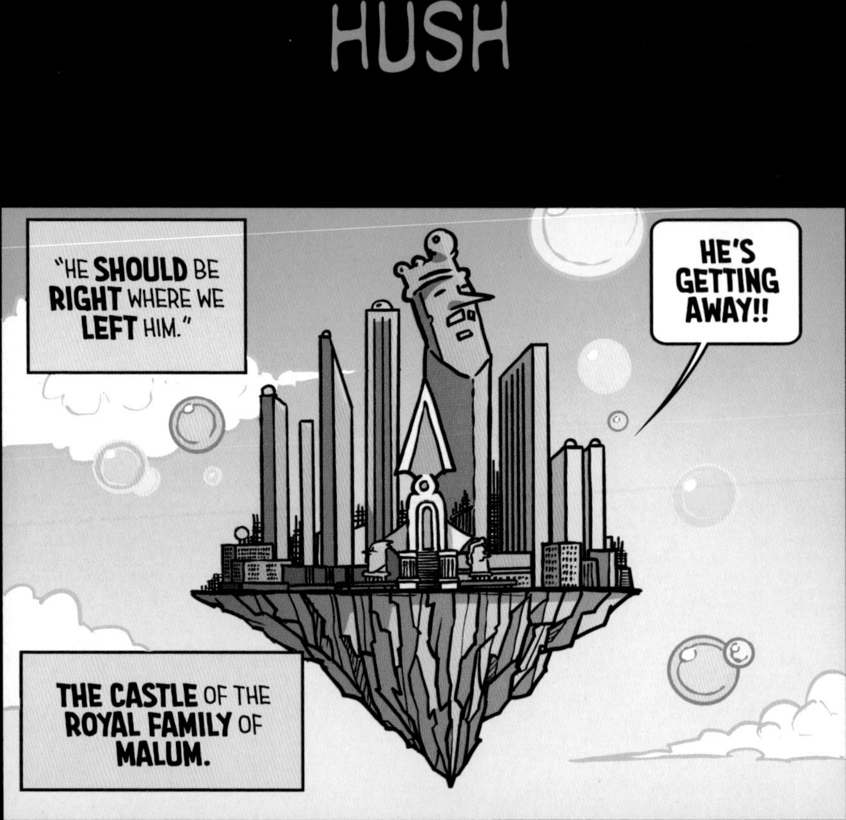
HUSH
"HE SHOULD BE RIGHT WHERE WE LEFT HIM."
HE'S GETTING AWAY!!
THE CASTLE OF THE ROYAL FAMILY OF MALUM.

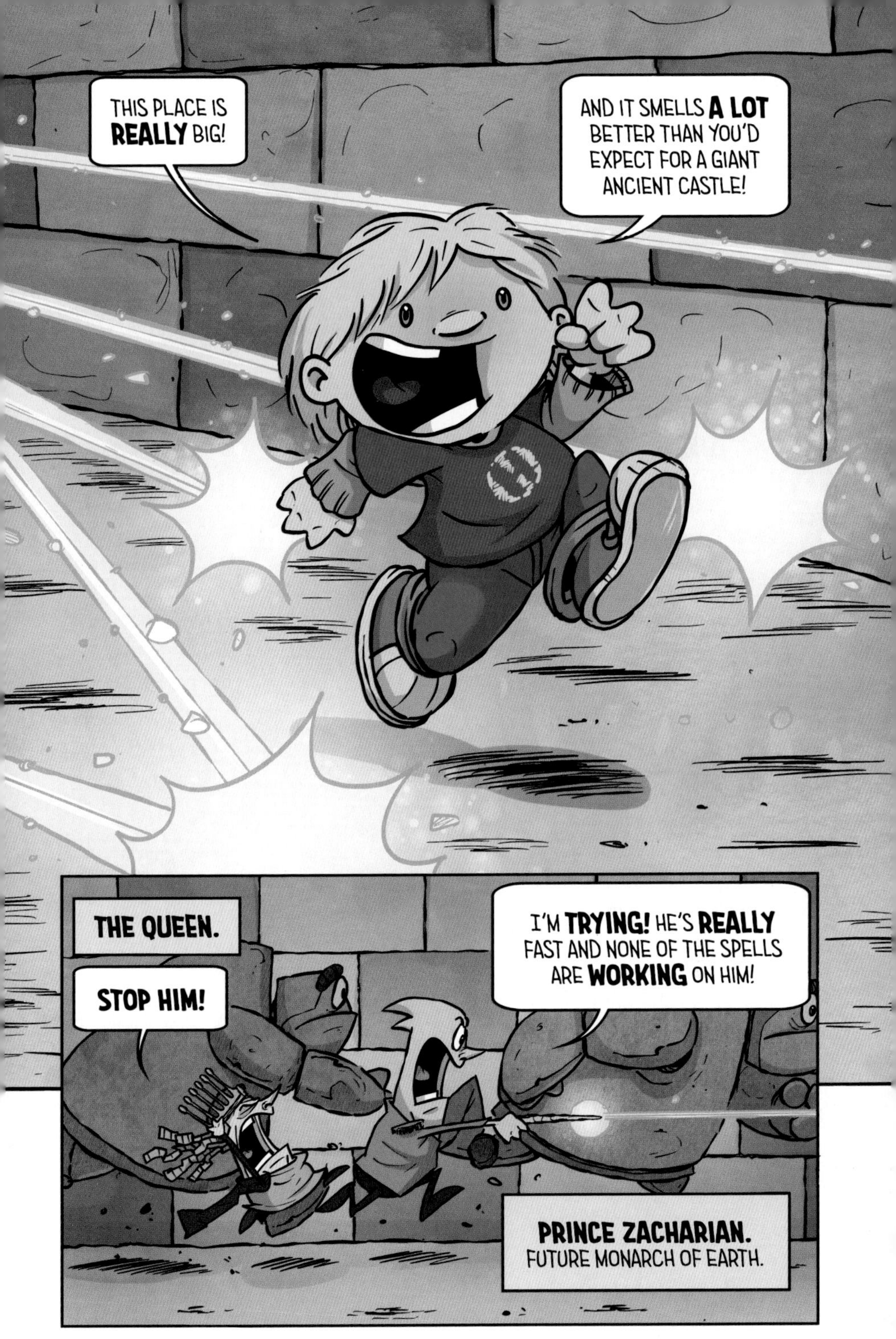

THIS PLACE IS **REALLY** BIG!
AND IT SMELLS **A LOT** BETTER THAN YOU'D EXPECT FOR A GIANT ANCIENT CASTLE!
THE QUEEN.
STOP HIM!
I'M **TRYING!** HE'S **REALLY** FAST AND NONE OF THE SPELLS ARE **WORKING** ON HIM!
PRINCE ZACHARIAN. FUTURE MONARCH OF EARTH.

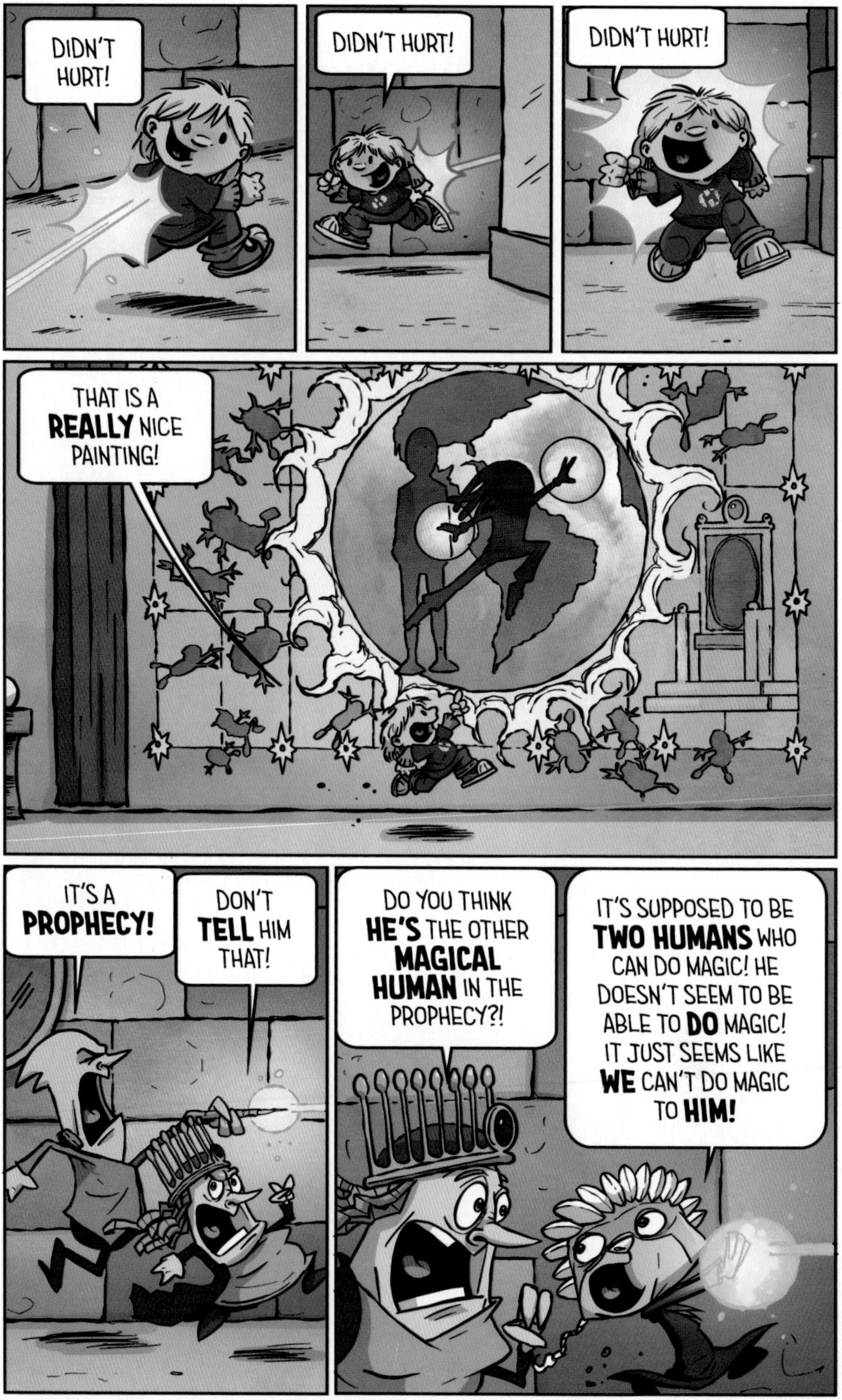
DIDN'T HURT!
DIDN'T HURT!
DIDN'T HURT!
THAT IS A **REALLY** NICE PAINTING!
IT'S A **PROPHECY!**
DON'T **TELL** HIM THAT!
DO YOU THINK **HE'S** THE OTHER **MAGICAL HUMAN** IN THE PROPHECY?!
IT'S SUPPOSED TO BE **TWO HUMANS** WHO CAN DO MAGIC! HE DOESN'T SEEM TO BE ABLE TO **DO** MAGIC! IT JUST SEEMS LIKE **WE** CAN'T DO MAGIC TO **HIM!**

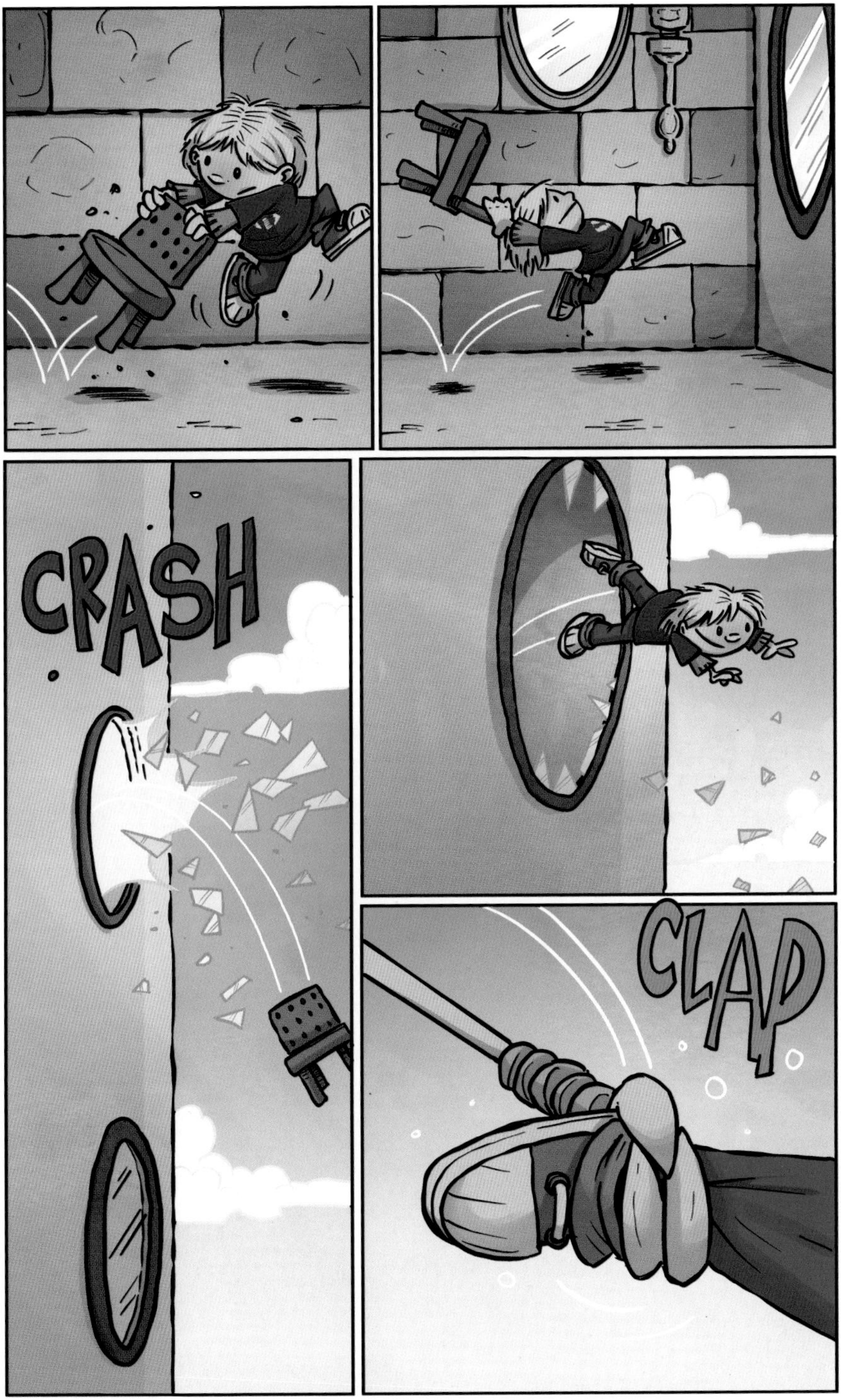
CRASH
CLAP

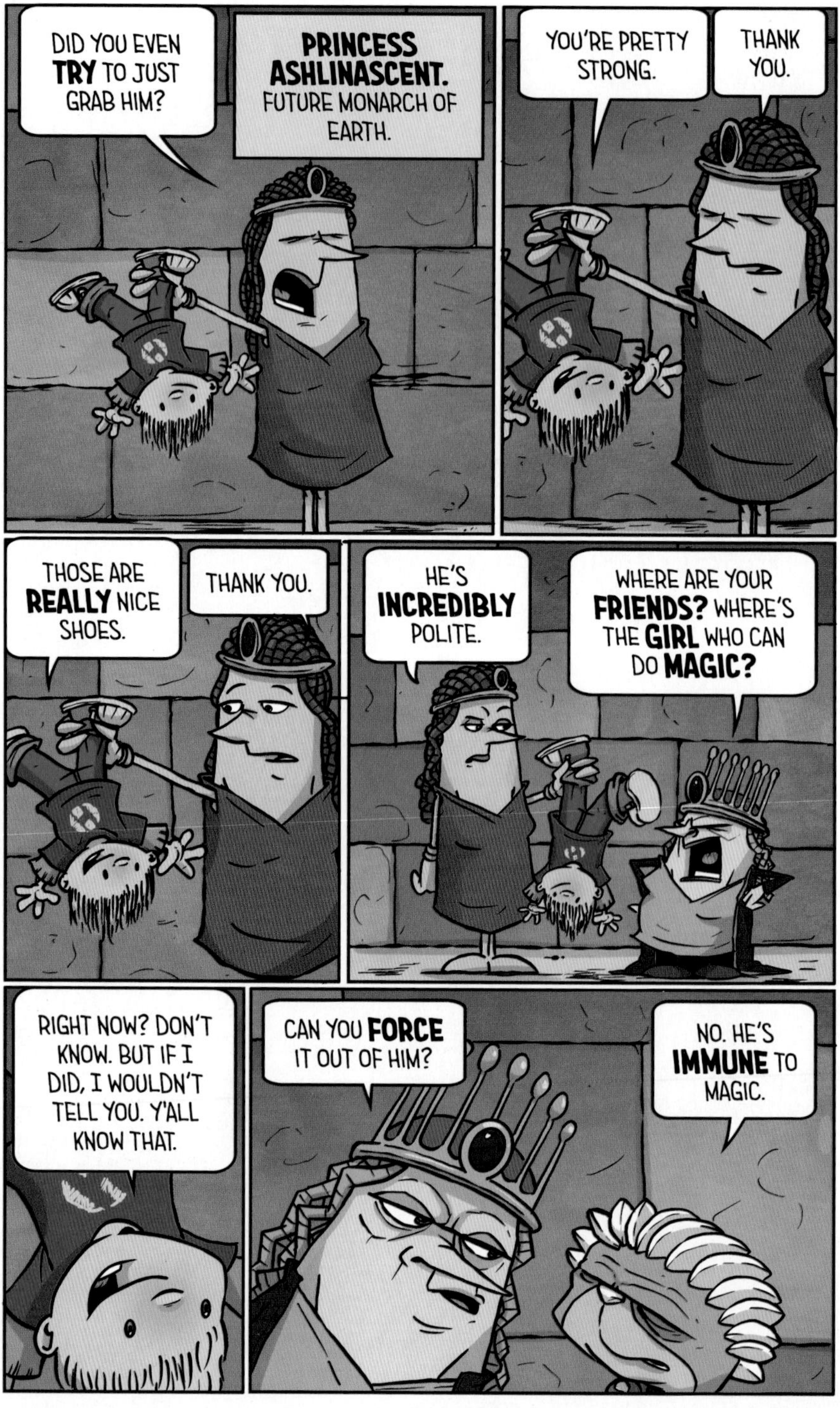
DID YOU EVEN TRY TO JUST GRAB HIM?
PRINCESS ASHLINASCENT. FUTURE MONARCH OF EARTH.
YOU'RE PRETTY STRONG.
THANK YOU.
THOSE ARE REALLY NICE SHOES.
THANK YOU.
HE'S INCREDIBLY POLITE.
WHERE ARE YOUR FRIENDS? WHERE'S THE GIRL WHO CAN DO MAGIC?
RIGHT NOW? DON'T KNOW. BUT IF I DID, I WOULDN'T TELL YOU. Y'ALL KNOW THAT.
CAN YOU FORCE IT OUT OF HIM?
NO. HE'S IMMUNE TO MAGIC.

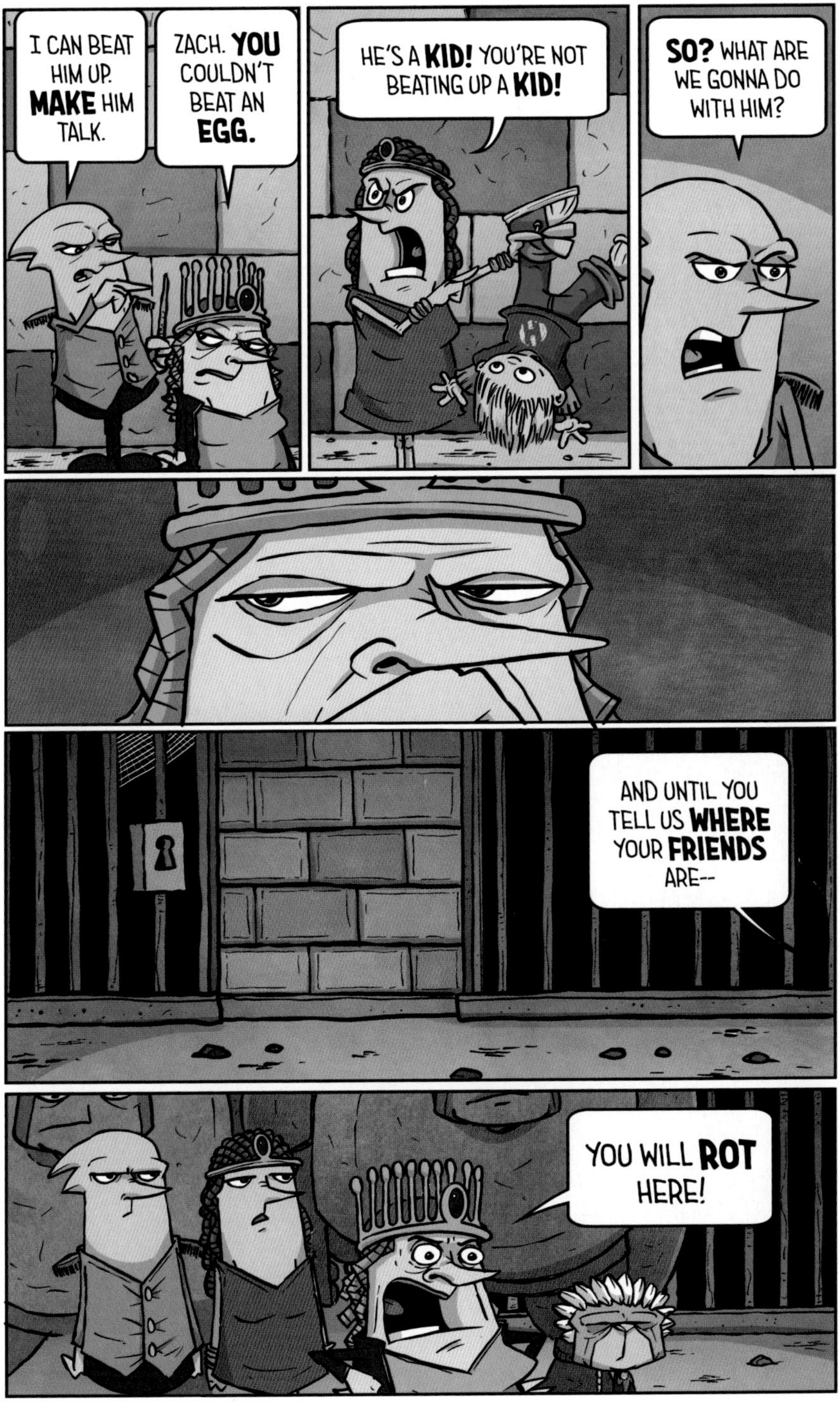
I CAN BEAT HIM UP. **MAKE** HIM TALK.
ZACH. **YOU** COULDN'T BEAT AN **EGG.**
HE'S A **KID!** YOU'RE NOT BEATING UP A **KID!**
SO? WHAT ARE WE GONNA DO WITH HIM?
AND UNTIL YOU TELL US **WHERE** YOUR **FRIENDS** ARE--
YOU WILL **ROT** HERE!

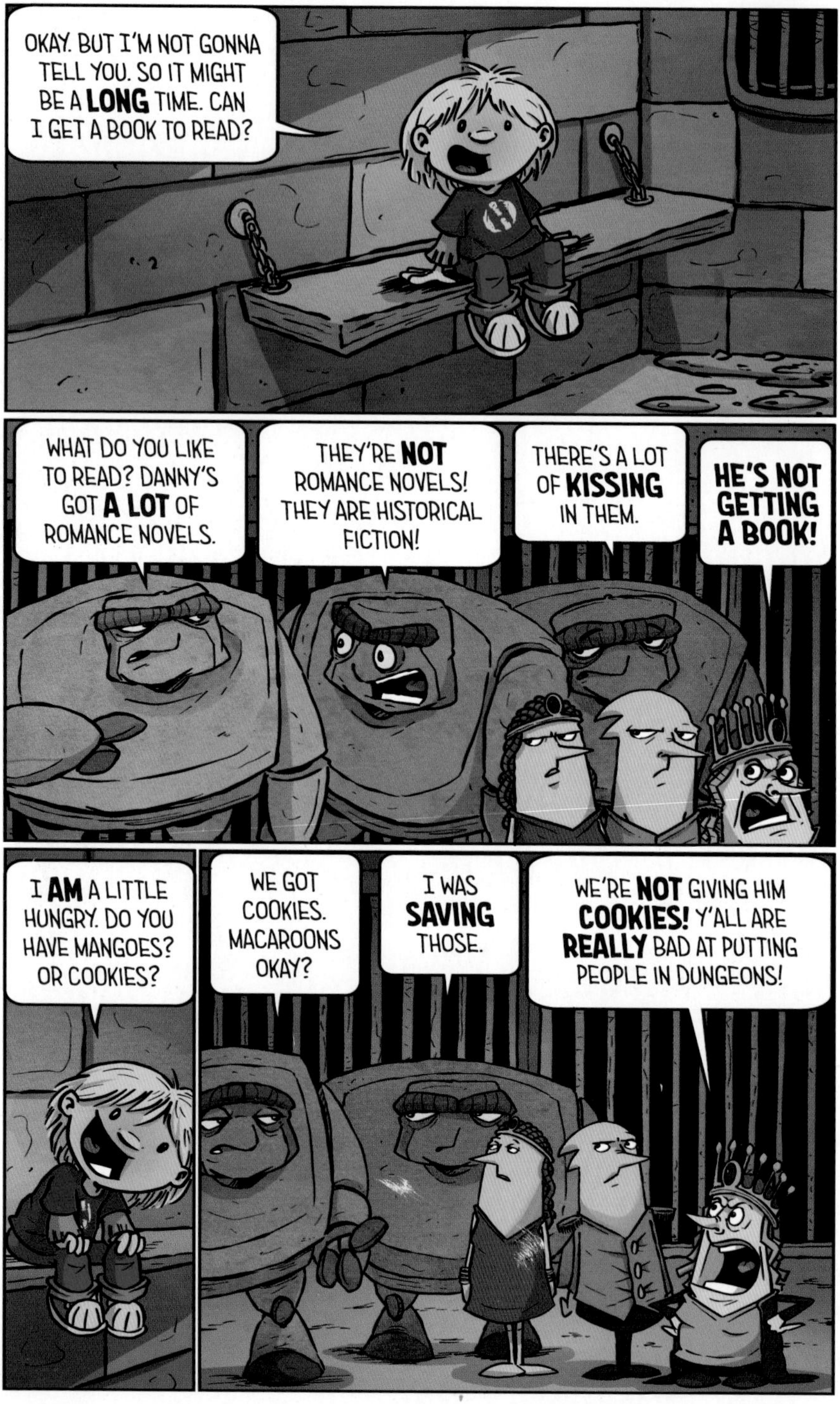
OKAY. BUT I'M NOT GONNA TELL YOU. SO IT MIGHT BE A **LONG** TIME. CAN I GET A BOOK TO READ?
WHAT DO YOU LIKE TO READ? DANNY'S GOT **A LOT** OF ROMANCE NOVELS.
THEY'RE **NOT** ROMANCE NOVELS! THEY ARE HISTORICAL FICTION!
THERE'S A LOT OF **KISSING** IN THEM.
HE'S NOT GETTING A BOOK!
I **AM** A LITTLE HUNGRY. DO YOU HAVE MANGOES? OR COOKIES?
WE GOT COOKIES. MACAROONS OKAY?
I WAS **SAVING** THOSE.
WE'RE **NOT** GIVING HIM **COOKIES!** Y'ALL ARE **REALLY** BAD AT PUTTING PEOPLE IN DUNGEONS!

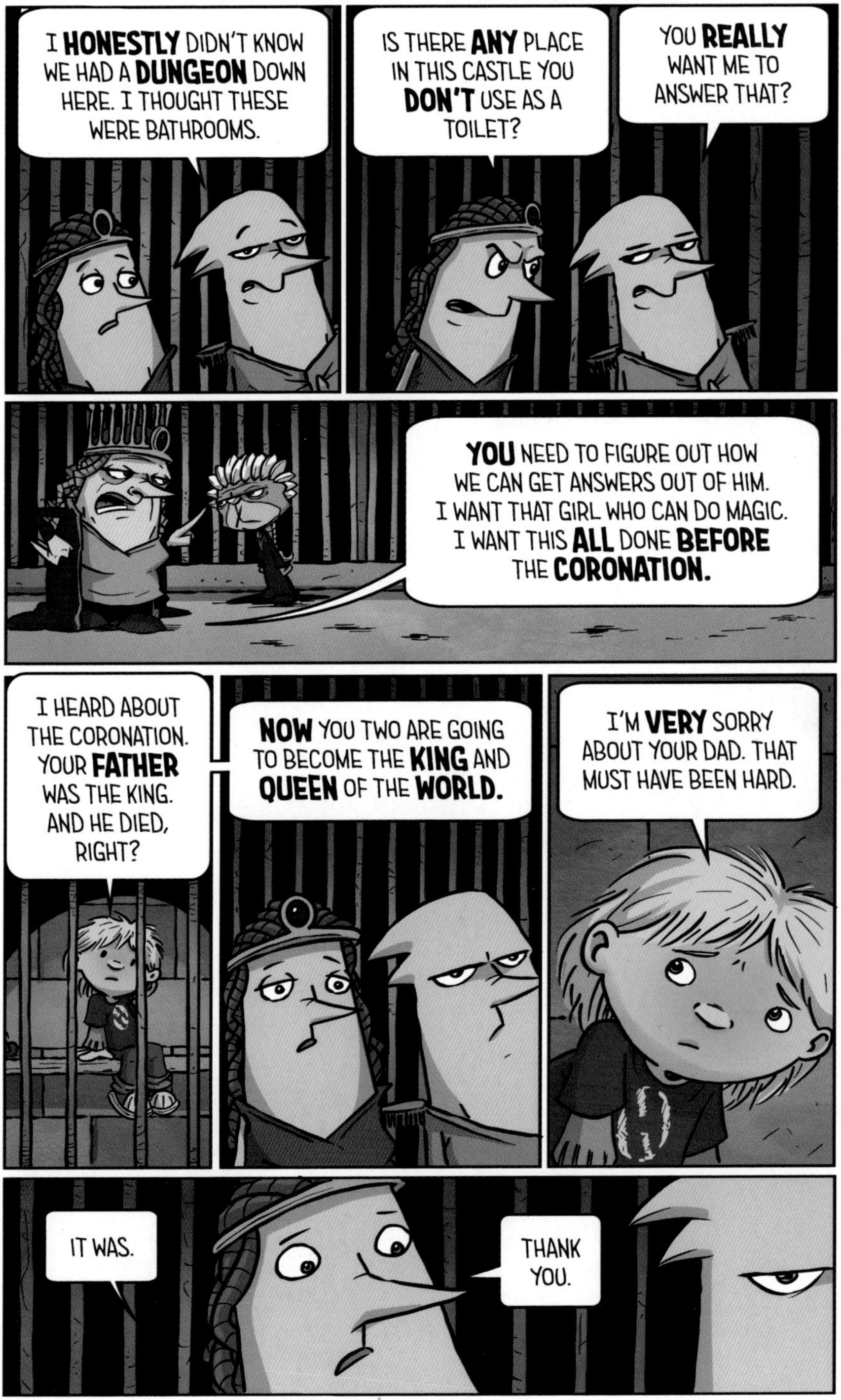
I HONESTLY DIDN'T KNOW WE HAD A DUNGEON DOWN HERE. I THOUGHT THESE WERE BATHROOMS.
IS THERE ANY PLACE IN THIS CASTLE YOU DON'T USE AS A TOILET?
YOU REALLY WANT ME TO ANSWER THAT?
YOU NEED TO FIGURE OUT HOW WE CAN GET ANSWERS OUT OF HIM. I WANT THAT GIRL WHO CAN DO MAGIC. I WANT THIS ALL DONE BEFORE THE CORONATION.
I HEARD ABOUT THE CORONATION. YOUR FATHER WAS THE KING. AND HE DIED, RIGHT?
NOW YOU TWO ARE GOING TO BECOME THE KING AND QUEEN OF THE WORLD.
I'M VERY SORRY ABOUT YOUR DAD. THAT MUST HAVE BEEN HARD.
IT WAS.
THANK YOU.

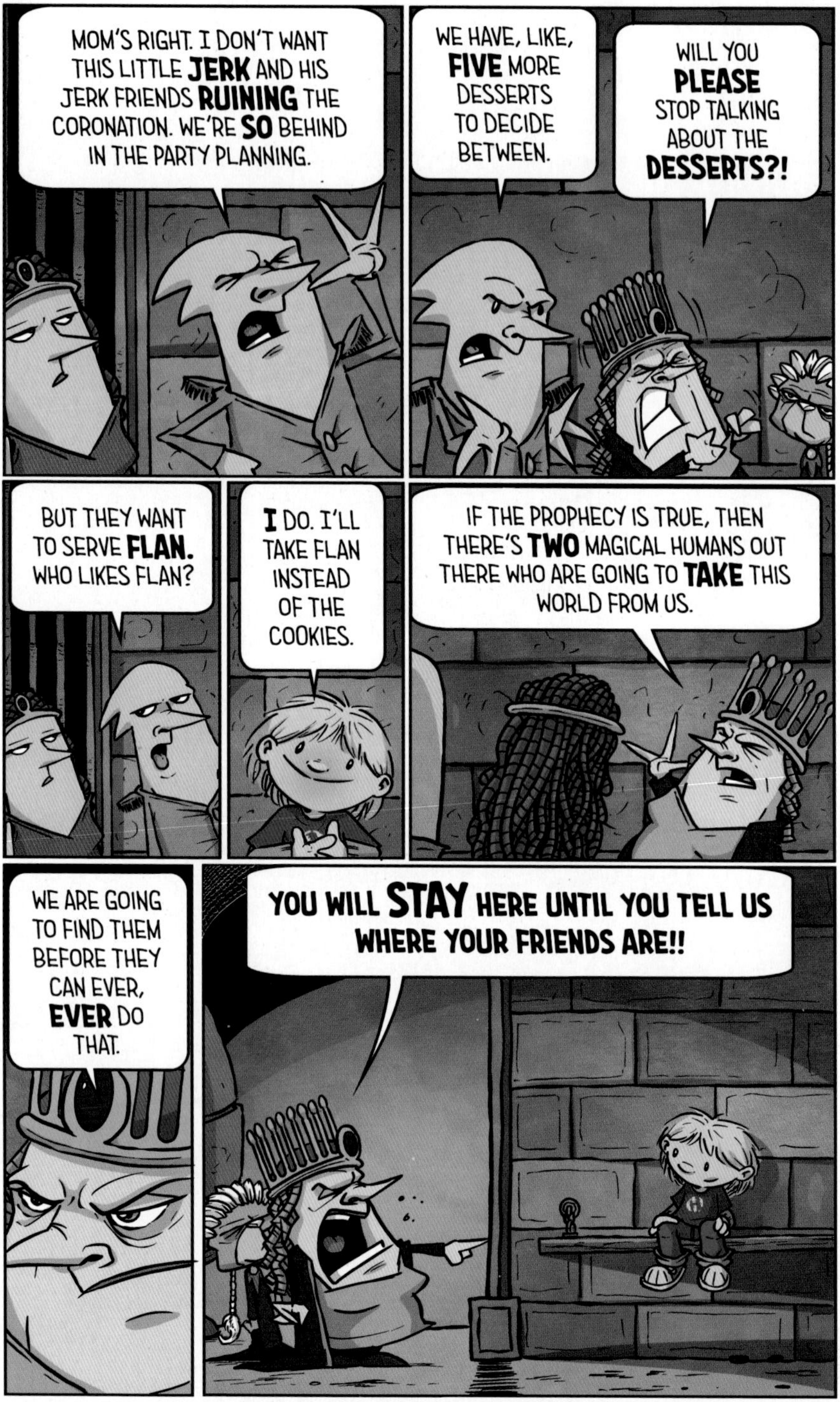
MOM'S RIGHT. I DON'T WANT THIS LITTLE JERK AND HIS JERK FRIENDS RUINING THE CORONATION. WE'RE SO BEHIND IN THE PARTY PLANNING.
WE HAVE, LIKE, FIVE MORE DESSERTS TO DECIDE BETWEEN.
WILL YOU PLEASE STOP TALKING ABOUT THE DESSERTS?!
BUT THEY WANT TO SERVE FLAN. WHO LIKES FLAN?
I DO. I'LL TAKE FLAN INSTEAD OF THE COOKIES.
IF THE PROPHECY IS TRUE, THEN THERE'S TWO MAGICAL HUMANS OUT THERE WHO ARE GOING TO TAKE THIS WORLD FROM US.
WE ARE GOING TO FIND THEM BEFORE THEY CAN EVER, EVER DO THAT.
YOU WILL STAY HERE UNTIL YOU TELL US WHERE YOUR FRIENDS ARE!!

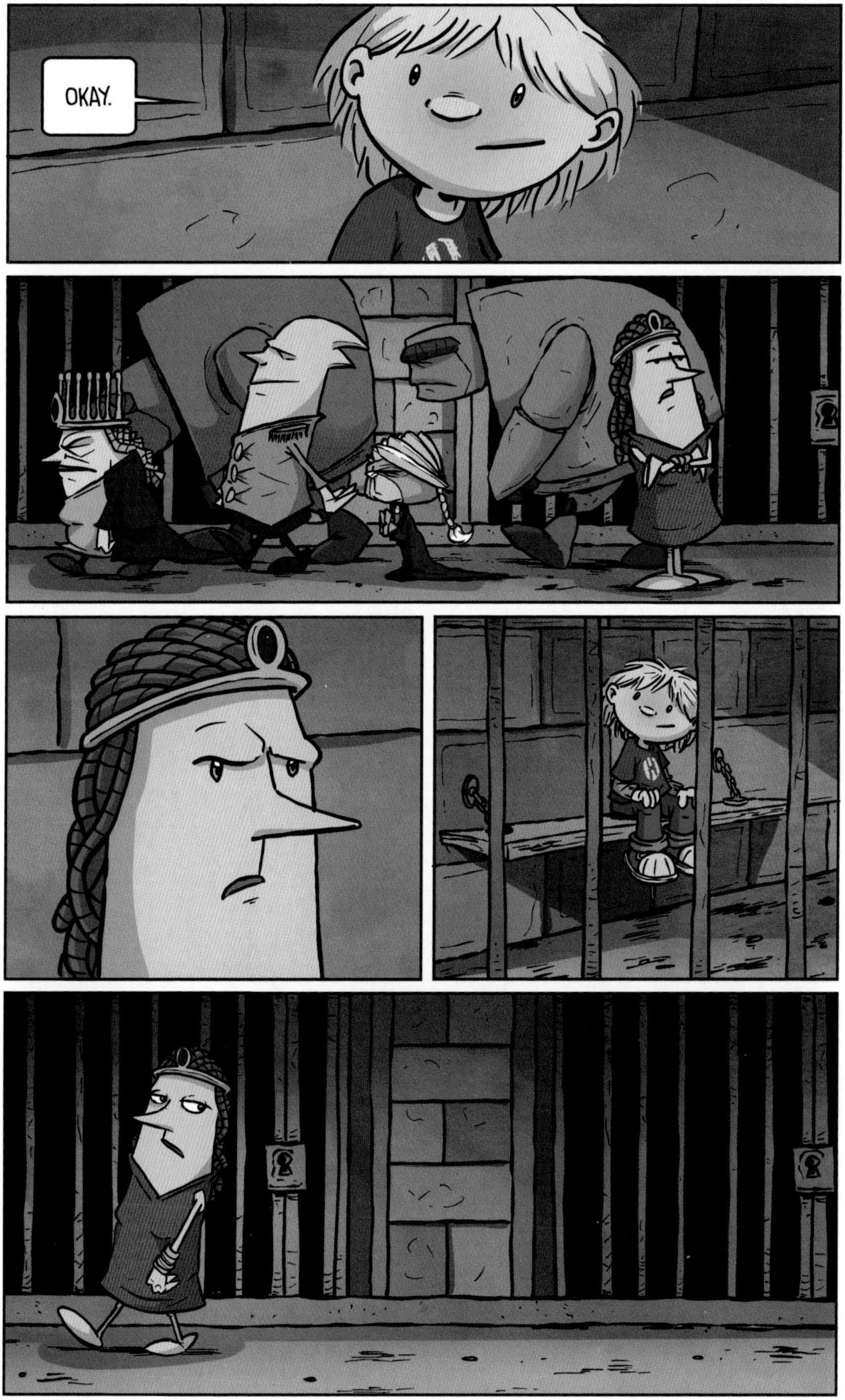
OKAY.

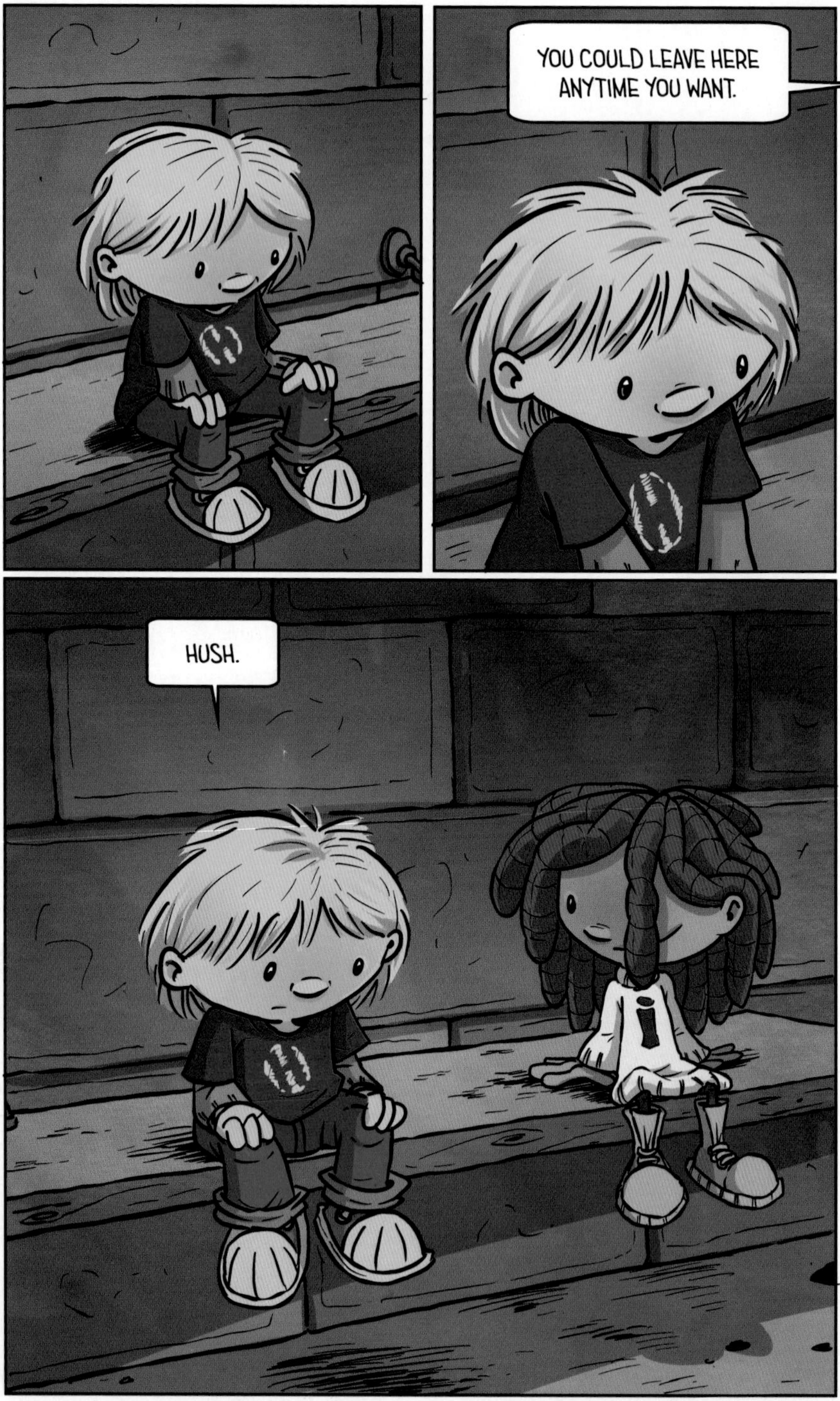
YOU COULD LEAVE HERE ANYTIME YOU WANT.
HUSH.

CHAPTER 3

BATTLE ROYALE

YOU **LOST** HILO?!
NO, I DIDN'T **LOSE** HIM! WE KNOW **EXACTLY** WHERE HE IS. HE'S IN THE **CASTLE** WITH THE REST OF THOSE ROYAL GARBAGE PAILS.

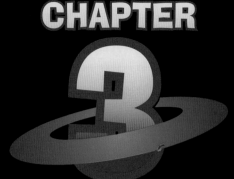

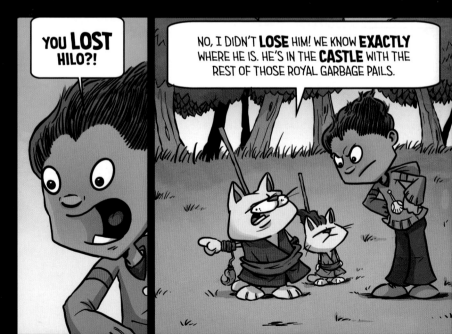

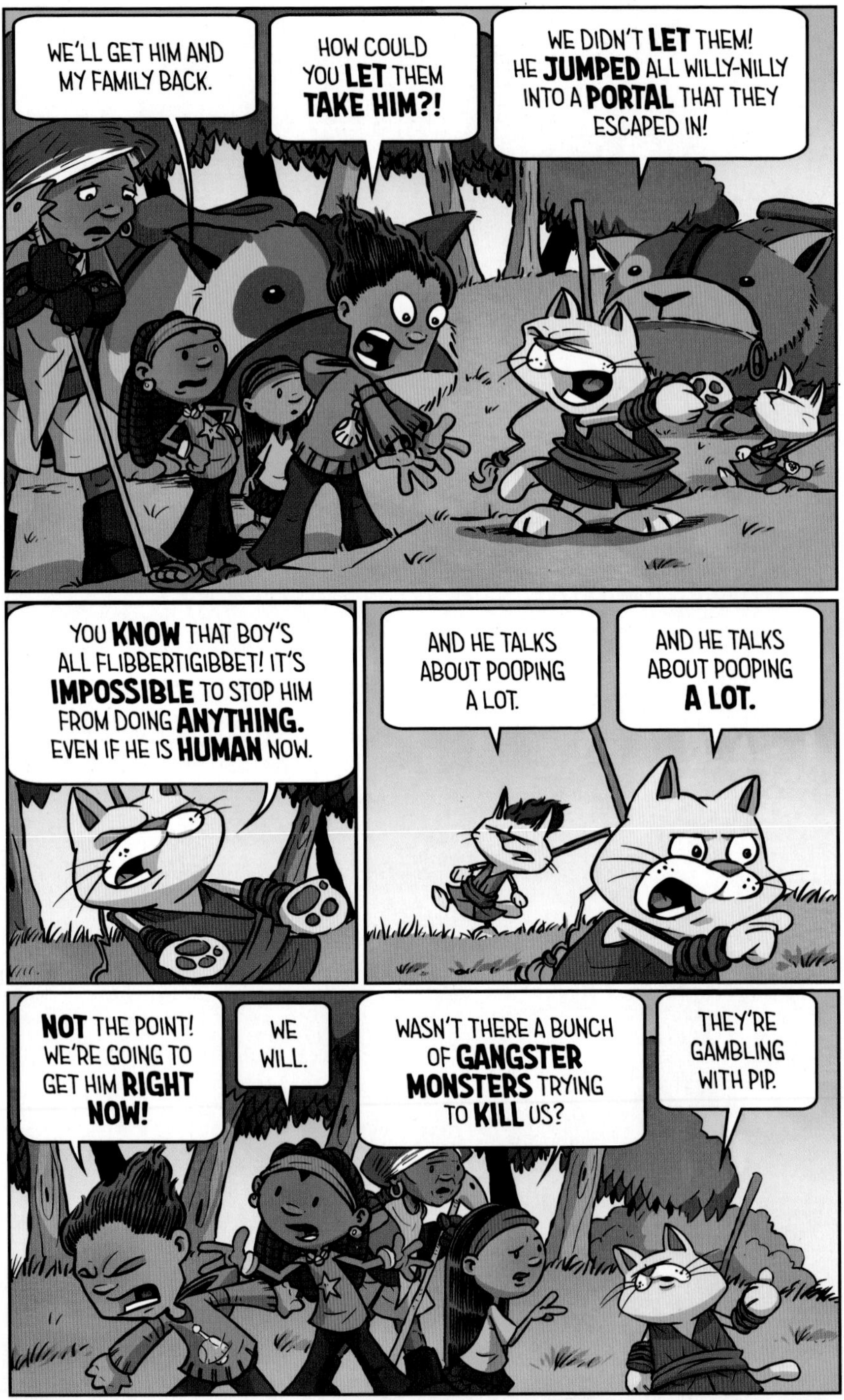
WE'LL GET HIM AND MY FAMILY BACK.
HOW COULD YOU LET THEM TAKE HIM?!
WE DIDN'T LET THEM! HE JUMPED ALL WILLY-NILLY INTO A PORTAL THAT THEY ESCAPED IN!
YOU KNOW THAT BOY'S ALL FLIBBERTIGIBBET! IT'S IMPOSSIBLE TO STOP HIM FROM DOING ANYTHING. EVEN IF HE IS HUMAN NOW.
AND HE TALKS ABOUT POOPING A LOT.
AND HE TALKS ABOUT POOPING A LOT.
NOT THE POINT! WE'RE GOING TO GET HIM RIGHT NOW!
WE WILL.
WASN'T THERE A BUNCH OF GANGSTER MONSTERS TRYING TO KILL US?
THEY'RE GAMBLING WITH PIP.

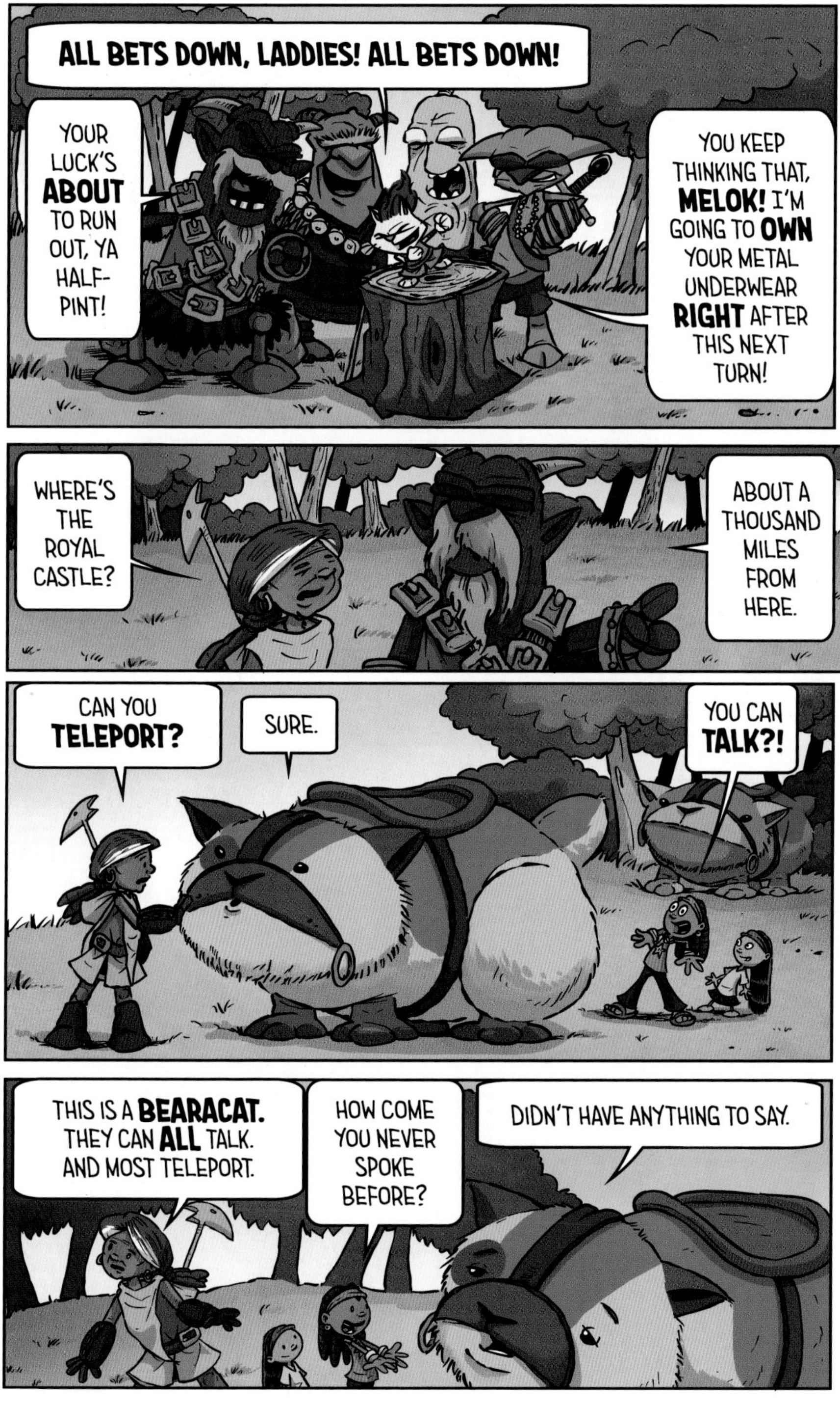
ALL BETS DOWN, LADDIES! ALL BETS DOWN!
YOUR LUCK'S ABOUT TO RUN OUT, YA HALF-PINT!
YOU KEEP THINKING THAT, MELOK! I'M GOING TO OWN YOUR METAL UNDERWEAR RIGHT AFTER THIS NEXT TURN!
WHERE'S THE ROYAL CASTLE?
ABOUT A THOUSAND MILES FROM HERE.
CAN YOU TELEPORT?
SURE.
YOU CAN TALK?!
THIS IS A BEARACAT. THEY CAN ALL TALK. AND MOST TELEPORT.
HOW COME YOU NEVER SPOKE BEFORE?
DIDN'T HAVE ANYTHING TO SAY.

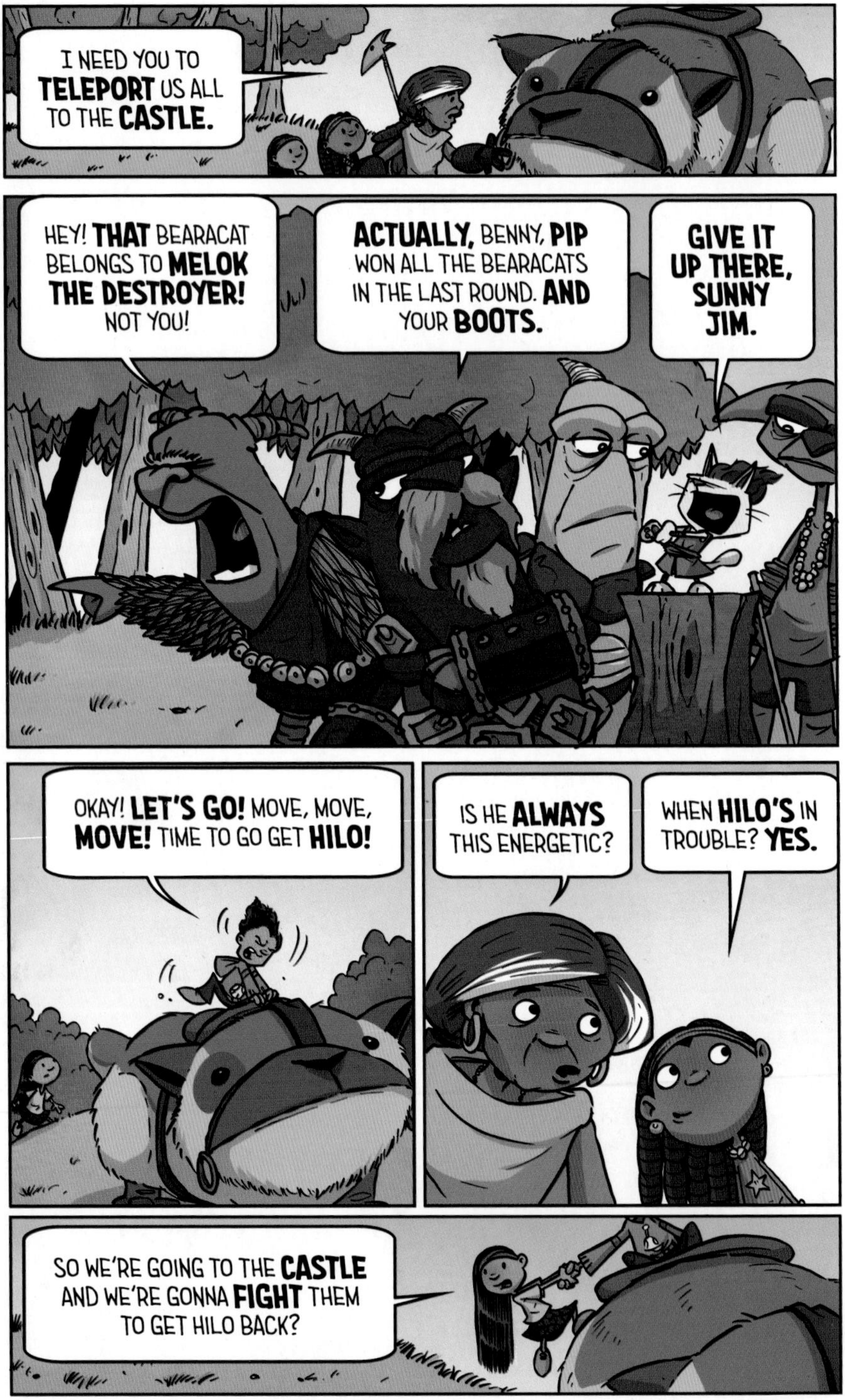
I NEED YOU TO TELEPORT US ALL TO THE CASTLE.
HEY! THAT BEARACAT BELONGS TO MELOK THE DESTROYER! NOT YOU!
ACTUALLY, BENNY, PIP WON ALL THE BEARACATS IN THE LAST ROUND. AND YOUR BOOTS.
GIVE IT UP THERE, SUNNY JIM.
OKAY! LET'S GO! MOVE, MOVE, MOVE! TIME TO GO GET HILO!
IS HE ALWAYS THIS ENERGETIC?
WHEN HILO'S IN TROUBLE? YES.
SO WE'RE GOING TO THE CASTLE AND WE'RE GONNA FIGHT THEM TO GET HILO BACK?

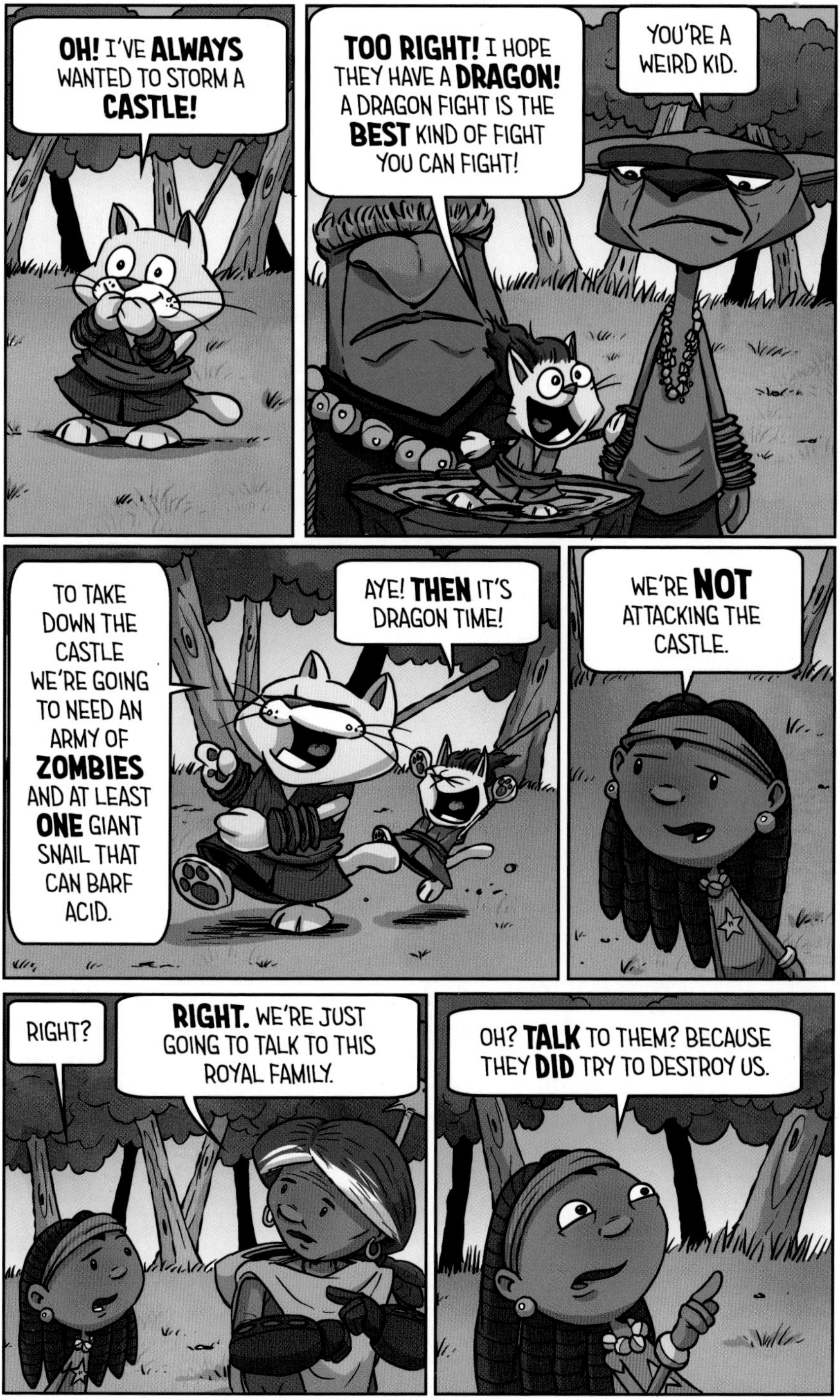
OH! I'VE ALWAYS WANTED TO STORM A CASTLE!
TOO RIGHT! I HOPE THEY HAVE A DRAGON! A DRAGON FIGHT IS THE BEST KIND OF FIGHT YOU CAN FIGHT!
YOU'RE A WEIRD KID.
TO TAKE DOWN THE CASTLE WE'RE GOING TO NEED AN ARMY OF ZOMBIES AND AT LEAST ONE GIANT SNAIL THAT CAN BARF ACID.
AYE! THEN IT'S DRAGON TIME!
WE'RE NOT ATTACKING THE CASTLE.
RIGHT?
RIGHT. WE'RE JUST GOING TO TALK TO THIS ROYAL FAMILY.
OH? TALK TO THEM? BECAUSE THEY DID TRY TO DESTROY US.

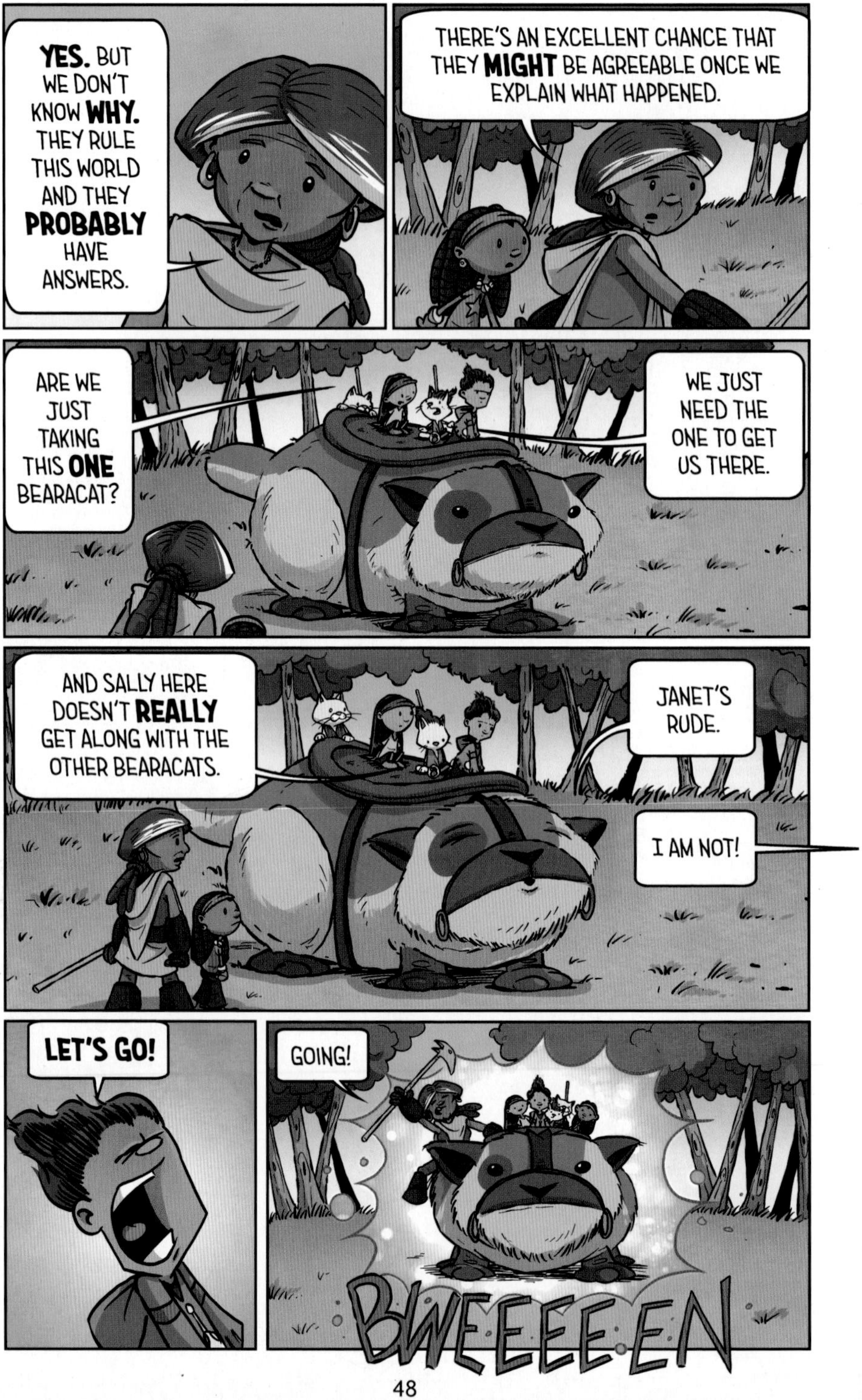

YES. BUT WE DON'T KNOW **WHY.** THEY RULE THIS WORLD AND THEY **PROBABLY** HAVE ANSWERS.
THERE'S AN EXCELLENT CHANCE THAT THEY **MIGHT** BE AGREEABLE ONCE WE EXPLAIN WHAT HAPPENED.
ARE WE JUST TAKING THIS **ONE** BEARACAT?
WE JUST NEED THE ONE TO GET US THERE.
AND SALLY HERE DOESN'T **REALLY** GET ALONG WITH THE OTHER BEARACATS.
JANET'S RUDE.
I AM NOT!
LET'S GO!
GOING!
BWEEEEEN

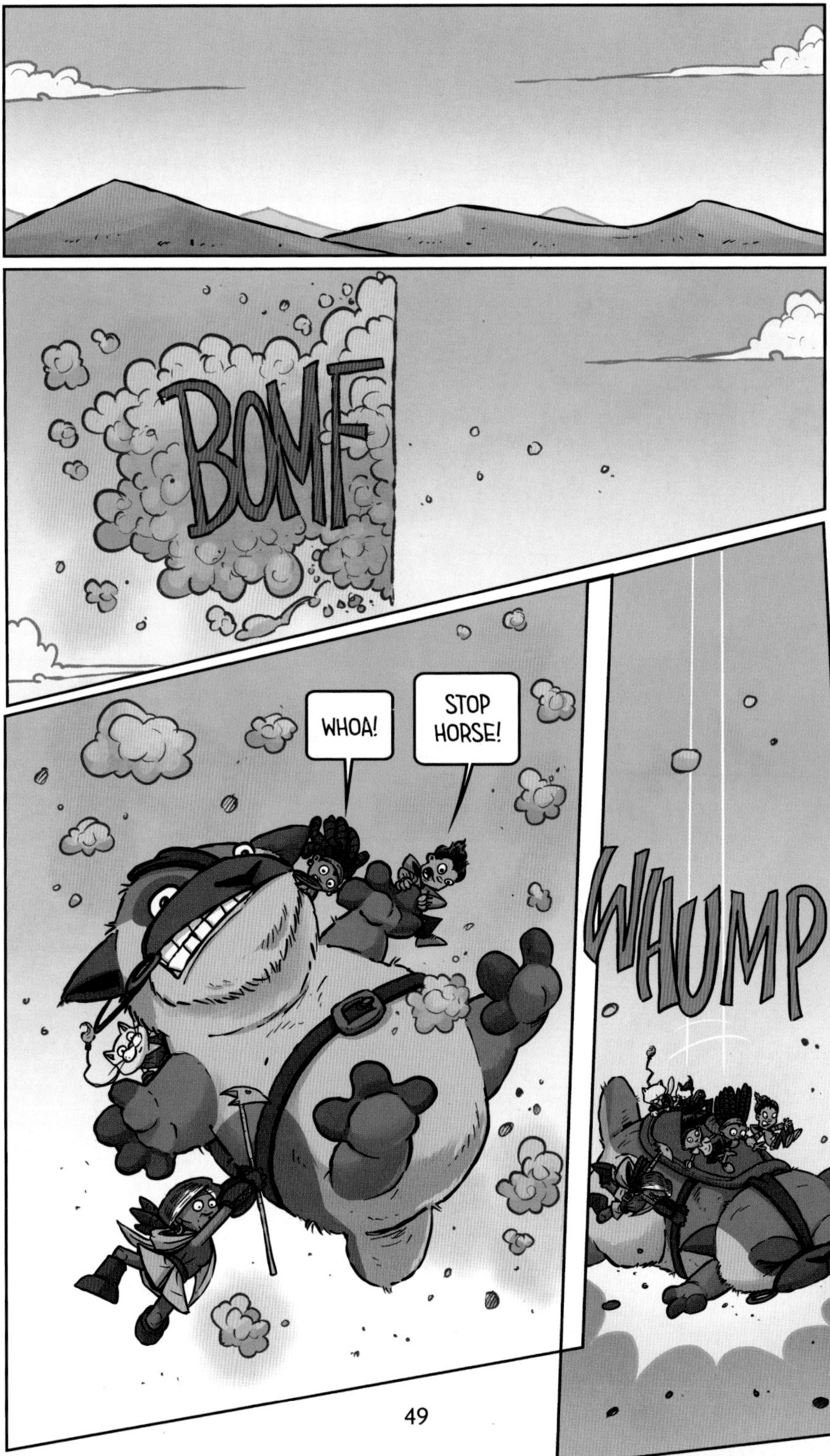
BOMF
WHOA!
STOP HORSE!
WHUMP

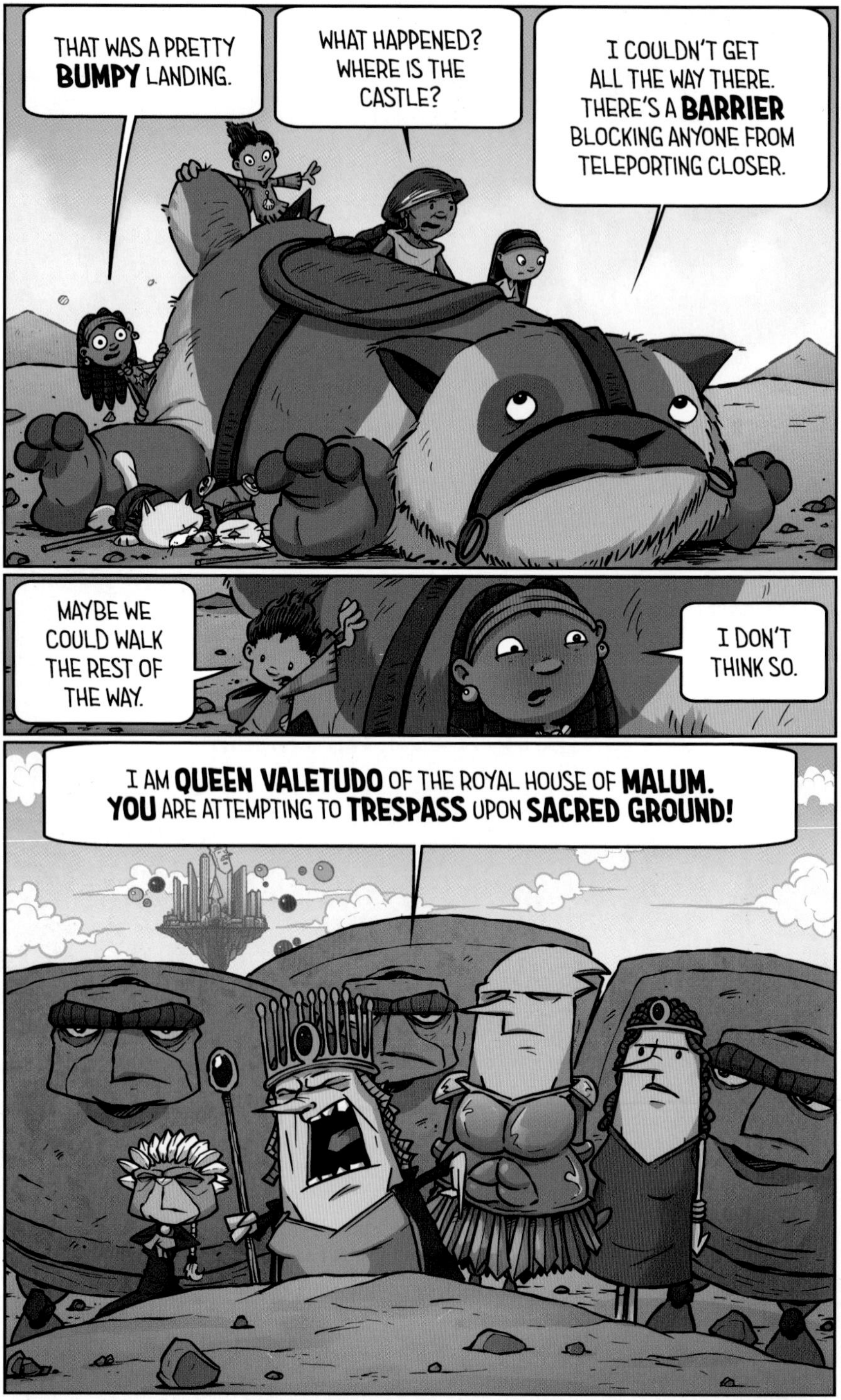
THAT WAS A PRETTY **BUMPY** LANDING.
WHAT HAPPENED? WHERE IS THE CASTLE?
I COULDN'T GET ALL THE WAY THERE. THERE'S A **BARRIER** BLOCKING ANYONE FROM TELEPORTING CLOSER.
MAYBE WE COULD WALK THE REST OF THE WAY.
I DON'T THINK SO.
I AM **QUEEN VALETUDO** OF THE ROYAL HOUSE OF **MALUM.**
YOU ARE ATTEMPTING TO **TRESPASS** UPON **SACRED GROUND!**

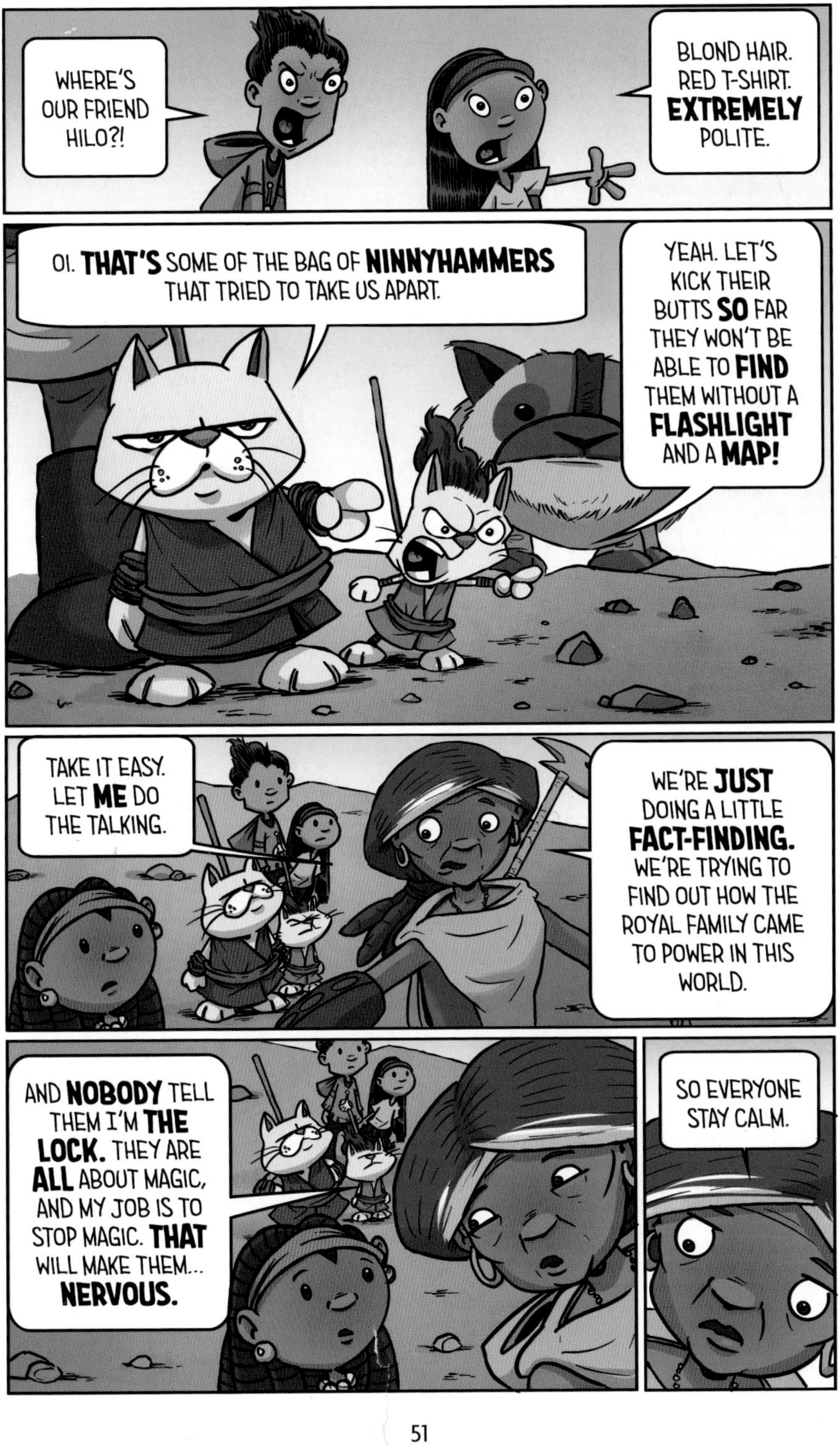
WHERE'S OUR FRIEND HILO?!
BLOND HAIR. RED T-SHIRT. **EXTREMELY** POLITE.
OI. **THAT'S** SOME OF THE BAG OF **NINNYHAMMERS** THAT TRIED TO TAKE US APART.
YEAH. LET'S KICK THEIR BUTTS **SO** FAR THEY WON'T BE ABLE TO **FIND** THEM WITHOUT A **FLASHLIGHT** AND A **MAP!**
TAKE IT EASY. LET **ME** DO THE TALKING.
WE'RE **JUST** DOING A LITTLE **FACT-FINDING.** WE'RE TRYING TO FIND OUT HOW THE ROYAL FAMILY CAME TO POWER IN THIS WORLD.
AND **NOBODY** TELL THEM I'M **THE LOCK.** THEY ARE **ALL** ABOUT MAGIC, AND MY JOB IS TO STOP MAGIC. **THAT** WILL MAKE THEM... **NERVOUS.**
SO EVERYONE STAY CALM.

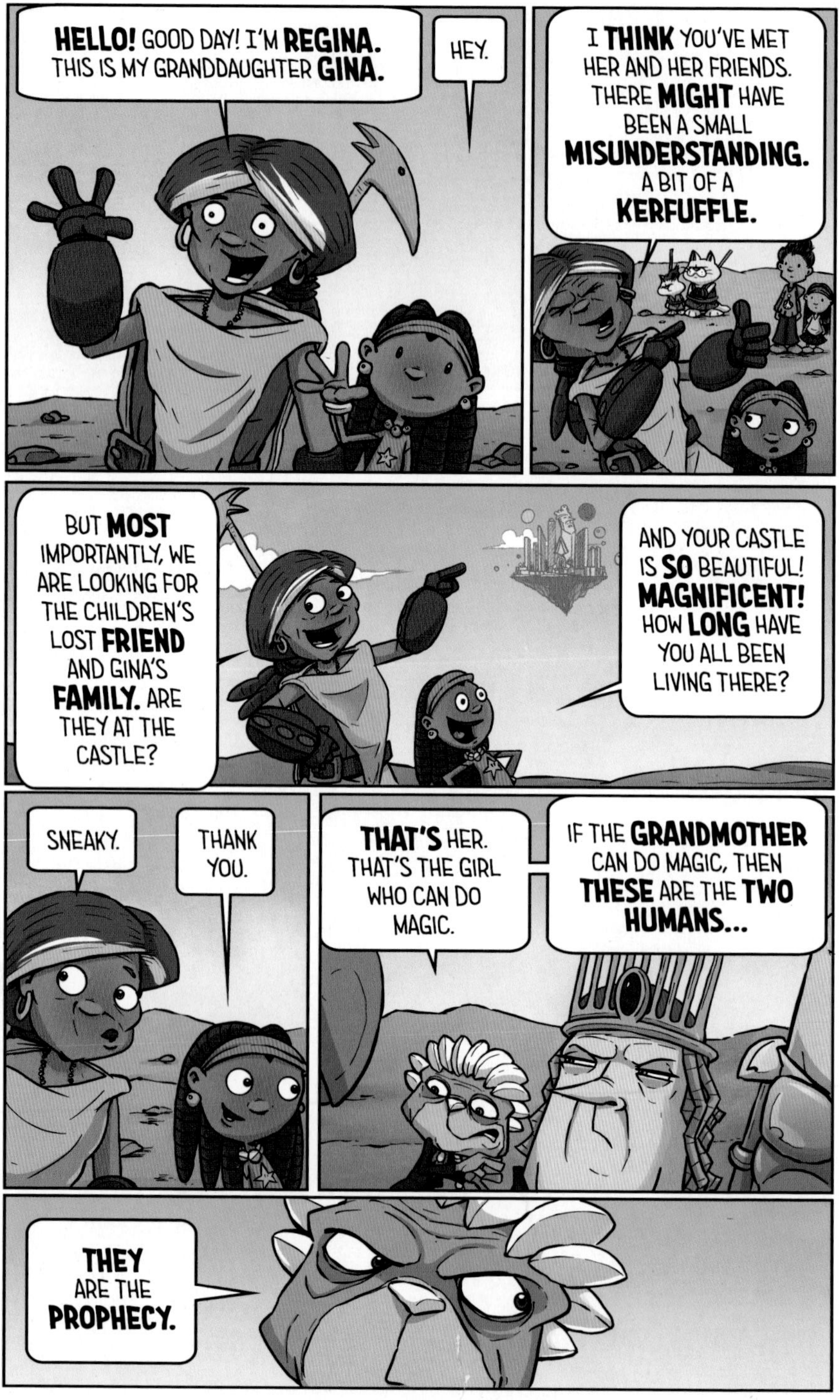

HELLO! GOOD DAY! I'M REGINA. THIS IS MY GRANDDAUGHTER GINA.
HEY.
I THINK YOU'VE MET HER AND HER FRIENDS. THERE MIGHT HAVE BEEN A SMALL MISUNDERSTANDING. A BIT OF A KERFUFFLE.
BUT MOST IMPORTANTLY, WE ARE LOOKING FOR THE CHILDREN'S LOST FRIEND AND GINA'S FAMILY. ARE THEY AT THE CASTLE?
AND YOUR CASTLE IS SO BEAUTIFUL! MAGNIFICENT! HOW LONG HAVE YOU ALL BEEN LIVING THERE?
SNEAKY.
THANK YOU.
THAT'S HER. THAT'S THE GIRL WHO CAN DO MAGIC.
IF THE GRANDMOTHER CAN DO MAGIC, THEN THESE ARE THE TWO HUMANS...
THEY ARE THE PROPHECY.

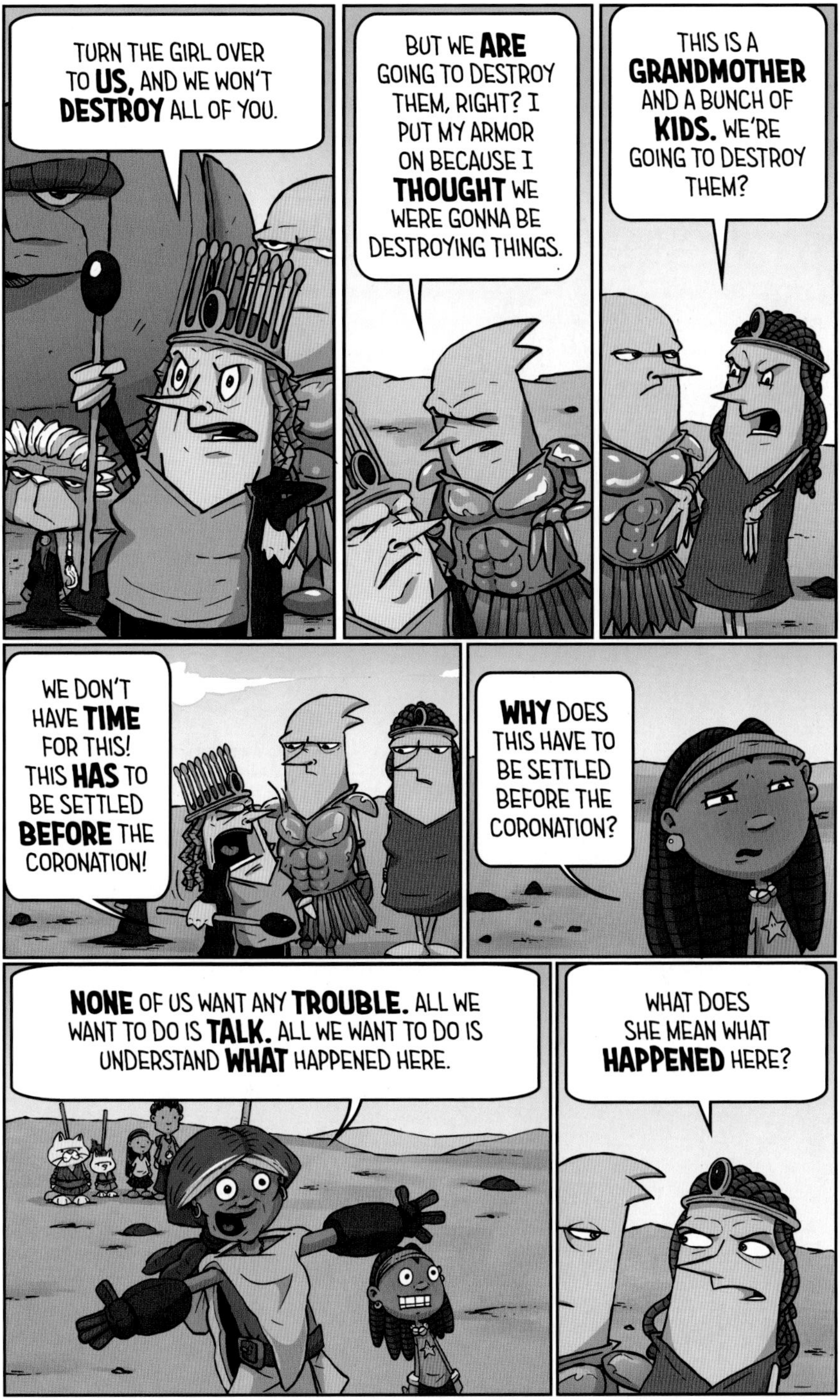
TURN THE GIRL OVER TO US, AND WE WON'T DESTROY ALL OF YOU.
BUT WE ARE GOING TO DESTROY THEM, RIGHT? I PUT MY ARMOR ON BECAUSE I THOUGHT WE WERE GONNA BE DESTROYING THINGS.
THIS IS A GRANDMOTHER AND A BUNCH OF KIDS. WE'RE GOING TO DESTROY THEM?
WE DON'T HAVE TIME FOR THIS! THIS HAS TO BE SETTLED BEFORE THE CORONATION!
WHY DOES THIS HAVE TO BE SETTLED BEFORE THE CORONATION?
NONE OF US WANT ANY TROUBLE. ALL WE WANT TO DO IS TALK. ALL WE WANT TO DO IS UNDERSTAND WHAT HAPPENED HERE.
WHAT DOES SHE MEAN WHAT HAPPENED HERE?

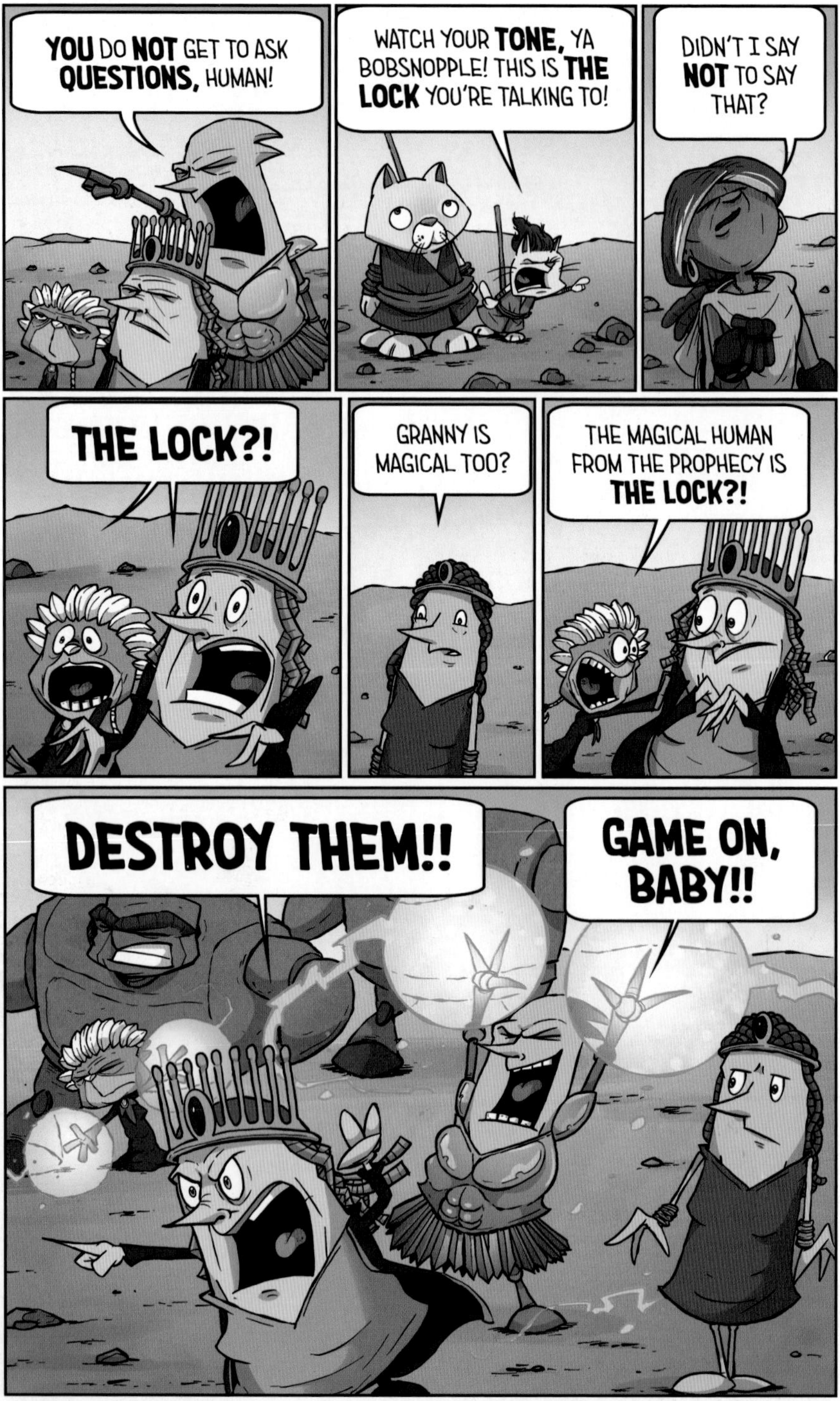
YOU DO NOT GET TO ASK QUESTIONS, HUMAN!
WATCH YOUR TONE, YA BOBSNOPPLE! THIS IS THE LOCK YOU'RE TALKING TO!
DIDN'T I SAY NOT TO SAY THAT?
THE LOCK?!
GRANNY IS MAGICAL TOO?
THE MAGICAL HUMAN FROM THE PROPHECY IS THE LOCK?!
DESTROY THEM!!
GAME ON, BABY!!

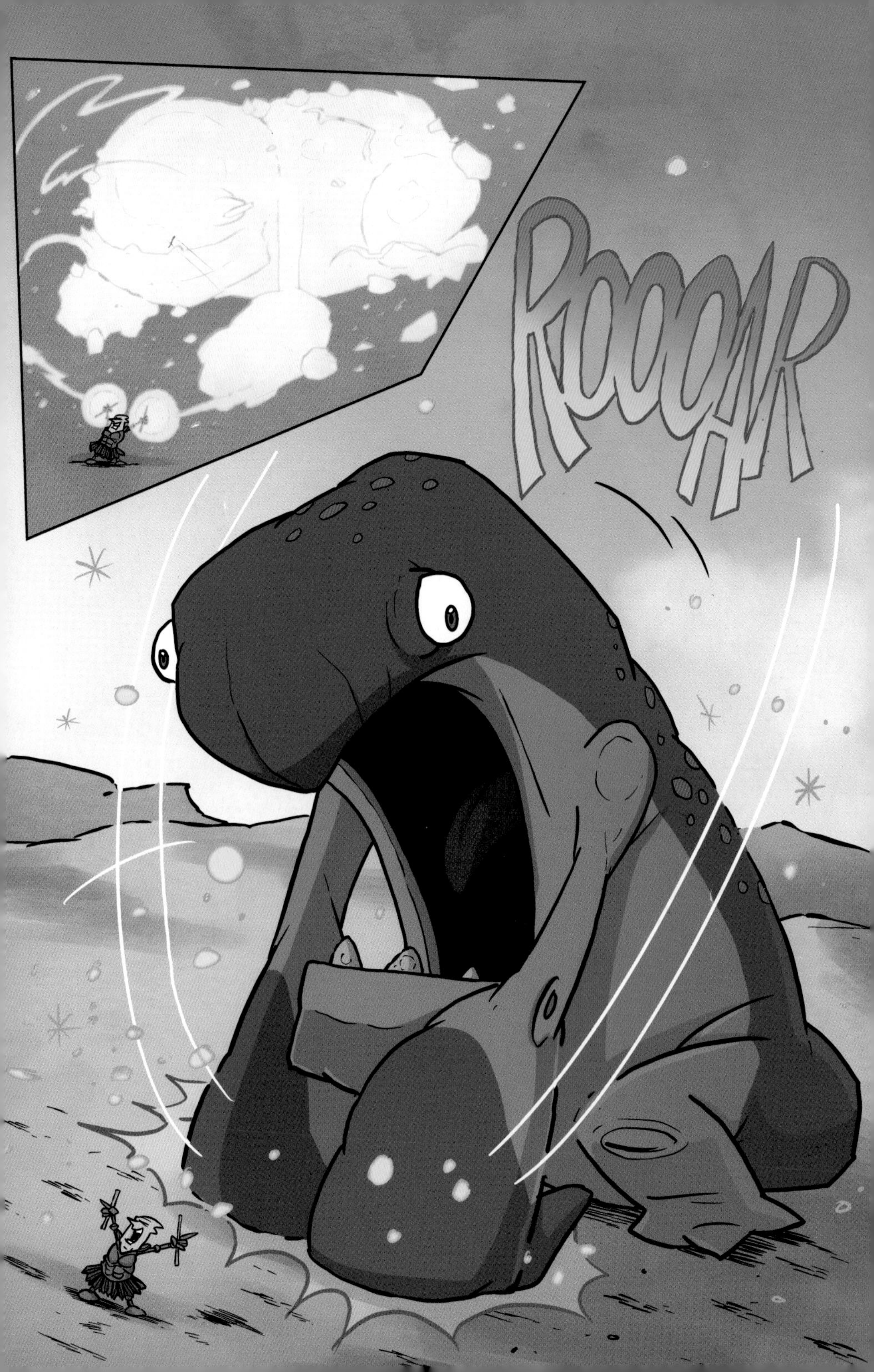
ROOOAR

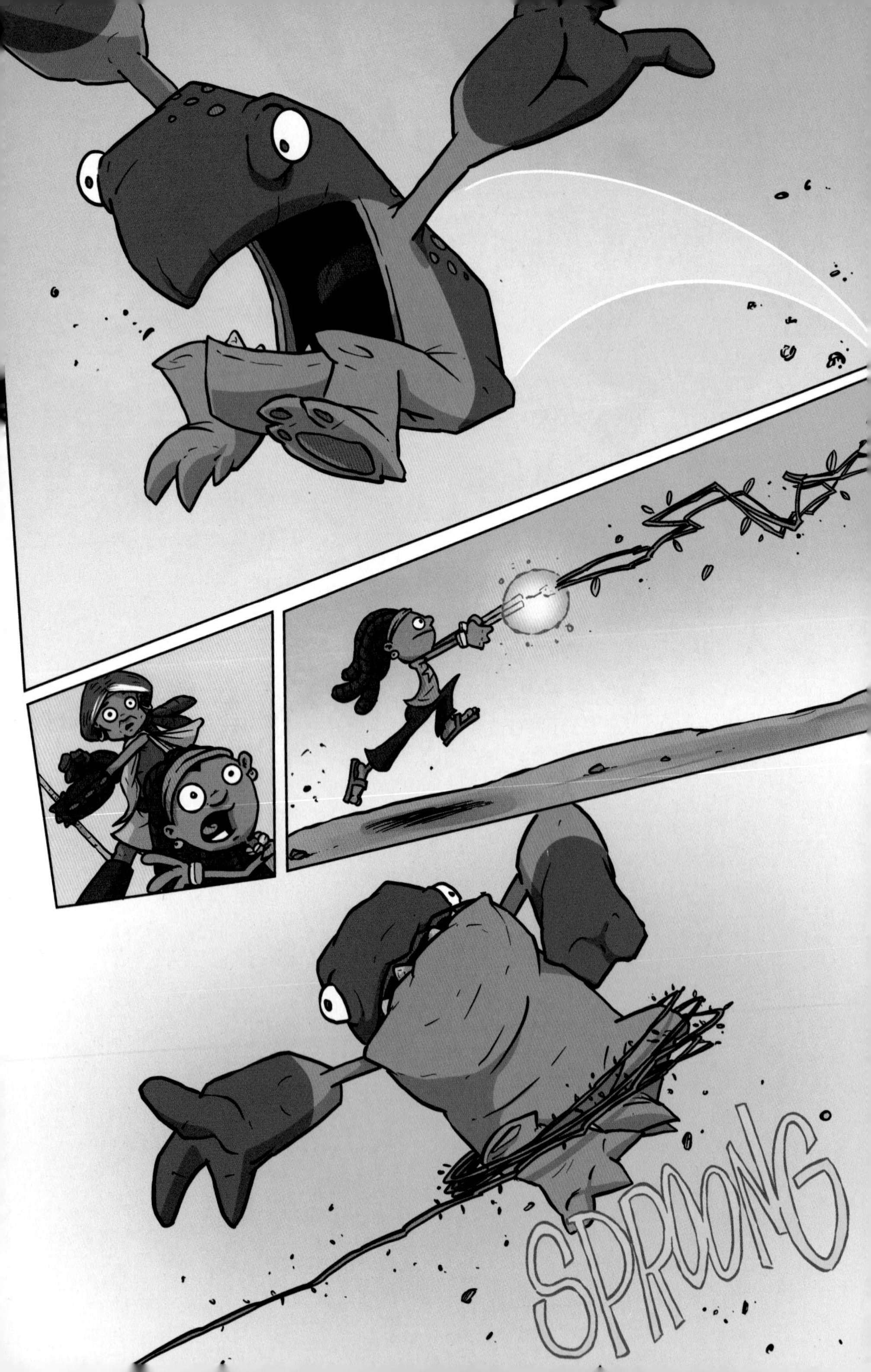
SPROONG

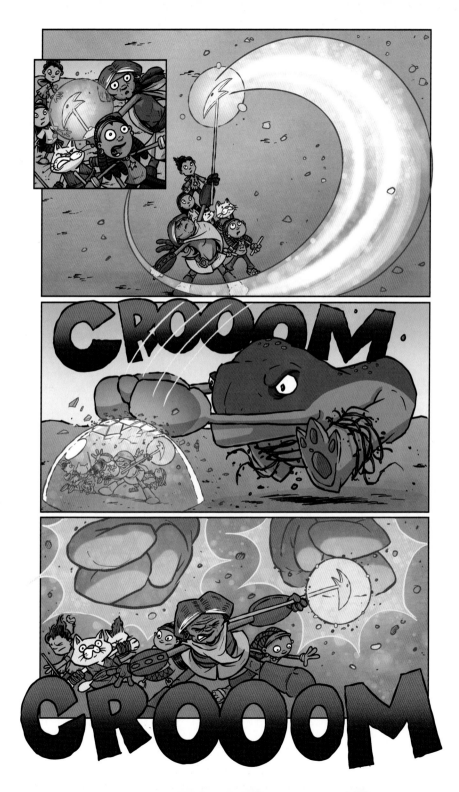

CROOOM

CROOOM

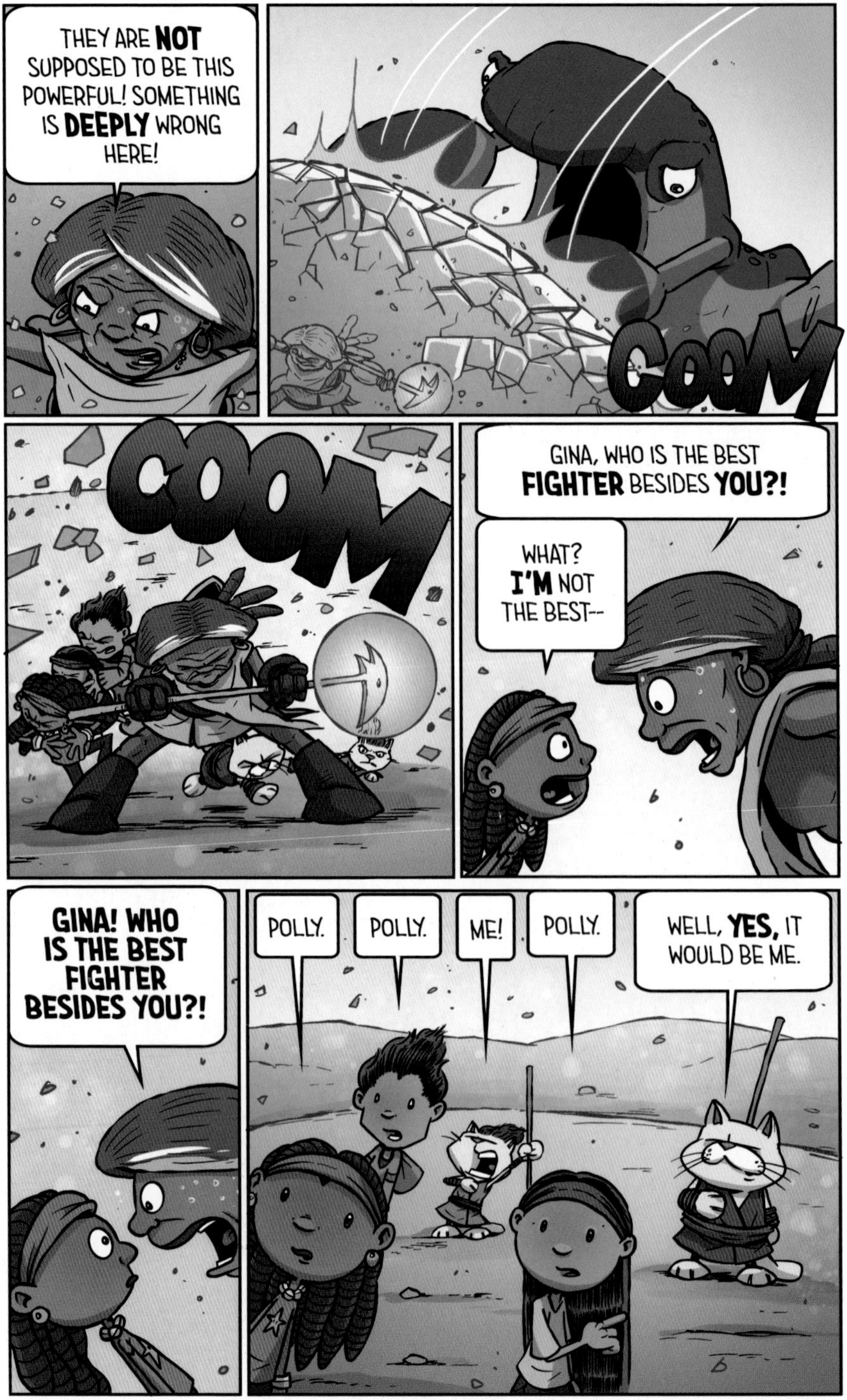
THEY ARE **NOT** SUPPOSED TO BE THIS POWERFUL! SOMETHING IS **DEEPLY** WRONG HERE!
GOOM
GOOM
GINA, WHO IS THE BEST **FIGHTER** BESIDES **YOU?!**
WHAT? **I'M** NOT THE BEST--
GINA! WHO IS THE BEST FIGHTER BESIDES YOU?!
POLLY.
POLLY.
ME!
POLLY.
WELL, **YES,** IT WOULD BE ME.

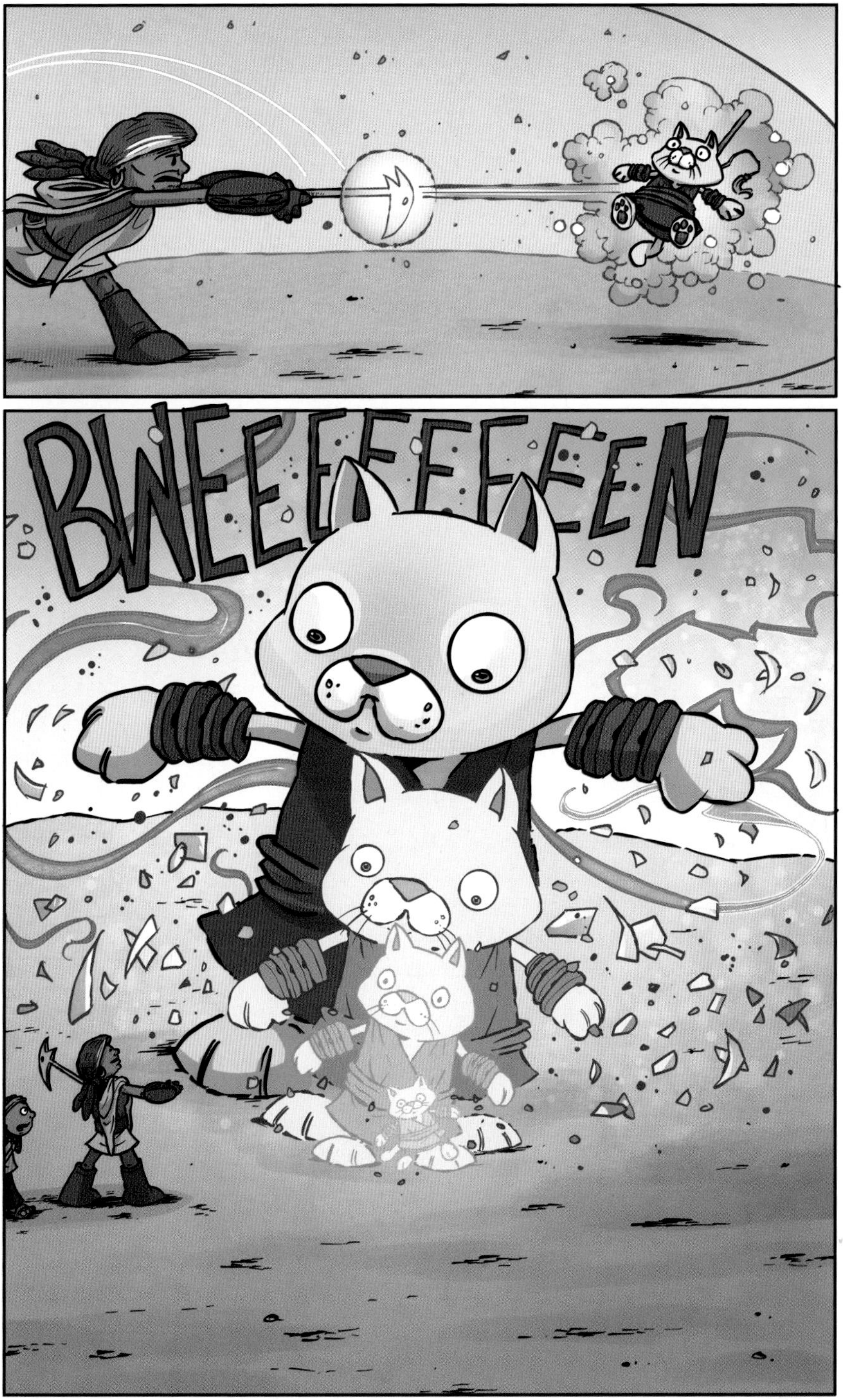
BWEEEEEEEN

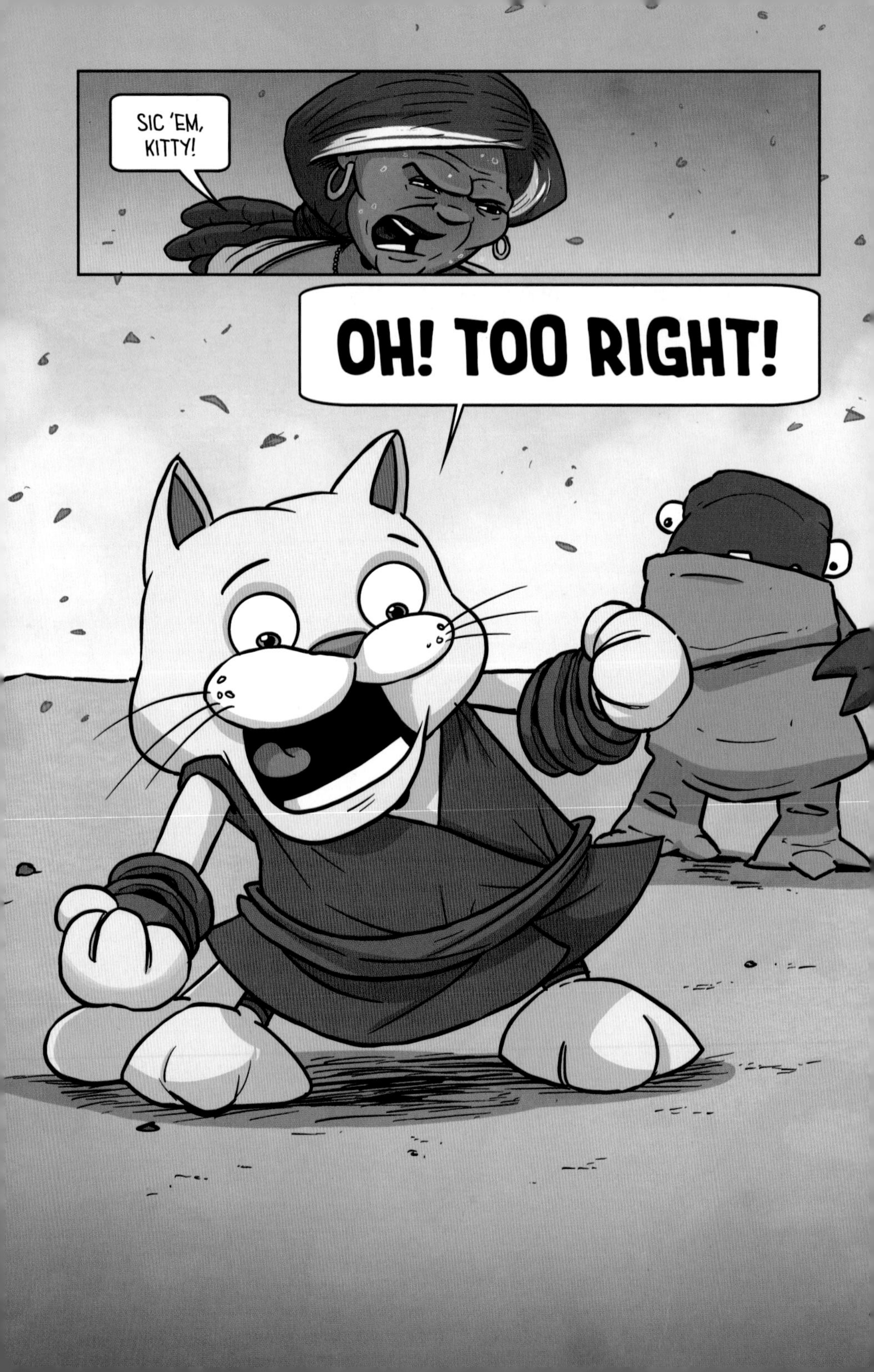
SIC 'EM, KITTY!
OH! TOO RIGHT!

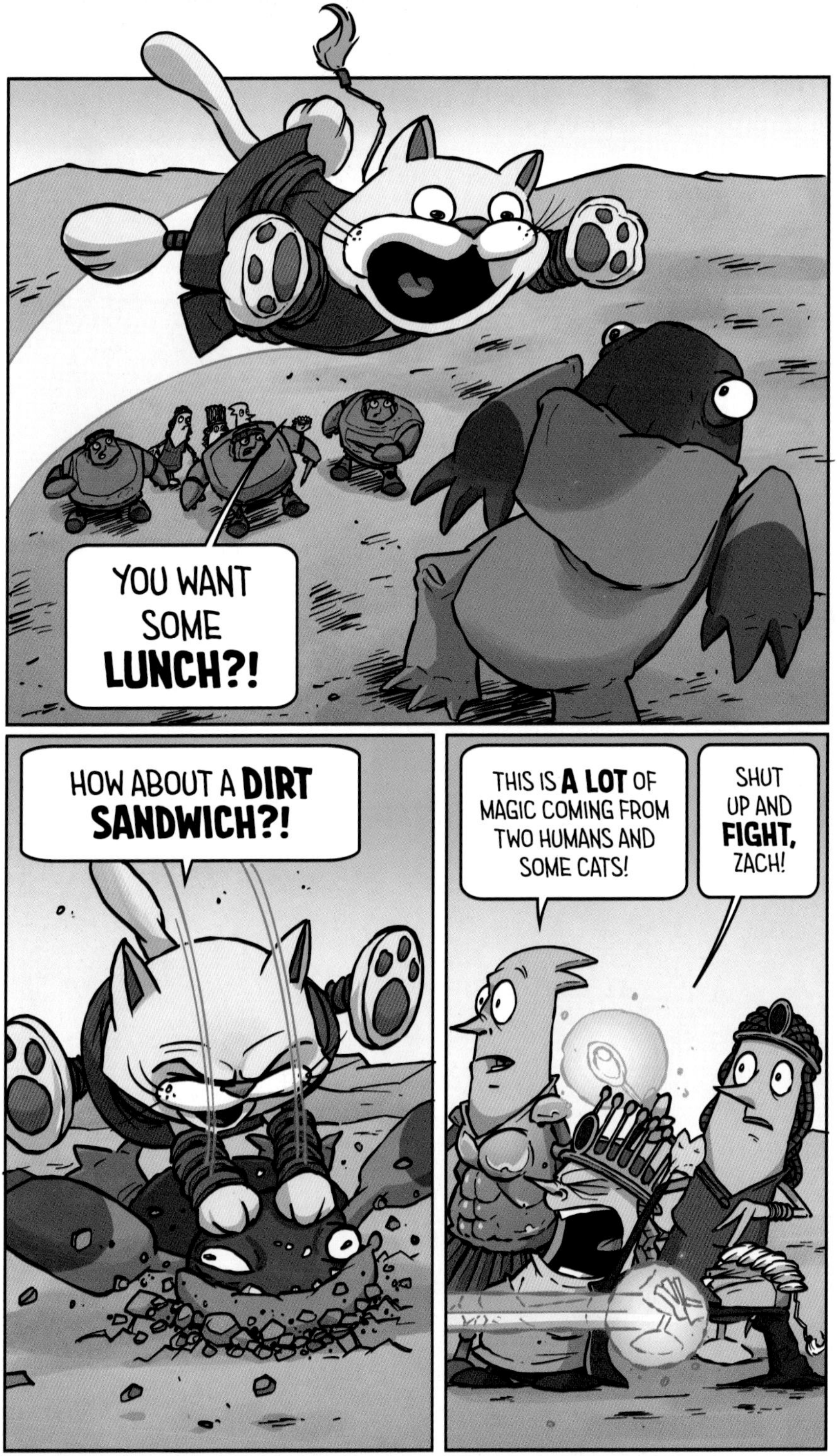
YOU WANT SOME **LUNCH?!**
HOW ABOUT A **DIRT SANDWICH?!**
THIS IS **A LOT** OF MAGIC COMING FROM TWO HUMANS AND SOME CATS!
SHUT UP AND **FIGHT,** ZACH!

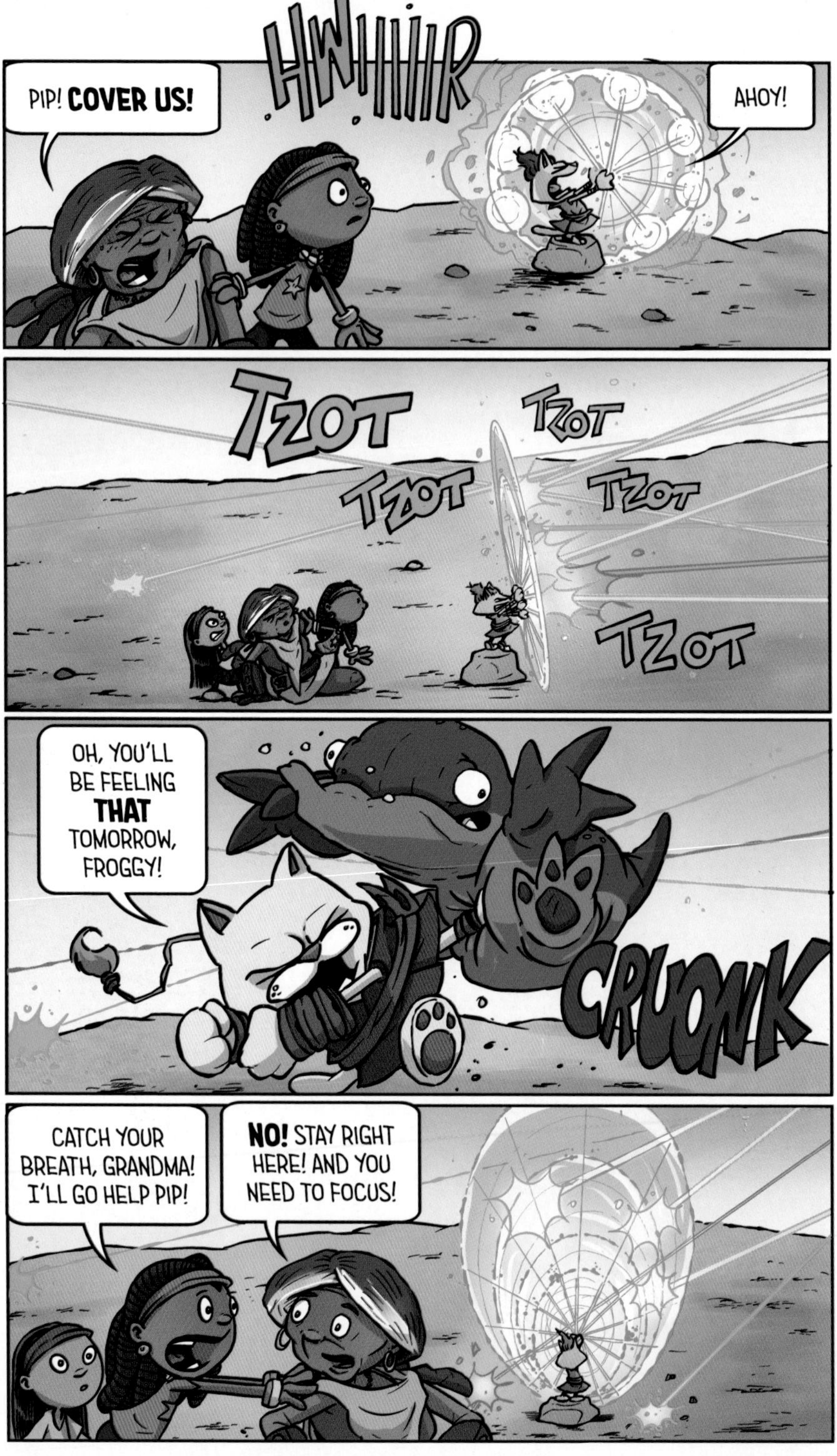
HWIIIIIR
PIP! **COVER US!**
AHOY!
TZOT
TZOT
TZOT
TZOT
TZOT
OH, YOU'LL BE FEELING **THAT** TOMORROW, FROGGY!
CRUONK
CATCH YOUR BREATH, GRANDMA! I'LL GO HELP PIP!
NO! STAY RIGHT HERE! AND YOU NEED TO FOCUS!

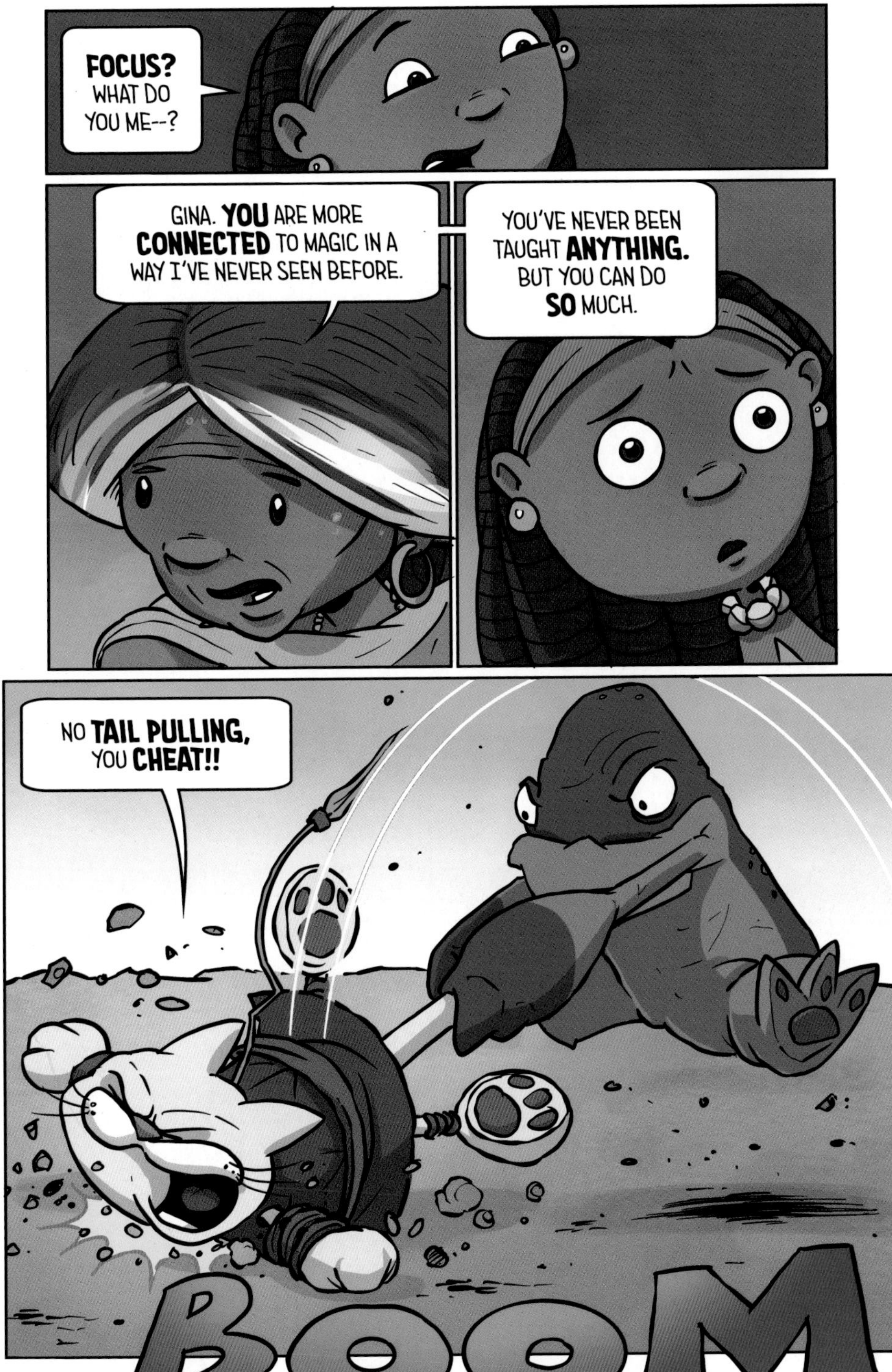
FOCUS? WHAT DO YOU ME--?
GINA. YOU ARE MORE CONNECTED TO MAGIC IN A WAY I'VE NEVER SEEN BEFORE.
YOU'VE NEVER BEEN TAUGHT ANYTHING. BUT YOU CAN DO SO MUCH.
NO TAIL PULLING, YOU CHEAT!!
BOOM

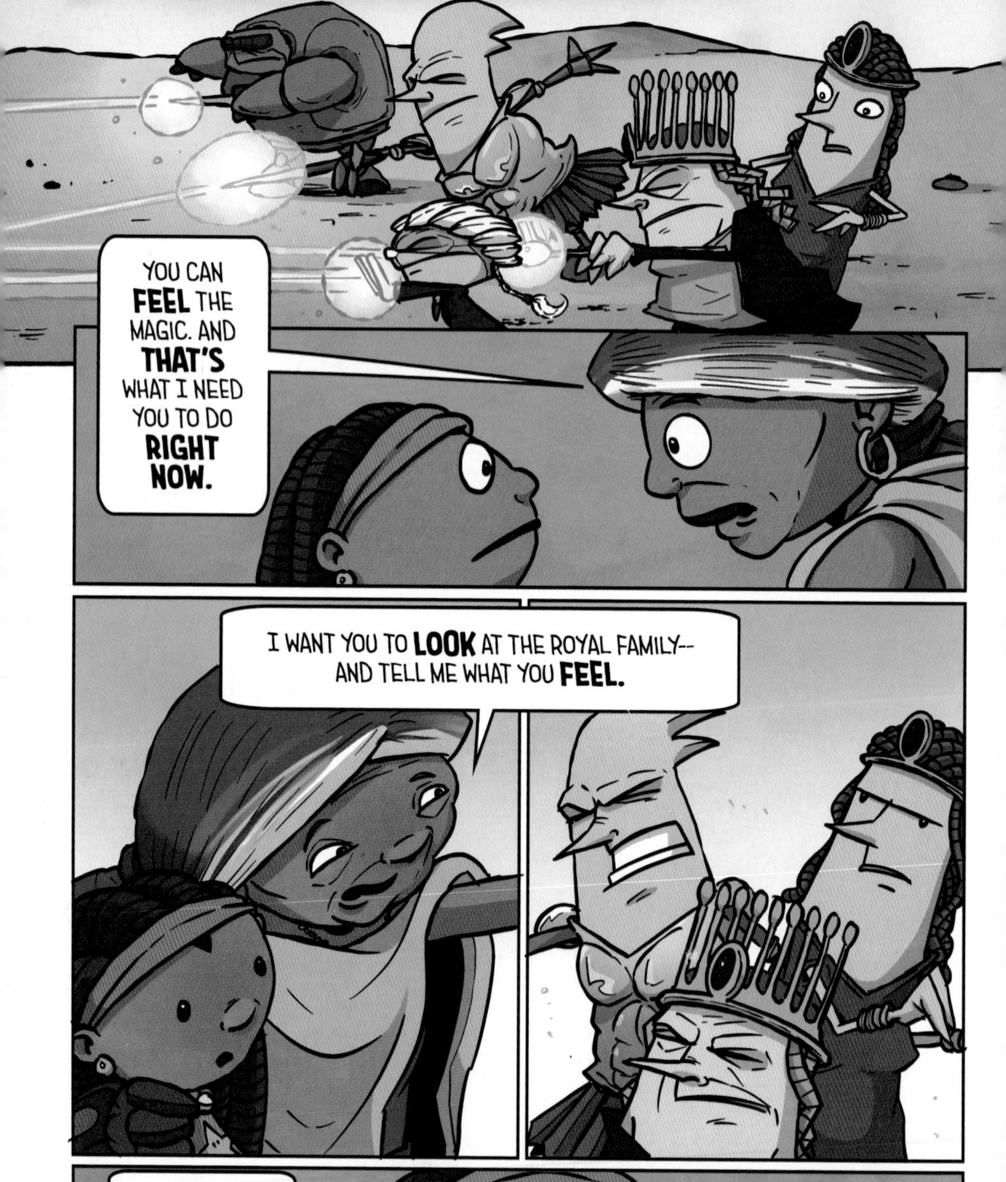
YOU CAN FEEL THE MAGIC. AND THAT'S WHAT I NEED YOU TO DO RIGHT NOW.
I WANT YOU TO LOOK AT THE ROYAL FAMILY-- AND TELL ME WHAT YOU FEEL.
WHAT I FEEL?

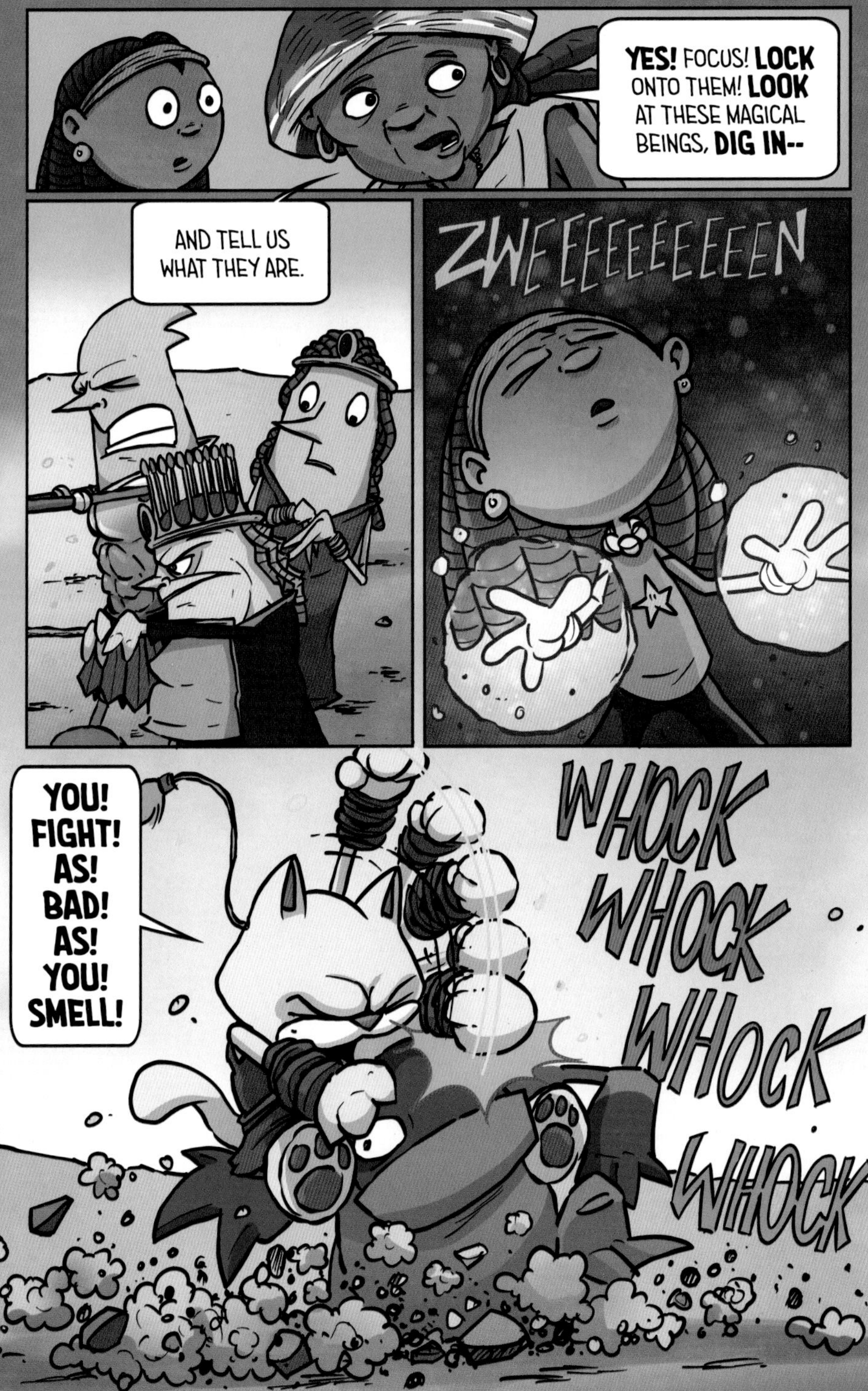
YES! FOCUS! LOCK ONTO THEM! LOOK AT THESE MAGICAL BEINGS, DIG IN--
AND TELL US WHAT THEY ARE.
ZWEEEEEEEEEEN
YOU! FIGHT! AS! BAD! AS! YOU! SMELL!
WHOCK
WHOCK
WHOCK
WHOCK

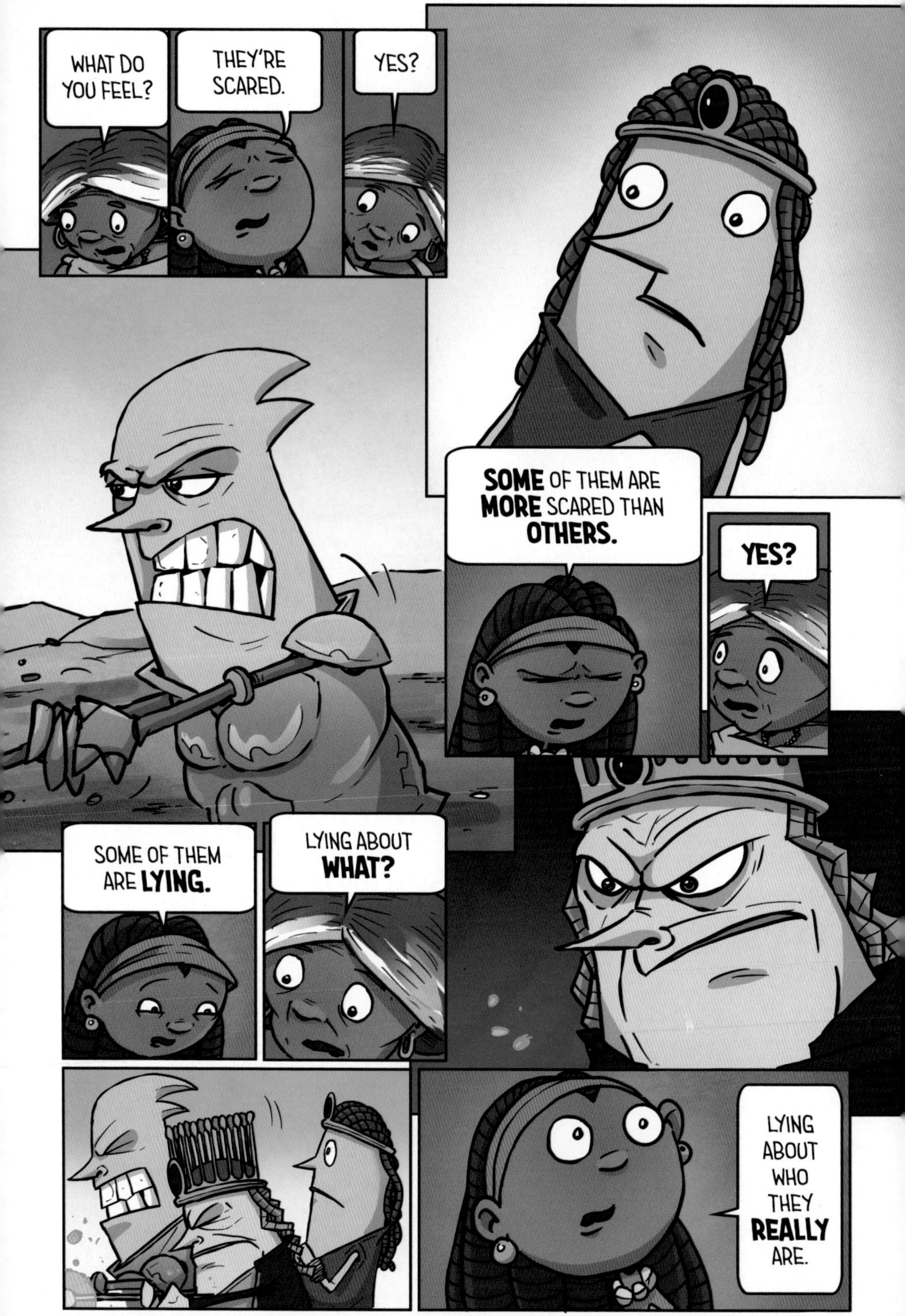
WHAT DO YOU FEEL?
THEY'RE SCARED.
YES?
SOME OF THEM ARE MORE SCARED THAN OTHERS.
YES?
SOME OF THEM ARE LYING.
LYING ABOUT WHAT?
LYING ABOUT WHO THEY REALLY ARE.

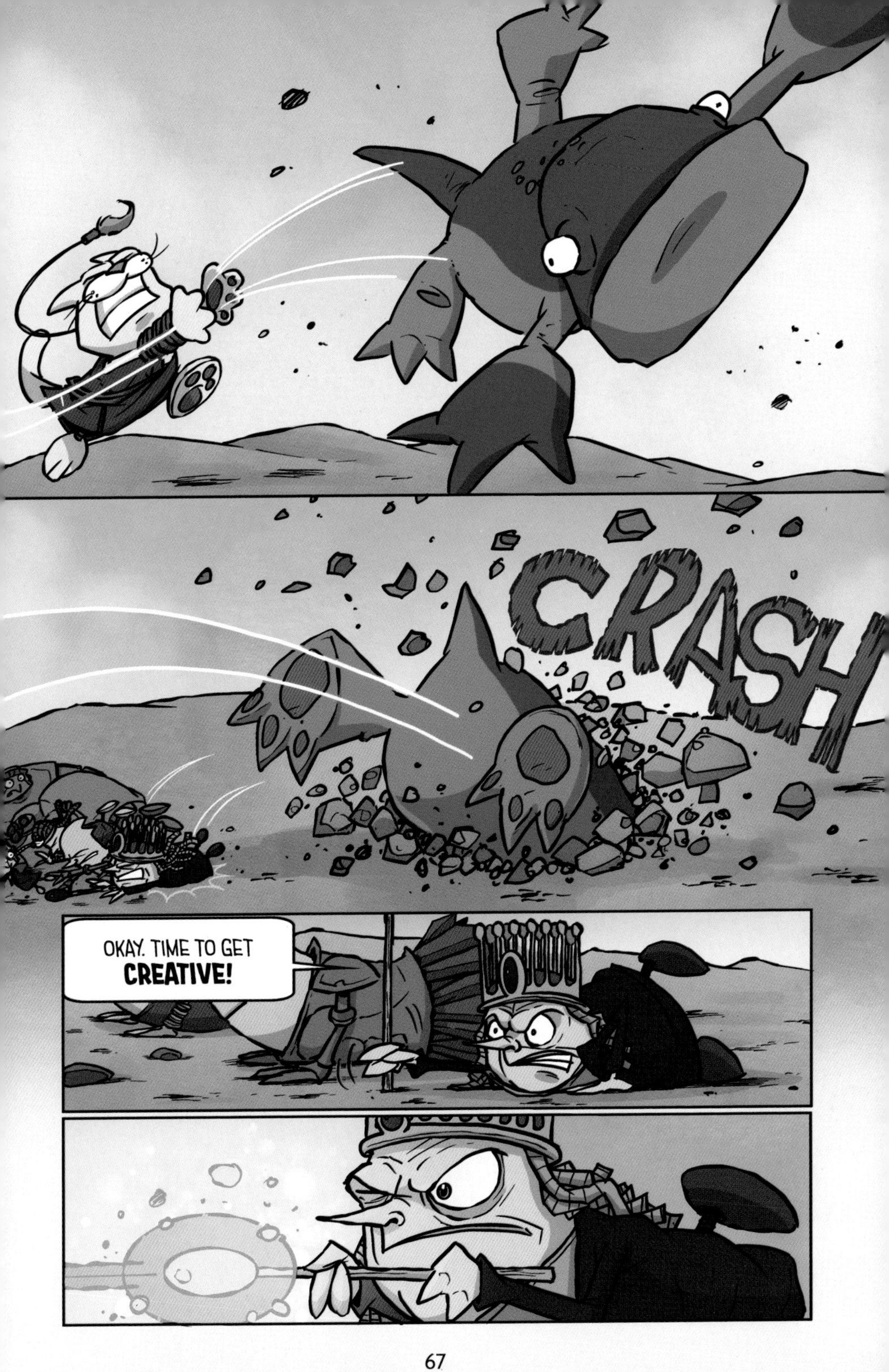
CRASH
OKAY. TIME TO GET CREATIVE!

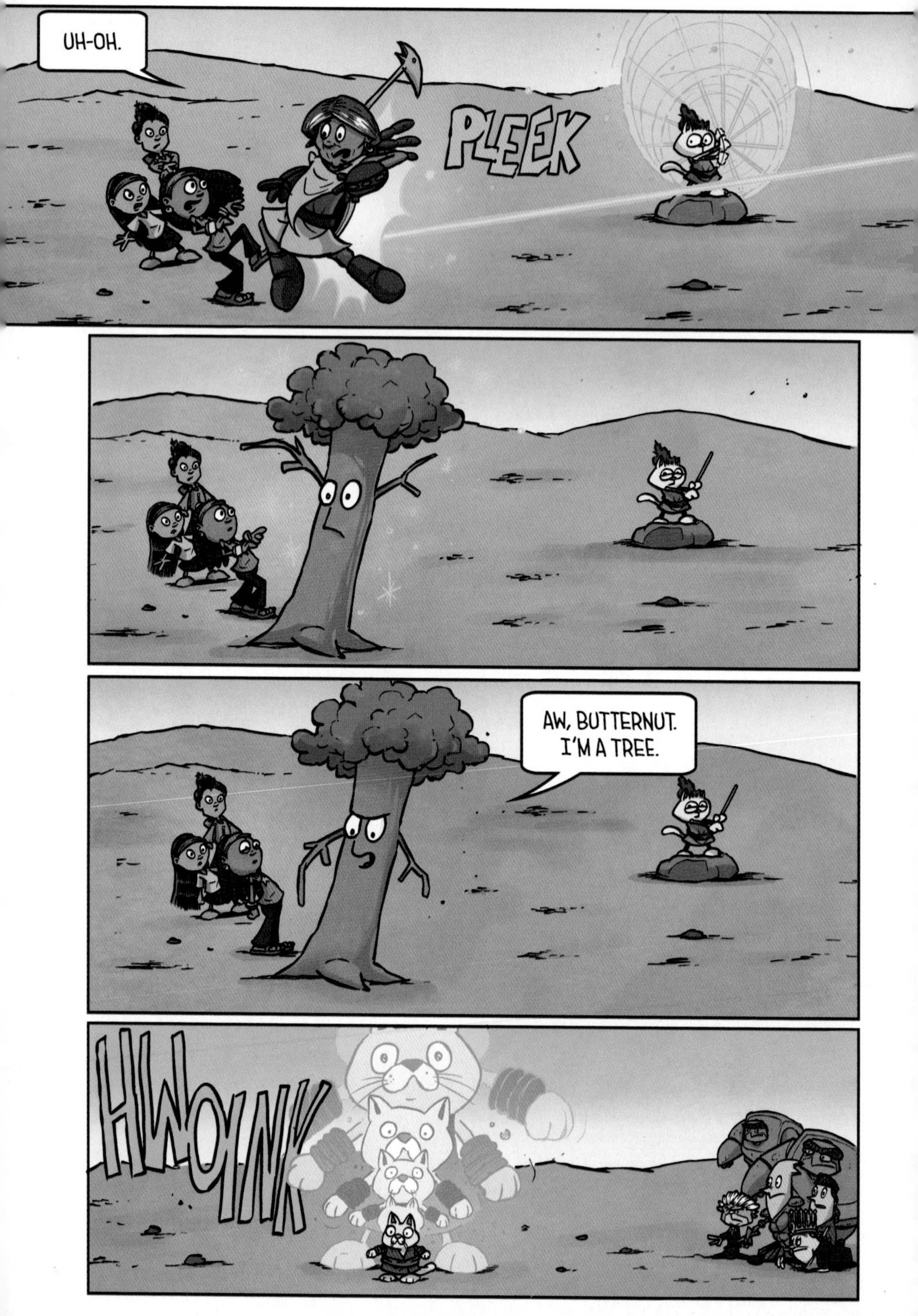
UH-OH.
PLEEK
AW, BUTTERNUT.
I'M A TREE.
HWONK

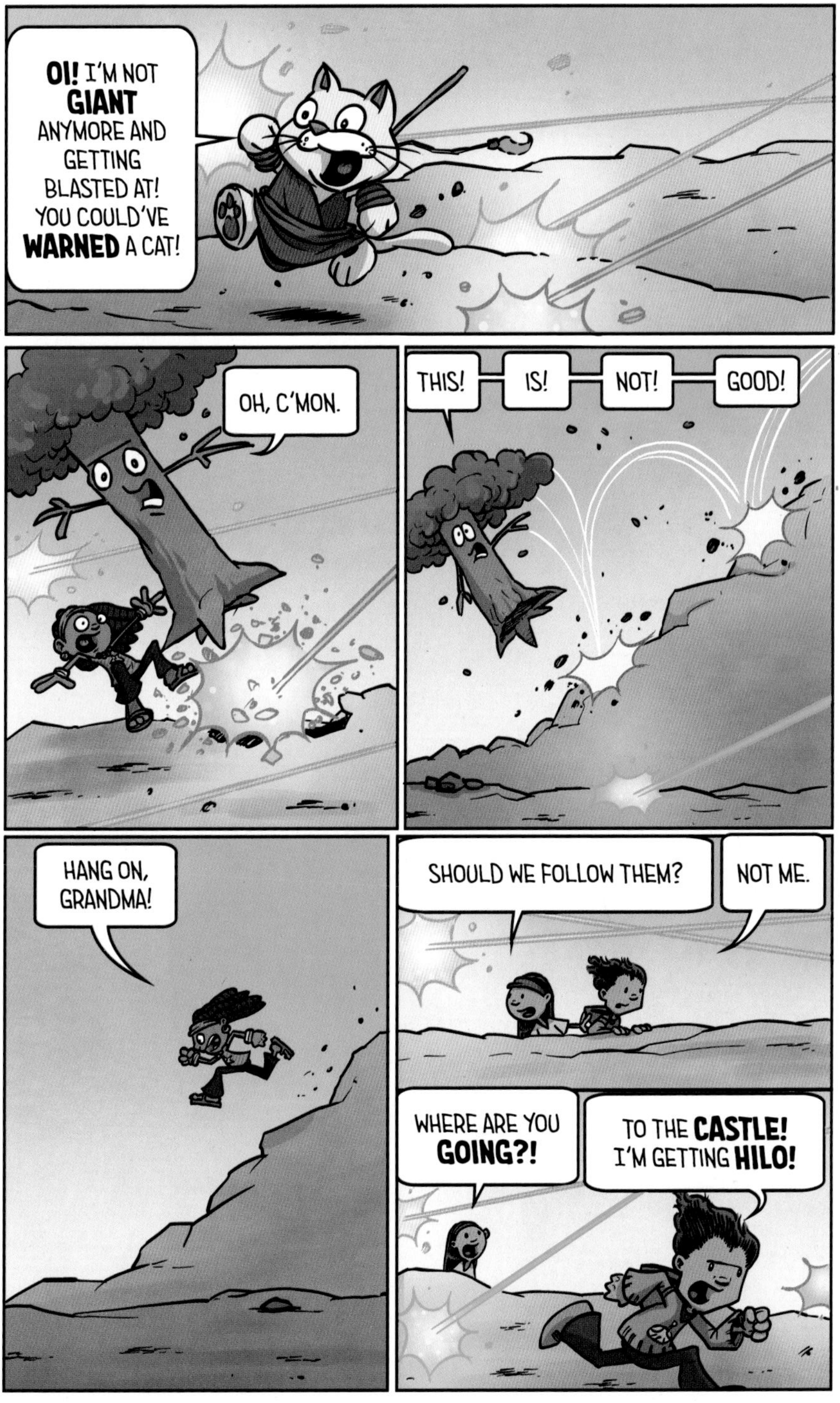
OI! I'M NOT GIANT ANYMORE AND GETTING BLASTED AT! YOU COULD'VE WARNED A CAT!
OH, C'MON.
THIS!
IS!
NOT!
GOOD!
HANG ON, GRANDMA!
SHOULD WE FOLLOW THEM?
NOT ME.
WHERE ARE YOU GOING?!
TO THE CASTLE! I'M GETTING HILO!

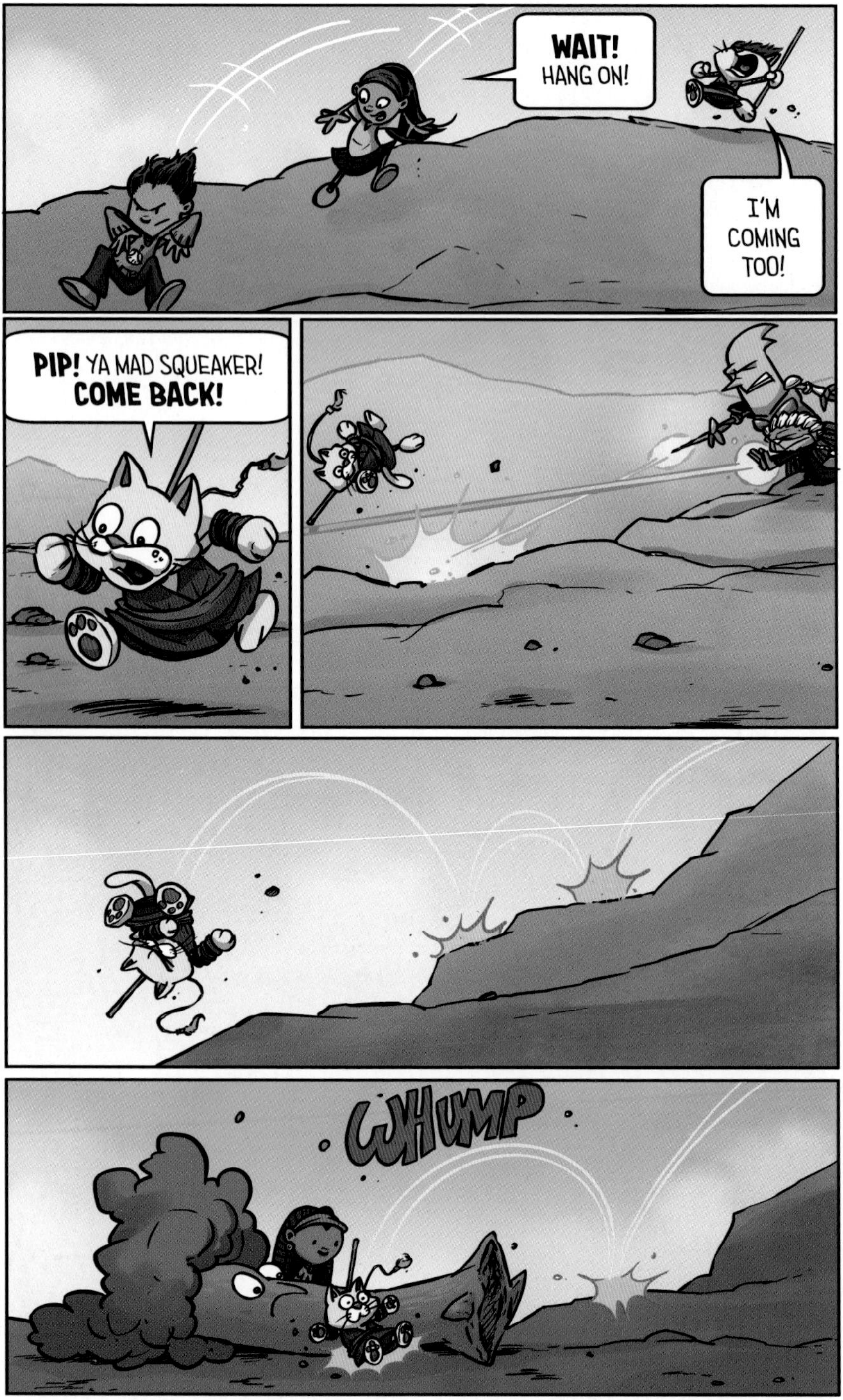
WAIT!
HANG ON!
I'M COMING TOO!
PIP! YA MAD SQUEAKER! COME BACK!
WHUMP

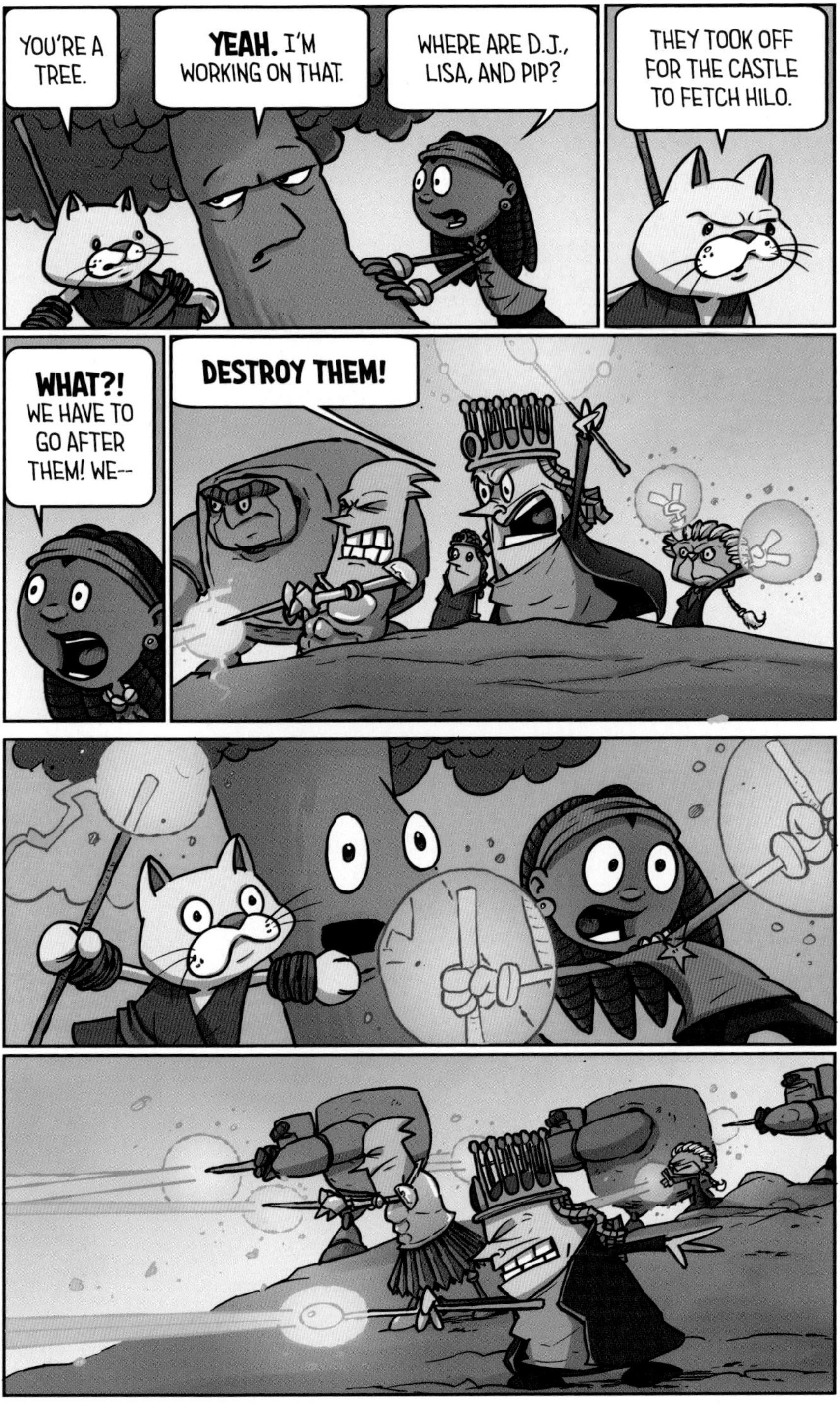
YOU'RE A TREE.
YEAH. I'M WORKING ON THAT.
WHERE ARE D.J., LISA, AND PIP?
THEY TOOK OFF FOR THE CASTLE TO FETCH HILO.
WHAT?! WE HAVE TO GO AFTER THEM! WE--
DESTROY THEM!

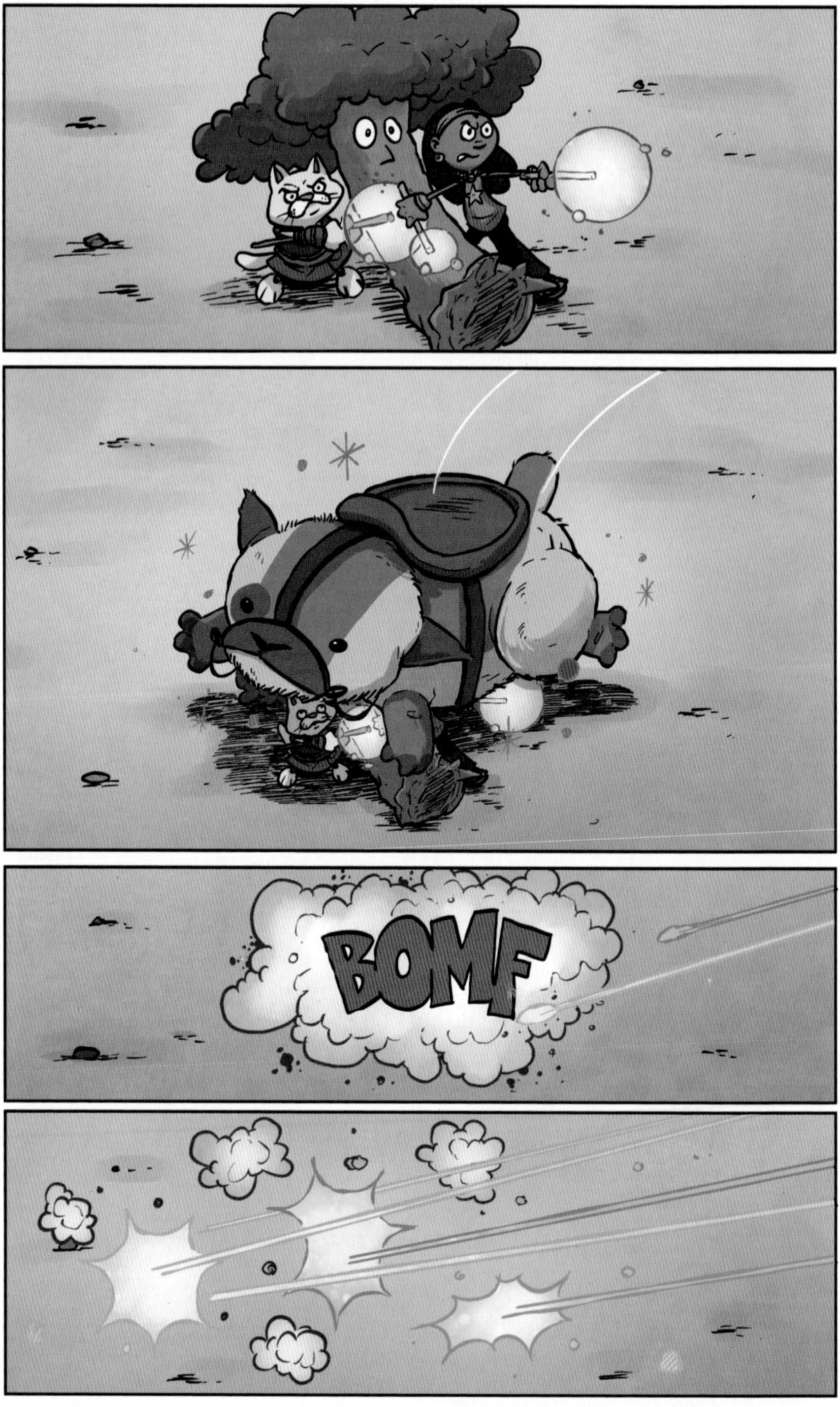
BOMF

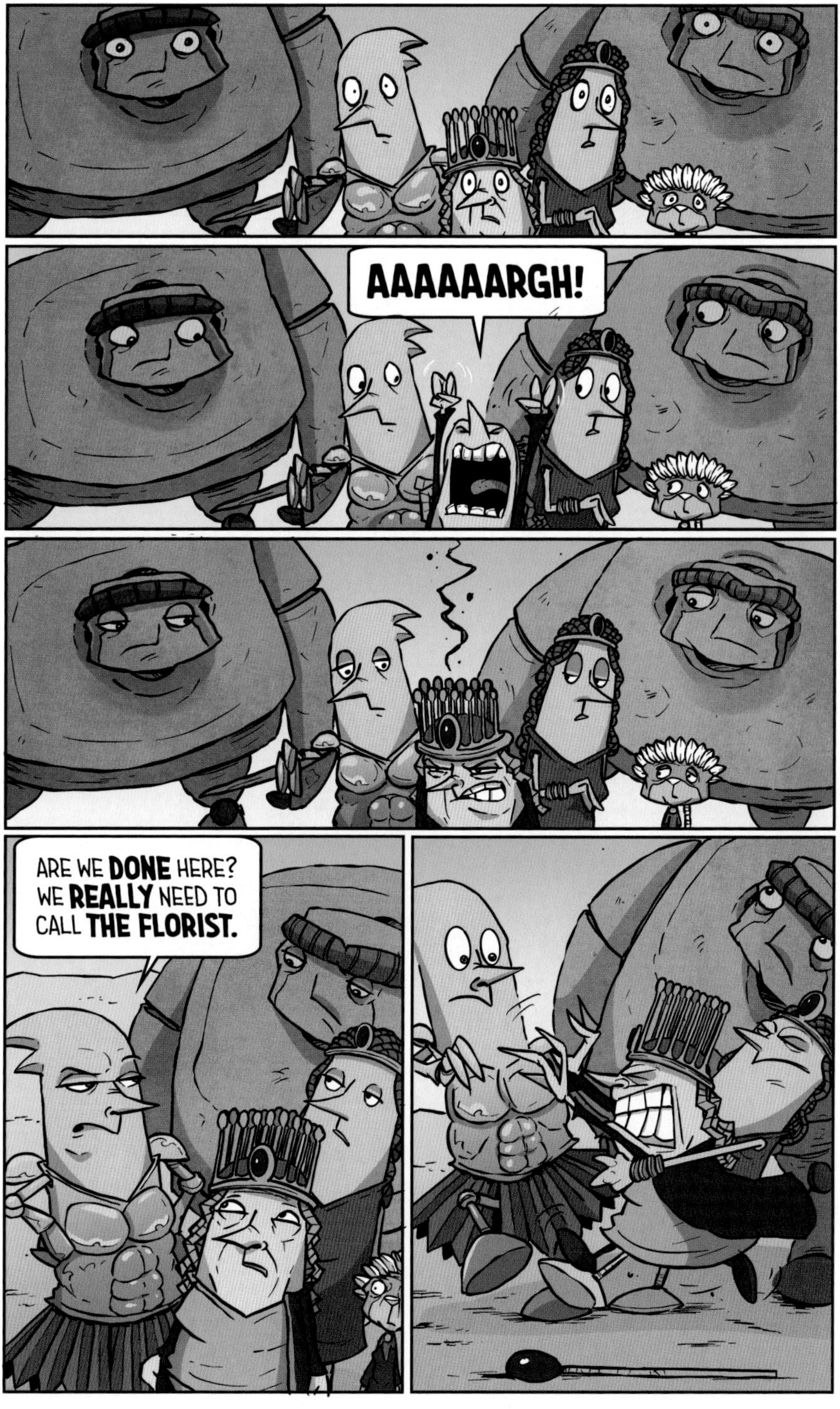
AAAAAARGH!
ARE WE DONE HERE? WE REALLY NEED TO CALL THE FLORIST.

CHAPTER 4

IT DOESN'T MAKE IT ANY LESS TRUE

WHAT ARE YOU DOING?
NOTHING.
I KNOW THAT.
BUT YOU **CAN'T** DO **NOTHING.**

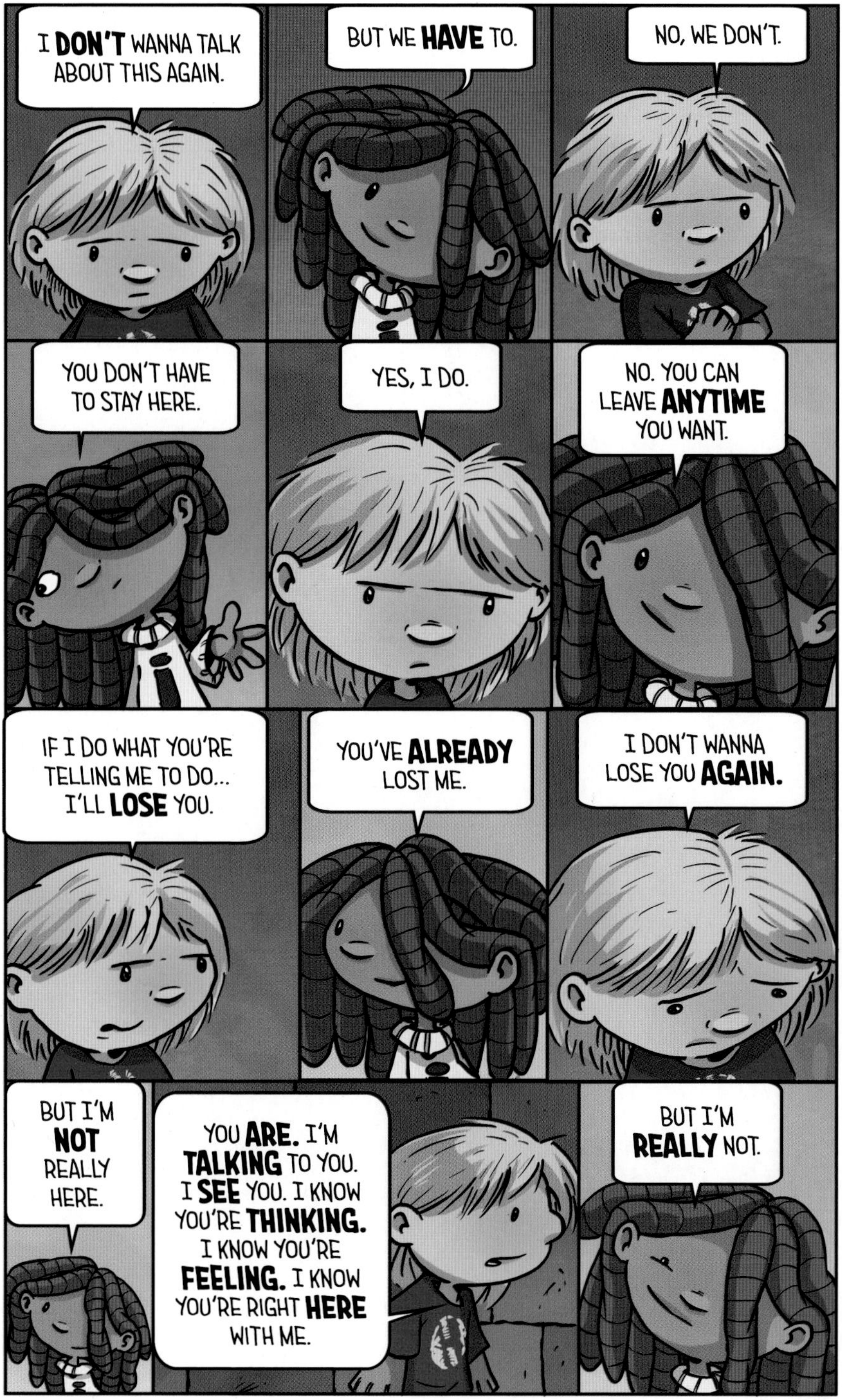
I DON'T WANNA TALK ABOUT THIS AGAIN.
BUT WE HAVE TO.
NO, WE DON'T.
YOU DON'T HAVE TO STAY HERE.
YES, I DO.
NO. YOU CAN LEAVE ANYTIME YOU WANT.
IF I DO WHAT YOU'RE TELLING ME TO DO... I'LL LOSE YOU.
YOU'VE ALREADY LOST ME.
I DON'T WANNA LOSE YOU AGAIN.
BUT I'M NOT REALLY HERE.
YOU ARE. I'M TALKING TO YOU. I SEE YOU. I KNOW YOU'RE THINKING. I KNOW YOU'RE FEELING. I KNOW YOU'RE RIGHT HERE WITH ME.
BUT I'M REALLY NOT.

78

CHAPTER 5

STEADY, BIRDIE

BOMF
WHAT DID YOU DO?!
WHAT DID YOU DO?!

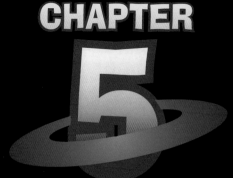

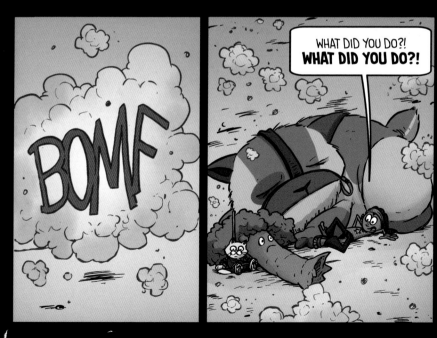

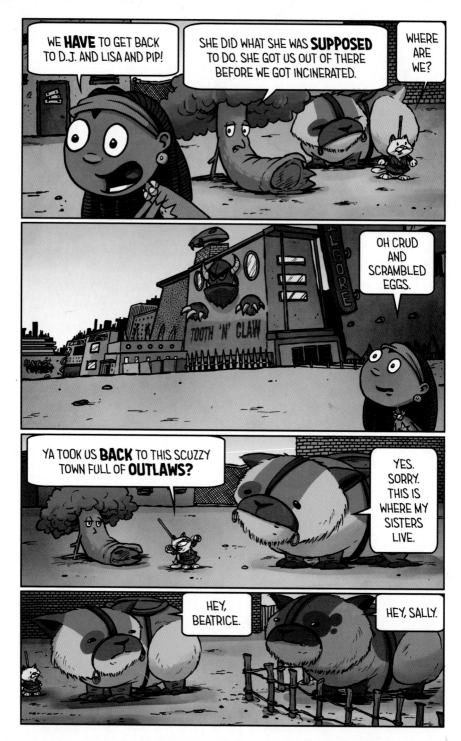

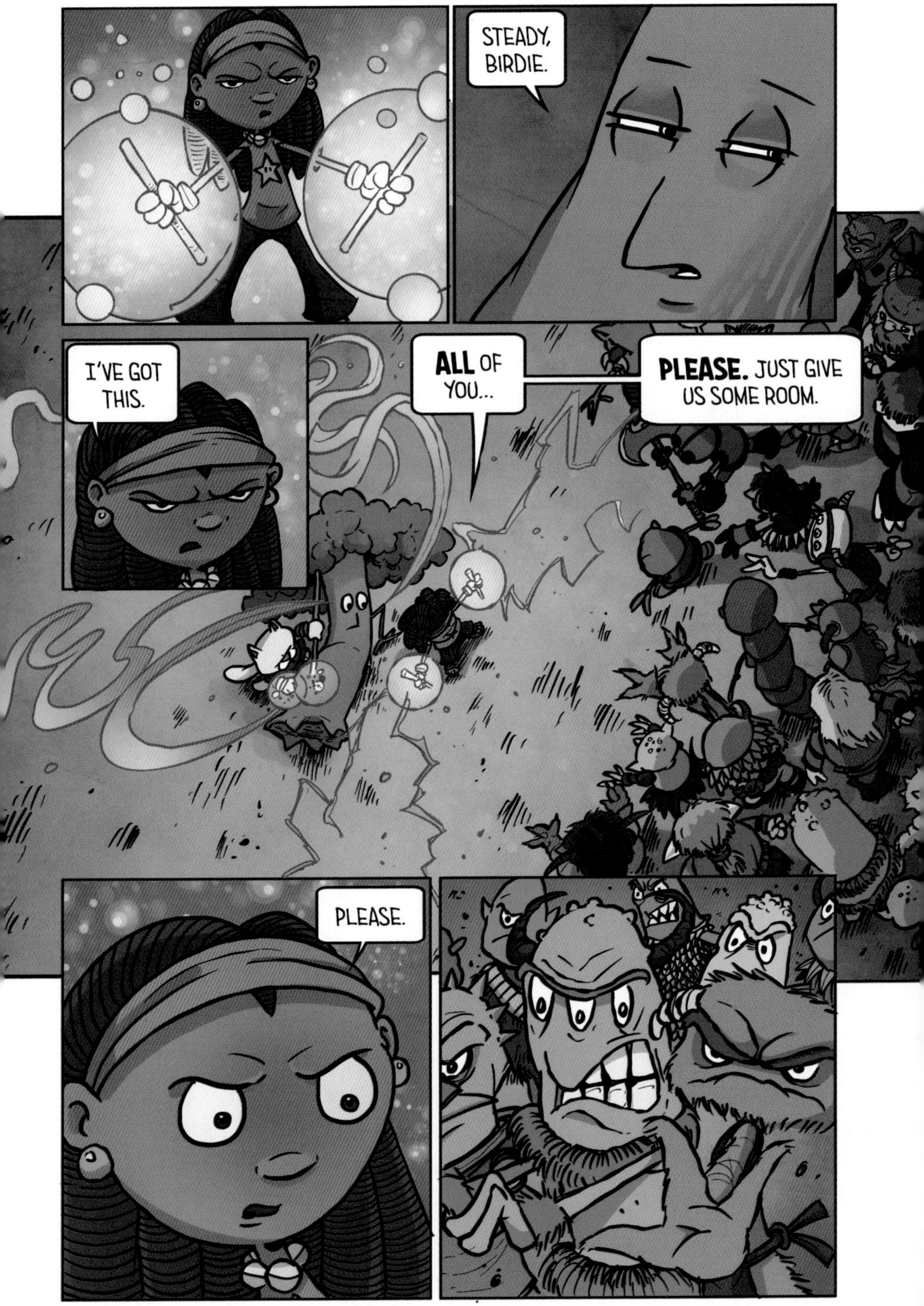
STEADY, BIRDIE.
I'VE GOT THIS.
ALL OF YOU...
PLEASE. JUST GIVE US SOME ROOM.
PLEASE.

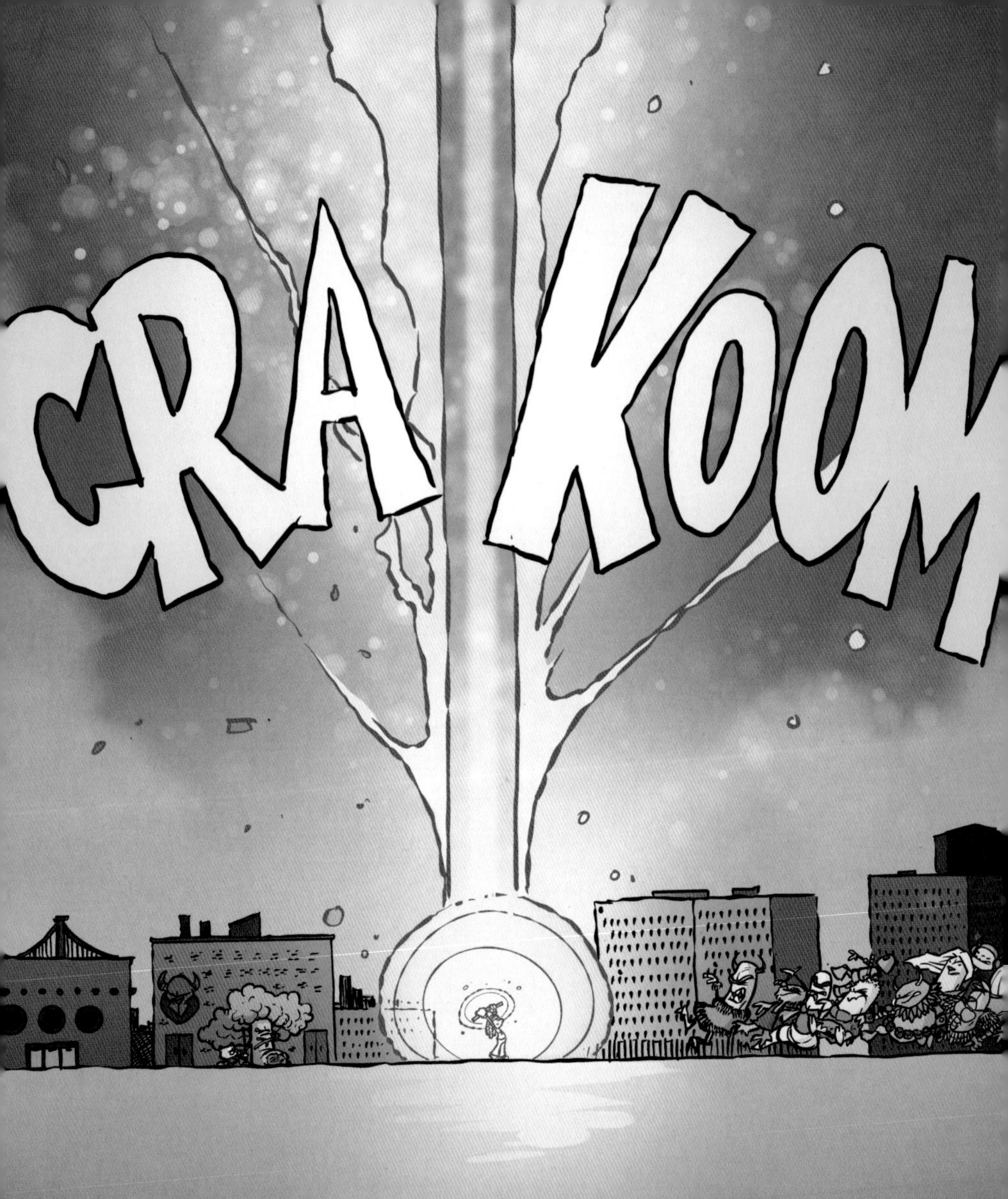
CRA KOOM

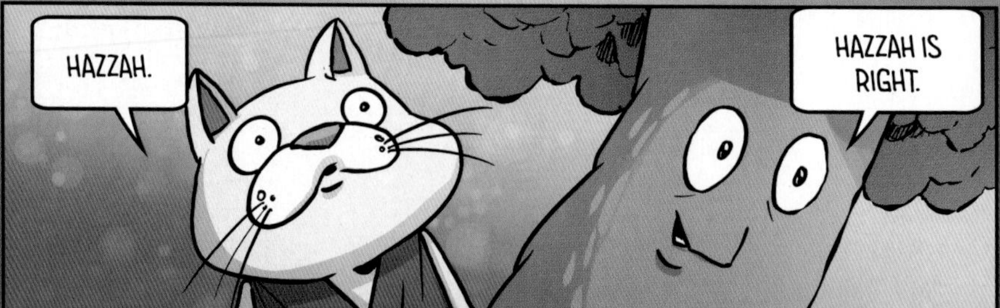
HAZZAH.
HAZZAH IS RIGHT.

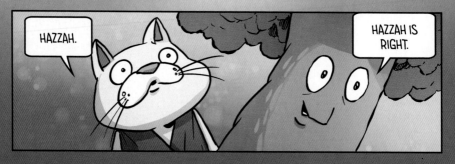

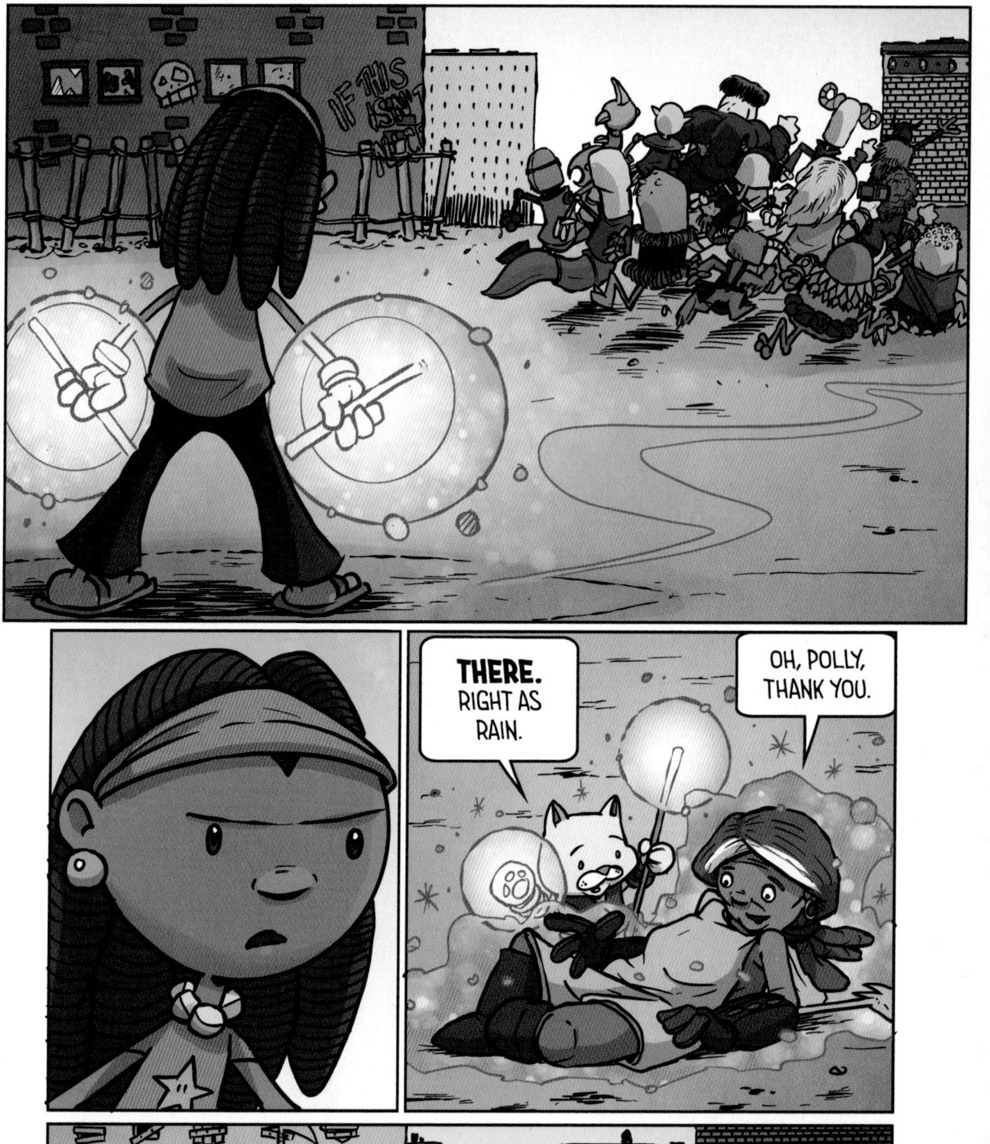
THERE. RIGHT AS RAIN.
OH, POLLY, THANK YOU.
HEY, FOLKS.

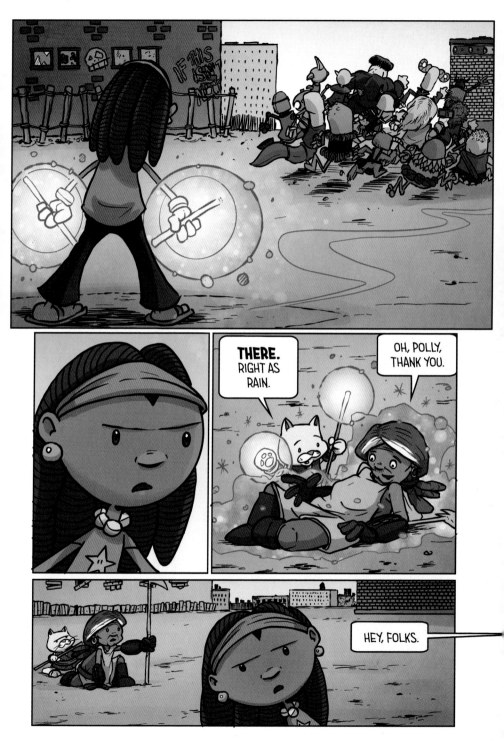

CHAPTER 6

WHEN PIGS FLY

THAT'S PRETTY FAR.

THE CASTLE OF THE **ROYAL FAMILY** OF **MALUM.**

HOW ARE WE GOING TO GET THERE?

CHAPTER 7

TO BE A PART OF IT

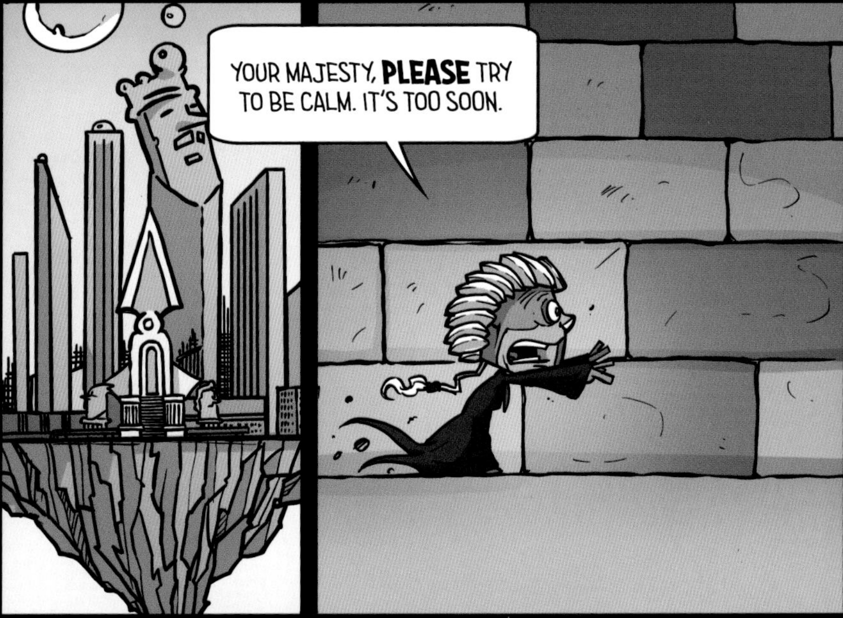
YOUR MAJESTY, **PLEASE** TRY TO BE CALM. IT'S TOO SOON.

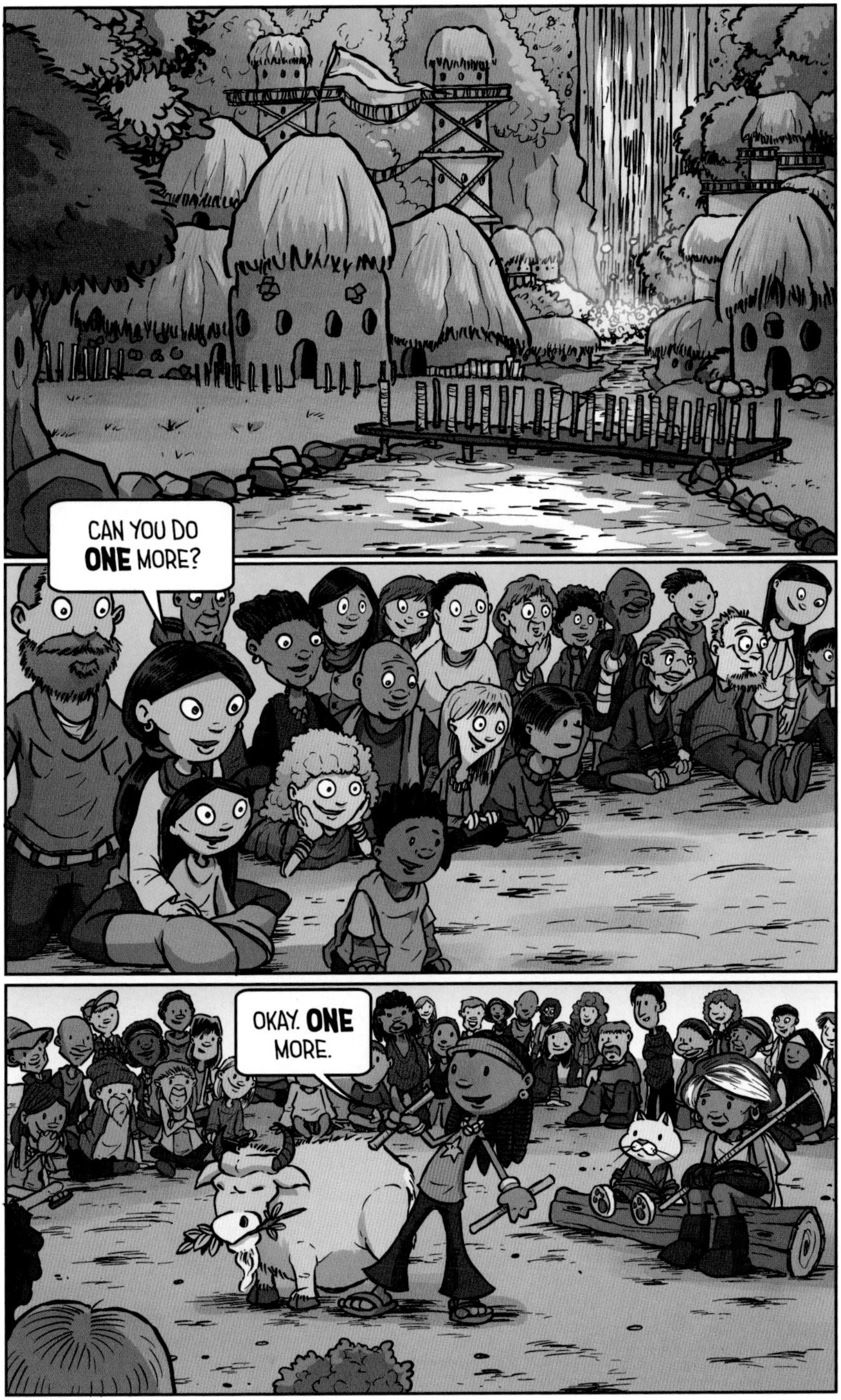
CAN YOU DO **ONE** MORE?
OKAY. **ONE** MORE.

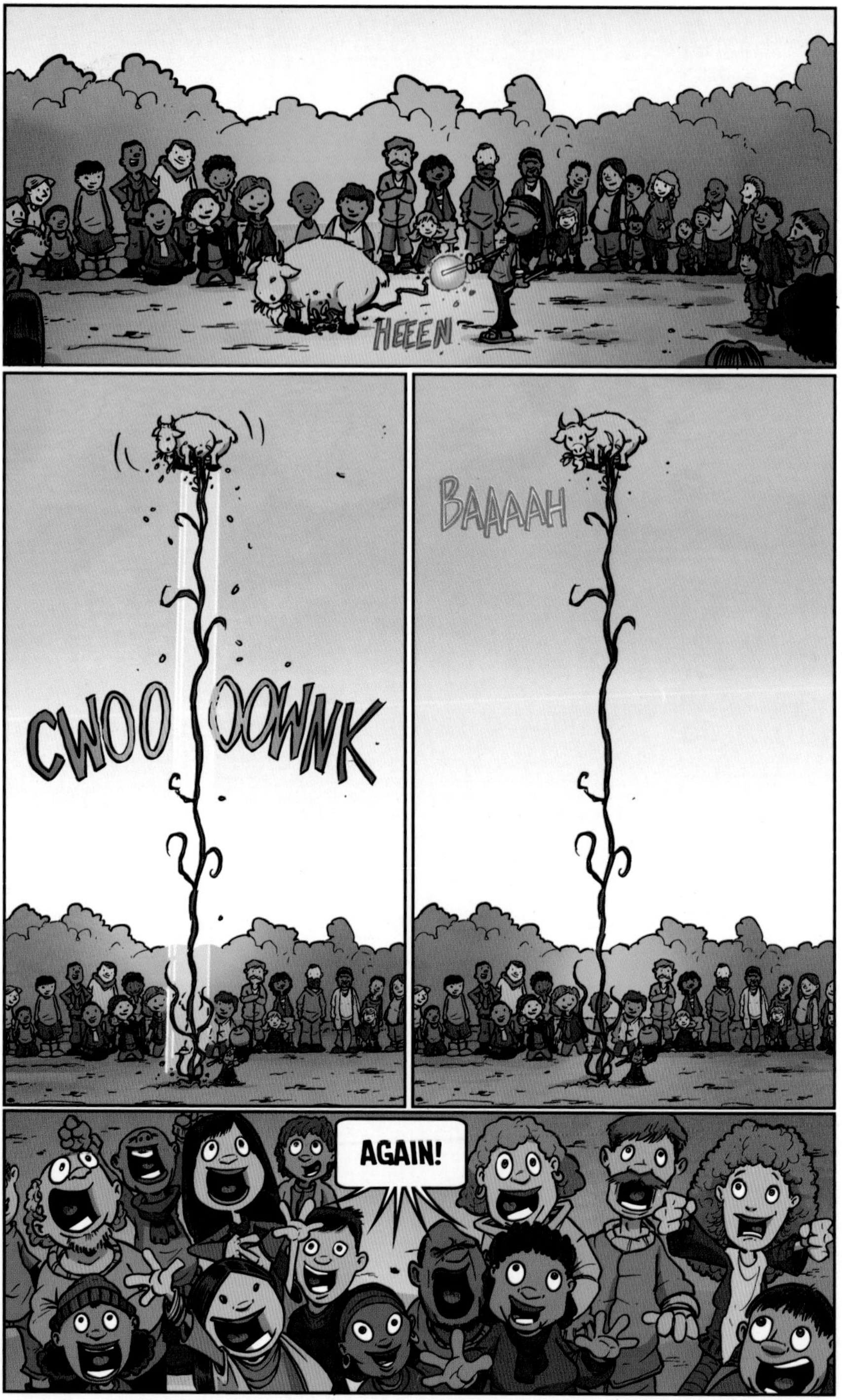
HEEEN
CWOOOOWNK
BAAAAH
AGAIN!

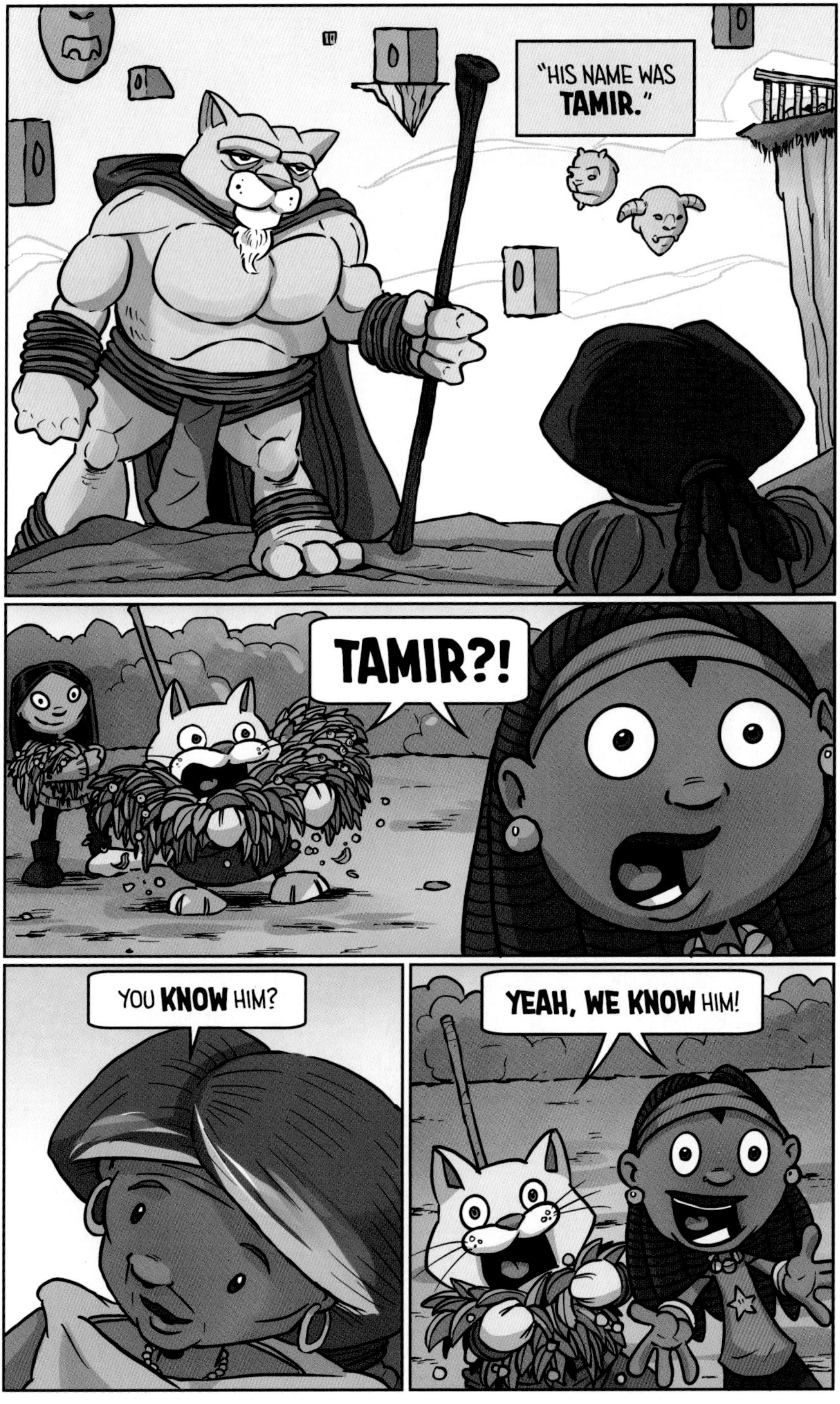
"HIS NAME WAS TAMIR."
TAMIR?!
YOU KNOW HIM?
YEAH, WE KNOW HIM!

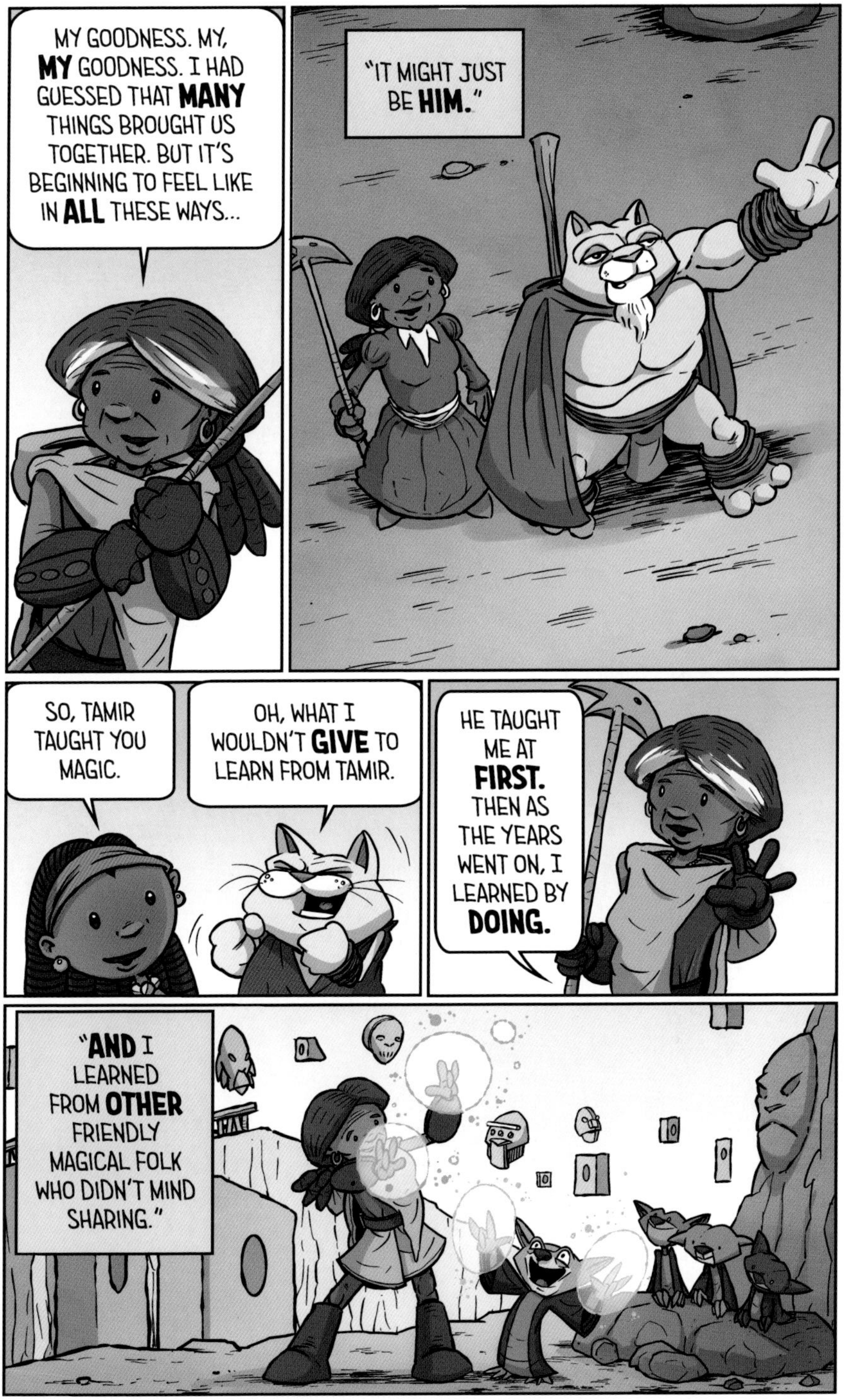
MY GOODNESS. MY, **MY** GOODNESS. I HAD GUESSED THAT **MANY** THINGS BROUGHT US TOGETHER. BUT IT'S BEGINNING TO FEEL LIKE IN **ALL** THESE WAYS...
"IT MIGHT JUST BE **HIM.**"
SO, TAMIR TAUGHT YOU MAGIC.
OH, WHAT I WOULDN'T **GIVE** TO LEARN FROM TAMIR.
HE TAUGHT ME AT **FIRST.** THEN AS THE YEARS WENT ON, I LEARNED BY **DOING.**
"**AND** I LEARNED FROM **OTHER** FRIENDLY MAGICAL FOLK WHO DIDN'T MIND SHARING."

CHAPTER 8

DUNGEONS, NO DRAGONS

CLACKA

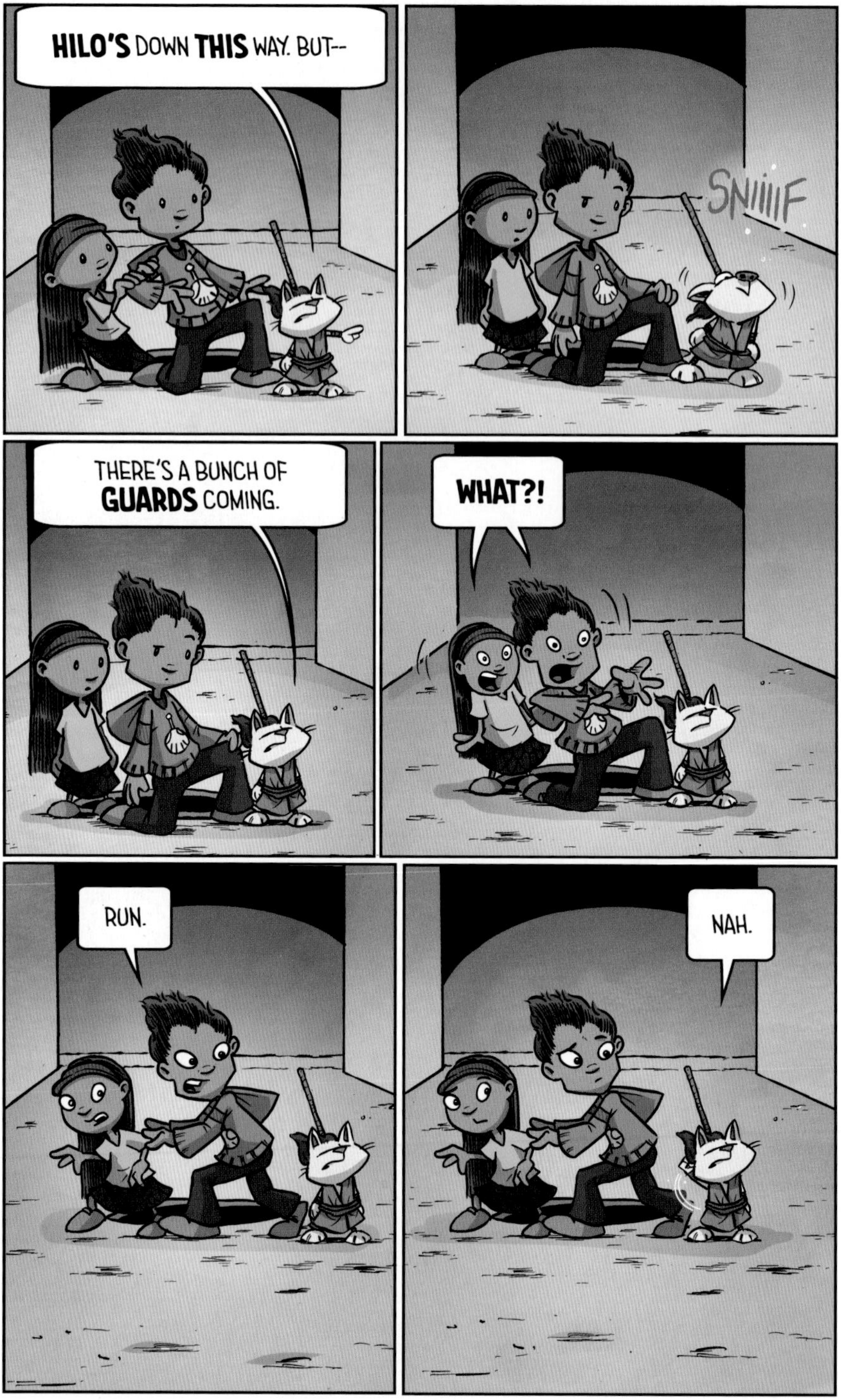
HILO'S DOWN THIS WAY. BUT--
SNIIIIF
THERE'S A BUNCH OF GUARDS COMING.
WHAT?!
RUN.
NAH.

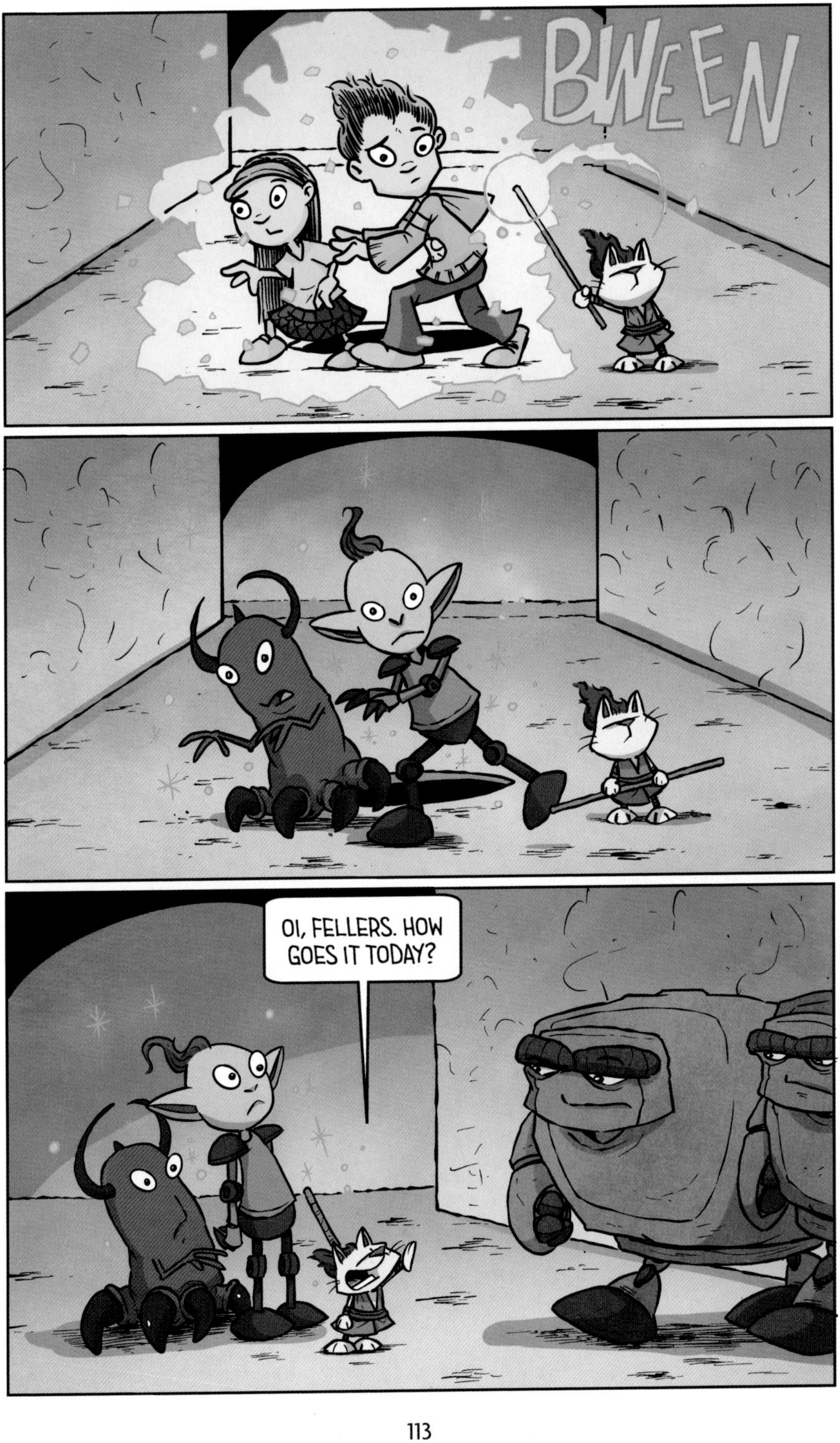
BWEEN
OI, FELLERS. HOW GOES IT TODAY?

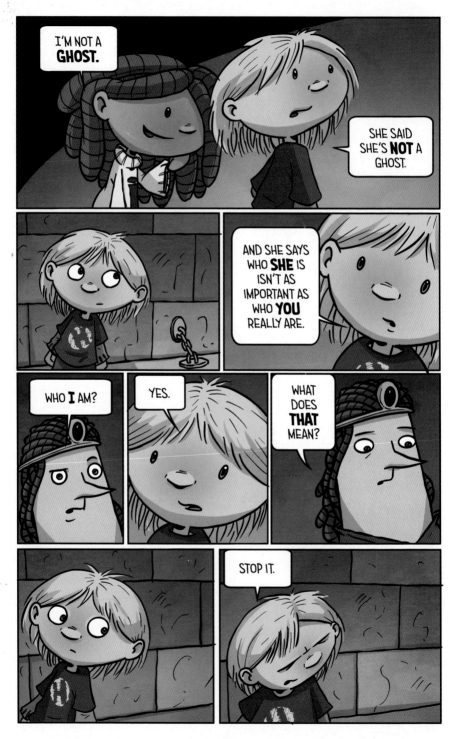

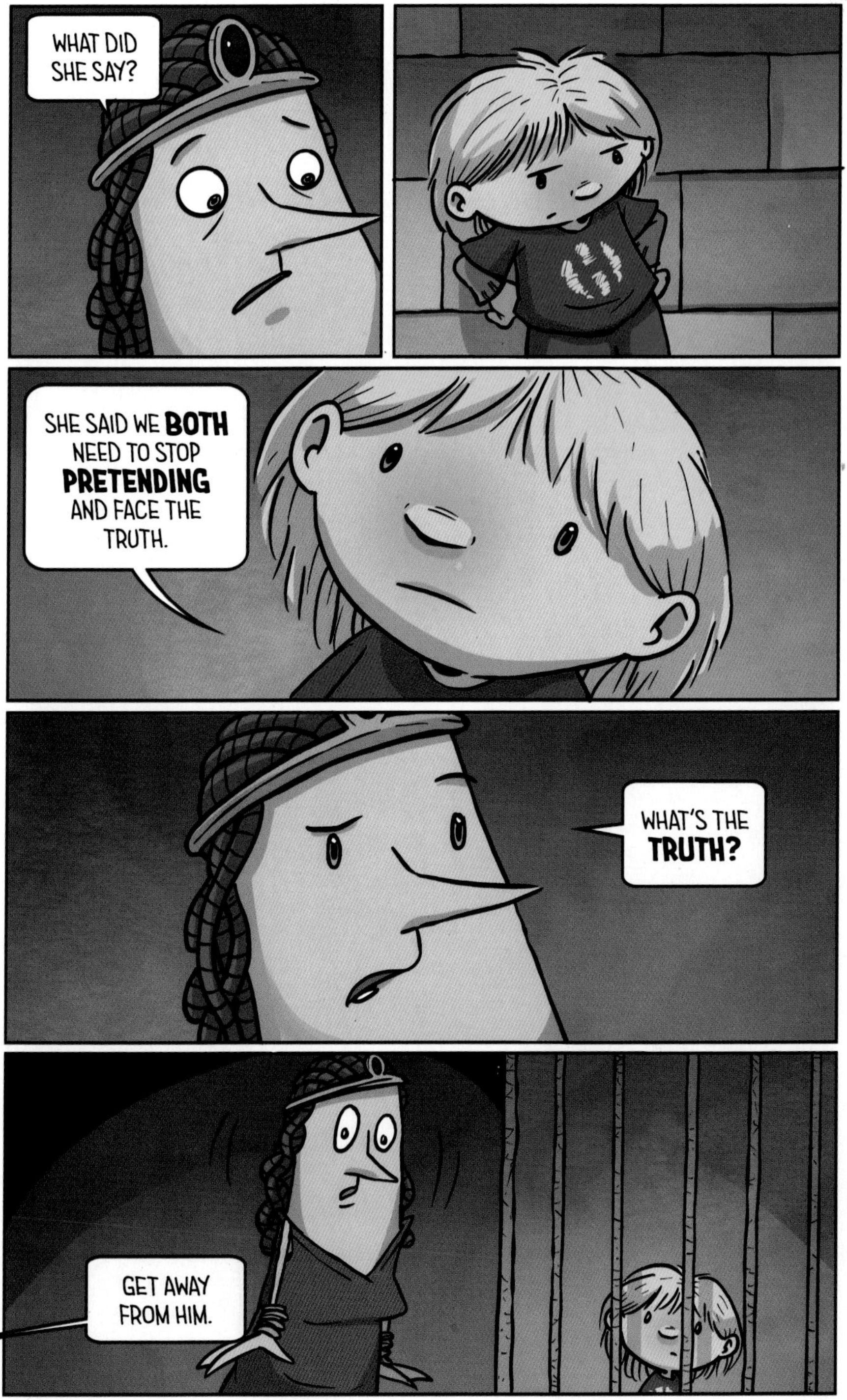
WHAT DID SHE SAY?
SHE SAID WE **BOTH** NEED TO STOP **PRETENDING** AND FACE THE TRUTH.
WHAT'S THE **TRUTH?**
GET AWAY FROM HIM.

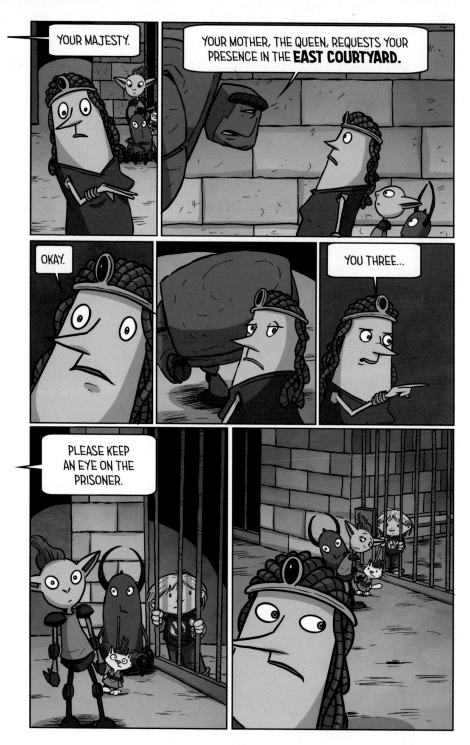

CHAPTER 9

THIS AIN'T NO PARTY

NOW! WE'RE DOING IT NOW!
YOUR MAJESTY, IT'S TOO SOON! WE'RE NOT READY!
WE'RE READY ENOUGH!

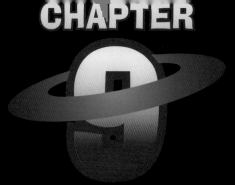

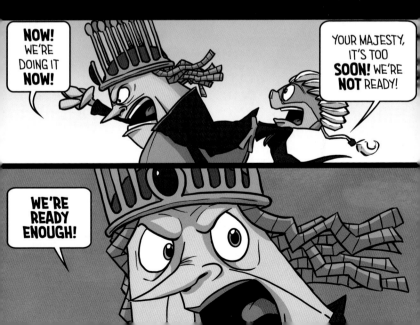

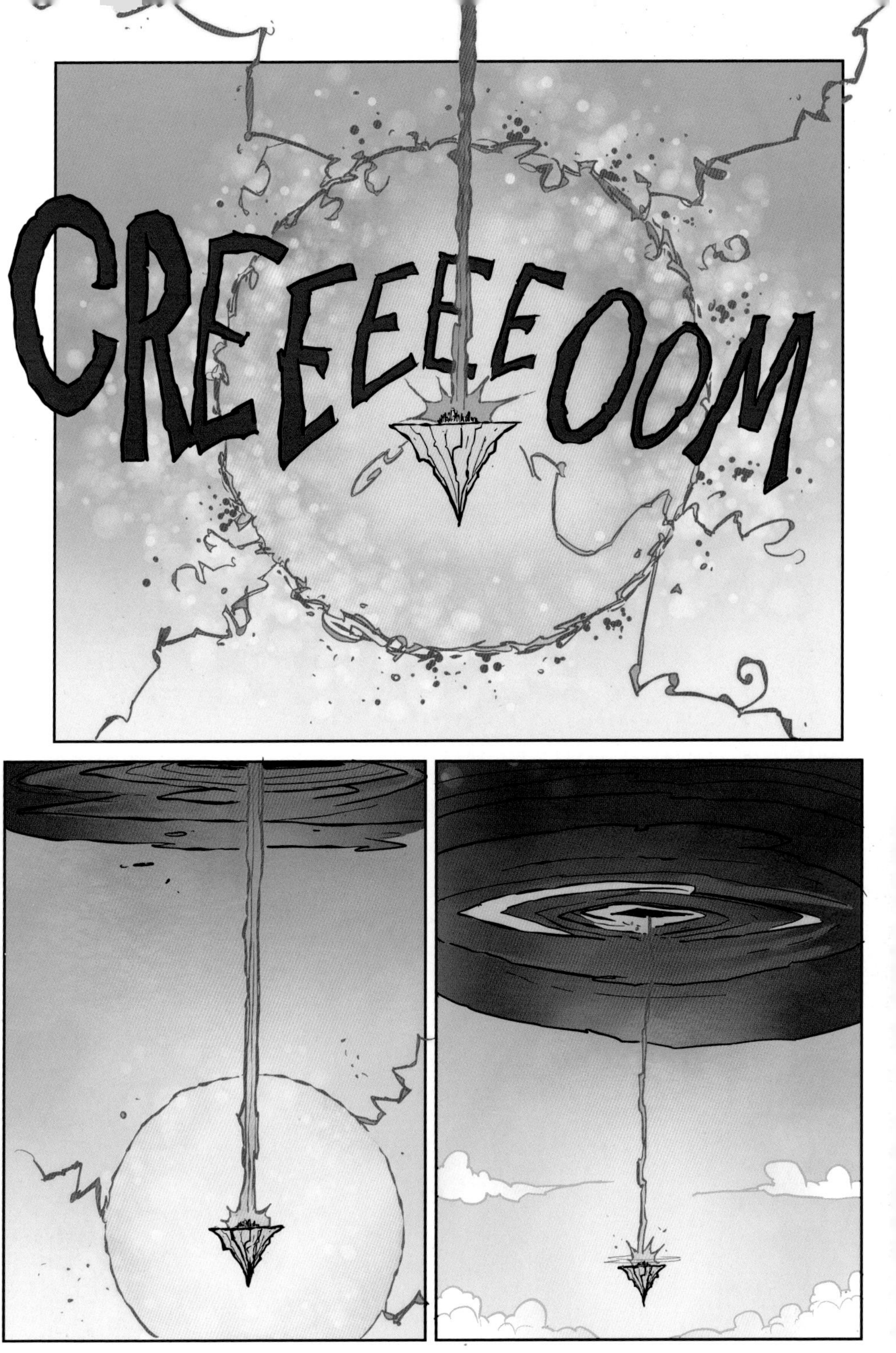
CREEEEEOOM

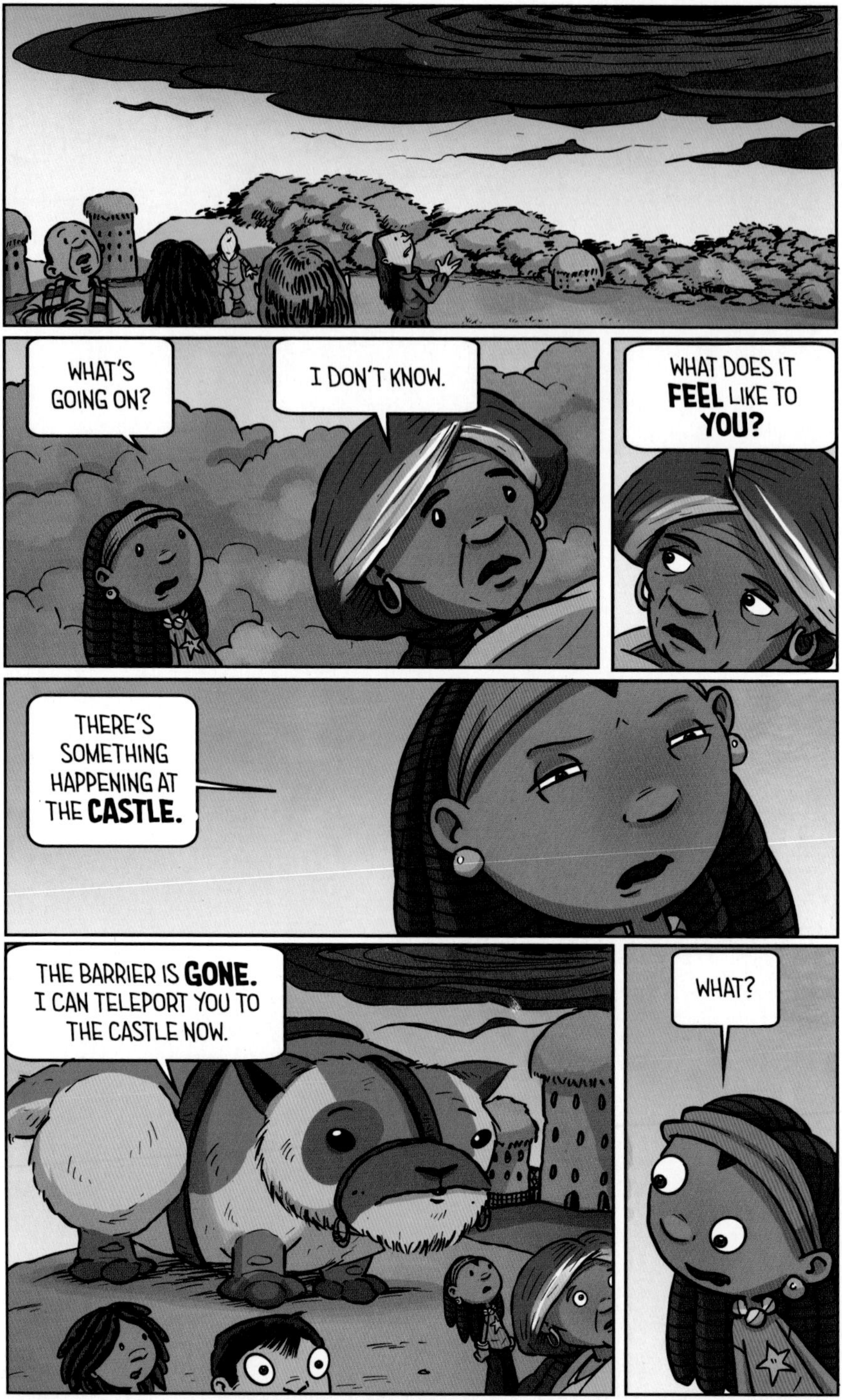
WHAT'S GOING ON?
I DON'T KNOW.
WHAT DOES IT FEEL LIKE TO YOU?
THERE'S SOMETHING HAPPENING AT THE CASTLE.
THE BARRIER IS GONE. I CAN TELEPORT YOU TO THE CASTLE NOW.
WHAT?

142

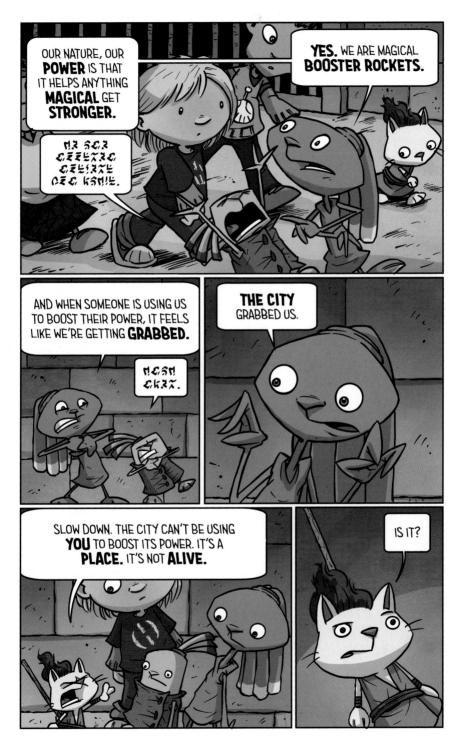

OUR NATURE, OUR **POWER** IS THAT IT HELPS ANYTHING **MAGICAL** GET **STRONGER**.

YES. WE ARE MAGICAL **BOOSTER ROCKETS.**

AND WHEN SOMEONE IS USING US TO BOOST THEIR POWER, IT FEELS LIKE WE'RE GETTING **GRABBED.**

THE CITY GRABBED US.

SLOW DOWN. THE CITY CAN'T BE USING **YOU** TO BOOST ITS POWER. IT'S A **PLACE.** IT'S NOT **ALIVE.**

IS IT?

143

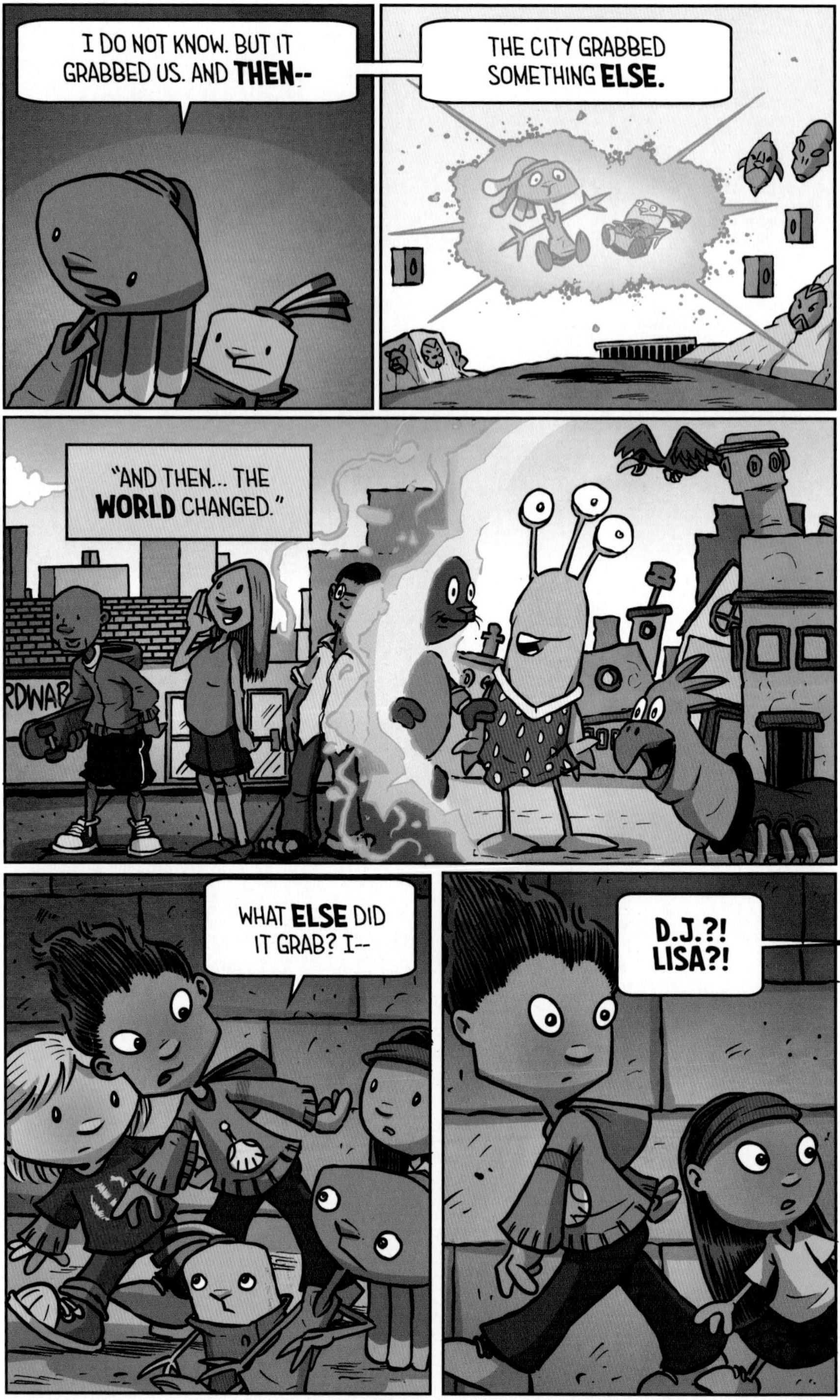
I DO NOT KNOW. BUT IT GRABBED US. AND **THEN**--
THE CITY GRABBED SOMETHING **ELSE.**
"AND THEN... THE **WORLD** CHANGED."
RDWAR
WHAT **ELSE** DID IT GRAB? I--
D.J.?! LISA?!

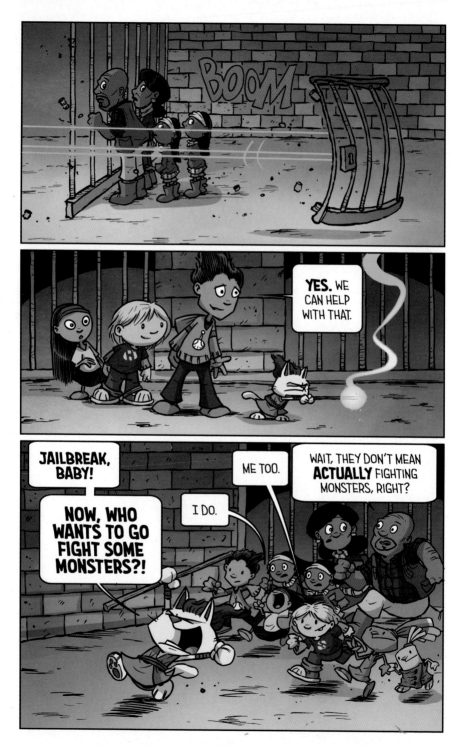

CHAPTER 10

STOP HORSE

MOM, PLEASE!
STOP!

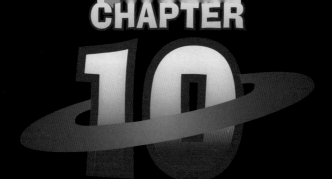

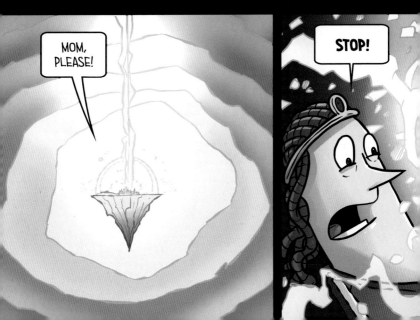

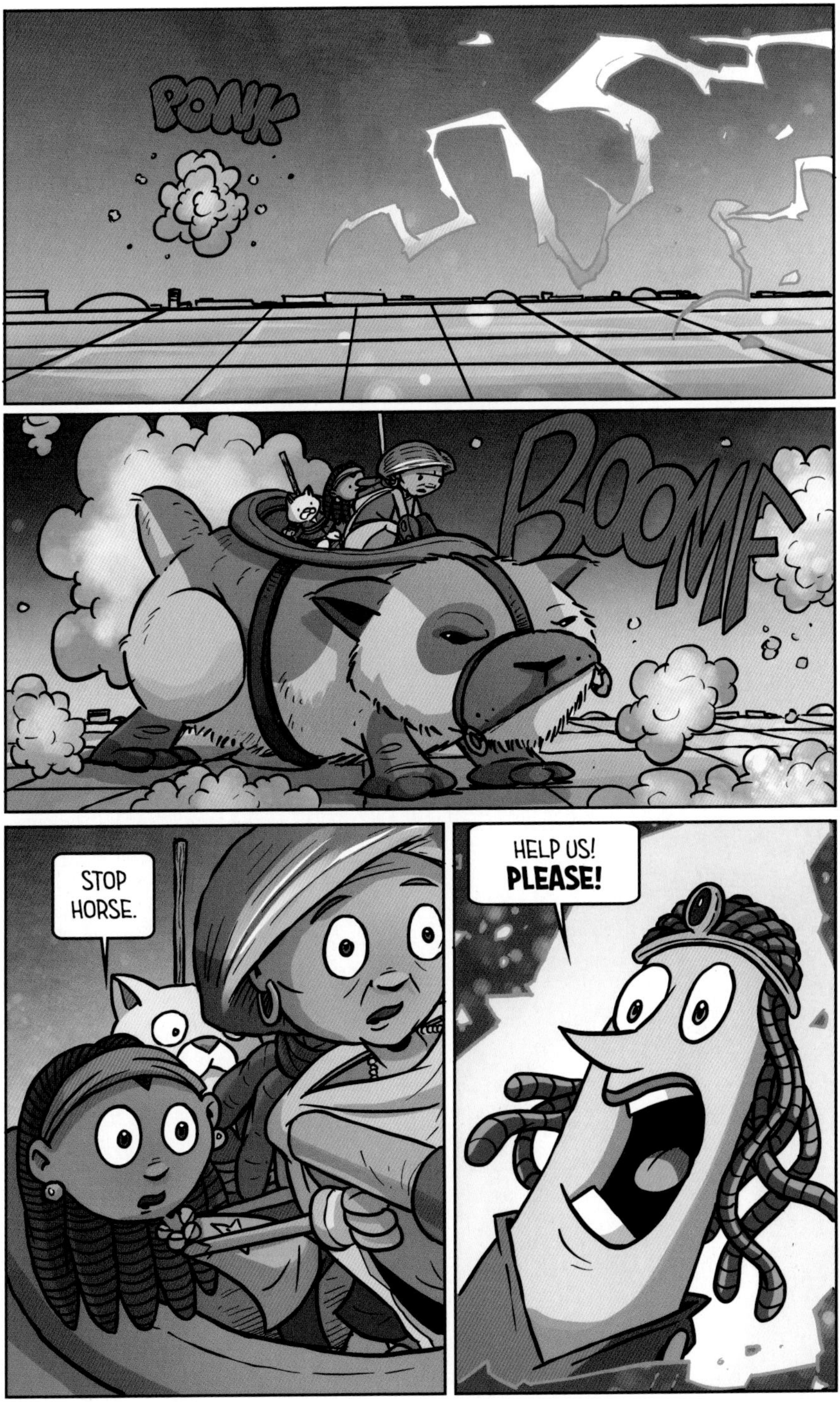
POINK
BOOMF
STOP HORSE.
HELP US! PLEASE!

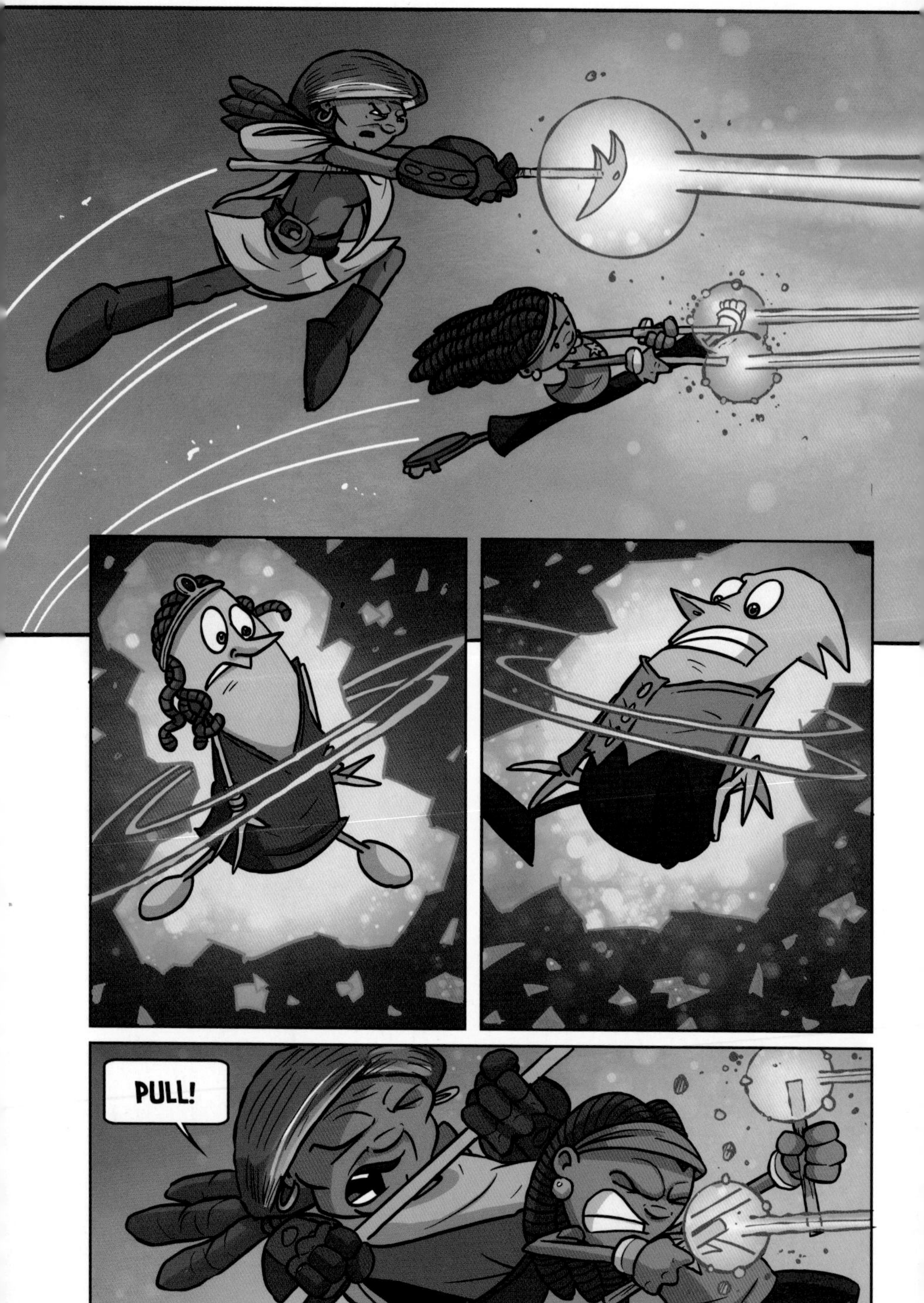
PULL!

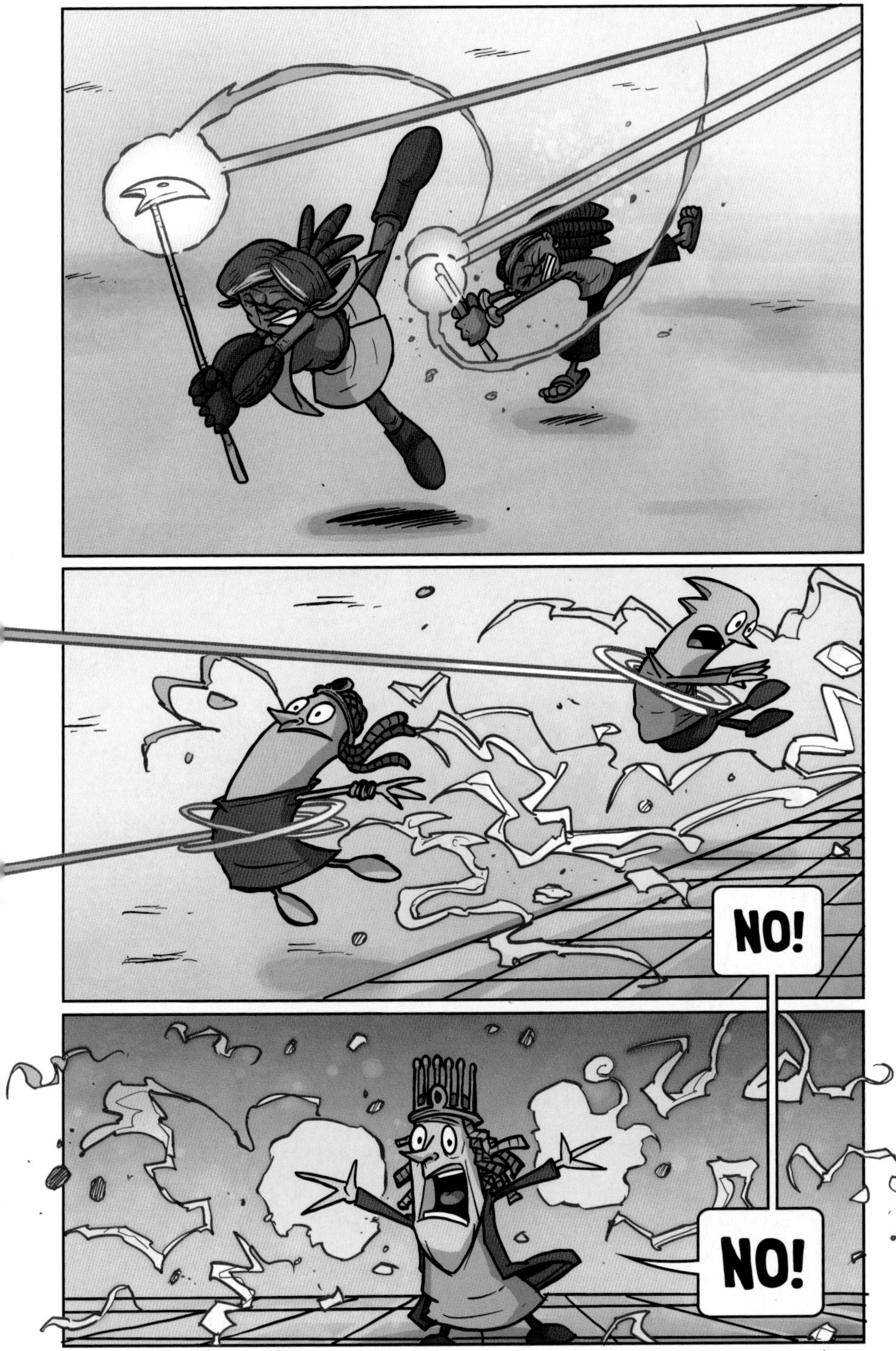
NO!
NO!

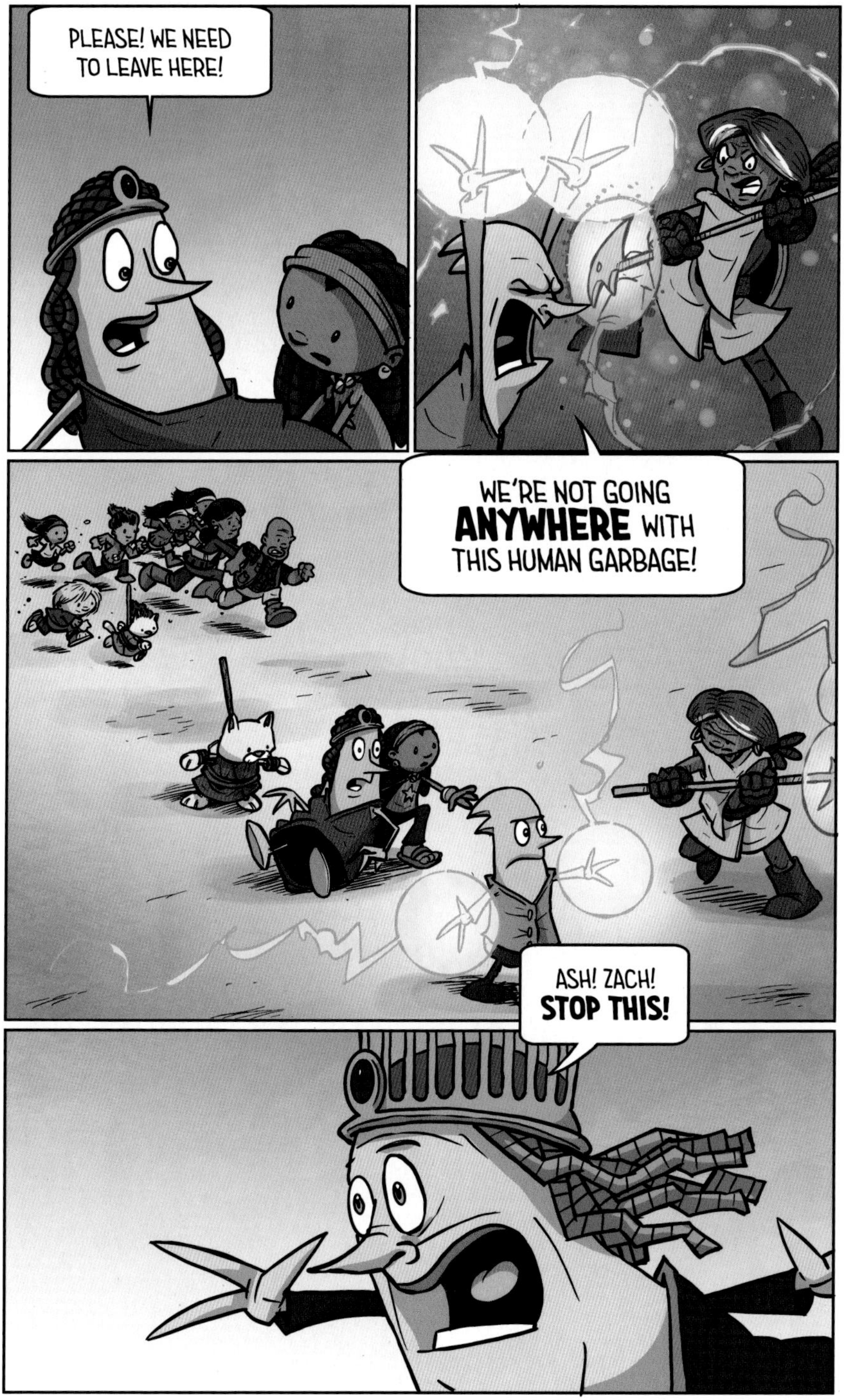
PLEASE! WE NEED TO LEAVE HERE!
WE'RE NOT GOING **ANYWHERE** WITH THIS HUMAN GARBAGE!
ASH! ZACH! **STOP THIS!**

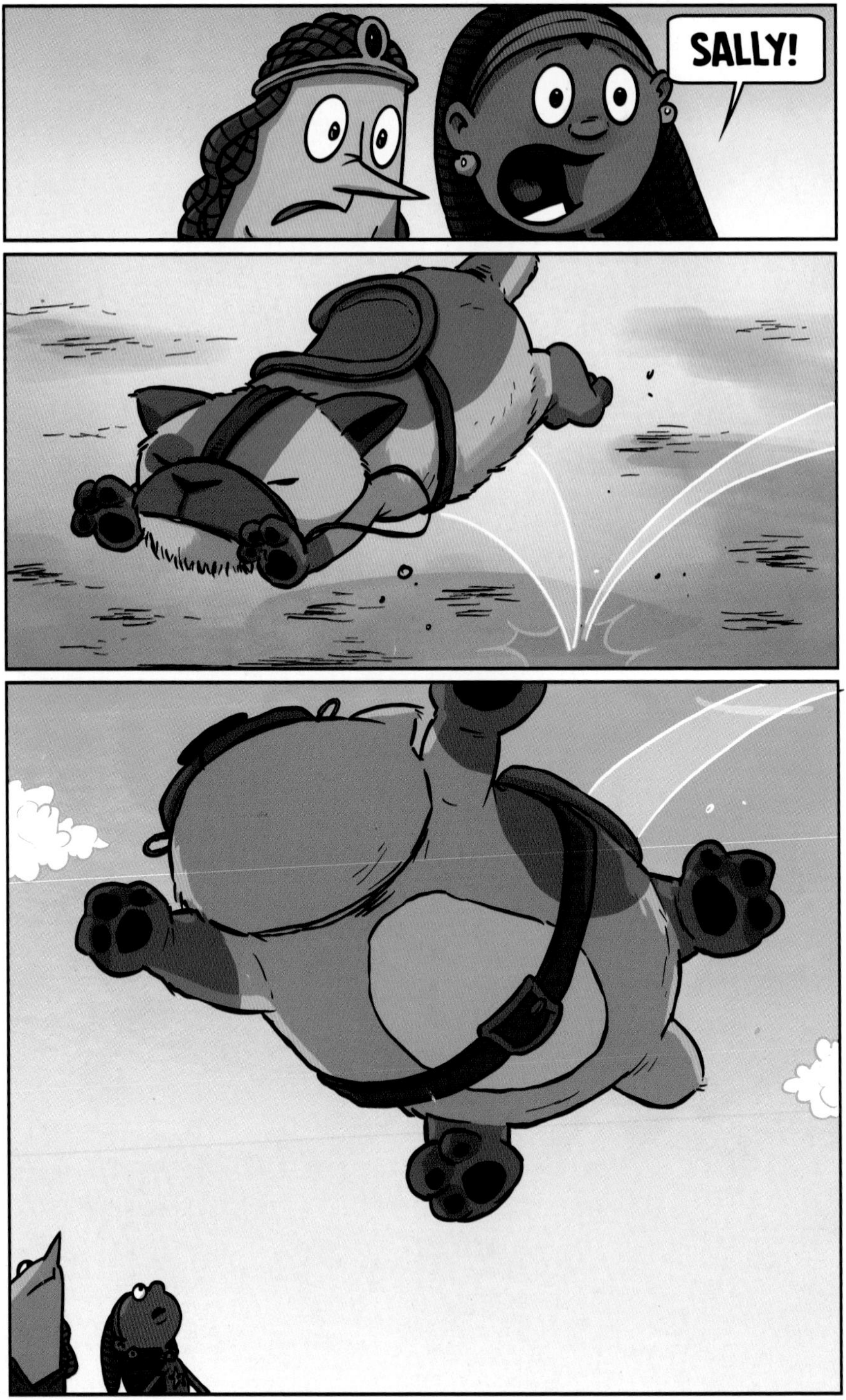
SALLY!

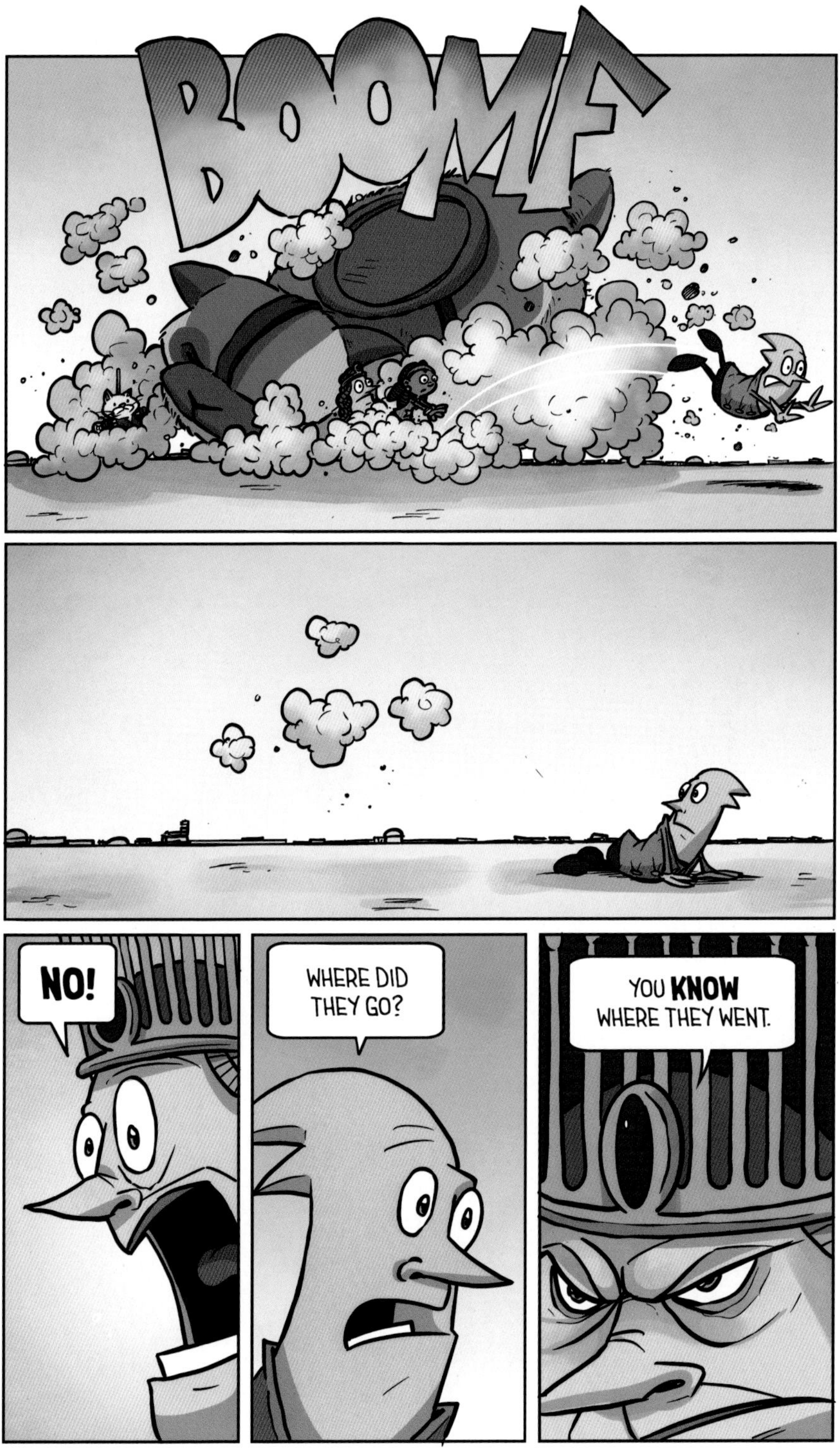
BOOMF
NO!
WHERE DID THEY GO?
YOU **KNOW** WHERE THEY WENT.

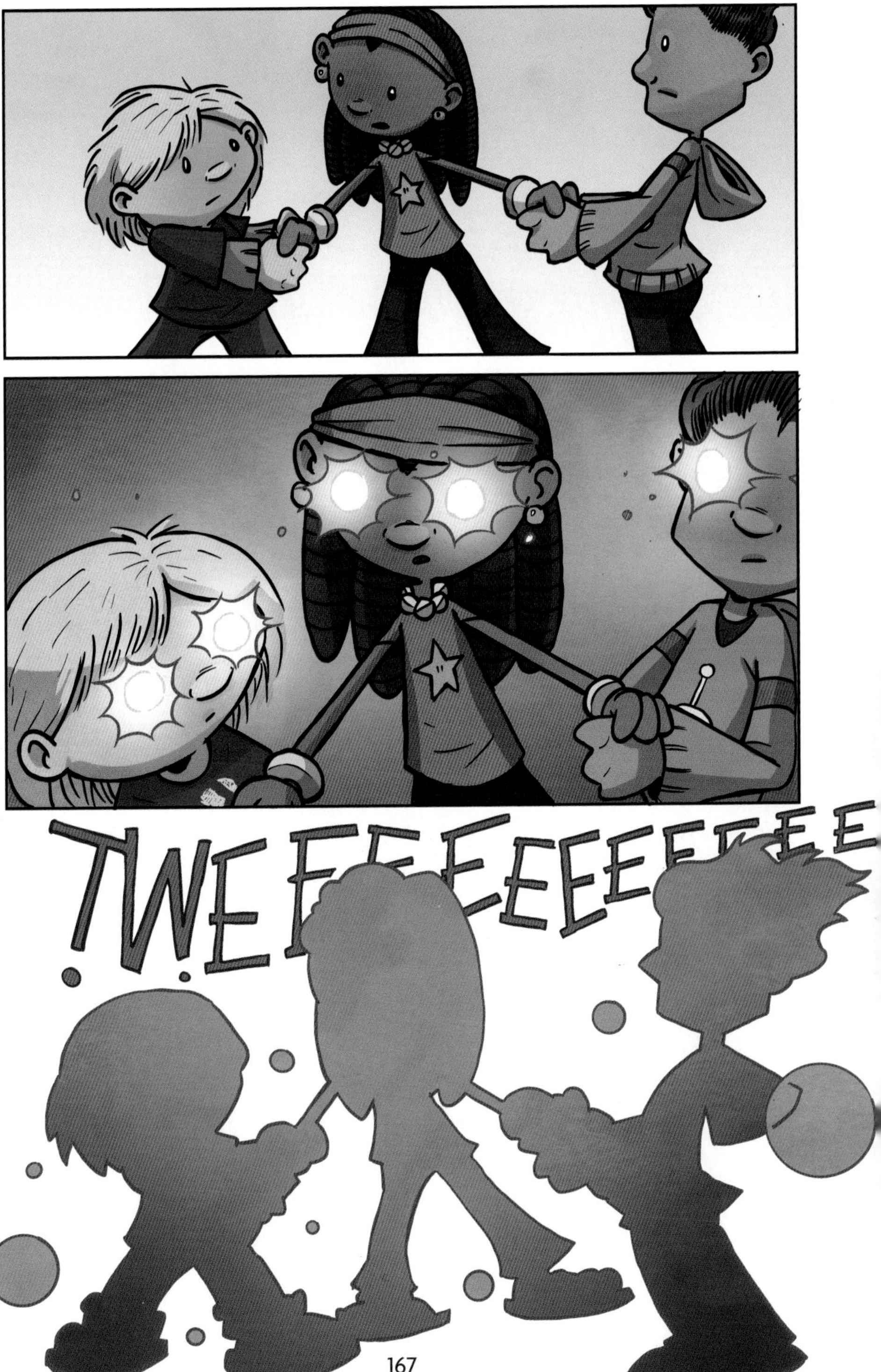
TWEEEEEEEEEEE

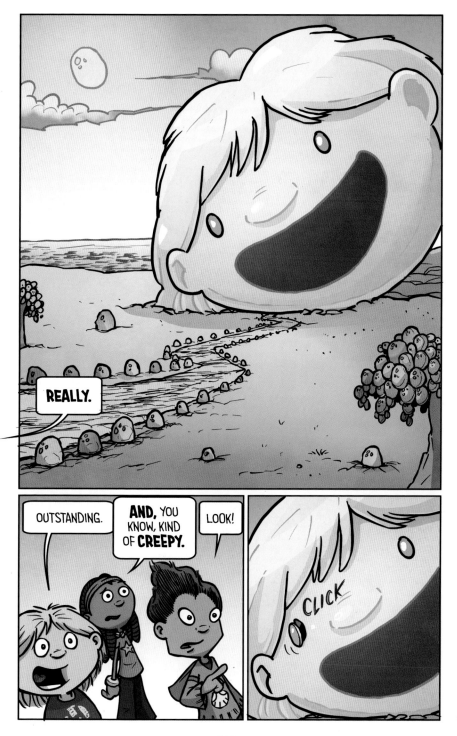

CHAPTER 11

THE LAST CITY ON EARTH

IT'S SO **NEAT** TO HAVE YOU HERE.

WHOMP

172

173

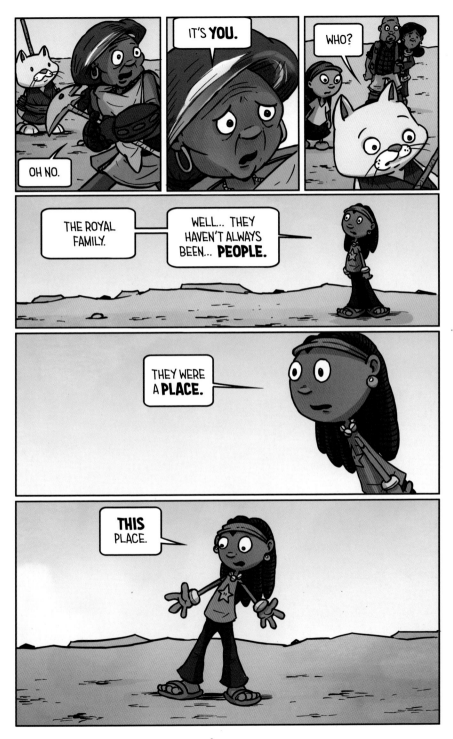

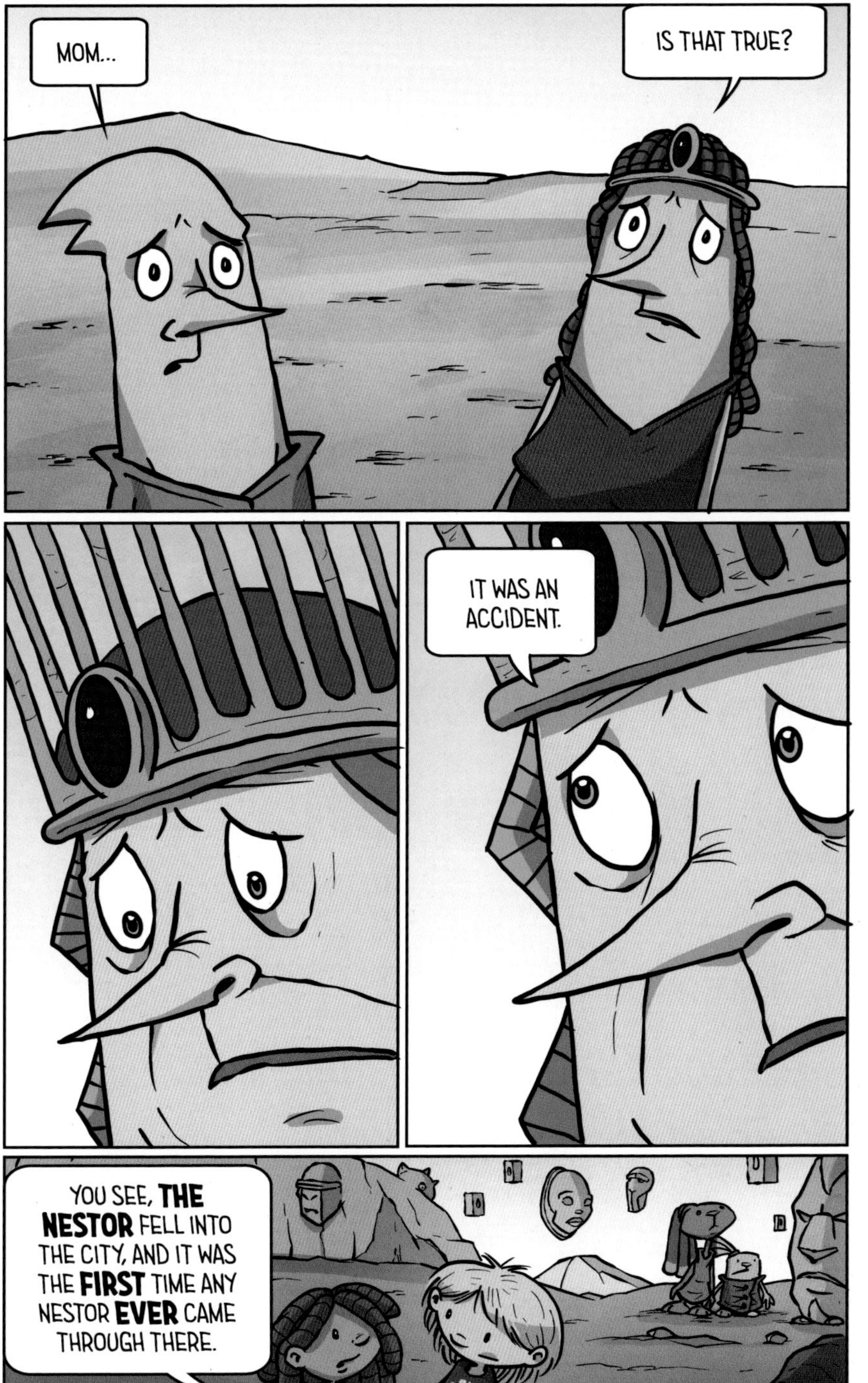
MOM...
IS THAT TRUE?
IT WAS AN ACCIDENT.
YOU SEE, **THE NESTOR** FELL INTO THE CITY, AND IT WAS THE **FIRST** TIME ANY NESTOR **EVER** CAME THROUGH THERE.

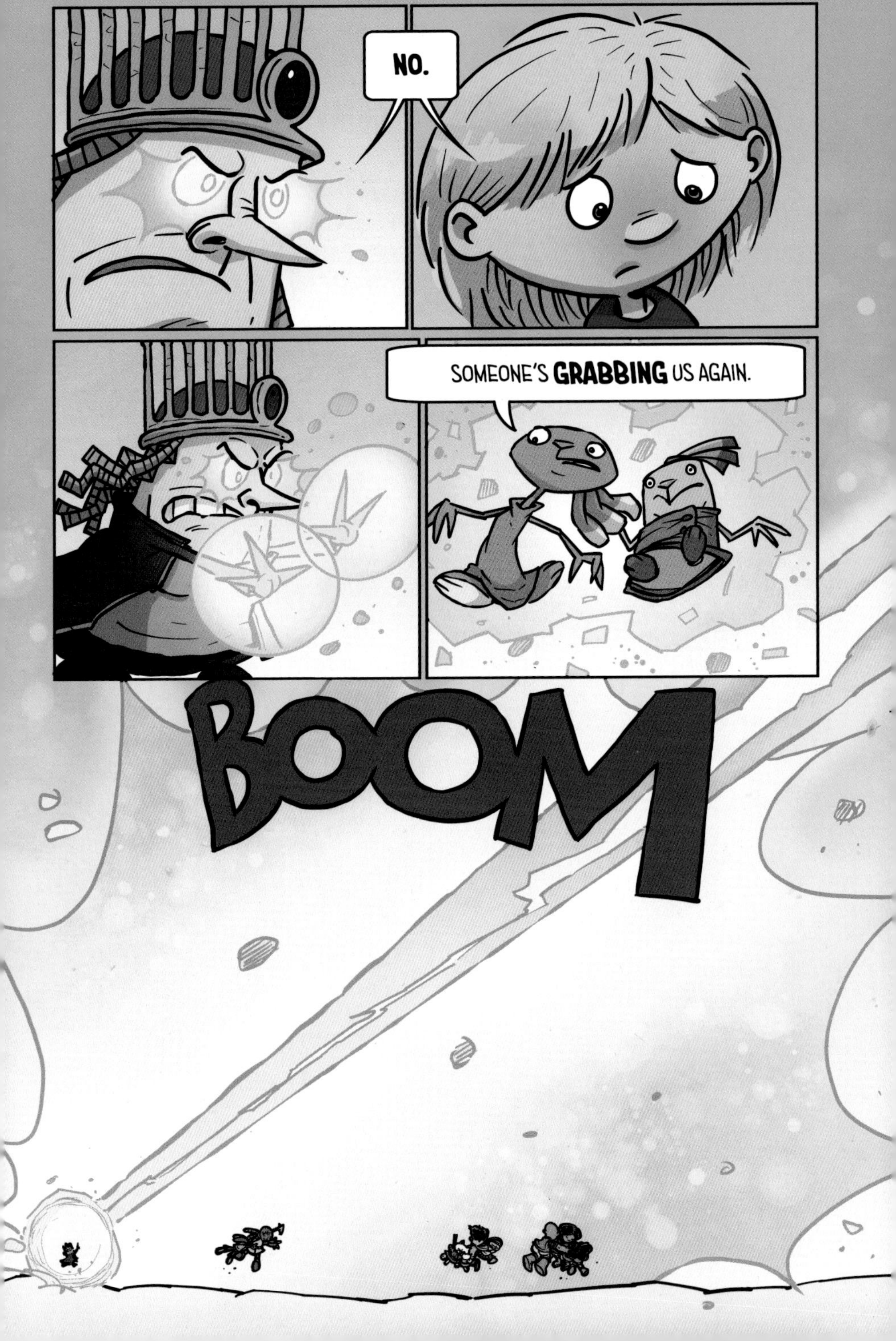
NO.
SOMEONE'S **GRABBING** US AGAIN.
BOOM

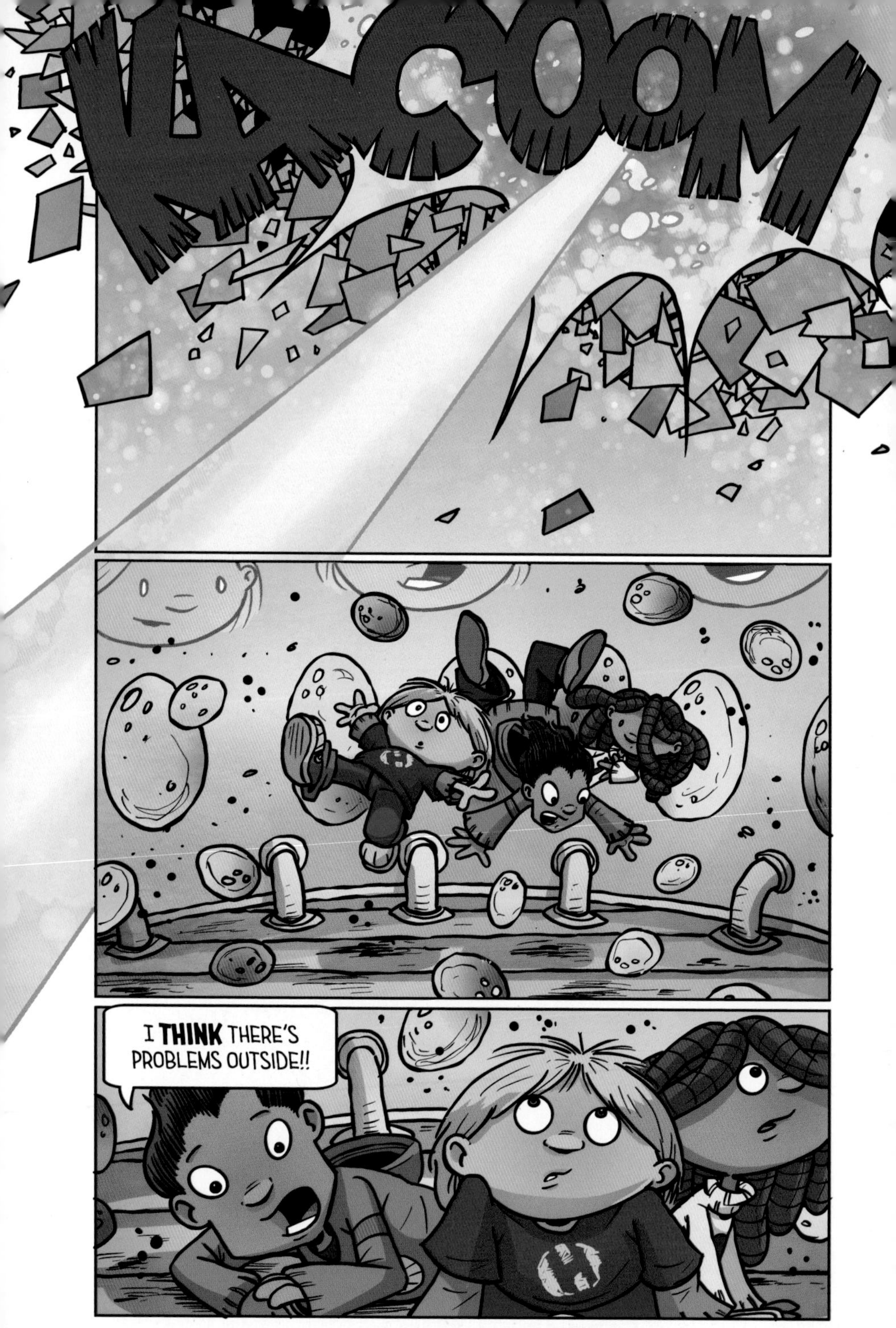
VACOOM
I THINK THERE'S PROBLEMS OUTSIDE!!

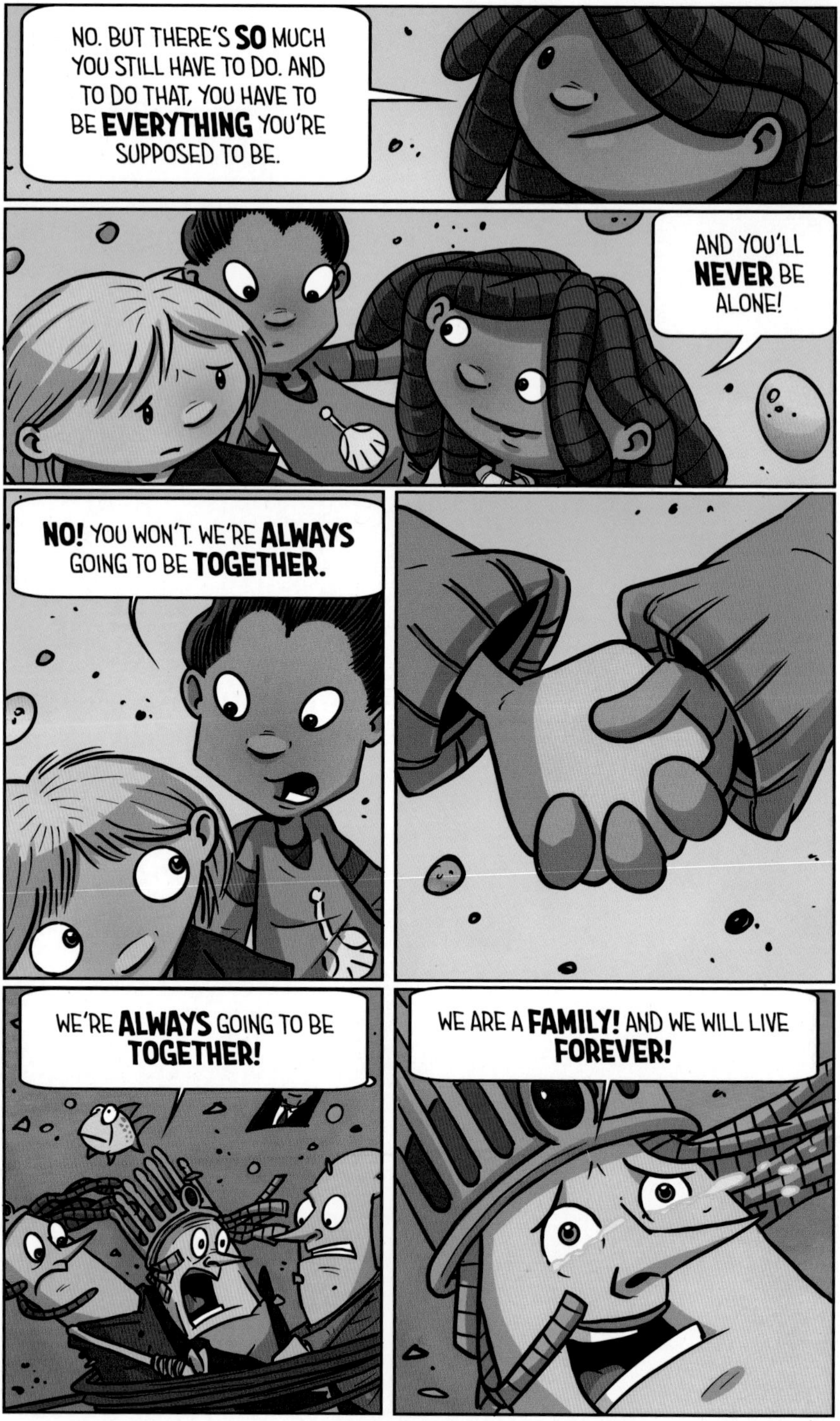
NO. BUT THERE'S **SO** MUCH YOU STILL HAVE TO DO. AND TO DO THAT, YOU HAVE TO BE **EVERYTHING** YOU'RE SUPPOSED TO BE.
AND YOU'LL **NEVER** BE ALONE!
NO! YOU WON'T. WE'RE **ALWAYS** GOING TO BE **TOGETHER.**
WE'RE **ALWAYS** GOING TO BE **TOGETHER!**
WE ARE A **FAMILY!** AND WE WILL LIVE **FOREVER!**

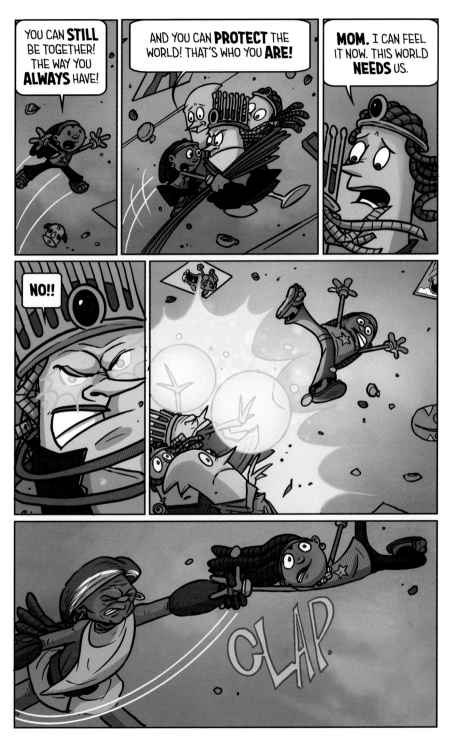

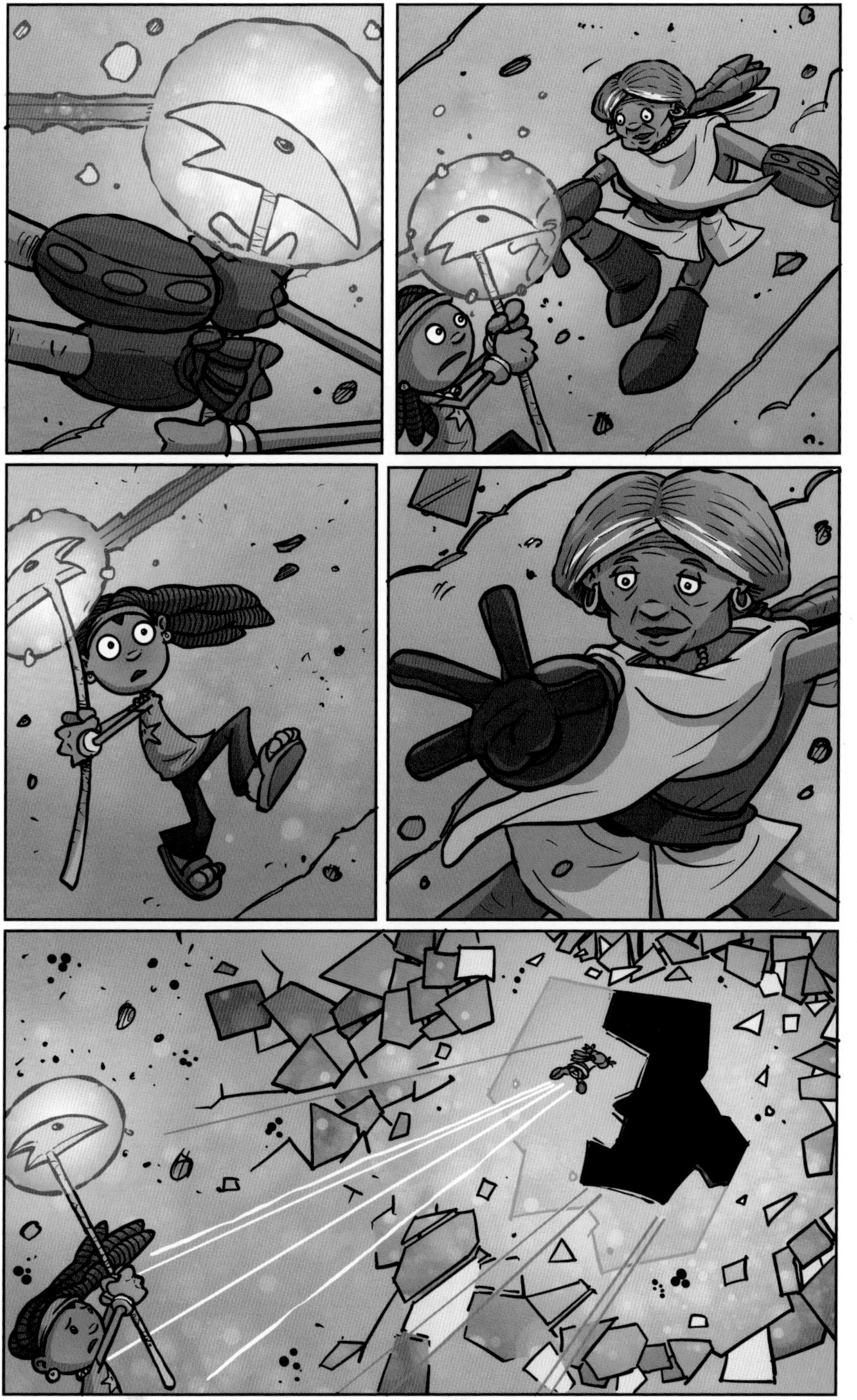

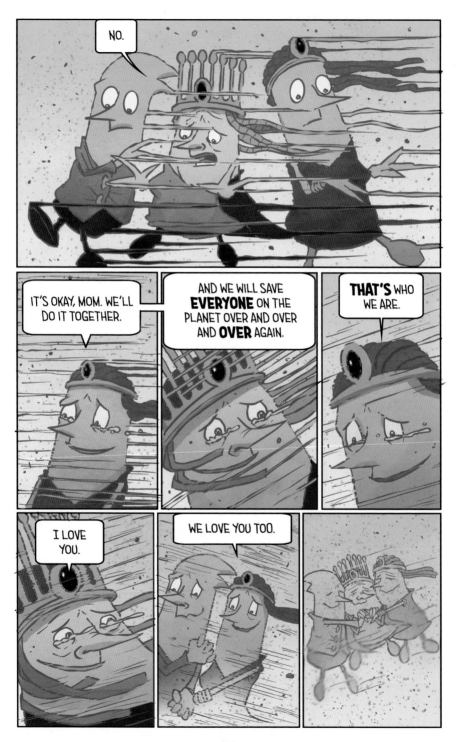

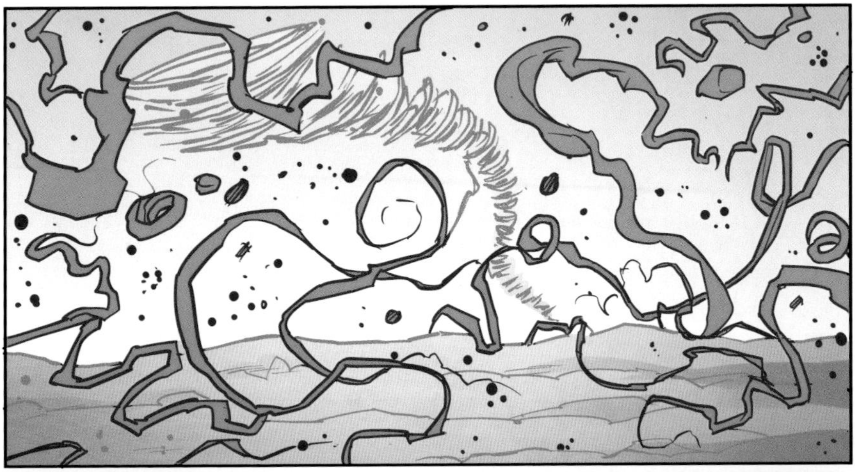

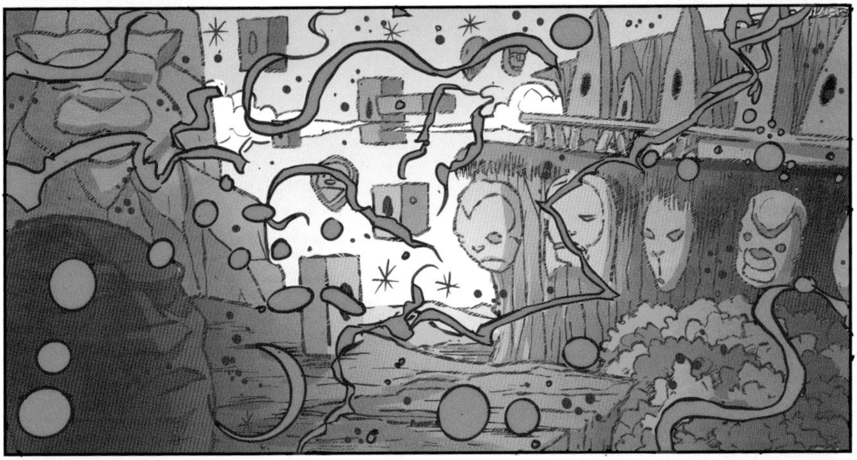

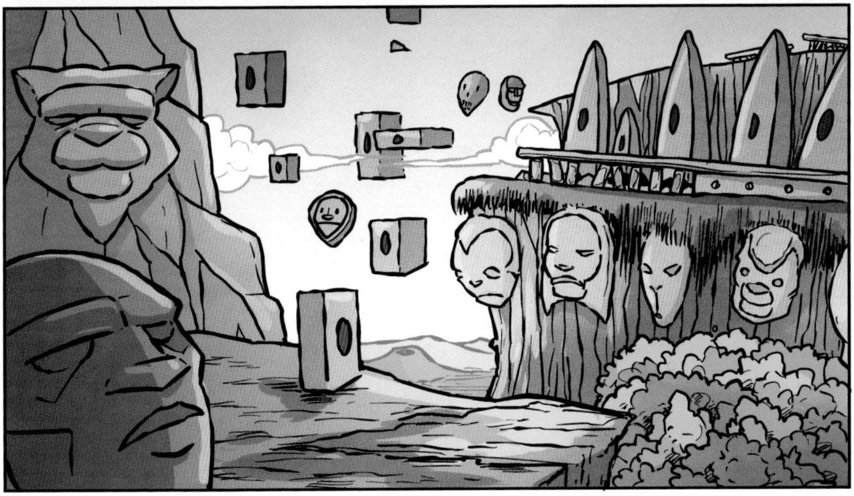

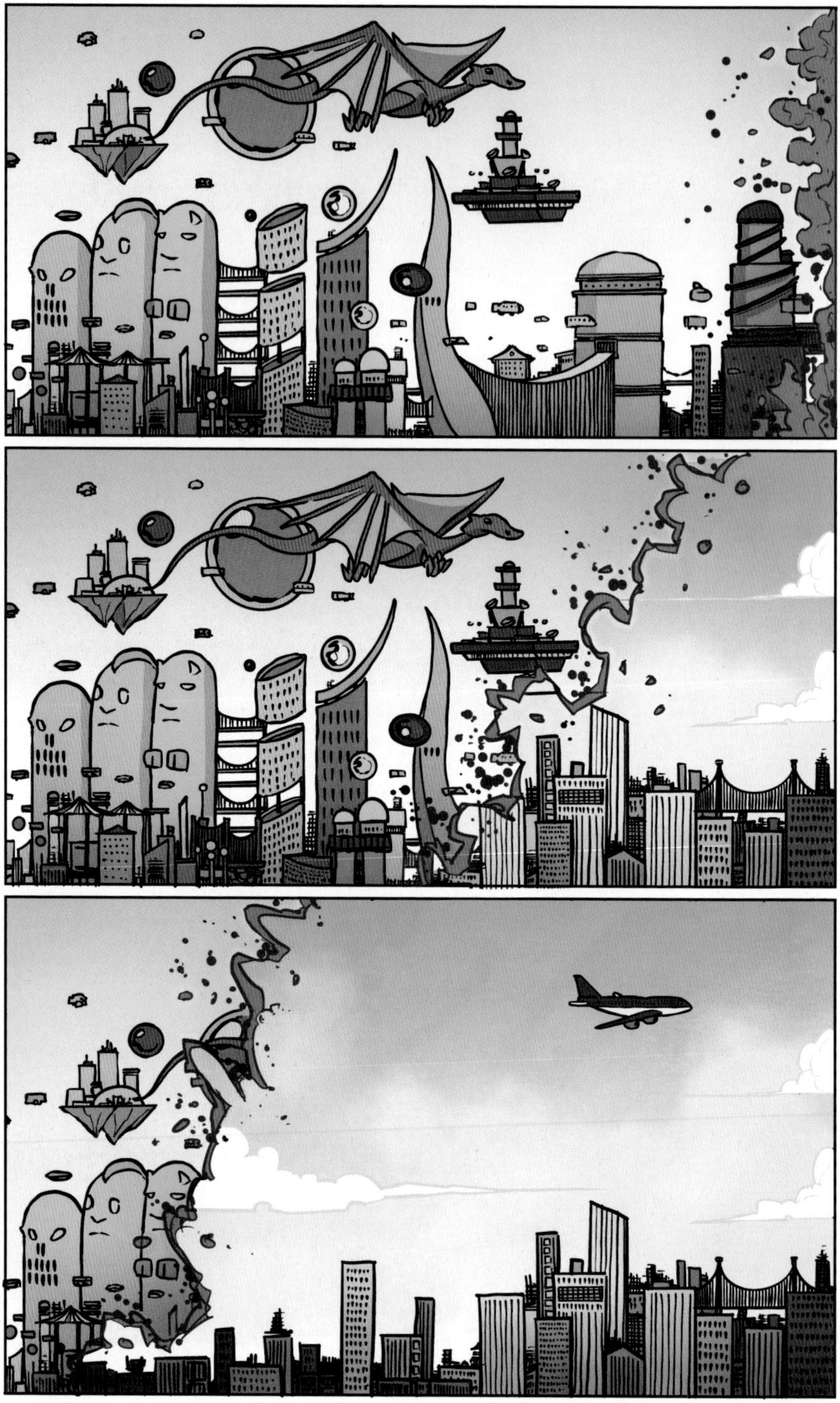

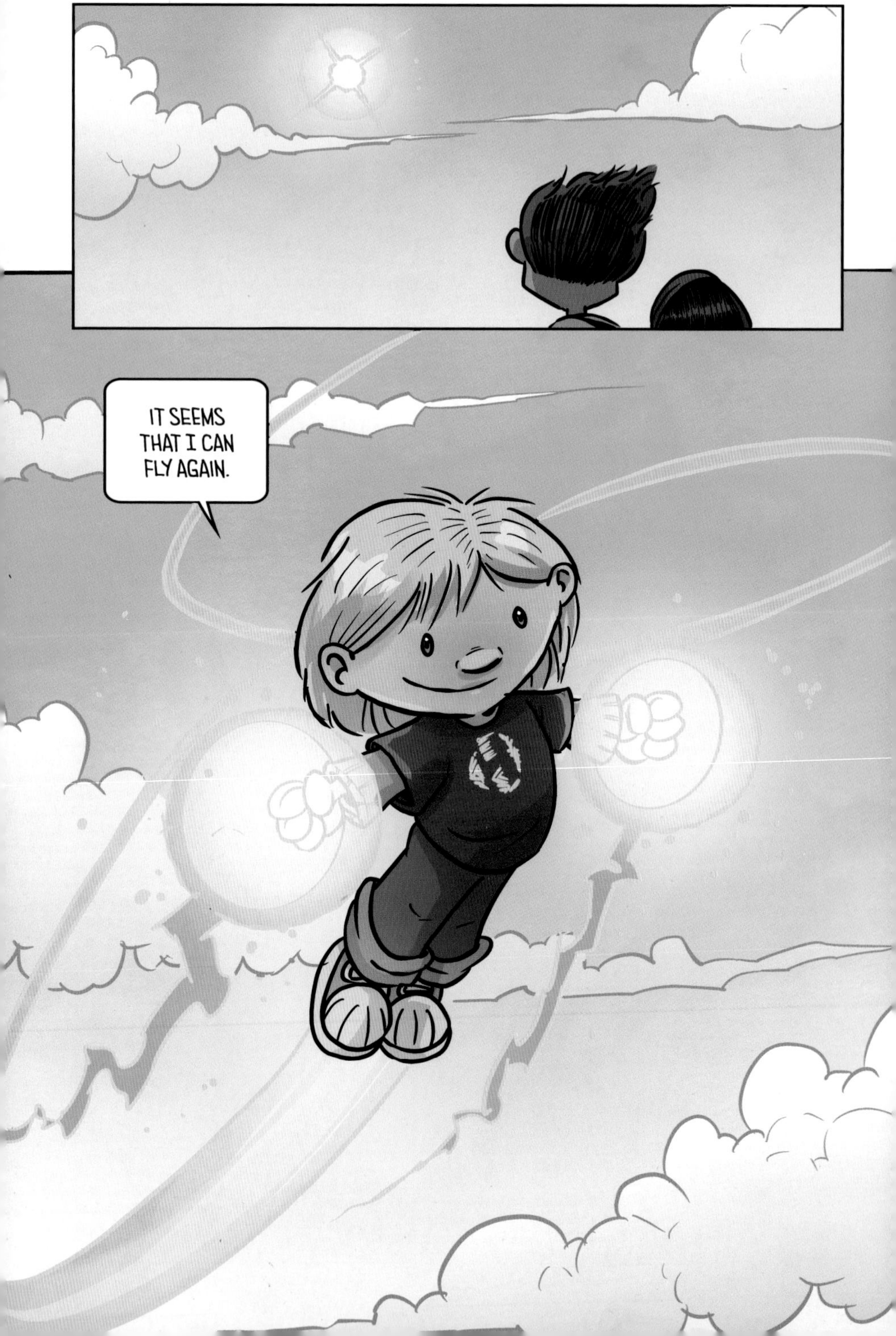
IT SEEMS THAT I CAN FLY AGAIN.

213

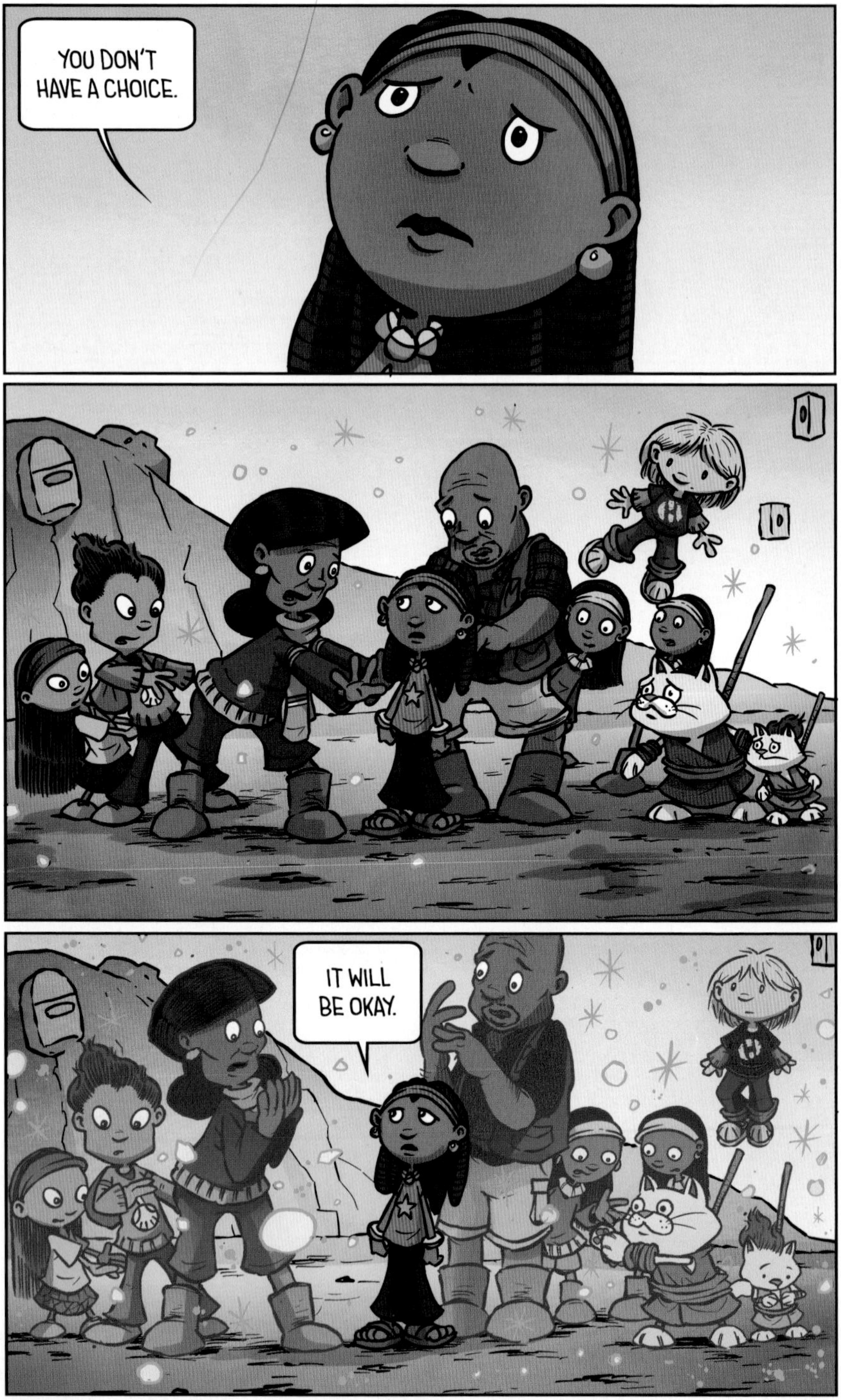
YOU DON'T HAVE A CHOICE.
IT WILL BE OKAY.

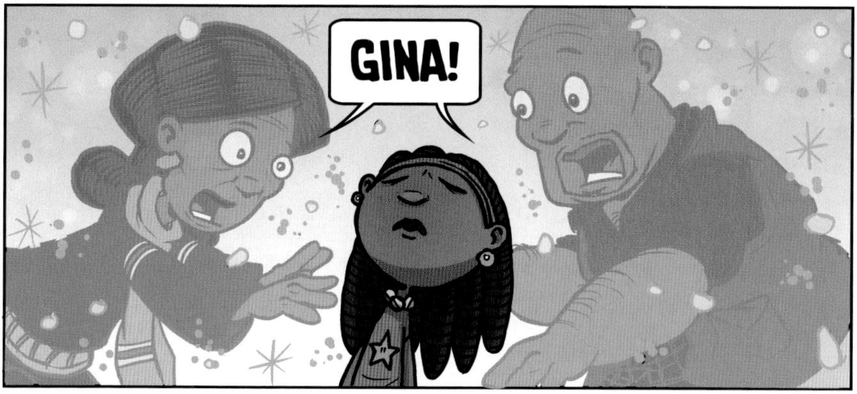
GINA!
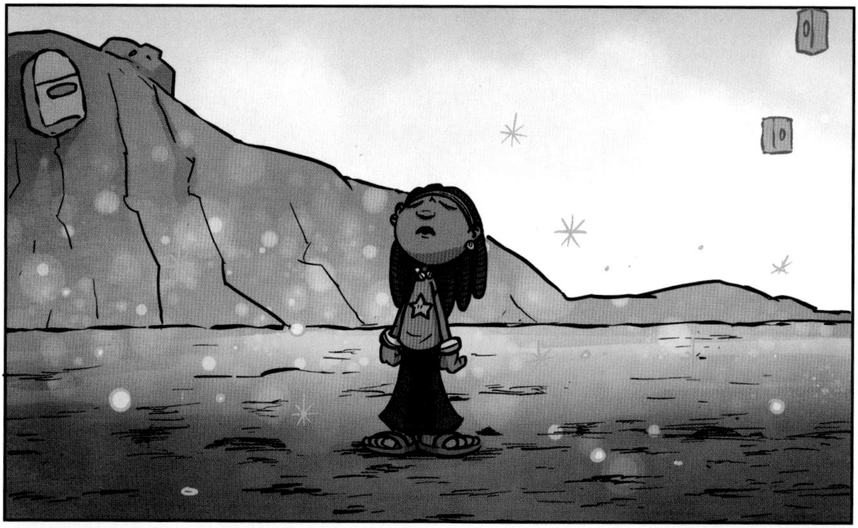
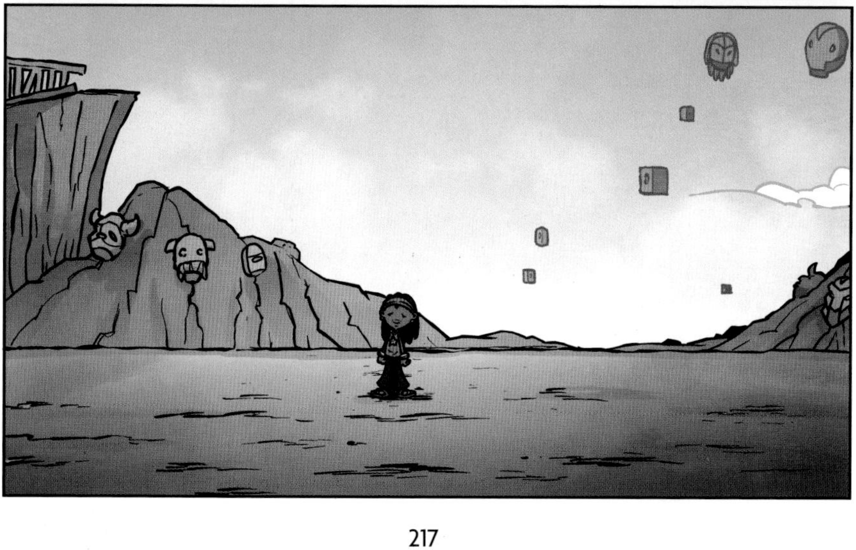

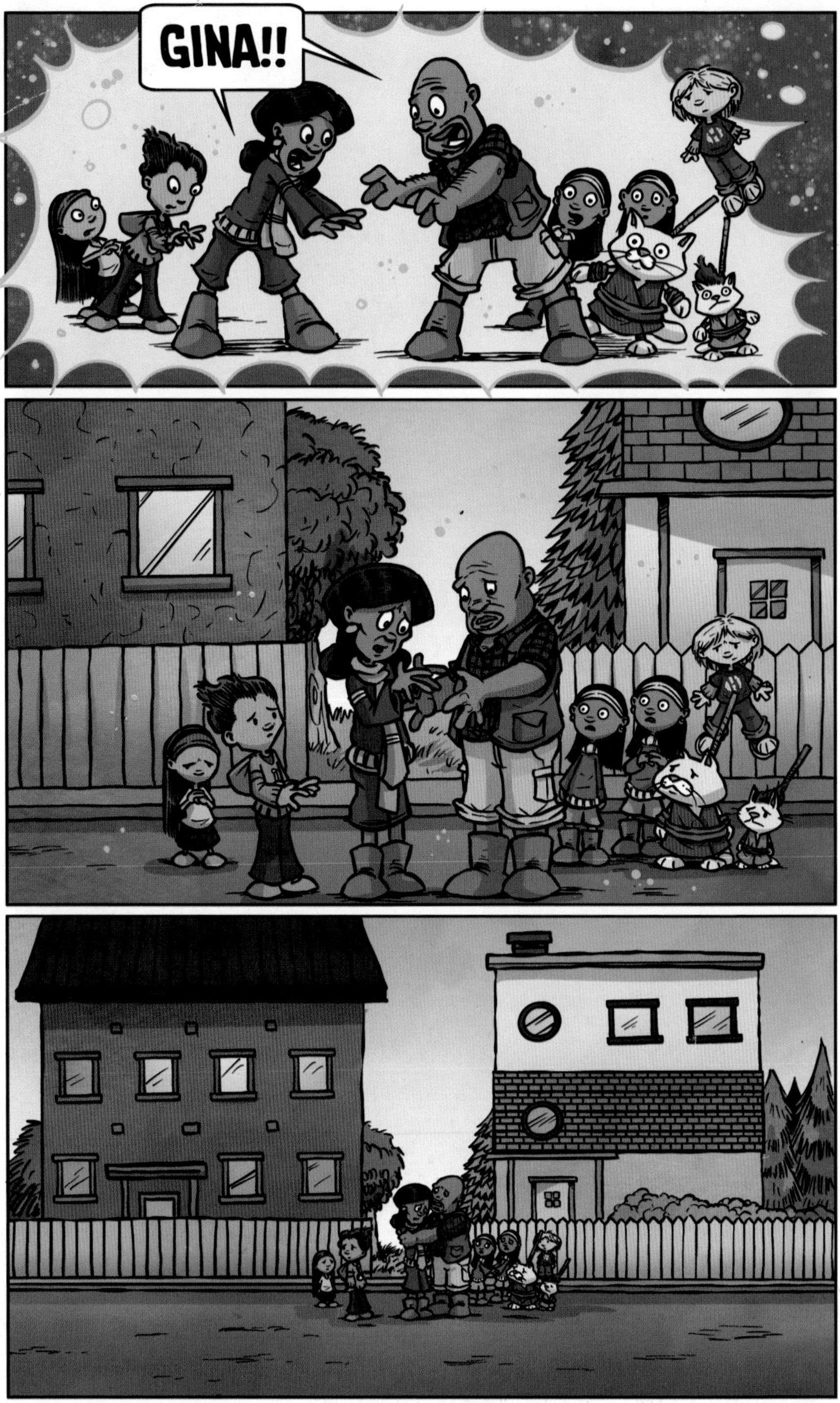
GINA!!

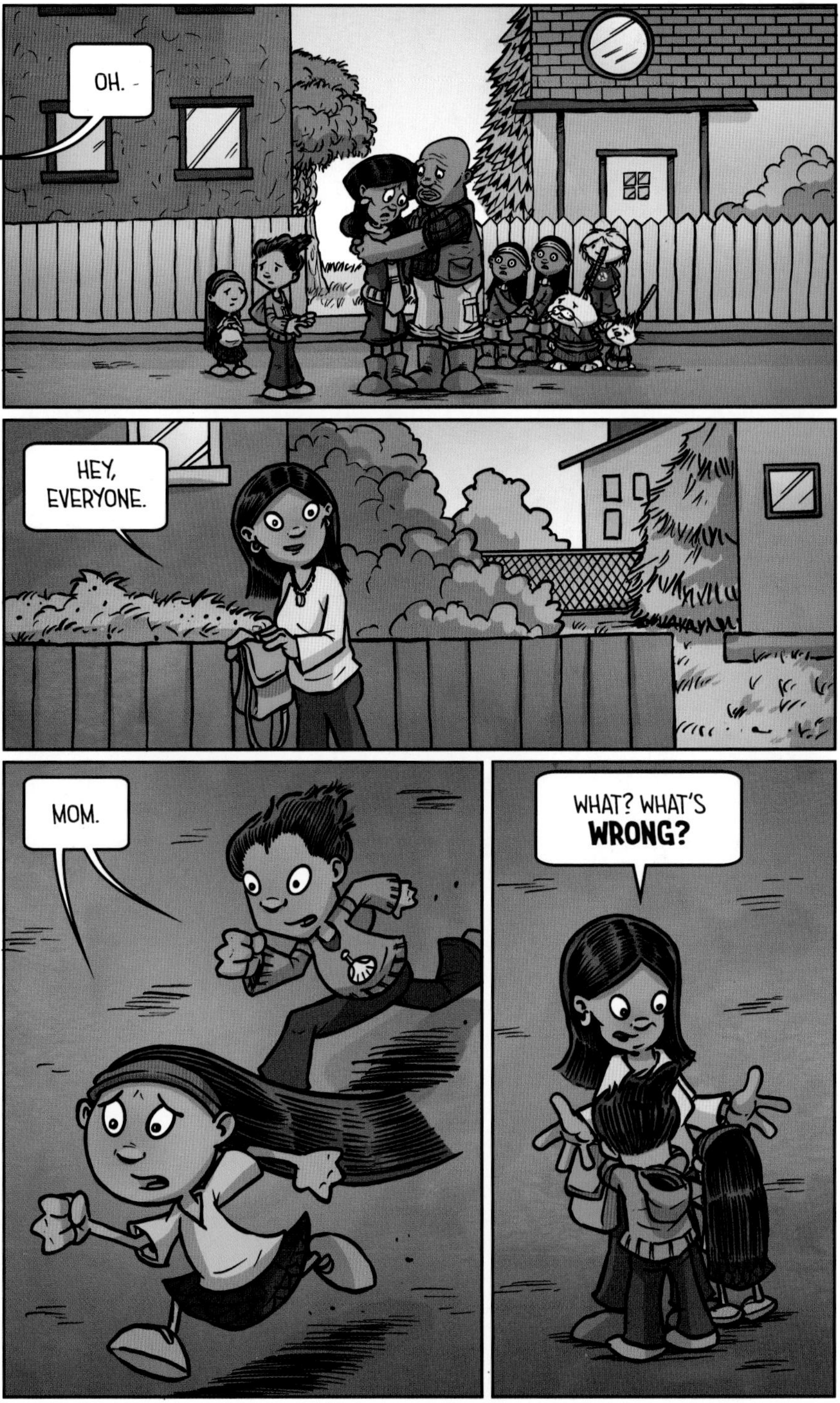
OH.
HEY, EVERYONE.
MOM.
WHAT? WHAT'S **WRONG?**

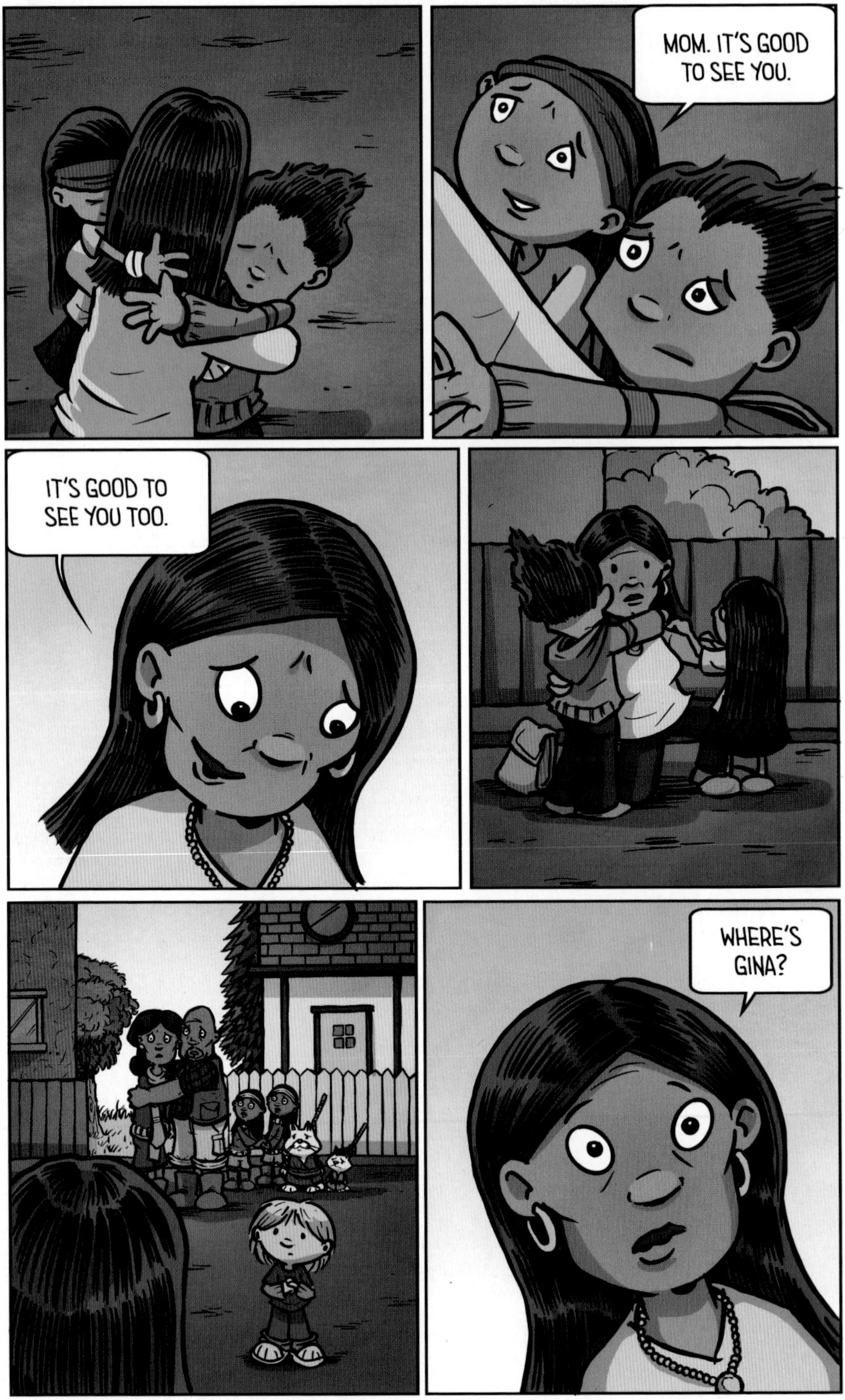
MOM. IT'S GOOD TO SEE YOU.
IT'S GOOD TO SEE YOU TOO.
WHERE'S GINA?

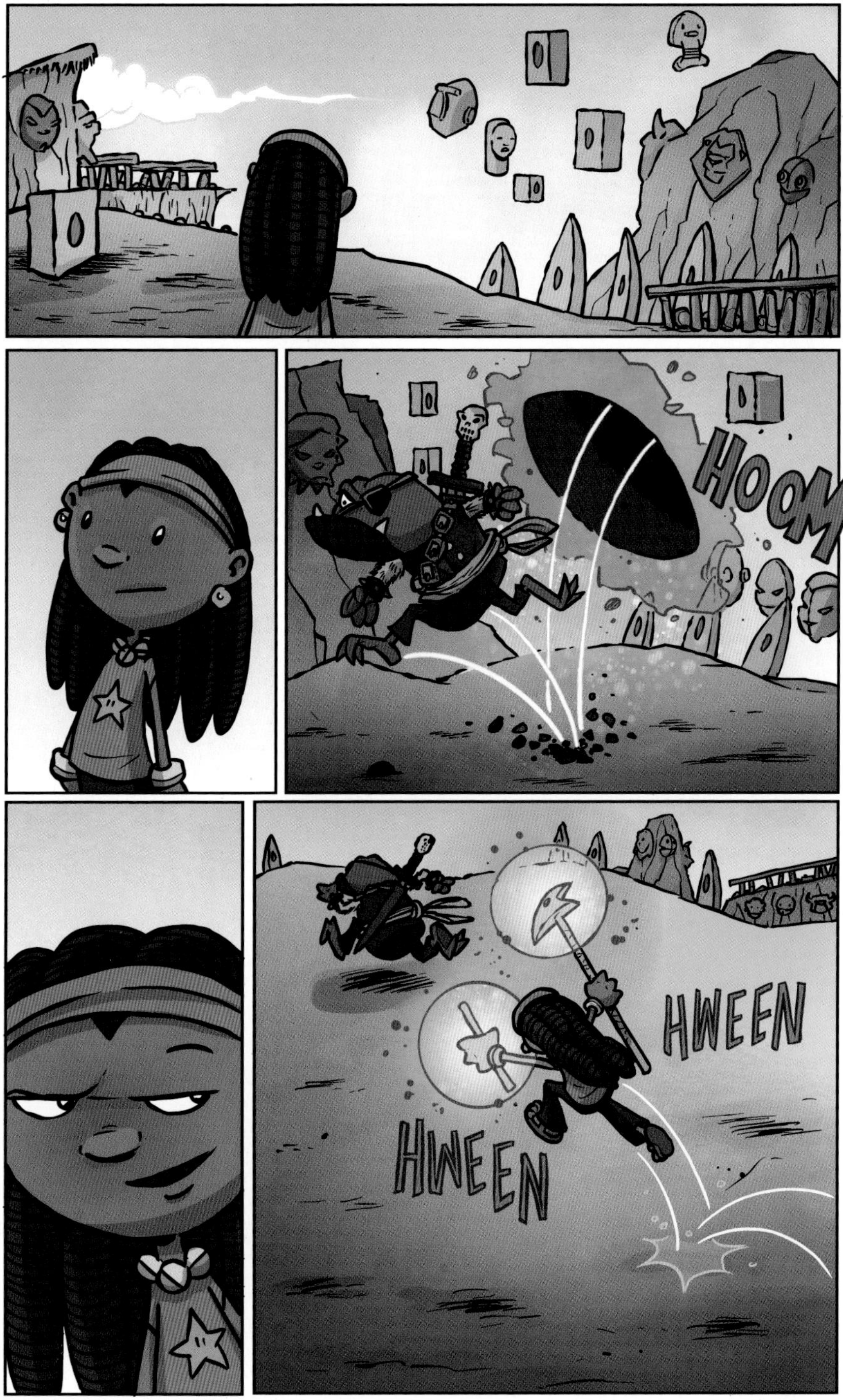
HOOM
HWEEN
HWEEN

CHAPTER 12

SOMETIME LATER

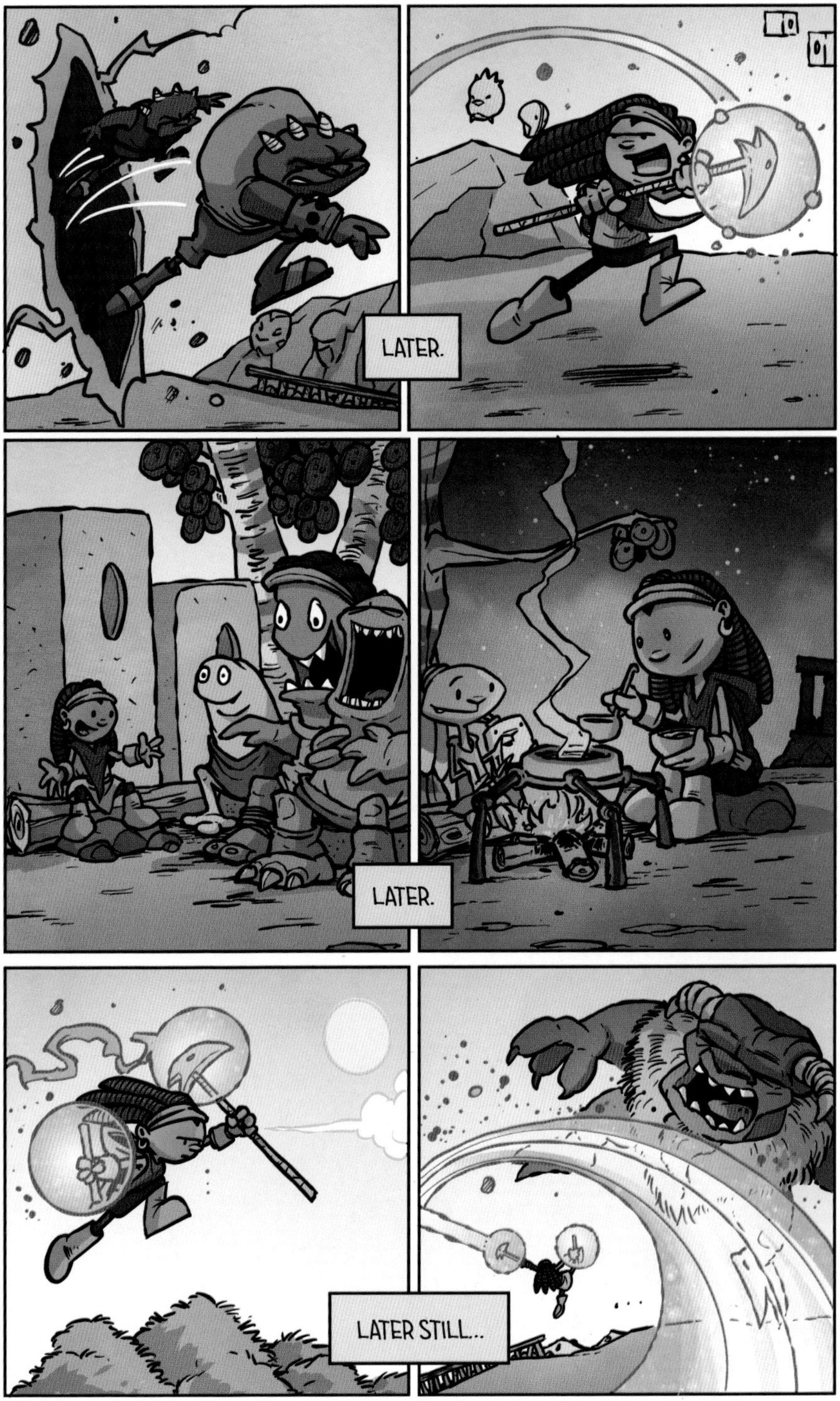
LATER.
LATER.
LATER STILL...

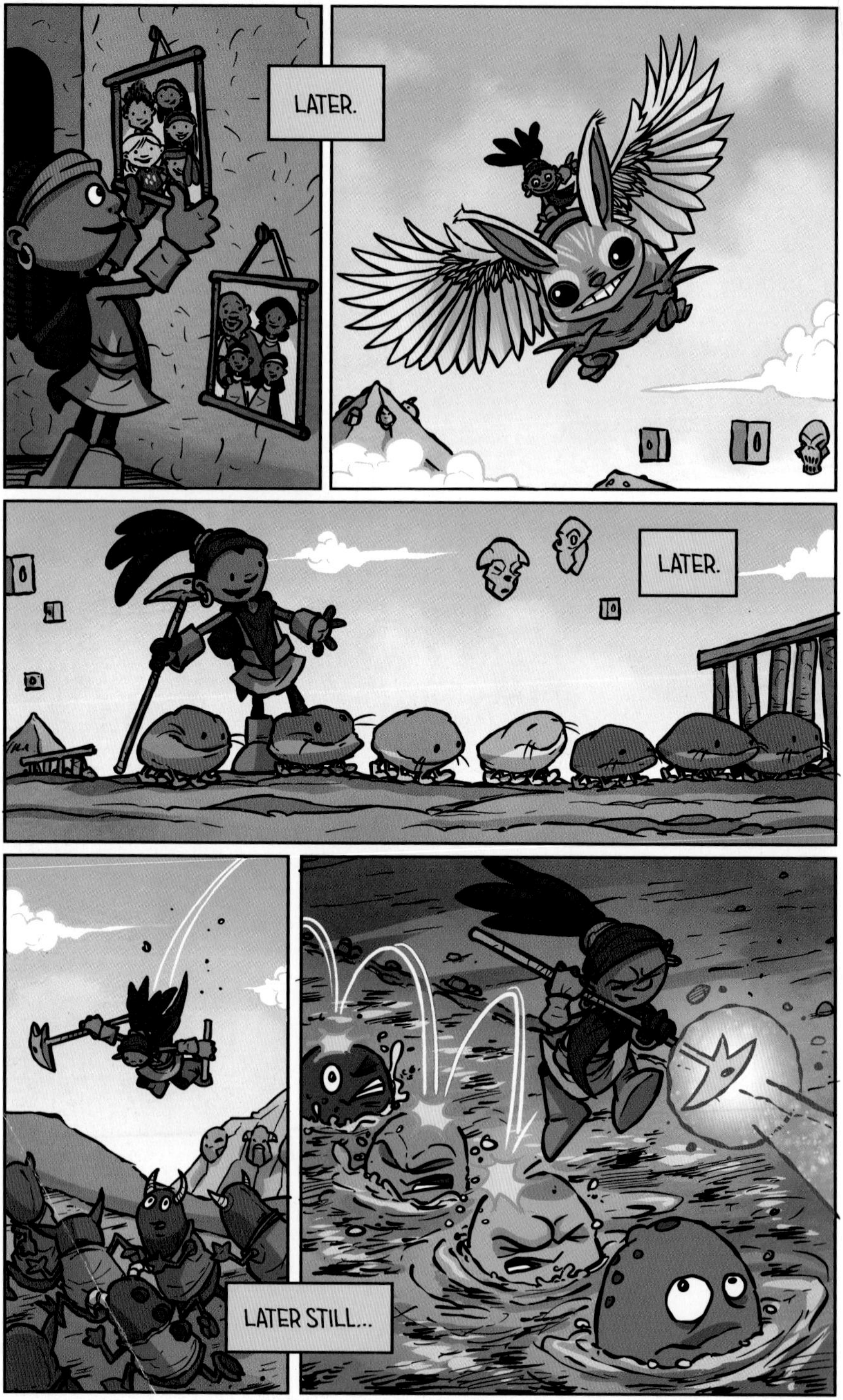
LATER.
LATER.
LATER STILL...

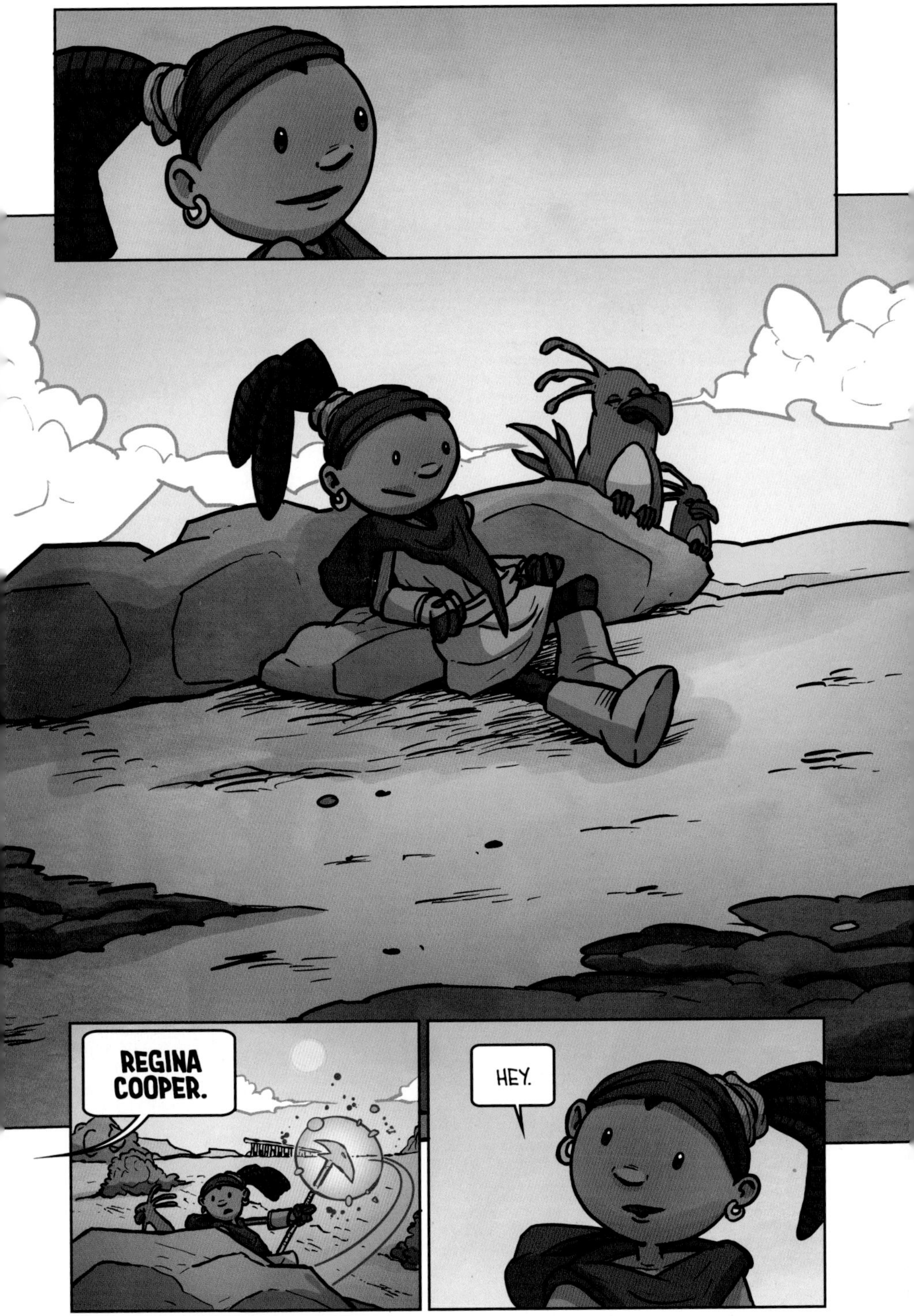
REGINA COOPER.
HEY.

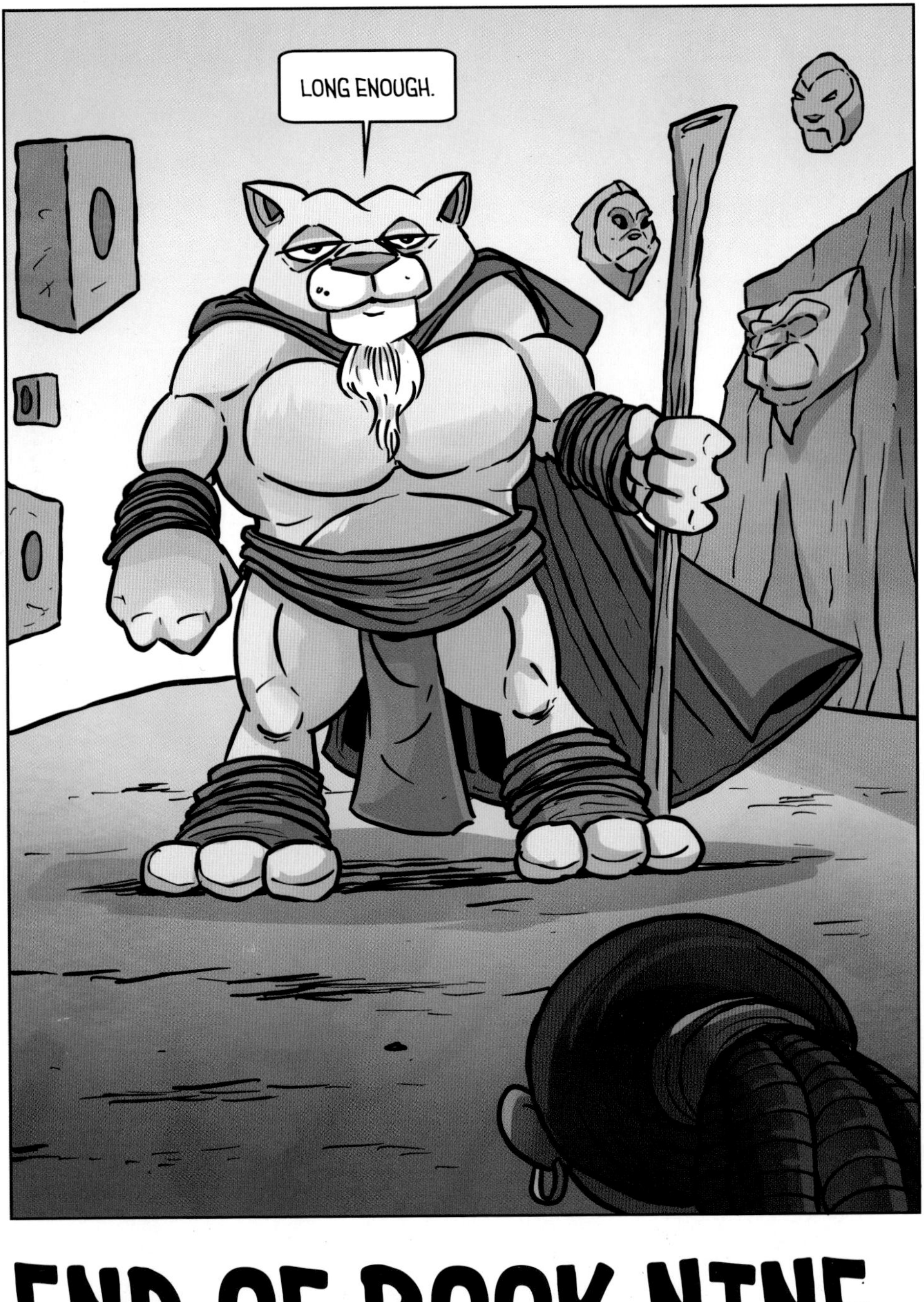
LONG ENOUGH.

END OF BOOK NINE.

Find out what happens next in—

HILO

THE RISE OF THE CAT

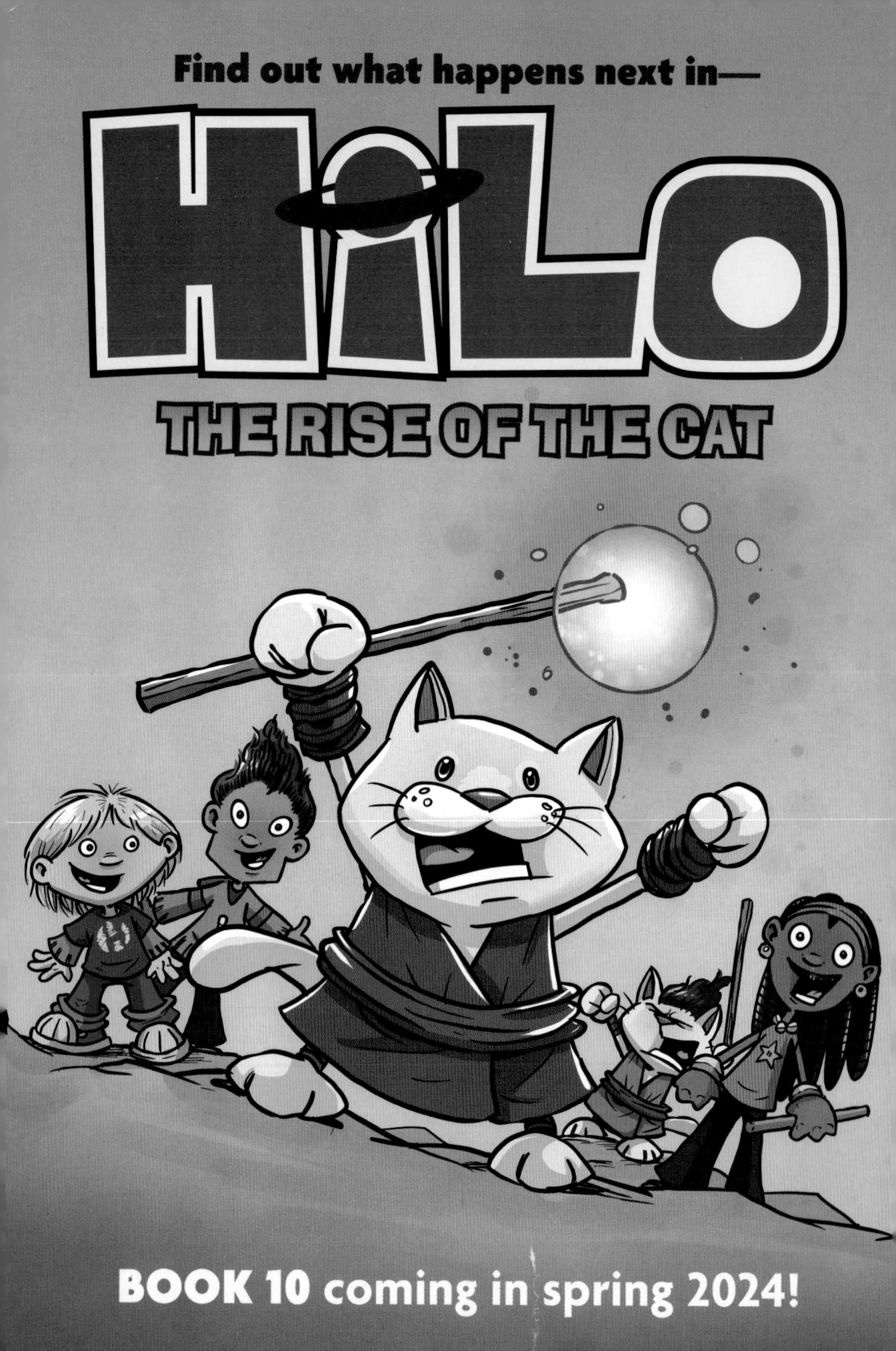

BOOK 10 coming in spring 2024!

JUDD WINICK is the creator of the award-winning, **New York Times** bestselling Hilo series. Judd grew up on Long Island with a healthy diet of doodling, **X-Men** comics, the newspaper strip **Bloom County,** and **Looney Tunes.** Today, he lives in San Francisco with his wife, Pam Ling; their two kids; their cats, Troy and Abed; and far too many action figures and vinyl toys for a normal adult. Judd created the Cartoon Network series **Juniper Lee;** has written superhero comics, including Batman, Green Lantern, and Green Arrow; and was a cast member of MTV's **The Real World: San Francisco.** Judd is also the author of the highly acclaimed graphic novel **Pedro and Me,** about his **Real World** roommate and friend, AIDS activist Pedro Zamora. Visit Judd and Hilo online at juddspillowfort.com or find him on Twitter at @JuddWinick.

SOMETIMES THE UNIVERSE

NEW YORK TIMES BESTSELLING SERIES
HILO
THE BOY WHO CRASHED TO EARTH
BY JUDD WINICK
HILO
SAVING THE WHOLE WIDE WORLD
BY JUDD WINICK
HILO
THE GREAT BIG BOOM
BY JUDD WINICK
HILO
WAKING THE MONSTERS
BY JUDD WINICK
HILO
THEN EVERYTHING WENT WRONG
BY JUDD WINICK
HILO
ALL THE PIECES FIT
BY JUDD WINICK
HILO
GINA THE GIRL WHO BROKE THE WORLD
BY JUDD WINICK
HILO
GINA AND THE BIG SECRET
BY JUDD WINICK
HILO
GINA AND THE LAST CITY ON EARTH
BY JUDD WINICK

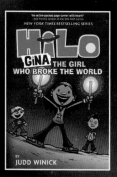